NORTH TO THE TALLGRASS

NORTH TO THE TALLGRASS

Osage Legacy

A Novel

Lonnie Magee

iUniverse, Inc.
New York Lincoln Shanghai

North to the Tallgrass
Osage Legacy

iUniverse books may be ordered through booksellers or by contacting:

iUniverse
2021 Pine Lake Road, Suite 100
Lincoln, NE 68512
www.iuniverse.com
1-800-Authors (1-800-288-4677)

This is a work of fiction. All of the characters, names, incidents, organizations and dialogue in this novel are either the products of the author's imagination or are used fictitiously.

ISBN-13: 978-0-595-41685-1 (pbk)
ISBN-13: 978-0-595-86029-6 (ebk)
ISBN-10: 0-595-41685-3 (pbk)
ISBN-10: 0-595-86029-X (ebk)

Printed in the United States of America

With Love

With Love,
To Joan, my late wife and best friend for 26 wonderful years raising
seven kids and fast thoroughbred horses was our passion.
See you on the Hill, Darlin'

Acknowledgements

I would like to thank everyone who has helped me with my three books but I find that the page is not large enough.

I've met some wonderful people and made a lot of new friends as well as fans from my books.

The time I've spent with the trilogy has been one of the highlights of my life. I have been fortunate enough to own and ride a fine calf roping horse and own a Champion Thoroughbred.

All of these things were great, but I have to admit the three books are pushing the thrill to a whole new level

The thrill of having strangers call and want the next book is indeed a new high. Telling them they will have to wait is not what some of them want to hear. Almost all of them have understood and were kind enough to give me their names and addresses so I can mail them the book when it is ready.

"Osage Legacy" completes the North of the Tallgrass series. I hope my readers enjoy reading it as much as I have enjoyed creating the story

I have several more works in progress and hope my fans enjoy them as much as I am enjoying watching the characters grow and become old friends of mine.

Lonnie Magee "06"

Foreword

The thought of being a cowboy has appealed to a broad range of people for over 120 years. However, there are few that have actually lived the lifestyle of the "bronc bustin, cow chasin, woman catchin American hero that has captivated imaginations of folks around the world. Even among the modern cowboys of today that make their living working cattle on horseback everyday, they too have that wonderment of how their life would have played out on the range in 1820.

Thanks to this magnificent series of books by Lonnie Magee, the city slicker as well as the seasoned cowhand can take a trip back in time and ride through the tall grass of Northeast Oklahoma. Lonnie's take on the post-Civil War Texas family that gathered wild longhorn cattle and headed north to Indian Territory is colorful and exciting. As if you were there, you'll be able to see the herds of cattle and horses, the landscape and you'll get to know the personalities of this daring western family. Magee's writing is so vivid that you can taste the coffee and smell the smoke from the Indian camp. You will sense that you are riding right through the middle of the Osage Hills fighting gun battles and chasing rustlers.

One of the reasons that this novel is so real is that the writer based most of this story on the true history of the Osage country during its developing years. Lonnie Magee grew up near Pawhuska Oklahoma and kept notes on many of th stories he had heard as a youth from the "old timers" in the area. So get ready to saddle up for the exciting ride in the Osage Hills of yesteryear.

Justin McKee

PRCA Rodeo Announcer, Rancher, Steer roper and PBR Commentator.

CHAPTER 1

▼

My wife Mary sat beside me on the porch swing watching the warm spring sun set in the west. We were having our evening cup of cowboy coffee (boiled) and were relaxing after a busy day.

"Remember how it all started James?"

"Sure do Mary, I think about it now and then."

"I know you do, I can see it in your eyes every now and then. You've always got that funny little grin of yours on your face."

"I can't help it Mary, I remember the place down in southwest Texas and how bad things were. The pastures were non-existent, water was almost gone and we had Longhorns coming out our ears."

"Remember how you got Comanche?"

"Sure, the Comanche attacked ma and me one morning. I'd traded for old Devil the week or so before and he smelled them, it's how we ended up surviving."

"You also got your Sharps in the trade for Devil didn't you?"

"Sure did, that rifle almost broke my shoulder the first time I fired it. When I shot the chief with it and got Comanche I had no idea how a horse could affect one's life."

"Even though the Comanche's attacked you, you still didn't hate them."

"I never hated them, they were fighting for what was or had been theirs for hundreds of years. They couldn't see what was going to happen. Their way of life was ending."

"Your mother died shortly after that didn't she?"

"Yes, my life seemed to end that day. I was mad at pa for being gone off to the war. I was mad at everything it seemed."

"But James, he came home."

"He did and I was glad to see him. I'd had almost a year to cool down and figure things out. Then pa suggested the drive."

"You've never been back have you?"

"Nope, one of these days I'd like to go back and say goodbye to mom."

"She knows James, she's with you all the time. You found Sam about that time didn't you?"

"I'd been gathering cattle for the drive and had gone back to the house to get our spare horses. Two men had Sam tied up and had him laying on the tack room floor. He helped me get both the boys who had murdered a neighbor to the North of us."

"That's how you met Harold and his family."

"Sure was, I'd knocked one of them out and shot the other. Harold and his brothers showed up and hung the one who was alive. Afterwards they decided to join us on the drive. Pa hired Paco, Cookie and another man to help us on the drive."

"Everyone thought you all were crazy to try and make the drive didn't they?"

"They sure did, we made the drive on the word of a stranger. He'd told pa the Army needed beef to feed the tribes here in Oklahoma. We didn't see that we had a choice, with no grass or water and four years of drought, we were out of options. The cattle weren't worth anything at home."

"You really enjoyed the drive?"

"Oh yes, I did a bunch of growing up on that drive. We fought rustlers, Indians and crooked cattle buyers. Really it was an adventure.

I'll never forget seeing the Red River for the first time. It was so unreal to me."

"You also found me."

"You bet I did, fighting the rustlers who had kidnapped you wasn't so bad. But when I found you, you were so mad you scared me half to death."

"That's always amazed me dear, you could walk into a gun fight with a smile on your face yet you were afraid of me."

"You understand now Mary, but I'd not had any experience with girls. Besides, you have to admit you gave me a pretty tough time."

"Well I guess I did but I'd been treated pretty rough for a couple of days and I was so mad. Then you uncovered me and had the shotgun in my face. It was just too much."

"I remember the tornado we got caught in down south, that was something I'll always remember."

"How about the tree cattle?"

"Oh yes, that was a sight, but that was after Thumb slipped up on me. I'd never been so embarrassed in my life. He always laughed about my sneaking abilities."

"And mother almost shot you."

"She sure did, I'll never forget it. It was her eyes that tipped me off as to who she was."

"She still gets a laugh out of that time."

"I know, she reminds me of it every now and then."

"Remember when we got to Fort Gibson and the buyers showed up? I'll always be thankful I was there to see your father and Harold's brothers faces when they heard the price they would receive for the herd."

"Mary, that was something I'll remember for the rest of my life. It saved a lot of families lives. It allowed Harold and his brothers to get through the drought and make a go of their ranches."

"I remember our getting married at Martha's store."

"That was a wonderful time. I remember the so-called outlaw who wanted Comanche. I saw your temper again when you told me to shoot him."

"I meant it James, he insulted me."

"I know, it never occurred to you he could have shot me."

"I frankly wasn't worried. He mistook you for a child. He really wasn't very smart."

"I remember our drive up to your folks place in Kansas. I'd never seen such a mess. I'm so glad they got moved down here.

"We all are dear, remember our lease and our first home that you and Sam built for us?"

"I most surely do. I think that was the first time I ever really hurt from work. That backsaw almost whipped me.

"Then Sam met Lesa and we had to build him a home. It was fun though wasn't it?"

"I'll admit it was fun, I felt sorry for Sam though I wasn't much of a hand as a carpenter."

"You learned dear, it only took half the time to build his cabin."

"I remember the bunch who tried to steal some of our cows."

"Oh yes and then there were the ones who pretended to be tax collectors."

"What I remember is the first ham Sam and Lesa smoked for us."

"Oh my goodness yes, it was wonderful. Who would have thought he'd have made his fortune smoking hams and bacon."

"At the time all I cared about was a big ole ham sandwich at noon hour."

"You haven't forgot Beth was born there."

"Not hardly, I was afraid to hold her. Little did I know how tough she was."

"I remember how you were made a Deputy U.S. Marshal. You were always busy settling disagreements. Really dear you were quite good at the job."

"I remember arresting the claim jumpers at your moms place and then shooting the Army Sergeant who was stirring up all the trouble."

"Oh yes, things did improve some after that."

"I'll never forget getting the coded telegram informing us the tribe was moving down here. After you and Beth left it was sure lonesome until we started our herd north up here. I really didn't like being alone again."

"Remember out tent and the tiny rope bed you made for Beth?"

"I sure do, I remember your mother picking on you. She said she told you if you married me you'd be living in a tent, never mind she was living in a tent too."

"I know, she loves picking on you."

"I know, but deep down I know she loves me."

"I should say so. She told father they were the luckiest people in the world. Their son had married a wonderful girl and their daughter had done just as well."

"Remember our first sorting of the calves?"

"My goodness yes, the tribe had never been treated fairly by a white man until you came along. Then Uncle Thumb made you his blood brother."

"Mary I had no idea what it meant at the time, all I knew was it was important to him."

"Oh yes, and got you involved in a lot of the tribal affairs didn't it?"

"Yes it did, but I enjoyed being the peace maker for the tribe. I really love these people. Besides Will was born that first year up here. Then Matt a couple of years later."

"Yes and then you and the Circle Four boys got the herd of Herfords and Angus from the crooks down at Tulsa."

"But that was after we got rid of the crooked agent who was going to lease all the land."

"Oh yes, the one Uncle Thumb shot after he'd tried to shoot you."

"You know Mary, I think all my hats had a bullet hole in them the first few years we were married."

"I know, I accused you of making a fashion statement."

Yes, I remember that."

It was fun to sit and talk about the past and the things we'd became involved in. We'd built our herd and helped the tribe each year by sharing our calf crop. Now that all the families had their own herd the tribes share of the calves now went to keep up the school, parks and special events that the council voted on. The "Celebration" as it was called, was still held every year at the sorting. There was dancing, horse races, rodeo and all sorts of games for the kids. Folks came from all over the country. Some of the people lived in different states and still came back for the weekend.

Mary, whose hair was now streaked with gray, was even more beautiful today than she was when we first married. I had indeed been a lucky man.

We now lived in our home up on the side of the hill, which over-looked the valley where I kept my Angus herd.

We could see the lights go on in Will and Tee's home. Soon lights were on in Matt and Deb's.

"Look James, our little community is coming to life. Your folk's lights are on, so are Sam and Lesa's. I even see lights in Mac and Bird's place."

"Looks like the boys are still up, down at the race barns too."

"We've created our own little world James."

"Sort of seems that way Mary, care for another cup?"

"That would be nice."

I went into the house and poured our cups full and returned to the porch swing.

"Mary, I've been thinking. How would you like to take a trip? I'm not talking about Kansas City, I mean a real trip?"

"Well yes, I'd love to go. Where do you have in mind?"

"I'd like to see the Rockies. All these years I've heard about them but just had too much to do. Now that things have settled down, Will can handle everything here. He's been handling things for the past year anyway. I'm thinking it's time we did some traveling."

"I thought we could talk to Dad and Carla tomorrow and see when the best time to go would be."

"Sounds like a plan to me, we'll ride down after breakfast and check things out. James, what about inviting Harold and Flower to go? Besides, their kids are pretty much running things anyway."

"Sounds good, we'll talk to the folks and then go see Harold & Flower."

CHAPTER 2

▼

The next morning after breakfast Mary and I saddled a couple of Comanche's colts we kept in our small barn out back and rode down to the folks place.

Pa and Carla were out working in their small garden.

"Hey kids, I'm glad you all showed up. This woman is trying to work me to death."

"James, don't you and Mary believe a word he says."

"I don't Mom, I know who used to have to weed the garden."

"I'll bet you do."

"Son, you're not being much help."

We were all laughing as we went into their neat little house. They could have had a much larger one but hadn't wanted one.

Carla poured everyone coffee then inquired what we needed.

"We were wondering when would be the best time to go see the Rockies up around Denver. Or what ever you think we should see?"

"Carla, what about contacting our old friend Mel Foster? I'll bet he could show these kids some sights."

"You know he would. Why don't you send him a wire and see what he has to say."

"Kids, I'll send him a wire first thing."

"James, he'll do anything to get out of weeding the garden."

Pa was already out the back door laughing. We told Carla goodbye and rode up to Harold and Flower's place.

They saw us coming and met us at the gate.

"Saw you coming a mile off on those two geldings."

"They do have a little color don't they?"

"James, those two are as loud colored as their pappy. And I swear they are as good looking."

"Now that we have discussed your horses what are you two up too?"

"Flower, James and I are going on a trip. We thought you all might want to come along."

"Oh that sounds grand. The boys are pretty much running the place anyway. When are you planning on leaving?"

"James' father wired an old friend in Denver. We should know in a day or so."

"Well in that case we'll come down in a day or so and see what's going on. We need to check on Thumb anyway."

"I saw him day before yesterday. He and one of his old friends were going fishing. His friend's wife was baking a cake."

"Well that explains the fishing. He went fishing for the cake. Father will do most anything for cake."

"Well I guess we'll see you all in a day or so."

"Looking forward to it. We'll have lunch ready when you get there."

Mary and I rode off toward home. We were looking at the country and enjoyed the ride. We rode around the Angus and checked the calf crop. They were the finest yet.

"James, your sale this year should do really well. The calves are really special, the best I've ever seen."

"Thanks Mary. I've worked hard at raising the best. I'm really proud of this herd."

"And well you should be, how many will you have for sale this year?"

"Twenty two cows, fourteen heifers and eleven young bulls."

"You should make a tidy sum."

"I hope so. I figure the trip is going to cost us some money and I don't plan on skimping. We've worked and saved and I have no intention of not enjoying our trip."

"Praise the Lord, my husband has seen the light."

"You bet I have, I plan on enjoying life and spending more time with you. I'm really looking forward to it. Will can run the ranch and Matt is handling the racing stables and taking care of the books so we can relax and enjoy ourselves."

CHAPTER 3

▼

The next morning I rode down to Will and Tee's place. I caught Will as he was coming out the back door."

"Morning Pa. What brings you down here so early?"

"Come to tell you that your mother and I will be leaving in a couple of weeks. We're going to go see the Rockies. It's going to be the honeymoon we never had."

"Oh, Pa! That sounds great, you all certainly deserve the trip."

"Thanks son, I've been thinking on it for a while and its just time to do it. We're both in good health and I feel your mom deserves a trip."

"Good morning Pa, did I hear you say something about taking a trip?"

"You sure did Tee, I've decided to take Mary on a vacation honeymoon trip."

"That sounds wonderful. Lord knows you all deserve it. We'll look after things while your gone."

"Figured you would."

"Pa, let me feed the stock in the lots and we'll have a cup if you're not in a hurry."

"I'll help you feed and then have a cup. Tee knows how to make a good cup of coffee."

"Thanks Pa, I'll take that as a compliment."

"You should, it was meant to be. You and Deb are about the finest daughter-in-laws a man could ask for."

We fed the stock and had our coffee, later I rode down to the race barn where Mac, Deb, Matt and Willie were all looking at a young horse.

"Morning James, coming down to check on things?"

"Heck no Mac, this place is out of my jurisdiction. I just came down to let the kids know Mary and I are planning a trip. The honeymoon we never had."

"That's great dad, where are you planning on going?"

"I thought we'd go up Denver way and see the Rockies. We've both heard so much about them. I just figured it was time. Besides you all will be leaving in a week or so for the track."

"That we will, there's a track down at Hot Springs, Arkansas we're thinking about taking a couple of the colts down there. Matt and Deb will take the young horses to Chicago and give them a try. We're looking forward to having a good year, some of the colts are really showing a lot of talent."

"Great! Mac, I hope you all have a great year. Willie, are you still happy here?"

"Mr. James, you know I am. You folks are like family to me. Besides I'm getting to work with fine horses. Man can't ask for much more than that."

"Good, well kids I'd better get going. I've got to go see Pa and see if his friend answered his telegram."

I rode on to Pa's place and once again found him and Carla in the garden. He hadn't escaped after all.

"Morning folks, I see you're busy as usual."

"You know it son, I'm glad you're here. It saves me a trip. Our friend in Denver is retired and wants you all to come up to Jackson Hole then up North into the country they are trying to get made into a National Park. You all get tickets to Denver, he will have your tickets to the Hole as he calls it. He said to bring plenty of warn clothes and boots, you'll be camping out for a week or better. He said to tell you there may be a little snow. It doesn't leave until late June some times."

"I'm heading to town to book our tickets."

"I've already taken care of them son. You all leave a week from today at ten in the morning. You'll go to Kansas City then west to Denver."

"How much do I owe you Pa?"

"James Howard, don't you talk to us about those tickets. Your father and I were thrilled that you and Mary are finally going to get away. It's way past time, you all have been so busy taking care of everyone else you've forgotten about yourselves. Now go get ready and have a good time. Our friend or one of his people will meet you at the station in Denver. You kids just go have yourself a good time."

I rode back to the house and told Mary to grab her horse. We needed to talk to Harold and Flower.

We visited all the way to their place. Mary had a million questions, some of which I couldn't answer.

We told Harold and Flower about our plans and about the trip. Both of them were thrilled and said they would be down the afternoon before we were to leave.

"James Howard, I followed you up to this territory some years back, danged if I'm not ready to trail along after you again. The first time was so darn much fun."

Mary and I headed home, she was making a mental list of things we would need. I could see that the following week was going to be a hectic one.

Mary packed and unpacked suitcases for the third time by mid-week. I tried to stay out of her way and not get involved.

The day before we were to leave, Harold and Flower drove up in their buggy.

"Glad to see you folks."

"James, I want you to know I've carried luggage out to this buggy four times today."

"Only four times."

"I said today, James! She's had me loading and unloading it all day yesterday."

Mary and I both were laughing. Flower smiled at Harold and wagged her finger at him.

"No ma'am, I'm not getting close to you. No way!"

"Flower would you hit my friend?"

"You know James, I just might."

We all broke out laughing and had a wonderful afternoon. Then we had a wonderful afternoon meal and a bottle of wine that evening.

"James, I remember sleeping under a tarp on the ground and hoping it wouldn't rain. Now here we are a few years later setting on the porch of your fine home sipping on wine. Times have really changed haven't they?"

"They sure have Harold, I don't even sleep with my Sharps anymore."

CHAPTER 4

▼

The next morning we drove the buggy into town and left them at the livery after unloading our luggage at the train depot. The ride west from Kansas City was a lot of fun, neither Harold or Flower had ever seen western Kansas. The huge wheat fields had them glued to the train windows.

The next morning our train was nearing Colorado Springs we all got our first view of the snow capped Rockies.

"My Lord James, those things are enormous."

"Kind of makes you feel like a flat lander doesn't it Harold?"

"It sure does, now I understand why your mom gets that strange look on her face when she talks about them. Words just can't describe them, they just have to be seen to be believed."

We had a two-hour layover in Colorado Springs before going on to Denver. The women wandered around the train depot area looking in all the shops. People came here from all over for various reasons. Harold and I were content to just stand outside and look at the mountains. We were in awe of Pikes Peak, it was truly something special to see. Snow was still a good third of the way down the mountain.

"By gum James, this view from right here is worth the trip."

"It is sure enough something to see. Makes you want to saddle up and just see what's on the other side of them doesn't it?"

"Sure enough does but I'm not that fond of the snow. I don't reckon I'd make a very good mountain man."

"That could be, I reckon we'd better go check on the women."

We found Mary and Flower looking at a book.

"James, you should see this book it's the history of Colorado Springs, it's fantastic. The children will love it."

"Not to mention you'll like it too"

"Well of course I'm going to read it, dear. I'll read it while we're traveling."

"Mary you can read. I'm going to look. I don't want to miss a thing. This country is really something to see."

We caught our train a short while later and finally arrived in Denver. A friend of Mel's, Shirley Gibson met us at the train station.

"Mel said you'd be here today and I was to show you all around. I made hotel reservations for you and have a hack waiting."

"Thank you ma'am, we really appreciate you taking the time to help us.'

"You're James aren't you, and you'd have to be Mary. Mel has told me all about you. I feel like I've known you all for years."

"This is my friend Harold and his wife Flower. Harold came up the trail with me from Texas. Flower is Mary's cousin."

"I know, when Carla married your father she turned the boarding house over to me. We've written many letters back and forth over the years. She's told me all about her new extended family. She's so happy to have a family she never had before."

"I'm glad to hear that. We all love her an awful lot. She has made my father a very happy man and I'm proud to call her mom."

"Well let's get you all settled and tomorrow I'll show you the sights."

The hack Shirley had rented took us to our hotel. It was even finer than the one we had stayed in at Chicago. We ate in the hotel restaurant and had a wonderful meal. Afterwards we returned to our rooms and laid out our clothes for the next day. Shirley had told us to wear something warm.

We looked out our window at the magnificent mountains and finally went to bed.

The next morning Shirley showed up early and hustled us to a train station where we got on a train. As Harold put it a cute little train.

It was a retired narrow gage train that for years had hauled ore from the various mines in the area. It now hauled tourist up into the mountains past a lot of the now closed mines.

The train began the slow upward climb up the mountains. The bench seats on the car were comfortable and we were all in awe of the scenery around us.

Every turn in the track brought us a new and more spectacular view. Around noon the train pulled into a small town where we unloaded and got something to eat.

"My father would love to see this country."

"He sure would Flower, I wish he could have come with us."

"He is getting old James, he told me the other day that when he passes, many people will mourn his passing."

"You got that right, I for one will be lost. He's like a second father to me."

"He looks upon you and Harold as his sons. Your friend, Sam, is one of his best friends. He and Lesa make sure that father has all the bacon and ham he needs."

"He has taught my children about the old ways. We're writing them down so they won't be lost to those who come later."

"That's great, when I first moved up here I was so dumb about your people's ways. He took me under his wing (so to speak) and taught me."

"Flower, maybe we should get together and pool our work."

"I may do that we could pool our work and maybe make a book for the people."

Mary and Harold, along with Shirley, came back with sandwiches and drinks.

"Are you all enjoying the train ride?"

"We're having a ball Shirley. The scenery is something we'll never be able to describe."

"That's a fact James, I'm not sure I'll even want to try."

"Shirley, we want you to know how much we have enjoyed the day so far. I for one can't wait to see what the rest of the trip will bring."

"I'm so glad you all are enjoying the day. This is the first time I've ever taken the ride myself. A lot of the folks who stay at the boarding house have taken this trip and all of them have loved it."

"Well they certainly told you right, this is a fantastic trip."

The rest of the ride was as impressive as the first half. The sun was going down when we arrived back at our hotel and I was glad I had my lined jacket.

The next day we wandered around town and the women did some shopping. Harold and I actually found a saddle shop and I found a pair of silver mounted bits that I just had to have for my paint gelding, Slick.

"Harold, these bits cost as much as one of my good Herford cows but I don't care."

"James, you know I've done some thinking lately. We've worked our whole lives to get to where we are and by golly if we want something I think we should have it. Buy the bits, they'll look great on that wild colored horse of yours."

I bought the bits and another pair for Mary. I felt great. I found a couple of pairs of fancy reins with silver ferrules on them for Will and Tee.

Harold bought a couple of silver buckles for his two boys and a barrette for his daughter. When we left the shop we both felt great.

That evening I gave Mary her bits and showed her the pair I got for Slick.

"James, he's already one of the best looking horses in the country. With those bits it will only add to his eye catching appeal."

"You don't think they are too much?"

"I think they are beautiful, and I think they show extremely good taste. Besides you have the best horses in the country, why not show you're proud of them. I'm sure going to use the bits you got for me."

We met Harold and Flower and once more had supper in the hotel dinning room. We talked about our day and about our next day's travel.

"We go the Cheyenne and change trains there, James."

"That's right Harold we take the early morning train there and have an hour layover before we catch the train to Salt Lake then we catch another train to Jackson Hole."

"Well, I guess we'll get to see some country."

"I'm sure we will, I'm looking forward to the trip. Harold, this is almost as big an adventure as the drive up from Texas."

"I'll bet we'll be a lot cleaner at the end of this trip."

We all had a good laugh and went back to our rooms. The next day would start early.

We caught the train to Cheyenne the next morning. We enjoyed the trip because the country was changing. We were traveling across a rolling landscape with new plants, some of which we'd never seen.

It was high desert plains, a gentleman told us. He sold farm and ranch equipment supplies to businesses in the Denver area.

We were rolling along the desert country but to our left were the Rockies. It was a beautiful sight.

We arrived in Cheyenne and found our train was expected to be on time. The baggage clerk checked our bags and we went to get a sandwich and to see some of the local shops.

We soon realized that this was cattle country. Cowboys in big hats and chink chaps as they were called walked the streets. We grabbed a quick sandwich and were back at the station when our train pulled in from the east.

We had sleeper compartments for our trip to Salt Lake. We sat in the parlor car and looked at the high desert country. We began to see antelope, deer and even some elk in a far off creek bottom. It was fascinating.

We turned in early and were up having coffee when we pulled in to Salt Lake. Our train to Jackson Hole was loading for the two and half hour trip. We wanted to see the Great Salt Lake and the Morman Church but would do that on our return trip.

We found seats on the train and began the last leg of our trip to Jackson Hole or "The Hole" as the locals called it.

The Hole sat in a river bottom with mountains to the west and east. We heard people talking about snow up to four feet deep. I was looking forward to seeing what the town looked like.

The town of Jackson Hole was small and had some businesses that were only open for the short summer months and closed after the elk and deer season.

When we dismounted the train, an older gentleman waved to us from a wagon.

"You folks be the Howards?"

"We are, sir."

"Good, I'll get your baggage loaded then we'll head out to the cabin."

Harold and I helped the gentleman with our bags then loaded up into the large modified wagon.

We later found it was an ore wagon our friend had bought and had redone to his ideas. There were padded seats behind the driver with plenty of room for luggage behind. At the edge of town we turned off the main road and followed a narrow road up along the side of the mountain. Then we saw the cabin.

The cabin was made of logs and was two stories tall. It was huge, it looked more like a hotel than a cabin.

"My Lord James, it's huge."

"Mr. Foster entertains a lot of folks in the early fall months. Folks come here to hunt. The town really grows for a month or so, then it's just us locals up here for the winter."

"You have a lot of snow?"

"Four, five feet is usual. I've seen it a lot worse though."

"James, I'm sure glad it's summer time."

"Me too Harold, that much snow doesn't sound good to me at all."

"Mr. Dent will be at the cabin. He was checking on the horses that were delivered yesterday." We ship them down towards Salt Lake to a ranch for the winter."

We pulled up in front of the cabin. A tall gray haired gentleman in jeans and a wool plaid shirt came out the door.

"Welcome folks get down and come on in. I've been waiting for you. I'm Melvin Foster, but you folks call me Mel. Lets see, you would be James, Mary, Harold and Flower."

"That's right, sir."

"Your folks have told me all about you kids. Heavens, I feel like I've known you all for years. Now come on in and get yourselves warmed up. My men will bring your luggage into the cabin."

"Mel, James and I lived in a log cabin. Believe me, your place it not a cabin."

Mel burst into laughter.

"Mary, your father and mother-in-law told me you spoke your mind and they were right. What the kitchen is now, was the cabin. I have built the rest after I hit the big mine. Since then we've just added on a room or two."

"Well Mel, if you don't stop adding there won't be any trees left in the country."

Mel and the rest of us were laughing. The evening was so much fun just getting to know each other.

"Now tell me, what do you folks want to see while you're here."

"Whatever you want to show us Mel, we're on vacation and don't have a time limit on us."

"That's great, there's things North of here that will make your heart skip a beat. Mary, do you ladies know how to ride?"

"Mel, if it has hide and hoofs Flower and I can ride it."

"That's great, it will make the trip a lot faster and easier. Where I want to take you it's tough to get a wagon into. We'll take packhorses and meet them at night. That way we can roam about and take side trips during the day."

For the next two days Mel seemed to always be on the run. His men were shoeing horses, checking tents and packing gear. Harold and I helped to get things ready.

We rolled out of bed early and had a big breakfast. We put on plenty of clothes and our heavy coats. The horses were saddled and waiting for us outside the front door. We followed Mel out the door and mounted the horses he had chosen for us.

"Folks, the boys left with the camp stuff an hour ago. We'll cover a good amount of ground for a day or so. I'll show you what are called the Grand Tetons. Folks they are the most beautiful things you will every see. I'm serious! They will be in your mind the rest of your life."

Little did we know how right he was. We followed Mel north on a little used trail that wandered along a stream. As we rode along Mel pointed out various points of interest.

"Mel, what are those marks on the rock over there?"

"Snow marks Harold, it's where a trapper marked the snow depth."

"That mark must be close to eight feet."

"Yes it is. I managed to get hold of a few logbooks that some of the old time mountain men kept over the years. They are very interesting reading. I'll show them to you when we get back."

"Mel, those journals would be priceless. It would be wonderful if they were put into a book."

"Mary, I'd not thought of that, but by golly, you're right. You think folks would buy a thing like that?"

"Mel, I'm sure they would, think about it. They could cause history books to be rewritten."

"She's right Mel, you've got actual accounts of how the mountain men lived and died. Not just someone's thoughts about how they lived."

"James, I'll do it! I'll get one of my people on it as soon as I get back to Denver."

"How many journals do you have Mel?"

"Twelve or fourteen. I'm not even sure. I've just bought, or have been given them over the years. I have a couple of friends who have several copies. I'll see if I can borrow them."

"That would be wonderful Mel! Could I pay you for one, I'd love to have a copy for my children to read."

"Flower, I'll send you all a copy as soon as I get them printed and you'll not pay me for them."

"But Mel!"

"Folks, I'm wealthy, very wealthy. It will be fun to make up a book and do something for folks."

We stopped in a small meadow near a swift running stream and had lunch that had been left for us by the crew who were ahead of us.

Mel took a picnic basket from a rock storage pit and handed out sandwiches and fruit. Last, but not least, he took out a bottle of wine and glasses.

"My Lord Mel, all the comforts!"

"You bet! No need to have to rough it if you don't have too. We've built these pits along the trail over the last few years. I've been trying to get the place we're going made into a national park. I've spent some money but what's up ahead will be worth it. I think you all will agree with me after you see it."

We ate lunch then resumed our journey.

We saw deer, unlike our whitetail deer at home. Mel called them mule deer. It was easy to see where they got their name because of their huge ears.

"Now folks look over there to the west. That stand of mountains are called the Grand Tetons, what do you think?"

We all sat on our horses as if frozen. The stand of mountains were so beautiful, words could not begin to describe them.

"They are so……..."

"I know what you're trying to say, James. Come along we'll get to our camp sight and you all can look at them through my big telescope."

An hour or so before sunset we rode into a beautiful mountain meadow and saw our camp for the night was already set up and waiting for us.

It was plain to see that the men who worked for Mel had done this before. The camp cook already had his Dutch oven on the campfire and whatever he was cooking, smelled wonderful.

We got off our horses and tied them up where one of the men directed us and went over to the fire for a cup of coffee.

At home, we would have been seating in the heat. But here, we all wore vest and the sun was not yet down.

We had coffee and took turns looking through the large telescope at the Tetons. Harold spotted some mountain sheep high up on the side of the mountains.

We ate our evening meal and were assured by Mel that we'd not seen anything yet. We went to our tents and found cots set up and our bed made.

"I'll say this for Mel, he goes first class."

"He does that James. James, thank you for taking me on this vacation."

"For Lord's sake Mary, don't thank me. This had been one of the greatest times of my life. I've seen things and hope to see things our kids will have a chance to see later. Mary, this is something we'll never forget."

"That's a fact, James. But now we'd better get some rest, Mel says we'll be covering a good distance tomorrow."

The next morning we were having coffee and watched as Mel's crew tore down the tents packed them away on the packhorses and left. We finished our coffee and were careful to put out our fire.

Mounted on our horses we again headed north, riding into an area of huge tall pine trees. The air smelled wonderful.

As we rode along I rode up beside Mel and visited as the trail continued north. We covered a good piece of ground that day and when we had finished our meal, I asked Mel how he had met Pa.

"Met your pa at Carla's boarding house. I knew her husband before he was killed in a mine cave in. I had a claim and was making expenses and not much more. A fellow had a claim above mine on the mountain. One day he just up and quit. He offered to sell me his claim. I told him I didn't have any money. He just up and signed the claim over to me and said if I made it pay I was to send him a hundred dollars."

"A week or so later a couple of new fellers set a charge of powder up the mountain from me. They set off the charge and at the time seemed to have blown half the mountain up."

"The explosion killed one and darned near killed the other. Later that day after things settled down, I walked up to my new claim and discovered a good vein of ore had been exposed but it was running straight down, right towards my original claim. Problem was I needed money for equipment. A pick and shovel just wasn't going to do the job."

"I collected a few samples and headed for Carla's place, she always new someone who had money to invest in a grubstake. Well I walked into Carla's place and found her pouring your father a cup of coffee. There he sat in his fine black suit, handmade boots, white shirt and string tie. He was younger then and had just enough gray in his hair at his temples to look distinguished."

"I didn't like him at all. He was talking to Carla and she had a big smile on her face."

"I spoke to Carla and went out back to wash up a mite, now I wanted to talk to her but I sure didn't want any stranger listening in on the conversation."

"Carla wanted to know what I needed. All I could do was stand there looking dumb."

"Then your pa spoke up and asked me if I needed a grubstake. All I could do was shake my head. He mentioned a figure and I nodded."

"A minute or two later he came out of his room and handed me a bank draft."

"Make it work Mel."

"Well I didn't know what to say. I finally asked him how much the interest would be."

"Your Pa just smiled and said for me to bring Carla enough gold to make herself a wedding ring. Danged if he hadn't proposed to her right in front of me."

"Carla asked him if that was a proposal and he said he reckoned it was. Well danged my hide if she didn't up and kiss him right there."

"That's when I decided your father had to be all right."

"That sounds like pa, for a fact."

"Well I went out and bought equipment and went to work. Five month's later I went to Carla's place with your Pa's money. I found Shirley had taken over the boarding house. Your Pa had come back a month later and got Carla. They were married and he had taken her back to your town."

"After that, everything I touched seemed to go well. I bought another claim and it later turned out to be a fine buy. I was suddenly a very wealthy man."

"I was sitting in a restaurant in Denver a few months later when your father walked in. I invited him to sit with me and before I could ask about Carla he told me she was home to help with her grandchild."

"That would have been Will, James."

"Sure was! Paco and Rosa were in New Mexico selling her ranch at the time. I remember Pa was upset because he had to leave."

"He was upset alright, he was waiting on the railroad to let him know when they could ship the cattle he had bought."

"I gave him a check for what I owed him and told me I'd ship him the block of gold for the ring."

"Kids, he was thrilled that I had done well and wouldn't take any interest in the mine when I offered it to him. He said he'd already knew I had gold I just needed money to get to it."

"That told me a whole lot about your father. So later, when I bought another claim and it also came in, I put your folks down for a share. They should be quite well-to-do by now."

"Is that right? I never knew anything about it. He has never said a word."

They sure haven't, Carla still makes most of the dresses and all of your fathers shirts."

"That sounds like Carla, she never was one to waste money."

"Well they've been getting a monthly check for about three years now. My accountant came to me to get your father's address."

"Well Mel, if he sent it to Pawhuska, Oklahoma, he would have certainly got it. After all I think half of the town is related or claim to be."

"That's what I've heard Mary. James' father has told me all about your extended family."

"Mel, how did you come to be here in Jackson Hole?"

"Came out here with a business friend on a fall elk hunt and fell in love with the place. The cabin we stayed in was for sale so I bought it. This is where I come to get away from all the business dealings."

"I've got people working for me who take care of the day to day business. I check in every now and then but during the summer I try and stay up here and promote the park."

"Your folk's telegram arrived the day before I was going to start up here. I sure hope you all enjoy seeing it as much as I do."

"Don't worry Mel, we're having a ball. Everything here is so beautiful."

"Good, Mary, you and Flower are cousins?"

"Yes we are."

"These boys from Texas moved in and tried to marry the whole tribe"

"Oh no, I had James cornered long before we reached home. It took Harold a little longer."

Mary told Mel about how we met and it was late when we finally turned it. It seemed Mel had laughed all evening long listening to Mary tell the tales of the drive.

The next day we again left early and things we saw amazed us all.

We lunched close to a hot mud flat. It was wild. The mud was hot to the touch and we watched as the mud bubbled up over an area of two or three acres.

After lunch we rode on and began to hear a roar that got louder as we continued north. Then we were finally able to see what was making all the noise. It was a waterfall, something none of us had ever seen. It seemed the water fell forever.

"My Lord James, have you ever seen anything like it?"

"You know I haven't Mary, it's just unreal."

Flower and Harold stood watching, as if hypnotized.

"What do you think kids?"

"It's unreal Mel, totally unreal!"

"Mel, there's been more water coming over the falls since we been here than James and I saw the whole time we lived in Texas."

"That's no joke Harold! Can you imagine trying to get cattle across this river?"

"No way James, I'd just stay on the other side and look at the falls."

We visited a while longer then mounted up and rode on a mile or so to our campsite.

Mel had a surprise for us when we arrived.

"Who wants a hot bath?"

"Mel, you're kidding us right?"

"Not hardly, you all follow me."

We followed Mel down the riverbank until we came upon a small stream coming down from the mountain.

"Mary, check the water!"

Mary kneeled down and checked the water with her finger.

"It's hot, Mel."

"You bet, but if you move right over here you'll find it's just about right."

Mary moved over and again tested the water.

"Oh my, this feels wonderful. Mel, where does this water come from?"

"A hot underground spring just up the mountain. If you ladies want a bath just get your things and try the water."

"Flower, let's get our things, I for one, want a bath!"

"I'm with you, Mary; I brought a couple of bars of soap."

"Gentlemen, I guess we'd better go back to camp until the ladies are finished with their bath."

We sat in camp and had coffee as Mary and Flower went down the path to the hot spring.

"James, a couple of years ago there was a mare running back east called Princess Mary, is their any connections?"

"She belonged to my sons Mel"

"Good Lord, it never occurred to me! I saw her run in New York. She won the race easy. Do you have any colts out of her?"

"We have a two year old and she has a colt by her side now. We sold her first colt to a gentleman from England. The colt has done very well over there. The two year old is a filly and is one good looking animal."

"Have you named her yet?"

"Oh yes, our youngest son who named her mother has named her Princess II."

"That's great, when will you run her?"

"The kids will be taking her to Chicago this week. She'll get a start in late July or early August."

"I'll be watching the racing form for her. What's your stable name?"

"It's the "Five HHHHH Stable.""

"How neat! An H for every family member."

"You have to understand Mel, everyone had a hand in training the Princess, and it was a real family affair."

I told him about getting Willie to work for us. How we'd built our own track and how Mary and Beth would ride different horses for her to catch.

"That would have been a thrill. I'd love to see your place."

"Then come Thanksgiving Mel, that way you can meet the whole family."

"Mary, I didn't hear you all come back."

"It's the Indian way Mel, we're sneaky."

"How was your bath?"

"Wonderful, if you want more hot water just move upstream."

"James, the soap and a towel are on a rock next to the stream. Now go get a bath."

"Harold, you go with him."

"Yes ladies, we're gone."

Harold and I got our bath and were just finishing dressing when he suddenly seemed to freeze in place.

"James, don't move he said softly. There's a bear, a very big bear! Just up stream from us."

I slowly turned my head and saw the bear. He was huge with rough hair but most impressive was the bear's muzzle. It was almost snow white. The way the bear moved, it was plain to see he was old. He shuffled along slowly and when he reached the hot stream, he waded right in and laid down with a groan.

I spoke softly to Harold.

"Let's move, the wind is in our favor."

We moved slowly away down the path. The bear never moved, he appeared to be enjoying the hot bath.

When we returned to camp we told Mel about the bear.

"Oh, you saw Old Timer. He's old and the hot stream makes him feel better. We've been seeing him ever since I moved up here. He's big isn't he?"

"I should say! If he stood up he would be near eight feet tall."

"Closer to nine, Harold. I've seen him standing up. I'm glad he made the winter. It's almost like he's an old friend."

"James, Mel is going to come down for Thanksgiving."

"Great, I know the folks will be tickled to see you. Besides, he will get to meet the family."

"Mary has told me about them. I'm really looking forward to the holiday."

That night, after we went into our tent, Mary had just gotten under the covers. I turned the lantern out.

"James."

"Yes Mary."

"I' sure glad Pa got Carla. Mel's nice but she just belongs with us."

"You bet she does Mary. I'm one lucky fellow. I've had two great moms."

"That's true dear."

The next four days were wonderful. We saw sulfur pits, mud pits, water falls but most impressive were the geysers.

Mel sat us down in the shade and told us to watch.

About twenty minutes later the biggest dome like mound began to throw hot water into the air. We heard and felt a rumble then suddenly, steam and water began blowing up into the air. Then and with a great roar, steam and water blew fifty or sixty feet into the air. It lasted only a minute or so but was something none of us would ever forget.

"Mel, that beats anything I've ever seen!"

"It is impressive, isn't it Harold."

"It sure enough is how often does it go off?"

"Once every hour or there abouts."

"Lord have mercy!"

"See why I'm working so hard to get this made into a park. No one should own this valley, it should be open for everyone to see."

"You're right about that Mel. Everyone should be able to see this place. It's wonderful!"

"Mel, you're wanting to get this made into a park. Ever thought about running an ad in the newspapers? You know, advertise pack trips back into this country. Your boys could run the operation. Lord knows they know how to make folks comfortable. Instead of catering to all the big money folks, make it something the public. You know, the more common man can afford."

"James, you may be right. Yes sir! I'll give that some thought."

"Mel with what you spend on the trips for the Washington big shots, you could take a hundred common folks and have a hundred folks talking for the park instead of one."

"Mary, you two folks are right. I'll get my people working on it. I'll need to hire some folks but the boys here know a lot of folks who could use the money."

"Don't worry about our area of the country Mel. We'll be telling everybody!"

"Oh yes, I want my children to be able to see this for themselves someday."

"Folks, we'll start drifting back towards the Hole tomorrow. There's plenty of things to see so you won't be bored."

He was right! We weren't. We saw herds of elk grazing on the mountain meadows. They were fun to watch. The calves ran and played while the cows grazed on the lush grasses. There were deer, a couple of grizzlies and we even saw a pair of mountain lions trailing a deer herd.

"James, you and Harold should come up and go elk hunting with me this fall. It's something to see and hear. The bulls are chasing the cows and there are fights a plenty."

To hear one of those bulls bugle is one of the strangest and weirdest sounds you'll ever hear."

"I told Mel about the cougar I'd killed after it had caused Thumb's grandson's horse to run away and throw him."

"They can be a problem. A few years back we lost a pack mule to a large female. One of the boys shot her but I've always felt bad about that."

"Sometimes you have to do things you don't like, but don't have a choice."

We watched Mel fly fish and found it amazing how he could catch a trout on the feathered flies he tied one night in camp. Harold gave it a try and after a few attempts he managed to catch a nice brown trout.

He was thrilled with his accomplishment. The trip was a complete success.

A couple of days later we pulled into Mel's place. It had indeed been a wonderful trip. We were all sad to see it end.

We all bathed and after a grand meal sat in front of the huge fireplace. We enjoyed the rest of the evening.

Mel promised to come to our place for Thanksgiving. Afterwards, we went to bed. The train would leave early in the morning.

Mel met us at breakfast and told me to tell Pa and Carla he was looking forward to seeing them.

"I'll be sure and tell them Mel. I'm sure they will be looking forward to seeing you too."

Mel took us to the train station. After handshakes and kisses, he waved to us as we pulled out of the station.

We found our seats and sat down for the short ride to Salt Lake.

"James, we've had a grand time but I sure do feel sorry for Mel. He's got more money than he'll ever spend and he's lonesome."

"You're right Harold, Mary and I talked about that last night. He enjoyed himself with us because he knew all we wanted from him was to show us his country. Every time someone tries to get close to him he's afraid that all they want is his money. He doesn't have any real friends."

"James, we're not rich in his league but in one since we're far richer. We have our wives and family. Mel only has his money. I really feel sorry for him."

"You're both wrong about one thing, Mel doesn't have a family but he has the park. That has replaced a family for him. One of the hands told me how much he'd enjoyed the trip. He told me, Mel had never gone to so many different places with any of the folks before and never for near as long as we were gone."

"Flower, you're probably right, he does love the country up there."

Our plans were changed in Salt Lake. Our train west was loading when we arrived. We'd have to see things in Salt Lake another time. We barely made the train.

A couple of days later we pulled into Pawhuska.

As I helped Mary and Flower from the train I heard Pa call my name.

"Son, did you have a good time?"

"Pa it was wonderful, Mel took us to see the most wonderful things. I made him promise me he'd come down here for Thanksgiving."

"He did, Mary how did you get that done?"

"Just sweet talked him Pa."

"I believe you did."

"Pa you should take mom up there, you all would have a wonderful time."

"I don't know how she would take to camping out."

"Oh Mr. Howard, she would love it, Mel has tents with cots and everything is set up and done for you."

"That's true just like Flower said. We had a camp cook who prepared our meals and is almost as good as Cookie. We even had wine every night with supper."

"Harold, the cook must be good if you compare him to Cookie."

"He's good Pa, Mel hired him away from some fancy restaurant in Denver. He's Mel's personal cook and just loves the outdoors."

"Sounds good to me kids. I may just talk to Carla about a trip like you all said. We'll talk to Mel about it when he's here."

"Carla said for you kids to come to the house for pie and coffee. She told me not to take "no" for an answer."

In that case I guess we'd better get our luggage."

We followed Pa out to his place and we're met at the gate by mom. I'd never call her Carla anymore. She was just mom, my mom.

We had pie and coffee and tried to explain to the folks everything we had seen.

Mary had to tell mom about the food and the hot stream bathes. Flower was excited and told her about the napkins and wine used every night.

"My goodness, maybe we should go up there and see things for ourselves. I can still ride a horse and I'd like to see all the things the children have tried to describe."

"We'll get with Mel and plan a trip dear."

We went home later. Harold and Flower spent the night and headed out the next morning. We spent the next two days explaining to the kids about the trip. It was hard for them to imagine the geyser we described. Tee wanted to go see the valley when her children were old enough.

The summer moved on. Mac and Willie had traveled north to New York with the main race string and were having a very good year.

Matt and Deb had just returned from Chicago to give the two year olds a rest. The filly Princess II was three for three in her starts and was showing signs of maybe being as good as her mother. The kids also informed us we would be grandparents again. Deb was expecting in January.

Tee did a lot of riding with Matt. With Mack gone Bird was free to watch the two grandkids and give Tee a break. All in all everyone was happy.

Mary's mom and Dad had taken a trip to Washington to visit some of his old friends.

Pa and mom came by the house one day after lunch. Mary had lemonade made, so we sat out on the porch.

"Pa, I've got a question to ask you."

"Fire away son."

"Not that I care, but what have you done with all the money Mel has sent you?"

"What money son?" Mel doesn't owe me any money. He paid me back years ago."

"No Pa, I mean the money you get from the mine every month."

"Haven't seen any money son, Mel wrote and said he'd given us a share in a mine but we've never seen any money. Figured it had went sour and closed."

I looked at Mary and she looked at me.

"Pa we've seen the mine and, believe me, it wasn't a bust. Mel thinks you've been getting a check every month since it opened."

"Carla, you know anything about this?"

"Not a thing, if there's any money coming into the bank its news to me."

We explained to them what Mel had told us. Now if they weren't getting the money, who was? Something was wrong, bad wrong.

"Pa, something isn't right. Mel told Mary and I about the mine and believes you all have been getting a check each month. If you don't mind me meddling in your business I'm going to see if I can find out where that money is going."

"Son you have your father and my permission to look into this. We'd like to know ourselves."

After the folks were gone Mary and I sat talking.

"James, Mel thinks your folks are getting a check which we know they are not. We know that Mel wrote your father a letter letting him know he and your mom had a share in the mine. I'm thinking Mel needs to do some checking and be very careful about how he does it."

"I think you're right Mary, how about we ride into town and send Mel a telegram. He's still at the Hole so maybe he can start checking things out, maybe the money's just being held in a bank in Denver."

Mary and I rode into town and sent the telegram to Mel letting him know folks had never seen any of the money from the mine.

Art sent the telegram and Mary and I walked across the street to Tom's office. His office had grown like our town and he had hired a couple of young men from the tribe to help in the office. He had been responsible for them going to law school and had hired them upon graduation. They all were kept busy looking after the tribe's business.

We were visiting with Tom when Art came into the office and handed me a telegram.

The telegram was short and to the point.

"IMPOSSIBLE" SIGN CHECKS MYSELF. (STOP) ON WAY TO DENVER (STOP) WILL FIND OUT WHERE. MEL.

"Oh my goodness, I'd hate to be in some ones shoes when Mel hits Denver. He's fit to be tied."

"You have that right Mary, someone's either putting the money in the wrong account or has been putting it somewhere behind Mel's back."

"Your father has never received a check James?"

"Not a one Tom, and it's been several years."

"Is it a big mine, James?"

"Sure is Tom. It's the biggest Mel has in operation."

"Then he has a problem. I can see how it could have happened. Your folks are retired and not likely to travel much, so if someone decided to try and divert the money it was a perfect opportunity. The only way they could get caught was if your folks were to travel to Denver and look Mel up. With Mel gone so much, I'd venture to guess it's someone who controls Mel's mail."

"They could screen any letter your folks might write to him."

"That's about it Mary."

"If that's the case Mel will be heartbroken, he tries so hard to treat everyone right."

"I know Mary, but we're talking about quite a lot of money and people do have weaknesses."

I hollered at Art and told him to send any telegrams from Mel out to me at the ranch.

"No problem James it's my pleasure."

CHAPTER 5

───────────────▼───────────────

Two days later just after breakfast a young man rode up to our gate.

"Mr. Howard, I have a telegram for you sir."

I took the telegram and reached to hand the young man some money.

"Sir you don't owe me anything. The banker has already paid me."

"Then thank you young man."

"You're welcome sir, see you later."

I walked back into the house and opened the telegram.

"FOUND MONEY (STOP) IN ACCOUNT HERE IN DENVER (STOP) WIRING FUNDS (STOP) HAVE NEW BOOKKEEPER (STOP) SEE YOU THANKSGIVING (STOP) MEL.

There was a note attached from the banker asking Pa to come to town at his earliest convenience.

"Mary, change your clothes. We've got to take the folks into town."

I handed her the telegram.

"Get the buggy ready, James. I'll be ready in a few minutes. Oh this is so exciting!"

When I drove around to the front of the house Mary stood waiting, a large smile on her face.

We drove to the folks and found them ready to go to town. Mom needed to do some shopping and Pa was getting ready to get their buggy.

"What are you kids smiling so big about?"

I handed him the telegram and when he finished reading it, I handed him the note from the banker.

"Carla, Carla get out here, woman!"

"My Lord dear, what's all the rush? James, Mary when did you kids get here?"

"Never mind that woman, look at what they have brought us."

Pa handed the telegram to here and then the note.

"Oh my goodness, James are you responsible for this?"

"I just called the matter to Mel's attention, Mom."

"Well apparently you got it son."

"I think so. Now if you all will allow us, we'd like to take you to town."

Pa helped mom into the buggy then stepped in himself.

"Son lets go to town."

CHAPTER 6

▼

We drove up to the front of the bank and found the banker waiting at the front door.

"Mr. and Mrs. Howard, come in"

"Be there in a moment sir. Kids, you come along with us."

"Pa you don't need my help."

"Son, please, honor my wishes. We want you to come along with us. We've discussed this every since you brought this matter to our attention."

"Yes Sir, be glad too."

I tied the buggy horse then Mary and I followed folks into the bank.

"You folks come on into my office."

Everyone found a chair and sat down.

"Would anyone care for coffee?"

"Not now sir, you said to come here and we did. Coffee can come later. Seems a friend of mine sent me some money."

"Oh yes sir, he surely did."

"Alright, now how much?"

"Six hundred fifty."

Pa looked at me, disappointment in his eyes.

"Well six hundred and fifty dollars is better than nothing."

"Thousand Mr. Howard, six hundred and fifty thousand."

Pa was pale as a ghost. Mom's face was frozen.

"You're telling us Pa just go six hundred and fifty thousand dollars"

"That is correct. With what he already has on deposit I'd say your father is a very wealthy man."

"Pa, it looks as if you're rich."

Pa looked at mom, who had tears in her eyes.

"Carla darling, we're going shopping. I mean really going shopping."

"Carla, you alright?"

"I'm fine Mary, I guess I'm shocked."

"Mr. Howard, I received a wire from the Kansas City Bank this morning. They want to know what you want done with the money. I'd suggest you get an attorney out to advise you what to do with your money if you don't mind."

"Mary, is my grandson over at Tom's office?"

"Yes sir, he has been working there for a week or so. They came back from the track and he came back to help Tom."

"Would you go get him and Tom for me please, daughter?"

"Yes sir, I'll be back in a moment."

"Good, I don't know if my legs would hold me right now."

"Son, this would never have happened if you'd not done your checking. Now here's what we're going to do."

"Pa, maybe you'd better wait a day or so before you make any decisions. There is no need to get in a hurry."

"Don't need to wait son, Carla and I have already discussed what we wanted to do. Right Carla?"

"That's right so James Howard you just set there and listen!"

"Yes ma'am."

Mary came back into the room with our son Matt and her brother Tom.

"You wanted to see me grandpa?"

"I did grandson, I've come into some money and I want you to handle it for me."

"Yes sir, I can do that. What do you want me to do?"

"First off I want you to draw up papers giving half of it to you folks."

"Fine sir, how much money are we talking about?"

Pa looked at Mary.

"I never said a word to him Pa, this is your business."

Pa smiled and looked at our son.

"Six hundred and fifty thousand dollars."

Our son's mouth dropped open in shock. He looked at me and I nodded my head.

"Grandpa, you're telling me you've just received six hundred and fifty thousand dollars and you want to give half of it to mom and dad."

"That's correct, Carla and I have talked it over and that's what we want to do. Now what do we have to do to make it legal?"

"First off grandpa, where did you get the money?"

"Friend of your grandma's and mine. He was starting up a mine, he gave your grandma and me a share a couple of years ago. The money was laying in a bank in Denver until your father here found it."

"James, I want to hear this whole story when you have time."

"I'll fill you in when we have time Tom."

"Matt, the banker here says I need a lawyer to look after my money."

"Well we can make some investments for you and your money should continue to grow."

"That's great, when your grandma and I are gone whatever is left goes to you three grandkids. So Matt, manage it wisely."

"Yes sir, I'll do my best. But you all will hang around for a good long while. Dad, what do you and mother want to do?"

"Truthfully son, I'm not sure. I guess you might as well manage our share too."

"How about the piece of ground just north of Aunt Dove's old place?"

"Is it still for sale?"

"Yes sir."

"Then get it bought! I'll put that little bunch of Longhorns I've had farmed out on it."

"I'll take care of it this afternoon. Grandpa, how much do you want to put in the bank here?"

"I'm not sure, how much would it cost your grandma and me to go to Paris?"

"Paris France, that sounds great. I'll make all the arrangements."

"How much will it cost grandson?"

"Why do you care grandpa, you've got another check coming next month. Don't worry about what you leave us kids. We're all doing fine. You just take grandma to Paris and both of you have a great time."

"James, wait until Harold hears about this. You know, he'll laugh."

"You bet he will, he's always said he'd rather have my luck than skill."

"James, may I get another couch for the living room?"

"Mary, get whatever you want."

"Matt, lets you and me go back to the office and put together a plan for the investments you'll need to make. Then you can have our banker here get the money in all the right places."

I looked at Mom and Pa. They were both now gray headed but were both still straight and tall. Not only that they both were smiling like a couple of teenagers. They were happy and looking forward to their upcoming trip.

Carla came over to Mary and me. She gave Mary a hug and I got a kiss.

"Thank you, son."

"It was my pleasure mom."

"Mary, he hasn't changed has he?"

"No mom he hasn't, he still can't take credit for things he gets done."

"James, thanks for just being you and most of all allowing me to have such a wonderful family."

"Mom, you deserve it, I've watched Pa build his business and not smile a lot. Then you came along and he's never quit smiling. I want to thank you."

I gave her a hug and a kiss on the cheek. We both had tears in our eyes.

Mary came over and gave me a hug.

"Grandpa, when do you all want to leave?"

"Sooner the better, I'm not getting any younger you know."

"I'll let you know when I have things set. I'll get things lined out, then Deb and I will be down."

"James, Mary if you'll take us home I feel like cooking and maybe have a glass of wine. Think you could eat something James?"

"You bet mom, I'll get the buggy ready."

"Pa, your son should weigh three hundred pounds. Lord I've tried to fatten him up but I guess he's just not an easy keeper."

"You should know Mary, you let him chase you until you caught him."

Folks and Mary were all laughing when they came out of the bank.

"What's so funny?"

"Private joke son, private joke."

Three days later Mary and I took the folks to the train station. They waved at us as they left to begin their Paris trip.

Mary and I walked over to Tom's office.

"Did they get off alright?"

"Sure did, they were like a couple of kids."

"I hope they don't get sea sick."

"I never said a word about it. Pa wanted to take her on this trip so bad. It seems it's the only thing Carla ever said she wanted to see."

"Well now, she's going to get to see it."

Mary and I headed home but decided to stop at her folks for a cup of coffee and get all the local news.

"James, what are you going to do with the money?"

"Well, Mary has ordered a new couch and I've bought a piece of ground on the north side of Dove's old place."

"That's a nice piece of property son. What are you going to with it?"

"I'm going to put my little group of Longhorns up there mom. They started this whole thing and I feel I owe them a good life."

"I know son, they are nearly all gone now. Will was by for a minute yesterday, as usual he was in a hurry."

"Always is mother, remember a few years ago James here was always on the run."

"Oh yes, daylight to dark, but look what he's done."

"I know mom, I'm very proud of him."

"And well you should be daughter. Why, I've even bragged on him a time or two myself, of course he has helped give me these wonderful grandchildren, an even great grandchildren. So I guess we'll just have to keep him!"

"Well now that you all have picked on me, can us men get a cup of coffee?"

After a good laugh Mary's father and I got a cup and I wheeled him out onto the front porch.

"They have always got to give you a bad time don't they?"

"It seems to make them happy."

"We got a letter from Beth. Seems Carrie is giving her fits. She wants a new jumper to show at the local horse shows and so far they haven't been able to find one. I guess she told Beth she'd just write grandpa, he'd fix her up."

"She's just like Beth, when they were here last, she wanted to cut cattle on Slick. I told her she wasn't ready and she got a little peeved with me. I saddled up my old gray horse and let her try him."

"I know, she told me he jumped right out from under her. You really got her attention. To her, you're a real cowboy."

"Dad, I may have the ideal horse for her. You remember the gelding Thumb helped us on?"

"Well yes I do, that was several years ago."

"That's right, the kids ran him and he made them some good cash. They have been trying to make a pony horse out of him. His problem is, he jumps the lot fence and goes out to eat grass. He's either eight or nine years old now and is sure enough broke."

"Sounds like just what she needs."

"I'll talk to Mary and if she thinks it's ok, I'll ship the horse to her."

"You'll be Grandpa of the Year, James."

"Well, what would you do?"

"Same thing I did with her mother, give her the horse!"

I discussed the horse with Mary on the way home. She thought it would be a good idea. Matt was getting tired of having to go catch the gelding every morning before he went to the office.

I would talk to Matt the next day about the gelding.

I talked to Matt the next morning and he was more than willing to give the horse away as he pointed to a horse out on the grass. He wanted to know if Mel was really coming down for Thanksgiving.

"Your mother made him promise he would."

"He's in for a shock, dad."

"I'm sure it will be, your grandmother is going to fix him one of her pecan pies."

"He's lost then, he'll probably want to come back for Christmas."

As I rode toward home I saw Tee outside hanging laundry.

"Hey Tee, looks like you're busy."

"I should say so. Those two grandkids of yours keep me hopping."

Their daughter Becca was now almost ten and cute as could be. She had Will's easy going way, her brother J.R. however was always on the move.

"They left a while ago to go down to mothers. I swear they always know when she is baking."

"Good thing Mack isn't home he'd run them off."

"Pa, he's as bad as you! He takes them to town and spoils them rotten. They are very lucky, they have two great grandfathers."

"Thanks Tee,"

"Pa, when I first came here I was scared to death you all would run me and mom off. After the first day I had never felt so at home, then mom found Mack. Everything is wonderful."

"Great Tee, I'd better be getting home. Tell the kids I said hello."

"I'll do that Pa, Will, will be up to your place later, mom's sending you all some of the French pastries you like so well."

"Oh Lord, now I can only eat part of my supper. I'll want to have room for them."

Tee was laughing as I rode off.

When I got to the house Mary was rearranging the living room.

"Good timing cowboy, I just got finished."

"Thank the Lord."

"There's a couple of cards from your folks on the table. Tom brought them out while you were gone."

I picked up the cards. Folks seemed to be having a wonderful time. They had seen Paris and were traveling around the countryside. They planned on starting home in a week or so.

"Will was by for a minute this morning too. He was riding over to check the west pasture."

"All he has to do is ask Boggs."

"I know James. Boggs looks after the west side like a tiger. You made a good decision when you hired him."

"I sure did, and until Fred got married I had two of the best hands in the country."

"That's true but you were glad Fred and the widow Brown got married."

"Sure was, she's a fine person. I saw Fred last week in town and he's as happy as a kid in a candy store."

CHAPTER 7

▼

We watched as fall began to set in. The trees down along the creek were the most beautiful things you'd ever see.

Folks had returned from their trip and had enjoyed their time away.

We'd received a letter from Mel and he was going to be here in three more days. Mary, Carla, Mary mom, Flower and Lisa were busy figuring out what all they would need to feed the folks.

Sam, Harold and I were sitting on the front porch when Mary came to the door.

"James, why don't you and your friends go hunting? We could use some venison and three turkeys."

"Mary, we'll get our things and go hunting we'll be back day after tomorrow."

"Fine, just be sure you get the turkeys."

We took the old pack mare and rode north. The three of us had not been hunting together in a while.

We rode along easy, talking and enjoying the day.

"James."

"Yes Sam."

"Is it true your father and mother are going to set up a trust for the outstanding students here at the school?"

"Yes, Mary and I also kicked in some money to set it up. It was Matt's idea."

"You think it would be alright if Lesa and I added to it?"

"Don't see why not Sam, we can talk to Tom when we get back."

"Good, I'd like to give something back to these folks. They really gave Lisa and me our start."

"Well then, I guess Flower and I better kick in too. After all, like Sam says, these folks gave us our start. I reckon it's time we pay them back."

Later we rode down into a small draw where we all knew a small spring was located. We tied our horses and unloaded the pack mare. We cut some straight young saplings and fashioned them together into a frame. We draped a tarp over the framework and had a rather nice tent-like structure in case of rain.

Harold built a stone fire ring while Sam and I gathered dry firewood. We filled the coffee pot with the clear spring water and set the pot on the coals.

"James did you bring some of Mary's bread?"

"Sure did, Sam."

"Better get it. I brought along a small ham. Figured we'd have a sandwich."

Needless to say, I got the bread.

We were waiting for the ham to warm in the skillet when we saw Thumb riding our way on one of my paint horses.

"Brother, is friend Sam's ham almost ready?"

"Real close brother, step down and fill your plate."

"Let me tie this horse. My niece thought mine was too old for me to ride up here. Brother you raise some very fine horses."

"Thank you Thumb, why don't you keep him. You will need him to go see your grandchildren and old friends."

"Thank you brother, my old horse was stumbling a good deal."

"I have plenty brother, and besides I like the way you look on him. It is fitting a warrior should ride a fine horse."

"Son-in-law, do you hear how my brother speaks? He speaks with much wisdom and as one of the people."

"That he does Broken Thumb! I too, am proud to call him my brother."

"Well said son-in-law, now take this sack that our friend Bird sent along with me to satisfy our sweet tooth."

After we had eaten, we opened the sack Bird had sent and found it contained some of her famous cherry turnovers. They were flaky and sweet just the way Thumb and I liked them.

"James, its a wonder Bird's husband, Mack, doesn't weigh three hundred pounds."

"That's true Sam, and he probably would if he wasn't working with the race horses every day."

"Brother, your wife said to tell you, your friend from Colorado was going to arrive tomorrow about ten. Your father and mother are going to pick him up."

"That's great! I'm glad he came. You boys will all like him."

Thumb sat next to the fire the next morning sipping on a cup of coffee while Harold cooked our eggs and ham.

"Brother, is it true that you and your parents are going to create a fund for our young school children?"

"It's true Thumb, Harold and Sam are going to help us also."

"I think I am very happy I didn't shoot you those long years ago."

"Me too, I've enjoyed meeting and becoming a member of the people."

"Thumb, do you think you could eat some of my wife's pumkin bread?"

"Of course friend Sam, does it have honey and nuts?"

"It sure does let me get the loaf."

We ate pumkin bread and drank coffee, relaxing and enjoying the company of old friends.

Later that afternoon we shot two deer and hung them on a rack next to camp. Both were young and fat. We had back strap with potatoes onions and carrots.

The next morning we broke camp and followed Thumb who said he knew where we could find the turkeys his niece needed for the Thanksgiving holiday dinner. As usual he was right, we got three nice toms and rode on towards home.

───────────────▼───────────────

CHAPTER 8

We arrived at the ranch about noon and saw Dad's rig tied out front.

"Looks like you have company James."

"Sure does, looks like Pa's brought Mel up to see the place."

Sure enough Mel and Pa came out of the house when we rode into the barn lot.

"Morning Mel, glad you could make it."

"So am I James, hello Harold."

"Mel how are you?"

"Fine, and full. You would have to be Sam."

"Yes sir I am."

"I've eaten your famous hams in some of the finest restaurants in Denver."

"I'm hoping you enjoyed it sir."

"Enjoyed it, why sir it was always excellent. I only hope I can get one to take home with me for Christmas holidays."

"I'm sure that can be arranged sir, I try and keep a couple of hams ready for special occasions."

"Sam, will you call me Mel."

"You bet I will."

"Good, and you must be James' advisor Broken Thumb."

"I am his brother in blood. My brother has grown over the years and now takes care of those less fortunate."

"I've heard that, he seems to have taken over the problems of many."

"This is true, he and his friends are a valued thing to my people. They have fed those who were hungry, helped those who were sick and now are helping to educate the children who will one day lead our people."

"I've heard about the plans they have made. I'd like to add something to the fund myself. I sure can't take the money with me so the least I can do is to put it to good use. From what I've seen here so far I've been amazed."

"You think we've done a pretty good job here Mel?"

"James, I've seen many reservations and none of them are anything like this. People here are happy. And this ranch of yours is truly something to see."

"Thanks Mel, we've worked hard to build it."

"I can see that. Your wife and father have been filling me in on the story. It's something that one day you should set down and write a book about the drive."

"Wouldn't know where to start Mel, I've never even thought about doing anything like that."

After putting the horses away we cleaned the turkeys and took them to the house. Mary and the women were thrilled with the birds and went to work on them.

We got coffee and got out of their way. It seemed Mel had a million questions and the evening quickly was gone.

"James may I watch the boys work the young colts tomorrow morning?"

"If you don't mind getting up early Mel. They begin working the colts at daylight."

"Not a problem, I'll meet you at the barn in the morning."

"Fine, see you there."

True to his word Mel was at the race barn when I showed up talking to Matt.

"Morning boys, I see you're getting to know my youngest Mel."

"Your dad introduced us yesterday James. I've been talking to Matt here about the young horses. I'm thinking of buying a colt or two if I can get Matt here to train them."

"I've not had a chance to explain to him dad that I only start the colts. Mack is the one who trains them at the track."

"Matt's father-in-law takes the horses to the track. Matt and his wife start the colts and evaluate them."

"Well it makes no difference to me as long as you all think he's good at his job."

"He's very good at his job. He's made our stable a very respected name. We've had some very good seasons."

"That's all I need to know. Now if you'll show me your colts and give me your opinion of them maybe we can do some business."

We watched the colts work and I listened as my youngest son stated blood pedigrees and gave his opinion of each colt.

When the last two colts came onto the track Matt told Mel that these two were the best of the bunch.

The colt was out of one of our best mares, she had already produced two nice stakes horses. His sire was one of our own studs, which we had leased last year to a farm in Kentucky.

"The filly Mel is something special. She's a daughter of Princess Mary and by a champion. I don't think I could sell her without the family's permission."

"I can understand that, how good is she Matt?"

"Good, real good. We think she may be as good or better than her mother. We'll know for sure in a couple of months. We're not going to get in any hurry and cripple her. She's far to valuable to us."

"I can understand. How good is the colt?"

"He's good, and seems to be getting better every day. We had problems getting his mind straighten out but he's come around and showing a lot of promise."

"Would you price him?"

Matt priced the colt and I gulped. The price seemed ridiculous.

Mel never blinked, he just said sold.

"That is if your trainer will take him."

"That will be no problem at all sir. Mack is looking forward to racing him, especially as a three year old."

"Why as a three year old?"

"The big money in Thoroughbreds is in their three year old year. In the Derbys, we only try and get a couple of races into the colts as two year olds. That way they get race experience and we can evaluate them. We had a colt two years ago who was lazy and didn't like to work. But when you put him in a race he became a real racehorse. We tried him as a pony horse after his career but then again he was lazy, so we are giving him to my sister's daughter for a hunter jumper. He probably will be great, he enjoys jumping out of his lot to go eat grass."

"Where does your daughter live James?"

"She lives in Kentucky Mel."

"Is the girl her only child?"

"No, she has a boy also. The girl is twelve and the boy nine."

"How many folks will be here Thanksgiving?"

Matt began to laugh.

"Did I say something funny?"

"Well yes you did Mel, we quit asking that question years ago. Whoever shows up is welcome and usually we have a house full."

"But James your house is not that big."

"Oh Mel we don't have it at our house, we have it down at Will and Tee's place."

"Mel, wait until Thursday. You'll see what a diverse family we have. As dad here says, half the country claims to be related to us. Dad, how many turkeys is mother fixing this year?"

"Three Matt why?"

"Well I know that Uncle Sam brought a huge ham so that's three turkeys and a large ham. See what I'm saying Mel, there will be a bunch of folks here. You're in for a real treat."

"I can hardly wait. I was shocked when I saw this ranch. You all almost have your own little town out here."

"Just family places Mel, when we came here we lived in tents until we got a house up. Some folks lived in tents all winter. Times were tough to say the least."

"They were tough but dad gave several head of cows away so some of the family's would not go hungry."

"Matt, I couldn't watch family's with kids go hungry."

"I know dad but you didn't tell anyone except Uncle Sam. I remember mother telling the story how she found out from one of her cousins. I remember her saying she sat down and cried, not because you lost cattle but because she was so proud of you."

"Now I'm beginning to understand some things. James, weren't you appointed a U.S. Marshall?"

"Yes, I was."

"I've heard some of the stories about how you caught some folks trying to steal an old women's place, returned a small herd to two kids that had been stolen from them. What else have you done for the folks here?"

"Mel, ask mom, getting dad to talk about his tales around here is almost impossible."

CHAPTER 9

▼

Thanksgiving day came. It was clear but cool. Sam and I had suffered all evening and had to fix our own breakfast. The women were busy cooking things that would be taken down to Will and Tee's place later.

Sam and I fed the stock and walked up to the ridge top to check on the Angus.

The Angus were feeding on the tall bluestem grass. They were in deed a sight to see. I had culled the herd from the start and fortunately for me everything had worked out. I had one of the finest herds anywhere. Each year buyers came from all over to our production sale.

"James, thee cattle of yours are something to see. I remember when they first arrived and you made your sort. You've brought them a long way."

"I think so Sam, I'm sure enough proud of them."

"James, who is that coming out here from town this early?"

I looked towards town and saw a team and buggy with three people coming our way at a good fast trot. I looked at the driver and then I knew. Beth and the grandkids were home.

"It's Beth and the kids Sam, now things will get lively."

"Lord I reckon you're right about that. Mary will be so happy. Did you know she was coming?"

"Never had a clue Sam."

"Oh boy, what a Thanksgiving this will be. I can hardly wait, I've sure missed her."

"I'm looking forward to seeing my granddaughter when she sees her new horse."

"You're giving her the gelding Matt can't keep in the pens?"

"Don't see why not Sam, he seems to want to jump. Might as well put the booger to work."

"Knowing your grandchild the way I do I'd almost guarantee that he'll be put to work. Probably a lot of work."

"Lets head down the hill Sam. I want to give my girl a hug."

We arrived at the house just as Beth and the kids drove up.

Grandpa, Carrie shouted as she launched herself from the buggy.

I caught her in mid air and swung her around.

"How's my girl?"

"Fine grandpa, but I need a new horse."

"I know, you've out grown yours."

"Beth, Carrie, Joe, oh my goodness. We didn't know you were coming."

"I know mother, but Mike had a meeting in Kansas City so we just loaded up and headed this way. Besides I wanted to see everyone."

"Where is Mike? Will he be here?"

"He's on his way, he should be here by one. He knew we wanted to come on so he sent us on ahead."

"James, how will he get here from town? No one will be at the station."

"Cookie said that he and Martha would pick him up on their way out."

"Well, that saves me from making a trip to town. How about you Joe are you doing all right? Looks to me as if you've grown a bunch since I saw you last."

"I'm fine grandfather, and yes I have grown."

My grandson was an extremely well mannered young man, but I really wished he had some of the fire his sister had.

"You all come in the house. I've got coffee and I'll have hot chocolate ready in a few moments."

"My Lord Beth!"

"Aunt Lesa, how are you?"

"Since we've moved back here, fine dear. Sam and I are both happy."

"That's grand, I'm happy for you. Uncle Sam, I've not got my bear hug yet!"

Sam smiled and proceeded to give Beth her hug, both were smiling as we went into the house.

My grandson came over to where I sat.

"Grandfather, my father said that he was looking forward to a deer hunt with Uncle Matt and Will."

"Seems as though they did go last time you all were here."

"I've talked to mother and she said to ask you if you'd take me deer hunting."

"Sure I'll take you deer hunting. Do you know how to shoot a rifle?"

"Yes sir, mother has taught me. Father is so busy most of the time."

"I can understand. I was pretty busy myself when my kids were growing up. Trying to make this ranch pay, don't blame your father too much. Now lets go see if your grandma will loan us her rifle for our hunt tomorrow."

I waved at Mary and when she came over I told her about Joe and my plans for a deer hunt. I wanted to borrow her rifle for our grandson if it would be all right.

"Of course Joe can use my rifle, you know where the shells are James?"

"Thank you grandmother, I'll take good care of it I promise."

"Just do me one favor Joe, Ok?"

"Yes grandmother."

"Please call me grandma like the rest of the kids. Grandmother sounds just a little too stiff for me."

"Yes Grand—Grandma."

"That's better, around here we're a little less formal than the folks back where you come from."

Sam and I took Joe out back of the house and let him fire Mary's rifle. He handled the rifle well and turned out to be an excellent shot.

"By gum Sam, looks like we've got a deer hunter on our hands."

"Sure does James, I'd go with you but my nephew is going to bring a girl over tomorrow."

"Not a problem Sam, Joe and I will be fine. We'll get out fitted tonight and get an early start tomorrow morning."

The women finished their cooking and Sam and I were put to work loading all the food to be moved down to Will and Tee's place. I told Joe to jump in and help. He seemed to be pleased. When the buggy was loaded I sat down on the back of the buggy with Sam and told him to drive us down to Will and Tee's.

"But Grandfa—Grandpa, I don't know how to drive a team."

"Just pick up the reins and cluck to them. When we get down to your Uncle's place pull back on the reins and say whoa. You can handle it."

Sam looked at me and smiled, he approved of my way of handling my grandson.

Joe clucked to the team and they started down the road. The older team was steady and slowly plodded down the hill. When we reached Will and Tee's place, Will stepped out the back door.

"Well my Lord Joe looks like your grandpa has put you to work."

"It's fun Uncle Will, I'd never driven a team like this before."

Looks like you've done a fine job. Now lets unload this stuff before we get in trouble."

We carried everything inside and sat it down where Tee and Bird wanted it put.

Joe got a hug from both Tee and Bird and I saw Bird slip him one of her special sweet tarts as we were leaving.

Sam and I gave him a hard time on the way back up to the house. He offered to share but we wouldn't hear of it.

We were all laughing when we pulled up in front of the house. My grandson was beginning to learn how to relax.

Mary and Lesa had changed clothes while we were gone. Sam and I were instructed to get changed.

I was changing my clothes when Mary came into the room.

"Well Mr. Grandpa, you've done it now."

"What have I done Mary?"

"Your grandson told us he drove you and Sam down to the kids. I swear that boy is so thrilled."

"I thought he enjoyed himself."

"Oh yes, and then you and Sam gave him a hard time about the sweet tart Bird gave him. He told Beth you all really had him concerned until you started laughing. James, his other grandparents expect him to be proper at all times. Would you mind if he spent the upcoming summer with us?"

"Not at all, in fact I think it would be good for him."

"Thank you dear, I'll ask Beth."

We all loaded into the buggies and drove off down to Will and Tee's. There were already several rigs outside when we arrived.

"Looks like folks and Mel are already here."

We walked into the back door and were greeted by the family. Will and Tee's two kids grabbed onto their cousins and left at a run.

"James, I've just had a good visit with Mack. He seems to think I made a good buy on the colt."

"Great Mel, I hope it all works out."

"James, I really don't care. I just want to have some fun like you folks. I've seen and heard more laughter this last week that I've heard in years."

"Good, I'm glad you're enjoying yourself."

"Mel, have you met our daughter Beth?"

"No Mary, I've not had the pleasure. Beth I'm very pleased to meet you."

"Thank you sir and thank you for showing my folks such a good time last summer."

"Beth the pleasure was all mine. I can't remember ever having a better time. Being invited down here has been the best thing that has happened to me in years. I've never seen such a family."

"Oh Mel, this isn't nearly all of them, wait awhile."

"There's more?"

"Lots more Mel, its only beginning."

Mel sat next to Pa and Carla and watched as the rest of the family began to arrive. Cookie, Martha and Beth's husband Mike arrived, followed by Mary's folks along with Tom and his family.

Matt, Deb and their family arrived next followed by Boggs, Willie and then Harold and Flower and their family. A few moments later, Thumb arrived with Sam's nephew. Mel was beginning to see the family.

"My lord what a bunch of folks to be called a family."

"There's one more family, my uncle and his family haven't arrived yet."

"Yes they have James, Bill and Willa just pulled up outside."

I greeted them at the door and introduced them to Mel. While they were visiting Mr. Conners arrived.

Mel came to me a short time later and was shaking his head.

"James, I've met your brother Thumb and your Uncle Bill. It seems you've been a rather busy fellow over the past few years. They have told me stories that I know are true. You never told me you were a Marshal."

"Mel, James doesn't tell anyone much of anything."

"I've found that out Mary, Thumb is very proud of him."

"I know Mel, the whole tribe loves him."

"That is apparent, I've never seen so many folks so happy."

CHAPTER 10

▼

Everyone was full and was sipping coffee and just enjoying the company when I heard Beth.

"Oh no!"

I ran over and out to see what had upset her.

Her daughter, my granddaughter was on her new horse, riding him around the small board lot with only a halter and lead rope.

"It's all right Beth, she's just riding around bareback. She'll be fine."

"You don't know her dad, she's going to jump him."

I watched as my young granddaughter suddenly picked up speed and suddenly drove the gelding at the fence. The gelding cleared the fence in good fashion all to the delight of my granddaughter who raced the gelding up the hill where we all stood.

"Mother, did you see him, he just flew over the fence. Grandpa he's wonderful, thank you."

"Better thank your uncle Matt and aunt Deb they broke him."

I took Beth's arm and whispered in her ear. "You deserve this child." Beth suddenly burst out laughing and a serious moment had passed.

"Carrie, go put him up for the evening. Don't forget to rub and wrap his legs"

"I'll show her how, I need to get back to the barn and check on things."

"Thank you Willie, I'd appreciate that a lot."

"Not a bother, I watched over her mother some if you'll remember. I guess I got another job to do and to tell the truth I'm looking forward to it."

As the day ended everyone was full and happy and looking forward to a goodnights rest. Mary, Joe and I returned to our house where Mary found a old pair of boots that with two pair of heavy socks fit Joe for the next days hunt. With one of her heavier coats, a pair of gloves, an old hat and a scarf for his ears had Joe ready for his first deer hunt.

He drank a cup of hot chocolate and went to bed, a very happy young man.

Mary and I sat down in front of the fireplace with a cup of hot chocolate and relaxed.

"Where do you plan on taking him?"

"Your mother told me about a buck she sees almost every morning out her kitchen window. He comes around the hillside and beds down in that little bunch of rocks. I thought we'd try there first."

"James, I hope he gets one. Tom, Will and Matt are going north of the valley and hunt the creek bottom."

"I know, they'll see and probably get their deer. I just want us to see one and let our grandson get a shot."

The next morning, well before daylight I rolled Joe out of bed and told him to get dressed. Mary fixed a quick breakfast while we went out and hitched the older pack mare to the light buggy. We went back into the house and got our rifles. I also grabbed a canteen and some sandwiches Mary had put together in case we didn't get our deer early.

I had Joe take the reins and drive the mare across the hilltop until we reached the spot we would try and ambush the buck. We tied the mare and walked carefully until I figured we were in a good spot. I laid a couple of burlap bags down on the grass in back of a rock crop-out and we sat down.

I had Joe load his rifle with three shells and put the same in mine.

We whispered back and forth as we watched the eastern skyline begin to turn pink. I saw a light come on down at Mary's mom's place.

As it began to get light I told Joe to begin looking for movement. I had told him to move his head slowly and keep a sharp eye.

About thirty minutes later Joe touched by leg. I turned my head slowly and saw what he was looking at.

A large buck was slowly picking his way along the hillside.

I told Joe to ease his rifle over the rock in front of us. He slowly slid the rifle in place and settled in behind it.

The buck continued along the trail and was getting nearer to us all the time. When he was within sixty yards I told Joe to take him when he was ready.

The buck took a few more steps and suddenly the small rifle spoke. The buck never moved. I watched as my grandson worked the lever of the rifle to load another shell. Just as he leveled the rifle for another shot, the buck collapsed in a heap.

"Joe! You got him."

"Do you think so grandpa?"

"Sure enough, I can see his antlers. We'll wait five minutes or so and then go take a look."

"Grandpa, I barely saw him, like you said look for movement."

"Let's go take a look at your deer Joe."

We made a small circle and came up behind the deer. The rack was wide and heavy and had long beautiful points.

"Joe, you've just got yourself a beautiful deer. I've only seen two that could compare to him. Your Uncle Matt has one and Uncle Thumb has the other. You may hunt the rest of your life and never see another like him."

"Grandpa, what do we do now?"

I had carried the sheath knife I'd taken off the Comanche chief years ago from behind my neck and handed it handle first to my grandson.

"It's you deer, you dress it. I'll tell you how."

I watched and helped where needed. I was proud of the way my grandson worked and listened. When he was finally finished I helped him spread the bucks ribs and insert a stick so that the buck would cool out quickly.

"Lets go get the wagon, we need to go down and show him to your great grandma and grandpa."

We got the wagon and with a lot of effort we managed to get the buck loaded.

"Take us down to your great grandma's place Joe. I know she heard you shoot."

Mary's mother and father were waiting at the back gate when Joe and I pulled up to their gate.

"Looks like you got a dandy Joe!"

"Great grandma, he's beautiful. He was sneaking along just like grandpa said he would be. It was so exciting."

"I'll bet it was, now get down and come have a cup of hot chocolate and a fresh cinnamon roll. I just took them out of the oven."

I'll race you Joe."

Needless to say, I lost the race.

Later after Mary's folks heard all about the hunt we mounted the buggy and headed to the house.

We stopped down at the track so that Matt could see the deer. He and Willie complimented Joe on his deer. Matt told Joe to ask Boggs if he would mount the head for him. Needless to say Joe was thrilled. It would be something he could show to his friends at home.

We drove up to the house and found the boys had just returned. They each had a nice buck but nothing that would compare to the one Joe had.

My grandson seemed to grow before my eyes. As Mary put it later he seemed to grow into a young man.

Beth and Mike were thrilled. Even his sister was impressed.

That evening Mary made me cowboy coffee and snuggled up close to me on the couch.

"Cowboy, your grandson will never forget this day."

"I won't either Mary, I had a ball. I was scared to death he had missed that first shot. I was thrilled when the buck fell."

"He asked to hunt with you next year."

"Sure did, in fact I'm looking forward to the trip."

"I think it's wonderful. Joe got his buck and Carrie is thrilled with her horse. Your grandkids think you're a great grandpa. Of course I've thought that for a long time now."

CHAPTER 11

▼

Mel came by before he left to tell us how much he had enjoyed himself. He promised he'd be back next fall to see the sorting. He'd heard so much about it from everyone he said he just had to see it. It would be after elk season in the Hole and winter would be settling in anyway.

We told him he was welcomed anytime he felt like showing up.

Christmas was approaching and I was in a quandary as to what to get Mary. Every year it became harder for me to find something for her. As it turned out Mr. Conner had the answer. He had painted a new portrait. Mary and I were in the center with Beth and her family across the top. Will and his family down the right side and Matt and his family down the left. Across the bottom were the faces of Pa and Carla.

I thought it was a wonderful painting and told him so.

"Thank you James, it's taken me a while to get it done. I've left enough space so that if Matt or Will's family increases I can add to it at a later date."

"What do I owe you sir?"

"James, you can't buy this painting. It's a gift from me to you. You folks have been family to me these last years when I had none. You all have made me welcome here and this is a gift."

"Thank you sir, I simply don't know what else to say."

"The look in your eyes when you saw the painting was payment enough for me. It will be here in this country long after you and I are gone James. People will look at it and remember James, that his more than enough payment for me."

When the presents were opened I got the painting and gave it to Mary. After she looked at it and wiped tears from her eyes she turned the painting around for the family to see.

I'd not seen either of my boys cry in years but both had to wipe tears from their eyes.

It was wonderful everyone was hugging everyone. My daughter-in-laws both came over to me and kissed my cheek. I hugged them both.

That night Mary snuggled up close and I held her until I knew she was asleep. I lay there thinking what a lucky man I had been to have my family and friends.

CHAPTER 12

▼

A couple of weeks later we had a snow. Four or five inches but it never lasted long.

I had helped Will check the cattle and had just got back to the house when Harold came riding in at a run.

"What's wrong Harold?"

"It's Thumb James, he wants to see you. James, I think he's near the end. He's had a bad cold for a week or so. Flower and the rest of the family are all over there now. He asked me to come and get you."

"I'll get my things and tell Mary, she'll want to come along. Go on back and be with Flower Harold, we'll be right there."

I ran into the house and told Mary what was happening.

"Saddle our horses James, I'll be ready in a few moments."

We left the place at a run and arrived at Thumb's small house a short time later.

Flower met us at the door.

"Go on in James, he wants to talk to you."

I walked into the small bedroom where Thumb lay propped up on a couple of big pillows. I had never realized it but Thumb was old. He'd just been there when I needed help or needed to laugh. I was beginning to feel the same way I felt when Ma had passed on.

"Brother, it is good to see you. My son-in-law said you were coming."

"Mary and I got here as soon as we could brother."

"That is good, ask my niece to come in brother, please."

I stepped to the door and asked Mary to come in. She gave Thumb a kiss on the cheek then came to stand by my side.

"Brother, my time is near, and you will have to take over more responsibility with the people. I feel there are troubled times ahead. I have heard they are drilling a hole in the ground over near the town of Bartlesville. If they get the oil they are seeking it will only be a matter of time before they are here to rob and steal like before."

"Maybe they won't find oil Thumb. We'll worry about that when the time comes. Right now we just want you to get better."

"Brother, don't be sad. I have had a good life. I've lived as a warrior and then had the pleasure of watching you build your ranch and help my people. It has been a pleasure watching you and my niece raise your family. Brother, I ask you to look after the people after I am gone. I think they may need you as never before. My son-in-law and friend Sam will help you. Remember the people need you and your wisdom."

"But Thumb."

"Brother my time is near, give me your word you'll help the people as before."

"You have my word Thumb."

"Good, now would you send my children in, please brother?"

We left the room and told Thumb's family he wanted to see them. I sat down on the porch step and cried. I was losing my brother, my best friend.

Later, Flower came out onto the porch and told us her father was gone. Both Mary and I sat down and cried.

Thumb's funeral was something I will never forget. The whole tribe was there as well as folks I'd never seen before from other tribes.

I was not myself for several days. Mary's mom came over to talk to me.

"Son, my brother would not want you to be sad. He would want you to be happy, remember the good times. Remember the times you rode against our enemies and allowed him to once more feel like a warrior. He loved you like his own James, don't dishonor him."

"I'm sorry mom, he was like a father to me."

"I know, but you must carry on and do as he asked. Tom is going to need your help and influence. I'm afraid the oil people are beginning to look our way and that means trouble for the people."

"I'll go talk to Tom this afternoon. Thanks mom."

"You're welcome son, I love to see a smile on your face. I've gotten rather used to your being around. Besides I love the grandchildren you and my daughter have given me.

I rode into town to see Tom and saw my first horseless carriage. It scared the living daylights out of my horse with its loud noise.

"Loud aren't they James?"

"Darn sure are Tom, I've heard of them but that's the first I've seen. Who is the feller herding the thing?"

"He's from over near Bartlesville."

"One of the oil folks I've heard about?"

"He sure is James."

"Trouble with a capital "T"."

"I'm afraid you're right. There are big changes getting ready to take place."

"What kind of changes Tom?"

"They'll be people here soon that will be wanting to drill wells James. You and I both know there is oil here on this land. What I have to do is figure out a way to keep the outside people from stealing the tribes land."

"Anything I can do to help Tom?"

"Right now I've got an idea but the council will have to approve it."

"Well if there's anything I can do to help just holler."

"James, I may want you to speak to the council when I make my proposal. They respect you and will listen to you. Besides, even though you're a member of the tribe you're still white. They see what you have done and many copy your ways."

"I'll be glad to help Tom, just tell me when you need me."

"Let me finish my proposal and then go over it with you. I want you to understand what I'm trying to do for the whole tribe. Matt has had a good deal of input to the proposal. He's very smart James, he's going to be a fine lawyer one day."

"I hope so, he's worked at it long enough."

"James, he's already a success with the Thoroughbreds. I've admired his determination to finish his education. It's not been easy."

"Tom, the boy has always finished what he started. I'm proud of him, he's never asked for a nickel since he and Willie first went to Chicago with the filly. He's made the operation pay and pay well. I have no idea how well because he handles the books and I've never asked."

"James, you're quite wealthy. I know you don't like to talk about it but your son has made investments that have paid you a very handsome return."

"If you say so Tom, Mary and I don't need much. We've got beef, chickens and Sam's bacon and hams. Mary still has a big garden and cans the vegetables."

"Money is not import to you James, but most folks wouldn't understand your ways."

"We're not most folks Tom. We've got the kids and each other so we're happy. Let me know when you've finished with your proposal and I'll go over it with you. Right now I've got to pick up a few things at the store for Mary."

I filled the list for Mary and headed home. I rode past the automobile as it as called on my way out of town. It might be progress but I'd still rather have a good horse under me.

CHAPTER 13

▼

A week later Tom showed up at the house with his proposal for the tribe. We spent better than two hours going over the paper work. When we were finished I saw how the plan would work for everyone's benefit. It would benefit the whole tribe and not just a lucky few.

"Think you can sell this idea to the council Tom?"

"I think I can with your help."

"Then call a council meeting, we need to get this done and let everyone know the agreement is in place."

Little did I know how this document would later affect the tribe, both good and bad.

After Tom left Mary poured us a cup of coffee. We sat for a while talking.

"James, you're wishing Uncle Thumb was here."

"I sure am Mary, he was always so respected by the people, when he spoke they listened and put all their petty things aside and pulled together."

"James, you remember what my Uncle told you on his death bed? He told you to take over and take care of the people, right?"

"That's what he said."

"Then why do you think he told you to do it dear. Because he's groomed you to take over for him from the time he made you his blood brother. Think about it, you've been doing the work for the last few years without even knowing you were doing them."

I sat there thinking. Mary was right, my brother had done it again. He'd slipped up on me without me knowing it. I had been doing his job while thinking I was only helping. I suddenly saw how it had all played out. He had indeed groomed me for the job.

"Mary, you're right. I guess I'll honor my brother and go with Tom and speak to the council like he wanted."

"Good, I know you will do well."

The council meeting was called. As Tom, Matt and I walked into the new headquarters building on the northwest side of town the room suddenly became quiet.

Tom's father who was still the leader of the council and motioned for us to come forward. Two gentlemen closed the tall doors behind us. What would happen here today must stay here until the tribe was called in for a vote.

Tom's father called the council to order and after a short opening statement asked Tom to speak.

"People of the Osage, this meeting today is or can be a great day for our tribe. We have an opportunity to protect our people from more troublesome times in the future. As you all know oil has been discovered just to the east of us and it is our belief that we of the Osage have the oil under our land here."

"My brother-in-law, his son and I have looked into this matter and came up with an idea where if and when the oil men come to our land we will not be cheated."

A murmur ran through the council.

Tom's father raised his hand.

"If the council will have patience my son will answer your questions. This is a problem we may not be able to solve in a days time so please use patience and listen carefully."

Tom began to explain his plan to the council. Sometime later he finished.

One of the council members raised his hand.

Tom recognized the man.

"You say that our brother James has looked over this agreement."

"Yes he has, and had some input into the agreement."

"This is good. We know that Broken Thumb was his teacher. He has shown us many times his love for the people, if he approves this agreement I will vote for it."

One by one the members of the council approved Tom's plan then he asked me to speak.

"Members of the council. For years my brother Broken Thumb tried to show and explain to me the ways of the people. He told me that sometime in the future I would need to help them as the times changed."

"We have managed to leave behind hunger by working together. Our families are prospering. But as my brother once said, our people will have more struggles. This new struggle will be a new and difficult test for the people. The people are not familiar with the ways of the people who will be coming among us. Therefore, we as the recognized leaders of the people must protect them as best we can."

"This plan is not a perfect one but it will at least get us started. Council members, we must start now. I am afraid the time is short. We must not let petty things come between us, today we must act like the leaders our people have elected."

An older member of the council raised his hand.

"Yes Lame Horse."

"We as members of the council are old and have seen many changes over the years. Do you think we are capable of handling this situation as you call it?"

"We must Lame Horse, the people depend on us for our wisdom."

"Do you think this plan will work?"

"I think this is a start, it will protect the people for now, but changes will have to be made by you as leaders of the tribe."

"Does this mean you will not help?"

"No it does not, I'll do what ever the tribe would like me to do, as I have always tried to do."

"Then I think it is time you join us."

"But Lame Horse, I can't. I'm not Osage."

"You were blood brother to Broken Thumb. You have helped our people over the past years. You have fed us and acted as our law when we had none. You and your family have helped settle disputes and have worked to educate our children far more in fact than many of us on this council. I for one believe you should be appointed by this council to the vacated spot of your brother Broken Thumb."

"I'd be honored but can you do this?"

"James, the council has the authority to do this."

Lame Horse spoke to the council.

"Members of the Osage Nation I think we should appoint this man to our council."

One by one the council voted. It was a unanimous decision. I had just been made a council member of the Osage Nation's Tribal Council. I sat there is awe. I couldn't believe it.

Mary's father spoke up.

"Members of the council, I think we should approve this plan and meet here again next month and discuss any new things that may have come forth in that time."

I made my first vote as a council member. I was proud because like Tom I could see big problems for the tribe if we did not get something in place.

The council members all welcomed me to the council and wished me well. Tom, Matt and I returned to his office and went to work.

"James, Matt, we're going to need some outside help on this thing. We can't have any holes for anyone to challenge us in court. These big money people will challenge us in court I'm sure."

"Uncle Tom, why don't we talk to Mr. Conners? He lived back in Pennsylvania where they have all the oil. Maybe one of his old friends would like to help us."

"Matt, you might just be right. Would you go talk to him and see if he knows of anyone we could talk too."

Matt left on the run.

"James, what are you going to tell Mary?"

"Better yet Tom, how am I going to tell her?"

"For gods sakes don't let her find it out before you tell her."

"I guess you're right. I guess I'd better head home, and quick."

"That would be best. Mom's going to have a fit. She told me a couple of years ago that this could happen."

"She did, how did she know?"

"Uncle Thumb told her. He's been talking to the various members of the council for the last couple of years."

My brother had bush whacked me again. He always told me he was sneaky.

"I know, he took great pride in his old warrior ways. But James the man looked on you as a son. He was always pointing out to folks how you had always put the peoples interest first. James you'll do a fine job, Uncle Thumb has taught you everything you need to know. All you have to do now is make him proud."

"I'll do my best Tom, see you later."

I rode home my mind a whirl. I had no idea what I would tell Mary. After putting my horse away I walked into the house.

"How did the council meeting go James? Did they approve Tom's plan?"

"The council approved his plan Mary. It was a unanimous vote."

"Great, anything else happen?"

"Well sort of, the council appointed me to take Thumbs place."

"They what!"

"Appointed me to take Thumbs place on the council."

"Who nominated you?"

"Lame Horse"

"It figures, he and Thumb were warriors together. I can't believe it, you're a council member. Mother will have a fit."

"Probably, but she already knew Thumb was trying to set it up."

"She never said a word."

"Since when did she ever say anything?"

"Well it's something else for me to live with."

"Has it been that hard Mary?"

"Not really dear, but just because you're on the council it doesn't mean that you get out of taking out the trash."

We both were laughing as I carried out the trash. Things weren't going to change around our place.

CHAPTER 14

▼

T he council met once a month for the next two months. Mr. Conners our local artist had known a gentleman who could help Tom with the legal wording of the tribe's agreement.

The gentleman was a retired attorney from one of the largest oil companies on the east coast. He came to town and was staying with Mr. Conners while working with Tom. Mr. Conners had brought him out to the ranch to meet our family and show him our place.

We were introduced to Bill Culbert. Bill was a tall gentleman who seemed at ease with himself. He did however seem in awe of everything around him. Mr. Conners had told him about how we had built our ranch from scratch.

"Mr. and Mrs. Howard you have a truly wonderful place. I've never seen anything quite like it."

"Thank you sir, my husband and I are quite proud of it ourselves."

"Your children all live here?

"No, our daughter lives in Kentucky with her family. Our oldest son manages the ranch, and our youngest manages the Thoroughbred operations and helps Tom with the tribe's legal work. James helps out of course but since he was appointed to the council he doesn't have much time.

"Mr. Howard, you're the first non Osage to become a member of the council. Do you foresee more non Osage to be appointed?"

"No sir I really don't, I was blood brother to one of the council members and over the years he sort of took over and groomed me for the job."

"From the stories I've heard you have earned the position."

"Thank you sir, I've tried to do the right thing for the people since we've been here."

"That seems to be the consensus of everyone I've talked too. Your brother-in-law and son have taken on quite a task. I've never seen anything quite like it. I think it will be good for the tribe as a whole. It will certainly give some of the big boys back east a hard time. I believe you folks are sitting on a tremendous oil field. Tom has shown me the sink holes, they are exactly the same as those found in Pennsylvania"

"Well sir, all I'm concerned about is that the tribe not get cheated we have fought over the years and so far been able to win but this is another matter. This will probably be settled in court and the people can't control what they will do. We need a plan in place so that they don't end up being poor again."

"I see why the council has taken you on to help them. They may need you to help them sort through things. You can add a lot of knowledge where and when they need it."

"I'm honored to be asked to help. I see why my friend moved here, the country is beautiful and the people are wonderful."

"Bill, we're honored to have you."

A month or so later Tom, Matt and Bill had finished their modifications to Tom's original plan.

The council convened and listened as Tom presented his plan to them. When he had finished, Mary's dad asked for questions.

Lame Horse again raised his hand.

"We have listened to this paper and I for one do not understand it all so I have a question for our new council member. James, do you have any questions about this paper?"

"No Lame Horse I don't, I have read and studied this paper and think it is good for the people. I feel that everyday we wait puts us closer to a danger the people can't control. I feel this paper will give the people something to rely on when the strangers show up. And believe me fellow council members, they will show up. It is simply a matter of time."

"Then I think we should approve this paper."

A vote was taken and was approved by the entire council.

Bill Culbert called me aside.

"Mr. Howard, may I call you James?"

"I wish you would."

"Thank you, I wish you would call me Bill. I think we're going to be in a dogfight in another few months. I was wondering, do you think it would be possible for me to buy or lease a building site here in town?"

"I'm sure it can be arranged, have you talked to Tom?"

"Not yet but if you don't mind it's what I'd like to do. I love the people and the country."

"Talk to Tom, I'm sure he can fix you up. We'd love to have you here to help as matters come up."

CHAPTER 15

▼

The next six months drifted by we had the gathering as it was now called and the holiday for the people. It drew people we had never seen before, only this time, not all of them stayed close. I asked several of the young men to keep an eye on some of them and report back to me.

Later that evening a young man began reporting to me. It seemed some of the men found the sinks and had taken samples. Some had actually had guides take them to various sinks. I was glad that Tom's proposal was in place. We were going to need it.

At the next council meeting the various members began by complaining about strange people coming and going on their property. They had had complaints from several tribal members. They all said something had to be done. They did not want another place like Kansas had been.

"James, do you have any suggestions?"

"Yes Tom I do. Let our tribal police start roaming the roads and send these folks packing."

"What if they won't leave like before?"

"Then I guess we'll carry them out."

"James, will you head up the tribal police?"

"Be glad to Tom, I guess my Marshal badge is still good."

"Unless you've been notified otherwise it's still in effect."

"In that case I'll go over to the tribal police station and set things up."

CHAPTER 16

▼

I walked into the tribal police office and showed the sergeant the papers from the council putting me in charge. Relief showed on the sergeant's face.

"Tell us what you want us to do Mr. Howard."

"First off how many officers are there?"

"Eight sir, five work days and three work nights."

"Alright, now how quick can you get all the men here?"

"An hour, maybe less sir."

"Good, bring them in. We're going to stop this mess now."

An hour later the eight men were sitting in the office.

"Gentlemen, we have a major problem. Outsiders are beginning to wander upon our land as if they owned it. We're going to try and stop it and stop it now."

"Each one of you will take one of these sections. I have marked here on the map. I want you to go to the different families living in these areas and have them notify us if they see any strangers on their land."

"I want every man here armed, a pistol, rifle and if you have one a shotgun. Now everyone understand me, move the people off and tell them that if they come back they will be arrested. If they give you any problems, bring them in and lock them up. In fact arrest all of them, they are trespassers and if we stop them now we may avoid trouble later on."

"Can we do this?"

"We can do it. They will not like being locked up but they also know this land is under federal control. I'm a U.S. Marshal and I am authorized to arrest anyone who is breaking the law here."

"Then we will arrest them."

The next couple of weeks were rather humorous. The officers arrested fifteen men for trespassing.

It was a lot of fun listening to their excuses for being on our land. Even the tribal officers enjoyed their stories. We kept all of the men overnight and told them that the next time they would be charged in Federal court. The last statement seemed to get their attention.

For several weeks we had no problems, then the other outsiders showed up on the morning train with their lawyers. The rush had started.

The men, all in suits and ties came to Tom's office to lodge their complaints and file papers to explore the Osage land for oil. Their lawyers were good but not good enough.

What they weren't prepared for was our new lawyer. In the short time he had been in town Bill Culbert had made many friends. His wit and jokes seemed to just draw people to him.

He had bought himself a pair of custom made boots, which he wore everyday along with his new silver belly hat, flannel shirt and jeans. He looked as if he'd been here for years.

Bill was sitting at his desk when the oil company lawyers came into Tom's office.

One of the lawyers looked at Bill in disbelief.

"Your Bill Culbert, you were lead attorney for Fathom Oil."

"I was until I got tired. I'm now working for the Osage people."

"But why? They can't begin to pay you what you're worth."

"What am I worth? They've allowed me to build a home and treat me with respect and have asked for nothing, which is a hell of lot more than I can say about the folks I left behind me."

"Now you boy's came looking to run over us with papers and such. Boys, it's not going to happen, your big steal isn't going to work. I'd suggest you listen to my associate here and let him explain how things are going to work here."

With that said Bill cocked his hat back on his head and put his fancy boots up on his desk. He was smiling all the time.

Tom informed them they were trespassing and then handed them the papers the council had approved and had been filed with the Indian Bureau in Washington.

The oil company lawyers were livid their first reaction was to say they would appeal. Tom told them to file, it would cost the tribe nothing but that he would keep it tied up for forty years if need be.

They suddenly realized they were not dealing with a dumb Indian, Tom was smart, very smart.

After they left the office Tom began to laugh.

"Did you see their faces? They were caught flatfooted. They were supposed to impress us with their suits and piles of paper work. I'm sure glad we had our program in place. The way Bill, Matt and I wrote it up, they will be working on it for weeks."

"Just as long as they stay off our land everything will be alright. When they come again there will be a new wrinkle for them to worry about."

"James, I know that look, what are you planning?"

"Well Tom if I arrest these boys and take them to Tulsa they will be out on bail in two hours."

"Probably, but what are you planning?"

"The Osage are a sovereign nation correct?"

"That is correct."

"Well I think it is time for the tribe to open a court. Elect a judge and a prosecutor. When the boys come back, they will get a surprise. We'll prosecute them for trespassing. Then after thirty days of mowing grass, painting and whatever else we need done gets done. We'll turn them loose."

"We do that, we'll have lawyers and law enforcement people all over us James."

"That's possible, but think about it. I'll bet the oil companies will have real trouble finding anyone to come scout out our area without our permission. We've got to get control now Tom or we'll be right back in the same situation you all had in Kansas. It's time for the tribe to stand up and take control of their lives."

"You're right James, it is time. Go ahead with your plan. Matt, Bill and I will start earning our pay."

So with those words, the "War" began.

By the end of the week we had nine men locked up and working. At first they refused to work, but after no food for two days they reconsidered their decision.

The oil company lawyers come calling, telling Tom he couldn't lock up their employees.

Tom explained to them he not only could lock them up but would lock up the lawyers after they had admitted to hiring the men to trespass on the Osage land. He sent word to me and I locked them up for the next twenty-four hours.

Tom in the mean time filed suit against two of the oil companies.

The Osage were taking the fight to the big companies on their own ground. This was the first and would take years to sort out in a courtroom. Exactly what we wanted.

We released the lawyers after twenty-four hours with the understanding that if any one from there company came back we would not only lock them up we would file more suits and shut their companies down.

Our point got across, we were notified a week later by mail that the two companies wanted to talk to the tribal council. As Bill put it "Things were looking up".

Mary and her mother were sitting on the porch visiting when I arrived back at the house.

"Well Mr. Council member what have you stirred up today?"

"Mom, I've tried to be a good little boy but it has been awful hard."

"I know what you mean. If you can't shoot it, it's no fun."

"Well sort of, but things were a lot simpler then. These slick talking lawyers are definitely not my sort of people."

"What about Bill, James?"

"Bill is a good person and only wants whatever is best for the people. The oil company folks are something different. They are already in Washington dealing with the politicians."

"How do you know that?"

"Tom got a telegram today from one of his friends. We're in for a fight folks and it's all going to depend on Matt, Bill and Tom. I don't see that there's much we can do. The agreement that we filed for control of our oil rights is about to be tested, big time."

CHAPTER 17

▼

$\mathbf{T}$he next two years I saw changes that were hard to believe. Automobiles were here to stay, and with them came a great need for oil. It seemed Tom, Bill and Matt were never home. They were busy putting out legal fires in Washington.

Finally the tribe's agreement was upheld in court. If the oil companies wanted to drill for oil on our lands they would have to deal with the tribal council. Bill, Matt and Tom had won. When we heard the news I told Mary to plan a party, a big party. It was time for the people to have a party, the biggest they had ever seen.

"I'll get mother and the girls to help me. How big do you want this thing to be?"

"I'll get hold of all the council members and have them notify the tribe. I want all of them to be here. We'll hold it down by the working pens just like an old gathering. Cookie has taught some of the boys how to use the pit. I figure it will take a dozen steers or so to feed everyone but I think Tom, Bill and Matt deserve something special. Real special when they return."

Mary and I walked down the hill to Will and Tee's place and told them the news and what I had planned.

"Dad we've got just about that many two year old steers over at the west pasture. Remember they weren't quite the quality we wanted in our last sale."

"I do now Will, have Boggs get them over here as soon as possible."

"Tee, if your mom will watch the kids you and I will go get Deb and head over to my mother's place. We have work to do."

Tee sent the kids over to get Deb and her kids. The kids would stay with Bird until the women got back.

"James, you go to your folks and tell Carla to meet us at mothers. Then go to Sam and Harold's. Tell Lesa and Flower I need them at mothers."

When I arrived at Pa's place he opened the door for me.

"Morning son, what's on your mind?"

"Need to talk to mom."

"Well I'm here son what do you need?"

"I told them about the court's decision and our plan for a party to honor Tom, Bill and Matt for their work. I told mom that Mary wanted her to come over to her mother's place and help plan the party.

"You gentlemen get the buggy ready, I'll change and be right out."

Pa and I hitched up the buggy; we had just finished when Carla came out of the house.

"Thank you, I'll be back when we get finished. There's plenty of food for you tonight dear."

She drove off in a hurry.

"Well son, looks like we've got the evening to ourselves."

"Not really sir, I've still got to go tell Sam and Lesa then go to Harold & Flower's. Mary wanted them over at her mom's place too."

"How about Rosa and Martha? They'll be heart broke if they don't get to help their grandkids."

"How about getting a hold of them Pa, I'll go on down to Sam's."

"Consider it done, it will give Cookie, Paco and I a chance to visit."

I rode down the Sam's place and found him outside his place working on his car.

"Broke down again Sam?"

"Not broke James, just a little bit bent. I'm cleaning the plugs. What brings you down this way?"

"I need to talk to Lesa."

"Lesa, someone here to see you."

"James Howard, what brings you over here this time of day?"

"Mary needs you over at her mother's place. We're planning a big party for Tom, Bill and Matt when they get back from Washington. The courts upheld the Osage right to manage their oil reserves."

"Praise the Lord. I'll change my clothes, Sam hook up the buggy."

"I can drive you over Lesa."

"Sam, I want to get there today. Hook up the buggy."

I helped Sam hook up the buggy. After Lesa left Sam began laughing.

"Lesa hates this automobile, but it keeps me busy. You'll have one someday James; it's one of those changes you'll make. You can't be left behind. You'll have to go forward to set the example for the tribe. Big changes are coming James and you're going to have to help lead the people, just like the trail drive up here. Your job has just started."

"Sam, you know Thumb set me up to be put on the council."

"Sure I do, he told me he was going to have you on the council one day."

"He did, you never said a word."

"I couldn't James, he made me promise. You know how he was."

"Yes, I know. He was something special. I sure do miss him."

"I know James, I do too. He sure loved my hams."

Sam and I visited for a while then I left for Harold's place. An automobile, what in the world did I need an automobile for. I had a fine horse.

The next couple of days were some of the busiest I'd ever known. The people of the tribe began to gather down near the working pens. Tents of every size and description dotted the tall grass prairie. Cookie was directing a dozen or so men who were building the pits for the beef.

Other members of the tribe were bringing wood up from the creek for the pit fires. It seemed everyone wanted to help.

Barrels were being set up and planks were being laid across them for make shift tables. It was wonderful to see the people all working together.

"James, you have a minute?"

"Sam, I didn't see you standing there. What can I do for you?"

"Figured I'd ask you to help me unload these sides of bacon and hams."

"Bacon and hams?"

"These folks can use the bacon, and the hams are for Cookie to put with the beef. James these folks helped me and I'm not about to forget it."

"Where do we need to unload them?"

We unloaded the hams into a box Cookie had brought out on a separate wagon from town. It seemed everyone was planning and working to make the coming day a success.

The women had been baking for the last two days. Cakes and pies from other tribal members now covered the make shift tables. The boys were going to arrive at nine-tomorrow morning and the party would start shortly thereafter.

Mary and I went to bed that night tired but happy.

"James, you had a wonderful idea. Everyone is thrilled to have the boys a party. They all know how hard they have worked to take care of the tribes business affairs."

"They deserve it Mary. I'm proud of them, but most of all I'm proud of our son. Will has taken over the ranch, Deb, Willie and Matt have the Thoroughbreds and Beth is happy. Damn Mary, we've done well."

"That we have, Cowboy, that we have."

CHAPTER 18

▼

The next morning Mary and I picked up Deb and headed to town to pick up the boys. We arrived at the train station twenty minutes before the train was to arrive from the north.

Art had coffee ready for us when we arrived.

"I wonder where Fran is I thought she would be here by now."

"I'm here Mary and so is my friend."

We turned around to not only see Tom's wife but Beth standing beside her.

"Oh my lord, Beth."

"Mother, you didn't think I'd miss the biggest party this place has ever seen. Besides my baby brother is being honored. I couldn't miss this."

"But what about your family?"

"The kids are in bed at Tom's house. Mike will be here this afternoon, he's in Tulsa taking care of business. We also have a surprise for you."

"What sort of surprise Beth?"

"We're moving to Tulsa. Mike is going to be the manager of the railroad business there."

"Oh my goodness, when will you be moving?"

"Sometime next month, we've got to find a place. A place where the kids can roam and have their horses."

"Reckon my grandson and I can do a little more hunting now."

"Dad, he has grown and become so much more outgoing. When he told his friends about his deer, they laughed at him and called him a liar. In fact he had several fights over it. Then the mounted head arrived and suddenly he became a big man at school."

"Mike's parents did not approve of him fighting but your grandson stood up to them. He told them a man had to stand up or he just wasn't much of a man. He told them his grandpa and uncles didn't let other fellers do their fighting."

"Dad, I was so proud of him. His sister is proud of him too."

"Beth, I didn't mean for him to stir up trouble with your in-laws."

"Dad, don't worry about it, Mike has been working on getting us out here to Tulsa for a couple of years. He loves it here, he told me he didn't know what a family meant until he came here."

"Well we're tickled to have you all home."

The train arrived at the station. Tom and Matt got off the train and were greeted by their wives. Bill followed them and came over to where Mary and I stood. Matt came over smiling.

"Mom, Dad, Sis what are you all doing here?"

"Well, we just thought maybe we could get a hug and a handshake."

Matt hugged his mother and gave her a kiss to boot. He shook my hand, a good firm handshake.

"Matt, I'm proud of you son."

Thanks dad, that means a lot to me you know."

"You've earned it son, I know how hard you've worked for this."

"Not near as hard as Bill and Uncle Tom. They didn't get much sleep while court was in session."

"Say James, where is everyone, this place looks like a ghost town."

"Well Tom, not that you mentioned it this place is rather quiet. Why don't you go home and see your kids for a while. Both of your boys need to be out at the working pens by eleven this morning. Bill, you need to be there too."

"The pens, James what's going on?"

"Well Tom it seems that your brother-in-law here is proud of you, Bill and our son here. It seems the council met and decided to have a party for the three of you."

"Mary, how many folks are out there?"

"Well Bill, I think the whole tribe. I mean everyone is there."

"Good Lord."

"Mother, you're telling us the whole tribe is out at the pens?"

"They were still arriving when we left but yes the whole tribe."

"My Lord, Deb, did you know about this?"

"I most surely did. In fact I've helped with the planning, but then I guess everyone did."

"Are we going to have some of Cookie's pit cooked beef?"

"We sure are son."

"Great, I'm hungry for some real food. The food in Washington wasn't really that great."

We loaded Matt's bags into the buggy and headed home. Tom, Fran and Beth loaded into their buggy and headed to Tom's place. They would be out after Tom unloaded his bags and cleaned up.

Art gave Bill a ride over to his small house. Bill would ride out with Art. Art had made arrangements for a man to take over for him for the afternoon. Art said he had no intentions of missing the party.

Matt and Deb sat close together on the buggy seat as we drove towards the ranch. Matt was shocked when we finally came into sight of the pens and he could see the people gathered there.

"Dad, how are you going to feed them all?"

"Well, I had twelve steers for Cookie and his boys to work with and the women have been baking stuff for the last two days. Plus your Uncle Sam brought some hams and bacon."

"Good lord, I've never seen this many folks here before."

"Maybe it's because we have never won a battle with the government before son. Your Uncle Thumb would have been proud of you, Matt. You and the other boys."

"Thanks mom, I've learned a lot these last few months. The oil companies have money to hire the best lawyers in the country and have a lot of clout with a bunch of the politicians. It was a tough fight but thanks should be given to Bill. He showed us how to close up a few loop holes Uncle Tom and I had missed."

"Well I figure before the day is over with you'll have time to thank him."

"I'll take care of it dad, all I want to do now is spend a day or so with my family and visit with Willie about this years colts."

Our serious son was getting back to business. The business he really loved.

CHAPTER 19

▼

Needless to day the day was a complete success. I had never seen Cookie, Paco, Rosa and Martha so happy. The young men Cookie had taught to cook the pit beef were running back and forth asking his advise.

"James, it's one heck of a party. It'll take the boys a couple of hours to feed these folks. Seems as if it's a very special day."

"Not everyday the tribe wins a battle against the politicians Cookie."

"That is a fact son, by golly I'd never thought of it like that. No wonder these folks are so happy."

Beth, Mike and their family arrived in plenty of time to get fed. Beth was smiling and visiting with old friends. It was easy to see she was happy to be back home.

When everyone had been fed Mary's father called for everyone to listen. He called Tom, Matt and Bill to step up on the wagon. He informed the tribe that the three were the new warriors of the Osage.

The people cheered the three men. He then asked the people to make Bill Culbert an honorary member of the tribe. He called for a voice vote. Bill stood tall and proud when the vote was taken, I saw him wipe a tear from his eyes.

Next Mary's father told the people how two of their own had fought and won for the tribe the right to control any minerals that lay beneath their lands. He pointed to Tom and Matt called them warriors of the first order.

The crowd cheered the two men. Next he said he wanted to thank Cookie for the wonderful meal he had again produced for the people. He told the crowd it had indeed been a great day when they had welcomed Cookie and Martha into their small town.

Again the crowd cheered loudly Cookie and Martha in return thanked the crowd for allowing them to be a part of the community.

Once more Mary's father called for quiet.

"Let us not forget our own tribal police force. They have been hard pressed these last few months to keep out the intruders who were roaming our lands. Remember they will still need your help so don't let up in your help for them."

Again the crowd cheered.

"Now, let's try the pies, cakes and other sweets the women of our tribe have prepared for us. Then the dancing can begin."

The deserts were served, and afterwards the musicians began tuning their instruments. The handshaking went on for a while and Mary and I enjoyed the whole thing. Bill Culbert came over to where Mary and I sat.

"May I have a moment of your time folks?"

"Sit down Bill, The dancing's just getting ready to start."

"James, I just want you and Mary to know how much these last few months have meant to me. I was speaking to a gentleman a few moments ago who was once your foreman. He indeed had high praise for you and your family. His wife told me you fed her and her boys the first winter you were here and didn't even tell Mary about your helping her. In fact I've heard several reports of things you've done like this over the years. No wonder these people love you so."

"Bill, my husband has done many things since we came here. Most of them you'd have to ask whoever he helped because he doesn't talk about these things. So don't be surprised if after a while you hear a lot more things about him."

"I'm beginning to understand why the tribe put you on the council. When I first came here I thought you were simply a prosperous cattleman. It shows that first impressions are sometimes wrong. Your son Matt is a very intelligent young man, the folks here are lucky to have him."

"Thank you Bill, his mother and I are quite proud of him. He's quite a good horseman too."

"I know, I saw the Princess run once in New York. She was a thing of beauty. What I stopped to tell you is that I will have my own house. The Swenson's are working on it now. I plan on going back east and sell my home and then I'll be back. This is where things are happening and I want to be a part of it."

"We're glad you're going to be here Bill."

"Don't thank me, this country seems to grab you. It's wonderful here, the people are so gracious."

"They simply appreciate your help."

"That may be but I now know where I want to stay, I'm in love with this place."

"We're proud to have you Bill, when you get back you'll have to come out and visit us."

"Oh I'll do that, I want to watch Matt work his horses."

The party didn't end until well after midnight. Folks began to head home the next day. Things were going to begin to get back to normal.

Beth and her family stayed a couple of days then returned home to Kentucky. They would be back in Tulsa in three weeks or so. They had a gentleman looking for a home for them.

My grandson had become a fine young man. He was quickly becoming as he put it my right hand. He wanted to learn how to do everything around the ranch.

I had asked him if he wanted to help with our Angus sale and he was truly excited. He had ran to his mother and asked her permission to come up and help.

"James, that boy is so much like you it's unreal."

"He's a dandy alright. I really enjoy having him around. Will's son is a good boy but is laid back like Will. Beth's son just has the fire inside."

I'm thrilled that Beth and her family are going to be close to home; I've missed her a lot these past years.

"Well they'll be here soon Mary, they will be here for Thanksgiving and Christmas that's what I'm looking forward too. The whole family will be home."

Things went well for the next few months then problems began to set in. Oil was discovered just outside the Osage land. Within a month a dozen rigs were drilling as hard and fast as they could go. It was only a matter of time until the boys would be going full blast.

One morning Mary and I were having our coffee on the porch swing watching the Thoroughbred colts at work when we saw Tom's automobile drive up to the race barn.

"Oh my, it looks like things are going to begin to happen."

"Looks that way Mary, It looks as if Tom is coming up this way."

Tom drove up the hill and stopped in front of the house.

"Morning James, got an extra cup?"

"Mary's already gone to get it Tom, come on up and sit down."

"What's going on Tom?"

"Looks like we're going to have to start our leasing program James. The oil companies are pushing us hard. They are willing to pay the royalties we have set forth."

"Does the council need to meet?"

"Probably James, we want everyone informed. We'll need to send out notices to all the oil companies letting them know when we'll have the auction."

"You've got the parcels of land numbered already?"

"Oh yes, Matt has had that done for some time. I just came out to inform Matt that I was going to mail the notices out today."

"I guess our quiet life is about to end."

"That is a fact James, I don't want to see it happen but at least we will have some control."

"That's how we have to look at it James. It will be both good and bad. Our children will be able to have fine schools and an opportunity to go to college. Some of our people will fall by the wayside, but we can't help that. We'll do the best we can do for them and go on."

CHAPTER 20

▼

So began the time of "Oil in the Osage".

The leases were bought and the drilling rigs and crews began to show up and dot the land. The thump of the drilling rigs could be heard night and day.

True to Tom's prediction oil was discovered on the tribes land. Vast pools of what the oil people called Black Gold.

A couple of leases on our land would be in the next offering and I was not looking forward to having them on our place but had no choice. You either had to move forward or get left behind.

Matt, Bill and Tom seemed to be running night and day looking after tribal affairs.

Willie, Mac and Deb continued working with the young horses. Mary and I sat out on our porch and gazed across our pastures at the cattle down below.

"Well cowboy, once cattle were the most important thing here. That seems to have changed."

"I know Mary, I can count six drilling rigs from here. Oil is the most important thing now."

"Well look at it this way James, it will mean more money for the ranch if the cattle market goes down."

"That's true but I still hate to see the changes. I just don't want the people hurt."

"Are the tribal police handling things alright?"

"They seem to be. They will have their hands full in a short while. It's only a matter of time until trouble will start. Where there's money you'll have whiskey, and fly by night schemes to get the money from the people."

"Then I guess we'll just have to keep watch and help when we can. By the way we got a letter from Beth today. They think they have found a place just north and west of Tulsa. It's a two-story home with a barn and forty acres. She seems to think it's just what they want."

"Want to run down and check it out?"

"Would you mind?"

"No, I've not been down to Tulsa in a while now. From what I've heard it's growing by leaps and bounds. They have discovered oil just south of Tulsa too."

"When do you want to go James?"

"Why not tomorrow, we've got all the time we need. We can find one of those nice hotels and then rent a rig and go out to the kid's place."

"I'll pack some things."

"Mary, we'll only be gone for a night or two so don't get carried away. I'll have to carry the bags you know."

"I can remember when all we had were the clothes on our backs. Times have sure changed haven't they cowboy?"

"I should say so, up until now change didn't worry me."

The next morning we drove the buggy into town and after unloading our bags at the train station I drove the team down to the livery and found things there hectic.

"Mr. Howard, how are you sir?"

"Fine Hank, looks like you're busy."

"Lord yes, I can't keep enough teams to do the work for the oil boys. We danged near had a fight here this morning over a team. Folk's tempers are sure short. Look at all the folks in town. I don't know a third of them."

"Times change Hank, do the best you can and go on."

"I'm doing that Mr. Howard, I have two of my boys staying here at night to be sure no one steals the teams. Never even had a lock on anything until now.

"I know Hank, things are changing for sure."

Mary and I caught the train to Tulsa and I could not believe how much the city had grown. Houses and buildings were going up everywhere. It was plain to see this town was on the move. I could only wonder if our small town would do the same.

We got off the train and I hailed a hack. I told him our daughter's address and sat back for the ride.

"James, I remember when there were only a dozen or so businesses here."

"It has changed Mary, it looks as if every block has a bar of some sort."

"I guess we'll see changes at home as well."

The kids had leased a small farmhouse just east of town. When the hack pulled into the lane leading up to their home I saw our granddaughter out in the nearby pasture riding her horse.

When she saw us she came charging across the field. When she reached the rail fence along the driveway her horse jumped and cleared it better than a foot, much to the delight of our granddaughter.

"Grandpa, Grandma, doesn't he jump just great?"

"He certainly does baby."

"Oh grandpa he's the best. The girls back home were glad to see me move. I think they were tired of loosing to him."

"How do you like your new school?"

"Oh it's fine, the kids for the most part are real nice."

"Most part, what do you mean?"

"A couple of the boys gave me a hard time for a while but Joe took care of them."

"Your brother took on a couple of older boys?"

"He sure did grandma, he's sort of quiet but when he gets mad my little brother is tough."

"Well what do you think about that James?"

"I think I'd better have a talk with the young man."

"Mother has already done that grandpa. When Joe told her what the boy said mother really got mad, and not at Joe."

"Oh my, this sounds serious. I'd better talk to Beth."

"Grandpa, would you hold Champ while I bathe him?"

"Be glad too Carrie, where do we go?"

I followed my granddaughter; it would not be the last time. My granddaughter had dreams and I was looking forward to see her try and achieve them.

Mike our son-in-law came home and we all drove out to see their new house. They were having it painted inside. It was a nice home and the out buildings were in good repair.

Mike told me they had been lucky to get it. A man he worked with lived just down the road and had told him about the widow who wanted to sell.

The kids had sold their place back east and had more than enough to buy the home. They seemed to be happy. My grandson and I had a little talk about the fighting. He told me what the other boy had said and then I understood why he had fought.

"Grandpa, I couldn't let them call sis those names!"

"No you couldn't, but remember fighting is not something to get in the habit of doing. Sooner or later you'll find someone who is tougher, and it's no fun."

"Grandpa, is it true that you've shot some men?"

"Yes, it's true, I've shot some men but I've sure never bragged about it. Things are changing; we have laws and lawmen to take care of folks like the ones I had trouble with. Where did you hear about me shooting folks?"

"The teacher at school was telling the class about people who were important in our state's history, she mentioned your name. She didn't know I was your grandson."

"She told the class about how you came here with cattle, and how you've built the ranch and have helped the tribe. She explained how you'd become a U.S. Marshal and helped clean up the peoples land. Grandpa, you're a very famous man."

"Not famous grandson, just a very lucky man who had friends to help him grow."

"But grandpa, our teacher said that you could run for governor and win."

"Well grandson, don't worry, I'll never run for any public office. Just being on the Tribal Council is all the responsibility I want."

"Besides, your grandma and I are enjoying being able to travel and see things we've never seen. Grandson, it may be hard for you to understand but in your young lifetime you've seen more of this country than I have. Your grandmother and I have worked hard to build the ranch and make something for our children. Your mother is a very strong willed person but she'll always be there for you so treat her with respect. Remember your father has made sacrifices for you and your sister. Moving our here and leaving everything he grew up with took a lot of courage. He moved here so you and your sister could grow up and learn things about your heritage. He wanted your mother to be happy."

"I know grandpa, he loves her an awful lot. My other grandma didn't like mother much."

"Probably because she has a tendency to speak her mind."

"Oh yes, mother did stir things up every now and again. She would take sis and I fishing or horseback riding rather than go to one of grandma's tea parties."

"I can believe that, it sounds just like her."

"Grandpa, are we sure enough going to go deer hunting again this fall?"

"You bet we are, you want to camp out like your father and uncles do?"

"Heck yes. I've never done anything like that before."

"Well I guess it's past time. We'll just get everything together and go."

"Oh boy, wait until I tell the kids at school. Oh Boy!"

CHAPTER 21

▼

Mary and I spent the night in the town's new hotel. We were quite pleased with the service. The town was growing and growing fast. I could see what the oil business was doing here and could see what was going to happen to our small town.

We did some shopping then caught our train home.

"James, is our town going to grow like Tulsa?"

"I hope not, the only hope we have is that the tribe controls the land and can restrict the sale of the land. It looks as if the big oil companies are building office buildings in Tulsa. Let's hope they stay here."

We caught the train and enjoyed the ride home.

Art met us at the station with the latest news. It seemed some men had indeed tried to as they told the tribal police borrow a couple of teams to finish up a well site.

They were rewarded with a couple of loads of birdshot in various parts of their bodies. It had taken Doc an hour or so to remove the shot.

A few days after our return home we saw the first of the drilling rigs pulled onto our ranch. A car came driving up the road to our house. A young man got out of the car.

"Mr. Howard?"

"Yes sir, what may I do for you?"

"Sir, I'm Leonard West foreman for Fourmost Oil Company."

"Alright Mr. West what can I do for you?"

"Sir, it's more like what I can do for you."

"What you can do for me, sir I don't understand."

"Let me explain Mr. Howard. First of all we'll try and keep the damage to your land at a minimum. We'll use your existing road to move our equipment over. In return we'll maintain the road at no cost to you. Second, we'll be drilling fourteen wells on your place here. We also will do our best to drill our wells while trying to keep the damage to a bare minimum. If you see anything you don't understand or approve of, just come to me and we'll work out the problem."

"Mr. West, I'm going to be truthful with you. First of all I really don't want you boys drilling on my place, but I don't have a choice. Now if you keep your word we won't have any problems, but if you don't then I'll come look you up."

"Thank you for being truthful with me Mr. Howard. We're here for the long run and we'd like to get along with everyone. I've heard a lot about you Mr. Howard and all of it good. I've heard you're a fair and honest man so I'll not lie to you. My company has ordered me to drill the wells but I've been instructed to try and work with you."

"Mr. West, you've got a job to do so I guess you'd better get to it."

"Thank you Mr. Howard, Mrs. Howard, I'll be on my way then."

We watched as the young man drove down the hill.

"Damn it Mary, I shouldn't have been so short with that young man, he's got a job to do."

"I know James, but I think he understands."

"I hope so, I'll ride down tomorrow and have a talk with him."

"That would be the thing to do James."

"I know, but it won't be easy."

"Dear, since when has anything been easy, now look around you. We've got our family, the ranch and more friends that most people ever dream of having."

"Look to the future James, that is what Uncle Thumb would want you to do. That's why he worked so hard to get you on the council. Darling you've always looked to the future don't stop now."

"I'll do my best Mary, maybe I'll just saddle my horse and go look at the Angus. That usually makes me feel better. I'm just upset about what this oil is going to do to the people. Mary, they're not ready for this."

"I know dear but we can't stop what's going to happen."

"I know, I guess my retirement just ended, reckon I better go talk to Tom and the boys."

"That would probably be a good idea. I talked to Bill last week and he said that he and Will had been working on a plan to help the people manage their newfound wealth. Maybe you should talk to him."

"You may be right Mary, Bill's been a big help to Tom and Will. Maybe together we can work things out.

CHAPTER 22

▼

I found the boys busy working on piles of paper, lease agreements, bids submitted for future oil leases and at the same time trying to take care of the day-to-day business of the tribe.

"Anything I can do to help boys?"

"James, there just might be something you can do."

"Name it Tom."

"We've received complaints about how some of the rigs are tearing things up out at the well sights. You still have your Marshal's badge so how about going out to a couple and see if you can get something done."

"I don't how much I can do Tom but I'll give it a try. What wells are we talking about?"

"Tom get a map and show me the locations."

"James, folks respect and trust you, you're the only hope we have right now.

"I'll do my best Tom, I think I'll ask Sam to ride along with me."

"Whatever you want to do James, we're snowed under with all this paper work."

I said goodbye to the boys and headed out of town. Wagons loaded with pipe and equipment filled the once quiet roads. The town was filled with strangers looking to make money. The boom as it was called was going full blast. Our quiet little town might never be the same.

I found Sam outside of his house working on his automobile again.

"Hey James, what are you up to?"

"Sam, what makes you think I'm up to anything?"

"The look on your face brother, I've known you for a long time and I sure enough know when your thinking about trouble. Now, what do you need?"

"I've got to go check on some complaints that members of the tribe have made against some of the drilling rigs. Want to ride along with me?"

"Let me get my hat. Put your horse in the barn, we'll take my automobile. It's quicker and if you've got several sights to look at we'll need it."

I put my horse in Sam's barn lot and walked back to his house. Sam was waiting for me.

"Here brother take this and put it on."

Sam was handing me the pistol and holster that my father had given him years before.

"You think I might need it Sam?"

"James, some of the drilling crews are some pretty salty boys. It might not be a bad idea. I'm going to take this other one myself."

"You may be right Sam, let's go. That is if you can get this mechanical monster to run."

"Hop in James, you're in for a treat."

Sam started the automobile and we left his place in a cloud of dust. Sam took the road east and then turned south after a few miles towards the first well site. We topped the rise and saw what the folks were upset about. The area around the drilling rig looked like a tornado had just gone through it.

A couple of men were working their teams of horses using what were called ships and were making a trench from the well site towards the nearby creek. Trash of all sorts littered the site. I could see why the tribal members were upset. The well site was within fifty yards of the tribal member's house.

"James, this place is a mess. I can't believe what these men have done."

"Why are they cutting that ditch?"

"No idea Sam, but we're going to find out."

Sam stopped the car and we got out. The tribal member came out of his house and quickly came to where we were looking at the mess.

"Mr. Howard, you have come to help?"

"I'm going to see what I can do Lone Eagle. I only heard about this mess this morning."

"They came in day before yesterday and began setting up. They were supposed to drill the well over there, pointing to a small red flag a couple of hundred yards from the present location."

"The men curse and show no respect for our families. My wife was hanging clothes and one of the men relieved him-self right in front of her. He laughed when she hurried my oldest daughter into the house."

"Lone Eagle go back into the house, let Sam and I see what we can do."

We watched as Lone Eagle walked slowly back towards his house.

"Sam, lets find out who is in charge down here."

"I think that's exactly what needs to be done James."

Sam and I slowly walked down to the drilling location. The first man we encountered was screwing some parts together.

"Who is in charge here?"

"The man looked up only long enough to point to a large man in a black shirt standing on what was called the floor.

Sam and I walked over close to the floor and I motioned for the man to come down.

He looked at me for a moment then gave me a gesture with his hand that I took offense to. He turned his back to me and went back to talking to a man we later found out was the driller.

I quickly mounted the floor and just as the man turned around towards me, I without thinking drew the pistol and brought it down along side his head. He dropped like a rock onto the floor. I turned to the driller.

"Shut this thing down, now!"

The man didn't argue and ran to the engine house where he quickly shut the engine down.

I turned to the man on the floor who was shaking his head.

"Why—you, I'll whip—"

He quit talking when I cocked the pistol in my hand.

"Now friend, you just lay there and listen because I'm only going to say this once."

"First you tear this rig down and move it over to the location where you're supposed to be and don't you leave any of this mess behind."

"Second, close up that ditch, you're not going to foul the water. The tribe down stream depends on it. Build yourself a holding pond and do it right."

"Third, you build yourself an outhouse. If I hear about you or one of your men exposing himself to another woman I'll come back and shoot it off. Understand?"

"Yeah, I understand. I'm calling the company and having you arrested."

Sam began to laugh.

"What's so funny?"

"Fellow, you're talking to the U.S. Marshal."

"You're a Marshal?

"That's right, so you do whatever you like with your company because I intend to get in touch with them myself. What is the name of your company?"

"Lucky Dollar Oil, sir."

"They're based down in Tulsa?"

"No sir, their office is in Kansas City."

"And your name is?"

"Bart Gibson."

"Alright Bart, now that we've had our little talk, if I have to come back out here I may not be so nice."

"No sir, we'll start moving the rig right now."

"Fine, but you can expect me to be back. You'll have no more trouble from me if you and your men do your work and don't cause the tribe anymore trouble."

One of the men nearby began to cuss. Sam drew himself up and stepped over to the man.

"Feller, if you don't like it here you'd better leave, because you start cussing my brother and I'm just liable to shoot you myself."

The man, much smaller than Sam began to back up. You could see the sudden fear in his eyes.

"You're his brother, you can't be!"

"He's my brother friend so maybe you better listen to him. We don't care what you boys do at night down in your saloons outside of town but if I catch one or any of you creating trouble in our town you'll answer to me. Understand?"

"Yes sir."

"You're not back east anymore, out here we sort of take care of things ourselves. Sometimes it can be rather sudden. Act like your mamma raised you and you won't have any more trouble."

Sam and I walked back to his car and headed on to the next well site. Sam had to chuckle as he drove.

"James, times have changed. There was a time folks like that foreman wouldn't have lasted a day out here."

"That's true Sam, I probably shouldn't have hit him but he made me mad."

"I've got a feeling we won't have anymore trouble from him in the future."

"I hope not but we may need help before this mess is over Sam, there's no way we can keep up with all these sites."

"James, I've noticed that big oil companies are a little more concerned about how they do their work."

"That's because they don't want to get shut down and drug into court."

"May be, but I think it's the smaller outfits trying to make things go on a shoe string."

"All we can do is try Sam."

CHAPTER 23

▼

T he next month was something I'll never forget. Sam and I went almost from dawn to dark.

I had returned home just at sundown one evening tired and hungry.

"James, your bath is ready. Your clean clothes are already laid out. I'll have your supper ready when you're finished."

"Thank you Mary, I'll admit I'm completely give out."

"You've been working too hard James, you and Sam are not twenty years old anymore."

"I know Mary, but I promised Thumb."

"You promised Uncle you'd help the people, you can't help them if you kill yourself dear. Now get your bath and after you've had your supper we'll talk. I may have an idea that will make things easier for both you and Sam."

I got a kiss on the check and headed to our bathroom for a hot bath. As I soaked in the tub I seemed to float in space. I was tired, bone tired. The last few years of good living had softened me, that and twenty years.

"James, hurry up before your supper gets cold."

I had dozed off in the hot tub. I quickly got dressed and went in to eat dinner.

"Well my dear what is this idea of you have?"

"Why not have the council appoint a group for overseeing the drilling sites. James, we can't save everything. I know you'd like to but there is no way, there are simply too many of them. Maybe with the money the tribe will receive we can restore things after the drilling is over with."

"Mary, you're probably right, Sam and I have been chasing our tails the last month or so, I'll ride into town and talk with Tom and the boys."

"James."

"Yes Mary."

"I'll drive you into town!"

"You'll do what Mary?"

"I'll drive you, I bought a car last week and I've learned to drive."

"My lord Mary, I've been too busy to even know what's going on in my own house."

"That's true dear but maybe now you can slow down enough to back up and look at things in a different light. You've always been able to figure something out."

"Lady, I'm the luckiest man in the world to have had you all these years."

I kissed her and held her close.

The next morning Mary took me down to the barn and showed me our new automobile. She explained to me how to start and operate it. I had watched Sam over the last month and had a good idea how things worked.

"When we get back dear I'll teach you how to drive."

"Guess I'd better learn, I've always told everyone to look ahead to the future. Looks like I'd better practice what I've preached."

Mary drove us into our bustling town and after an hour or so Tom, Bill, Matt and I came up with a plan to try and oversee the drilling. We would hire a dozen men to check on the various rigs and try to keep the damages to the people to a minimum.

"James, the tribe will begin receiving their money next month. We'll really have problems when this happens; we're going to need you more than ever then. We'll have every sort of riffraff you can think of here to try and steal the people's money."

"But Mary, it's going to be theirs, it's not up to me to tell them what they can and can't do."

"I know that James, but there will be those who will ask you for help."

"And I'll give it Mary but you have to understand, it's like Thumb told me. Some will survive and others won't. Those who have educated children and will listen to them will be fine. It's the older people I worry about. They are like children and as such, are the ones we have to watch out for more than anyone."

"James, do we have a chance?"

"I'm not sure Mary, we'll just have to work hard and pray."

"I guess so, sort of like your trying to teach me to drive our new beast."

Mary finally laughed and on the out skirts of town pulled the car over.

"Time to try your hand cowboy, let's see how you handle this bronc!"

God what a mess; I cussed and Mary laughed but finally I got the beast headed in the right direction. The gears would never be the same but I had it going. Stopping the first time was another treat. Mary had tears running down her checks she was laughing so hard.

Finally though I began to get the hang of things and even I began to laugh. When we reached our house without incident and I shut the beast down Mary smiled.

"Cowboy, for awhile there I thought it was going to throw you but you came through again. I'm proud of you. Now you drive down to Sam's and show him you can drive by yourself. He won't believe you unless you show up by yourself. Besides you'll get better the more you drive. You'll need all the practice you can get if you're going to be going all over the land."

"Well, guess I might as well get started then."

Mary got out and went into the house. I started the automobile
and managed a smooth start. I turned the car around and drove down
the hill. I waved at Tee as I drove by.

Sam saw me coming and met me at his front gate.

"Well I'll be, you finally saw the light."

"Reckon I did, you up to a little ride?"

"Sure, let me tell Lesa."

Sam went in to the house and came back out smiling.

"You're a brave sole to ride with me you know."

"Reckon I'll take a chance, been following you for a while now."

"I don't remember you ever following too much Sam, as I remember you were usually standing beside me when times got tough."

"That's true James, we been down the road together seems like forever, sometimes but then I wouldn't change a thing if I could."

"Now, where are we headed?"

"I thought we might just drive back out and check the Lucky Dollar, we'll see if anything has changed."

"Lets go, I'm sort of looking forward to seeing if we had any effect
on those boys."

The drive out to the well wasn't too bad. I was actually learning
how to change gears smoothly. I began to enjoy this new fangled
automobile.

What Sam and I found at the well site was even better. The old
sight had been cleaned up and the new one was in good shape. We
drove on past down to Lone Eagle's home. Both he and his wife met
us at the front gate.

"Mr. Howard, good to see you. Things are a lot better now. Your
talk with the men seemed to have worked. We have had no more
trouble."

"Thank you Mr. Howard, my daughters and I feel much better
since you talked to the men. At least now they seem to respect us."

"I'm glad Mrs. Lone Eagle, sometimes the only thing that some of
the boys need is a little talking to."

"I know sir, I saw how you talked to him with your pistol."

"It wasn't much of a thing, just something to get his attention."

"It was good enough, thank you sir."

As Sam and I drove away I felt good all over, we hadn't won the battle but it was a start. If we kept trying we might just make a difference.

CHAPTER 24

▼

$\mathbf{M}$ary and I were having our last cup of coffee out on the porch when we heard a blast and saw the flames off to the southwest.

"Lord James, I didn't know they were drilling down that way."

"They are not Mary, remember the Duck family opted out of the lease program. Lame Duck said he had cattle, hogs and a good garden. He didn't want the oil wells on his place."

"But James he had a head right.

"That's true but he didn't want the oil folks on his land. It was his choice, several others went along with him."

"James, maybe we'd better go check, that fire seems to be getting bigger.

"You're right Mary, we better go check."

We took our automobile and drove off towards the fire. Twenty minutes later we could see folks running around trying to put out fires that were burning all around the house location. The house itself had been flattened by the explosion.

I saw the Duck's oldest son standing off to one side, he seemed to be in a daze.

"Frankie, is there anything I can do for you?"

"Mr. Howard I'm not sure."

"What happened? Did your father have some dynamite stored near the house?"

"No sir, he wouldn't have know how to use it if he had."

"Then what caused the explosion?"

"I don't know sir. I was over at my girl friend's house and was on my way back when the house exploded.

"You were on the road?"

"No I was taking a shortcut across the pasture, that was when I saw the truck going down the road."

"Which way was it headed?"

"It was headed east Mr. Howard, towards town."

"Were you close enough to make out the color?"

"It was a dark color with white lettering on the door."

"You're sure?"

"Yes sir, they drove right by me but didn't see me."

"You couldn't see who was in the vehicle?"

"No sir, but since the oil folks moved in there are cars on the road all times of the day and night."

"How long was it after you saw the vehicle the house blew up?"

"Only a few seconds, the explosion nearly knocked me down. In fact I'd forgotten about seeing the automobile until right now."

"They didn't stop and come back to help?"

"I've not seen them Mr. Howard."

"Were your folks and you grandfather at home?"

"Yes sir, my sister is back east going to school."

"Frankie, do you have a place to stay for the next day or so?"

"I can stay at grandpa's old place Mr. Howard, but I want to know what happened here."

"So do I Frankie, so do I. Stay close, I'm going to wander around and see what I can find."

A few minutes later I spotted a man who was a driller helping put out the small grass fire.

"Hey Mike, good to see you here."

"Mr. Howard, I'd just finished my shift when I heard the explosion and saw the fire ball."

"If you were to guess, what would you say caused it?"

"Dynamite, Mr. Howard. I could smell it when I drove up. No doubt about it."

"You're sure Mike?"

"You bet I am. Mr. Howard I been around and used the stuff for years."

"Damn, I was afraid of that, we've got three murders on our hands. Mike, what company has dark colored cars with white lettering on the doors?"

"Mr. Howard, it this going to be between us?"

"Don't worry Mike, no one will know who told me."

"The only folks with their names on their doors is the high Rollin bunch from Tulsa called Queenland Oil."

"You don't seem to like them much?"

"Sure don't, I don't like their field men. Personally Mr. Howard I think they tried to get these folks to lease their place to them."

"Everyone knows they didn't want any drilling on their land Mike."

"I know that Mr. Howard, but it doesn't make these boys any difference. They didn't have enough money to buy any of the leases, so I think they are out trying to scare folks into leasing their land to them. I've seen their boys at several places over the last few weeks."

"Would you mind telling me where you have seen them?"

"Not at all, they've been to every property that wasn't leased this last week or so. It's a damn shame all the folks had to die here tonight."

"Mike, they didn't all die. The boy was on his way home when the house blew up."

"Mr. Howard, I'll bet the boys didn't know he was gone. They want the drilling rights. That boy had better be careful Mr. Howard those boys play rough."

"Looks that way Mike, we'll see what we can do about stopping them. Thanks for the help Mike."

"Not a problem Mr. Howard, there's oil a plenty for everyone. I just don't see why folks can't just play by the rules."

"Thanks again Mike, you hear anything I'd appreciate you letting me know."

"I'll do that Mr. Howard you're welcome at my rig anytime."

"Thanks Mike, see you later."

I walked away looking for Frankie. We had to have a talk and quick.

I found Mary and told her what had happened and what Mike had told me.

"James, this is terrible. What do you plan to do?"

"First thing I need to do is find Frankie, then have a talk with Tom and the boys. I need them to confirm who the mineral rights go to if something should happen to Frankie."

"James lets find Frankie, I've got an idea."

We found Frankie talking to some of the neighbors.

"Frankie, may I have a moment of your time please."

"Sure Mr. Howard be right with you."

Mary and I stepped away and waited for Frankie to finish talking to his friends.

"Mary, what's this idea you have?"

"James, someone's going to have to stay with Frankie until this mess is straightened out. Now give me a list of what you need and I'll go find Tom and get the information you need. Here take my pistol until I get back, you may need it. I'll stop and tell Sam, he should be able to be here in an hour or so."

"Sounds like a plan Mary, have Sam stop at our place and tell him to bring my old bed roll along with my pistol and Sharps. He knows where I keep them."

"Take care James I'll see you in a while."

"Come down by the timber there Mary. That's where Frankie and I will be. It's not safe for him to be up here. Those boys hear he's still alive they just may come back and try to finish the job."

"I'll tell Sam. See you later."

I watched as Mary drove off, headed back towards the road to town.

Frankie came walking over to where I stood.

"Mr. Howard, sorry for making you wait but the neighbors and I had to have a talk."

"Fine Frankie, we need to talk too. As you know I'm a member of the council."

"Yes sir, I've known you and your family ever since I can remember. You gave my grandparents beef the first winter they were here. I've heard the story many times from my grandfather."

"I remember Frankie, times were tough and folks were hungry, so I gave them beef. Frankie I had plenty so I gave them beef. Would you do the same for me?"

"Yes sir, I would."

"Then forget it, we've got bigger problems to work on. We've got to figure out who blew your grandparents home up tonight."

"I'll help any way I can sir."

"Good, now let's go over there in the timber and find a spot to sit down and rest. I've got some questions to ask you and we don't want to be interrupted."

"Follow me sir, I know just the place."

I followed Frankie down the hill and into the timber. We came to a spot where a large oak had fallen sometime in the past. Frankie sat down on the tree.

"Will this do Mr. Howard?"

"This will do just fine Frankie. Frankie, I've got some questions to ask. First, has there been anyone around talking to your grandfather the last few weeks?"

"Yes sir, there's been several but there has been one bunch in particular."

"One bunch, what do you mean bunch?"

"There were three all together. There was just one to start with but the next two times there were three. Grandpa was pretty upset when he came back into the house the last time."

"Did you know who the men were?"

"No sir, never seen them before. But then there are so many strangers running around now that's not a surprise."

"What did these boys look like?"

"The one in charge was about average height, the other two were big, more the size of your friend Sam."

"Alright, did your grandfather say anything about what they wanted?"

"Yes sir, they wanted to drill for oil."

"Anything else you can remember, anything at all?"

"Well, grandpa did say they talked funny."

"Talked funny, what did he mean by that?"

"They didn't sound like they were from around here sir."

"Alright, they are probably from out of state, brought in to scare folks."

"Frankie, do you have any other family?"

"Just my sister but she's off at school. Folks and I have lived with my grandparents for some time. My grandfather had a brother who lives down by Tulsa but grandfather didn't have any contact with him. Grandfather said he had shamed the people, about what I don't know."

"Well right now my main concern is you. I'm going to stay with you tonight. This was no accident Frankie, a friend of mine said he smelled dynamite when he arrived to help."

"Mr. Howard, why would anyone want to hurt my family? We really didn't have that much."

"It's the oil Frankie, some folks see a chance to become wealthy and don't care what they have to do to get it."

Folks had left after the fire burned down and was no more a threat to the surrounding countryside. A tribal policeman was up near the house and would spend the night. A search for Frankie's family would be done after the fire had cooled down.

"Mr. Howard, you think the men who did this will come back?"

"Yes I do, they have gone this far and they find out you're still alive they are going to want to talk to you. That's why we're going to keep you out of sight until we get this mess straightened out."

We had visited for a while when I heard my name being called, it was Sam. I hadn't heard his car so I was surprised.

"Over here Sam!"

I heard horses coming our way, Sam had brought my things but had come on horseback.

"Evening James, Sorry to hear about your family Frankie."

"Thank you sir."

"No thanks needed son, James I brought some sandwiches and your guns. You figure we're going to need them?"

"Not sure Sam, but I'd rather be safe than sorry."

"I know what you mean, help me unload this stuff."

CHAPTER 25

▼

We unloaded the things Sam had brought and quickly made a makeshift camp. I filled Sam in on what all Frankie had seen and heard.

"Sounds like we've got some bad boys in the neighborhood James."

"Looks that way Sam, I think the boys have been threatening some of our folks. Do you think you could do a little riding tomorrow for me?"

"Tell me what you want done."

"There are four more places over this way that are still un-bid on. Go to them and see if anyone has talked to them about leasing their land. The folks all know you so they will talk to you."

"Not a problem, I'll leave out first light. I've seen the maps and know the location of all the families. One of them backs up to Thumb's old place."

"You're right Sam, the way I got this figured we'll have to catch these boys in the act then get them to talk."

"May be hard to get them to talk James."

"Not the way I'm planning it Sam."

I explained my plan to Sam. He was laughing until tears ran down his cheeks. Frankie was laughing with him.

"Mr. Howard, may I round up the folks you'll need to pull this off."

"Think you can round up a half dozen or so Frankie?"

"You bet I do, in fact some of them are friends of my grandfather. They'll look forward to helping."

"Good, then get started. I figure we've got until at least noon before the boys find out you weren't in the house. They'll have to come back to find you."

"I'll be back before daylight."

Sam and I worked on my plan. He added a few suggestions that I thought were great. If we pulled this off we'd have to have some luck.

Frankie was back with eight men an hour before daylight. Four were younger and the other four were elders.

"Welcome brothers, sit down and I will explain my plan to you."

When I finished the men were smiling.

"It is a good plan brother, how do you intend to get the information to the men?"

"I figure they will come back to find Frankie. We'll inform the tribal police officer up at the house that Frankie here is staying over at Thumb's old place."

"You hope they will take the bait?"

"I'm hoping they do, otherwise we'll have to figure something else out."

"James, I'll inform the officer on my way over to the other lease holders."

"Thanks Sam, that will give us time to go over to Thumb's place and get things set up."

"Frankie, lets get over to Thumb's place. We'll need all the time we've got to get things set up."

When daylight finally came everyone was in place. I had found one of Thumb's old black flat brimmed hats and put it on. It was about two sizes to large and I figured it would work just fine for what I had in mind.

In the kitchen I found an old bottle of whiskey that Thumb and I had taken off a man several years before. It would be just what I needed to complete the plan.

An hour or so later I heard the signal we had arranged, I quickly sat down on the chair on the front porch after spilling some of the whiskey over my clothes. I pulled Thumb's hat down over my face and leaned back.

"Ready Frankie?"

"Yes sir, I think I am."

We heard the automobile coming slowly up the hill. I listened as it pulled to a stop. I listened as a man called out.

"Hello the house, anybody home?"

I heard Frankie come out of the house.

"May I help you sir?"

"Are you Frankie Duck?"

"Yes sir, how may I help you?"

"I understand your folks we burned up last night."

"Yes sir, I was just heading back over that way. They told me we'd have to wait until this morning before we could start searching for my folks' bodies."

"You're their only living relative?"

"My grandfather had a brother who last I heard lived down towards Tulsa."

"Who's the feller in the chair?"

"That's ole James, he sort of moved in here when my Uncle died a few years ago. He's a bad Indian, he stays drunk most of the time. I guess it's because he lost his hearing a few years back."

"You mean he's deaf?"

"Yes sir, he was blowing up stumps and didn't get far enough away."

"Playing with explosives can be dangerous."

"Yes sir, I understand that."

"You know your grandpa was going to lease his land to us."

"No sir, my grandfather never discussed his business with me."

"Well he was, I guess it's your land now."

"Yes sir, I hadn't thought about it but I guess your right."

"Well I have the papers here with me in the car, if you'll just sign them we'll get started next week."

"Sir, I don't know about that, the Chelsie Oil Company was out here last week and talked to grandpa. I think I should talk to them first. The man was very nice to my grandparents."

"Frankie, you might not want to do that."

"Why sir?"

"Frankie we know your Uncle from Tulsa, he will sign anything we want for a bottle of whiskey."

"But sir, he doesn't own the land, I do!"

"Frankie, what makes you think you're going to be alive?"

"Sir, are you threatening me?"

"Frankie my friends here don't mind hurting people so you figure it out."

"You were the ones who blew up my grandparents' house!"

"I'm not saying yes or no, I'm just saying maybe you'd like to rethink talking to Chelsie Oil."

"You're threatening me again aren't you?"

"I'm just advising you son."

"Hell Bert, let's just shoot him and hide the body, his Uncle will sign and we're done with this job."

"Now Hank relax, I'm sure the boy will see the error of his ways."

No one was looking at me as I slowly raised my head and cocked the pistol in my hand.

"Bert, you and your friend better step out of the automobile."

"Bert, the drunk's awake."

"Hank, I'm not drunk, I'm a U.S. Marshal and you boys are under arrest."

"For what, trying to do business with this boy?"

"Not really, on suspicion of blowing up his grandparents' house. Now get out of the automobile before I let this ole Colt start talking."

The men got out of the automobile and slowly began to grin.

"Something funny boys?"

"Marshal, our lawyers will have us out of jail ten minutes after you lock us up."

Just as the man made his statement, Frankie's friends walked out of the nearby woods dressed as the Osage warriors of long ago.

"Brother, are these the men who murdered our brother and his family?"

"I believe they are Lone Wolf, but they say their lawyer will have them out of jail in a short while."

"Brother, are you not a blood brother to the Osage, and a member of the council?"

"Well yes I am Lone Wolf, you know that."

"Then brother you have forgotten about the Osage blood law."

"Thank you for reminding me. The prisoners are yours, I'll be heading back to town."

"Wait a minute, what do you mean you're going back to town, you've got to take us with you!"

"I'm sorry Bert, I can't do that. You see I'm a member of the Osage tribe and as such I'm bound to live by their laws. Therefore, I have to turn you over to them."

"But we're entitled to a trial."

"By the white man's law that's right, but you've broken the Osage law and you're on their land so therefore I can't do a thing for you."

"You can't leave us here with these savages!"

"Bert, these are my blood brothers, I'd be careful how I talked about them. You just might make them mad, mad enough to use the ant treatment on you."

"Ant treatment, what are you talking about?"

"They are cousins to the Apache, they learned it from them. They bury you up to your neck then pour honey over your head. Those little ants just love their honey; of course they like tender flesh too. Heard of fellers being rescued but they never had any eyes, begged their rescuers to shoot them."

"You can't do this, it's not human."

"But Bert, you called my brothers savages. What do you expect? Lone Wolf, be sure whatever is left can't be found."

I started walking towards my horse that was tied to Thumb's old corral.

The third man of the group who had up until this time been quiet shouted to me.

"Hey Mr. Howard, you can't do this, it's not human."

"Fellow, as I said. I don't have a choice."

Just as I turned to get my horse Sam rode into the clearing.

"What's going on brother?"

"Not much Sam, I was just getting ready to leave."

"Who are these boys?"

"They are the ones who blew up Frankie's grandparents' house."

"Really, Lone Wolf and the boys going to settle up with them?"

"Yes, it's the tribe's right you know."

"Mind if I stay around and watch? I was at the last blood letting and it was really something to see."

"Makes no difference to me Sam, I've done my job so I think I'll ride home and get some breakfast. See you boys later."

I mounted my horse and started down the road.

I was so thrilled when one of the men began shouting for me to come back.

I stopped my horse and looked back over my shoulder.

"Please sir, you can't just ride off and leave us to be slaughtered."

"Why not, you blew the folks' house up and never thought anything about it. Why should I care what happens to you? I want your boss; he's the one I'm after. You all are going to cause me a lot of work to find out who ordered the house blown up."

"Give me a break and I'll tell you everything you need to know."

"Doug, you'd better shut your mouth."

"Shut up yourself Bert, I may go to jail but at least I'll be able to see."

"Doug, if you know anything I'd suggest you start talking. If you know anything of value I may be able to help you, otherwise I have no choice but to leave you to my brothers."

"You'll need to round up Richard Troop. His father owns Queensland Oil, his old man lives in Chicago, he sent junior down here to get him away from some trouble back home."

"How did you boys get involved?"

"He and Bert knew each other back home."

"Lone Wolf, may I keep this one to take to talk to our brother Tom?"

"I don't see why not brother we still have these two."

"Sam, may I borrow your horse to take this man into town? I'll bring him back later."

"Fine with me James, I'm in no hurry. I'll just hang around and watch the show. Take your time."

The boys put our witness on Sam's horse and we headed off towards town. A quarter mile or so down the road we heard a blood-curdling scream from back at the cabin.

"What was that?"

"I guess your friends are discovering how well the Osage can use their knives."

Sweat appeared on Doug's forehead and a shiver ran through his body.

I had a problem not smiling; I knew Sam's cougar imitation when I heard it.

CHAPTER 26

▼

I took the man straight to Tom's office.

Bill, Matt and Tom all questioned the man until we had all the information we needed. Tom had the man sign a statement. I asked Matt to go get one of our police officers and have him lock the man up.

"Matt, have them keep an eye on him. The boys down Tulsa way won't want him to talk in court."

"You're right dad, I'll tell them. Come on fella we'll put you in safe keeping."

When Matt took the prisoner out the door Tom spoke.

"James, how did you do it?"

I told them how we'd worked things, when I had finished Tom and Bill were laughing.

"The Blood Letting Ceremony, how did Lone Wolf come up with that one?"

"It was my idea Tom, by the way I have to go back out and get Sam."

"Go on James, by the way what are you going to do with the other two?"

"Keep them in the old ice house until we get this Mr. Troop in custody."

"Good idea, we don't want our witness having a lapse of memory."

Tom would send a telegram to the Marshal in Tulsa and tell him I'd be down his way on the first train out of here in the morning.

"James, I think I'll go along with you. I don't think there will be any need, but just the same I'll take a copy of the confession along with us. We'll get a judge to issue an arrest warrant for our Mr. Troop."

"Gentlemen, I'm the new kid on the block but if I were you I'd get on down to Tulsa as soon as possible. When these boys don't show up our Mr. Troop may run like a rabbit."

"He's right James."

"I agree with you Bill."

"James go change clothes and get back here. I'll send the Marshal a telegram. We'll take my car, we should be able to make it in a couple of hours or so."

"I'll send Mary down to pick up Sam. I'll be back in a hour or so Tom."

Mary met me at the door.

"I saw you coming and from the way you were riding I knew something was up."

"You're right Mary, Tom and I are heading down to Tulsa to get the man who ordered the family killed. I need you to take the automobile and go get Sam. I used his horse to take the prisoner to town."

"James, Sam was by here a short while ago. He was driving a strange car with two men in the back, he told me what happened. Hurry and get changed, if you don't mind I'd like to go along."

"Fine Mary but hurry, we don't want the snake to get away."

A short time later we headed into town. Tom was waiting for us when we drove up.

"I figured you'd be coming along sis, you'd want to be in on the action."

"Tom, get your automobile started, I can't wait to see this person behind bars."

The trip to Tulsa went well. We arrived at about three thirty. The Marshal and a deputy were waiting a few blocks down from Queensland Oil Company's office.

"He's there James, I saw him go in about twenty minutes ago. I've got the warrant in my coat pocket. Let's go get the snake Marshal, the quicker he's locked up the better."

As we neared the office two local men came out the door. Both were upset.

"Damn it Jeb, that bird was there I'm sure. He doesn't want to pay us."

"I think you're right Alf, but what can we do but wait."

"James, I've got an idea."

"Go ahead Mary."

"Let me go in ahead of you all. The man doesn't know me, so if I go in and ask to see him and say my name is Mary Duck."

"You could be right Mary, he wants that lease awfully bad."

The three of us stood outside where we could see through the window. Mary went in and asked to see Mr. Troop. The young lady went to a door and knocked. After a moment she opened the door and spoke to someone inside, then motioned for Mary to come in.

We watched as Mary went in the office and the door was closed. Then we entered the office.

The Marshal walked over to the young lady's desk, showed her his badge and gun while putting his finger to his lips for her to be quiet.

He motioned for Tom to come over and keep an eye on the young lady.

The Marshal and I walked to the door and stepped into the office of Mr. Troop.

Mr. Troop had his boots on top of his desk and was leaned back in his fancy chair. He had a look of surprise on his sharp featured face. He had black hair and was dressed like a dandy. Before he could speak the Marshal informed him he was under arrest.

A small nickel plated derringer suddenly appeared in his hand.

"You two bit local nothings, you think you can arrest me. Better men than you have tried and they aren't around anymore."

"Mr. Troop!"

"Shut up lady, I have more important things to worry about right now."

"Mr. Troop, I don't think so. This forty-four I'm holding is aimed at your head right now. I've shot men before so don't you be stupid enough to believe I might miss. Now lay that little pea shooter down on your desk, Now!"

I'll give Troop his due, he had sand. He tried to spin around and shoot Mary.

Mary's pistol fired and Troop was knocked backwards out of his chair where he lay screaming in agony on the floor.

Mary's shot had broken his shoulder. The shiny pistol lay on the floor near his desk. I picked it up and dropped it in my pocket.

"Nice shot Mary, that pistol I gave you came in handy."

"Thank you dear, I had plenty of time. He was in no position to move very fast."

"That may be but he had us caught flatfooted."

"That's a fact James, I never figured him for a sleeve gun. In fact, I haven't seen one in years. Mrs. Howard thanks."

"You're welcome Marshal, I just want this scum to get what he's got coming."

"Don't worry ma'am, I'm really going to enjoy seeing this dude go to trial. Now Deputy, how about helping me get him up. I'll need to get him to the doctor's office. We sure don't want him to die before his trial."

"No way do we want that to happen. Mary go keep an eye on the girl outside."

"Let Tom know we're fine."

"No need to hurry Mary, the young lady out front fainted when you shot Troop."

"Marshal let's get Troop up and get him moving before we have to carry him."

We left Mary to watch the secretary while we took Troop to a nearby doctor's office.

The doctor took one look and told his nurse to get ready for surgery. We waited out in the waiting room for almost two hours. The doctor finally came out.

"He'll live Marshall, but he'll never use his arm again. Whoever shot him completely shattered the joint. There was nothing I could do to repair it. If he gets an infection in the wound we'll have to take the arm off."

"When can we take him to jail doctor?"

"You move him now he'll not last to daylight tomorrow, he's lost too much blood."

"Well I guess I can have my deputies watch him until you say it's alright to move him."

"Fine Marshal, I'll put a chair in the room for them."

We walked back over to the oil company's office and found Mary and the secretary were both busy sorting through papers.

"James, Marshal, look what I've found. Sammye has only been here a few days but she did know where a lot of things were kept.

She handed the Marshal and I a stack of papers to look at. It was indeed interesting.

"Check this out Tom, it seems as though our boy had some friends who helped him hire the boys we've got locked up."

"James, there are three more companies involved in this oil steal."

"Looks that way Tom, Marshal is there anyway we can get these other boys?"

"I'm not sure James, if we can find a letter or two signed by them then we might stand a chance."

"I'll check his desk while you two check things here."

A few moments later Tom called us into Troop's office.

"How about these letters Marshal?"

The Marshal looked at a couple of the letters and smiled.

"This is what I need. Now I can go round up these boys. You know I'm looking forward to this. Some of these boys have been living the good life and giving a lot of folks a hard time. Yes sir, I'm looking forward to this."

"Better get started Marshal or those boys will be long gone."

"That's true James, I'll get a couple of my boys and round these dudes up. You folks going back home?"

"We thought we might spend the night Marshal. We'll head back in the morning. By the way, thanks for your help."

"No James, thank you. I don't know how you got your information but sometime later I'd like to hear the story."

"Anytime Marshal, when you come up to pick up the boys we're holding I'll tell you the story."

"Looking forward to it James, see you folks later."

"James, take a look here. Our boy had his bank right here in his drawer. Tom showed us a metal box filled with money."

"Sammye, your former boss owed some folks money."

"Yes sir, I know."

"Of course, Tom what do you think about leaving Sammye here to pay folks Troop owed as long as the money lasts."

"Well James, she is a company employee and it would only be right for her to pay the company bills like you say. But first I think she should take a full month's wages for her trouble."

"That sounds good to me Tom, Sammye, you take out a month's wages then stay and pay all the folks you can."

"But Mr. Howard, I've only been here two days."

"I know Sammye, but you might have to stay here for another week or so. It only seems fair to me that you should get paid for your time."

"He's right Sammye, besides you'll need money to live on until you find another job."

"Mr. Howard, that's true. I'm not a spring chicken and even though I've worked in law offices my whole life, jobs here are hard to come by."

"Wait a minute Sammye, you've worked in law offices?"

"Oh yes, my father was a judge, I've been raised in the law business all my life."

"Sammye, when you close this office down if you like you can come up to our office in Pawhuska. We'll have a job for you."

"Sir, as soon as I close this office I'll come up to see you. There's nothing here to hold me."

"Good, see you in a week or so."

We got rooms at one of the new hotels and after eating a good meal in the dining room we settled down for the night.

Next morning after a good breakfast we headed home, feeling good.

CHAPTER 27

▼

It took an hour or so to tell what had happened in Tulsa to Matt and Bill.

"Mary actually shot him?"

"Well of course I did Bill."

"James, she has always been like this hasn't she?"

"Of course she has, ever since she crawled out from under the blanket."

"Wait a minute, why have I not heard of this before?"

"Bill we've all been busy, we'll tell you the story when things slow down some."

"Dad, they found Frankie's folks. They buried them yesterday evening."

"I'm sorry I wasn't here for the service."

"Will and I went your place."

"Thank you son."

"You're welcome, but remember I've known Frankie for as long as he's been around. There were lots of folks there besides tribal members. It seems there's a lot of folks up here that want to be known as your friend."

"Well I don't guess that's all bad then."

"Oh yes dad, two of the oil companies representatives came by today and wanted to know when the sorting was going to take place.

They want to help pay for the beef expense. Besides they want to bring guest."

"More guests, anymore and we will just have to invite the whole territory."

"Mary, have you noticed how your husband complains when he knows he's going to have a great time?"

"You know Bill, I hadn't until now but now that you mention it, you could be right."

They both got a laugh at my expense.

"Oh Bill, did Tom tell you he hired you all a secretary?"

"Not to my knowledge, Matt did he tell you?"

"No he didn't."

"Boys relax, she's really nice. Her name is Sammye Burk. She's worked in law offices for years."

"I for one think it's great. Bill and Uncle Tom have run me ragged. I don't think they either one know how to file."

"But Matt, you're so good at it."

"Watch yourself Bill, I have friends in high places."

"Look out Bill, I've seen him when he gets started."

"I know Mary, I've seen him calm a couple of our tribal members down."

"He does seem to have a talent for that."

"Hey Bill did I ever tell you about how Matt found his wife?"

"James Howard, let's go home."

Mary and I both were laughing as we went out the door.

A few weeks later the men involved in the bombing appeared in court. Two of the actual bombers got the death sentence and were sent to the Federal penitentiary in Kansas. For his help in the case Doug received a ten-year sentence in the state facility. Mr. Troop received a forty-year sentence in the same Kansas facility as his two cohorts.

There would be an appeal on his behalf but no one expected the sentence to be overturned. We all got a laugh when the defense attorney brought up the Osage Blood Letting ceremony. Tom and several members of the council were there and told the judge they had never heard of any such ceremony. The defense seemed to be puzzled and had nothing more to say.

A week and a half after our return from Tulsa Miss Sammye Burk showed up at Tom's office and went to work. A week later the office was organized and everything was running smoother than it ever had before.

Not only was the office looking and operating great but our friend Bill was smiling a whole lot more. Sammye didn't seem to mind that attention either. It looked like we might just have created another couple for our already growing community.

We heard of other bombings and such but it was all over near the small settlement of Fairfax. The law officials over there had their hands full. We heard stories of law officers who were taking bribes. It was becoming a nightmare.

Once again things began to get back to normal.

"Dear, when are you and Will going to work the herds?"

"Probably in another month or so Mary, I've been a little busy and not had a chance to talk to him about it.

"Don't forget you've got to let Joie (Joe) know. You promised him he could help this year."

"I know Mary so I'll do it. It's really becoming a big deal to the kids. I was talking to Matt the other day and he was telling me that Joe, J.R. and Seth were all planning on me taking them deer hunting this fall. It seems that Joe had such a good time he thought they should all go along."

"Well grandpa, what are you going to do?"

"I reckon I'll take them hunting."

"You'll enjoy it too."

"Of course I will, those grandsons are growing and a lot of fun to be around. I figured I'd ask Sam to go along. I think he would enjoy himself."

"James, you know he will."

"I guess I better talk to Will this morning about when he plans to make the gather. The oil companies are helping supply beef for the party."

"James they should. Last year I think half of the oil companies people were here."

"I know Mary it's really become a holiday for the tribe. As one member told me the other day it's their own holiday."

"I know dear, even though they don't get a share of your herd anymore no one wants to see it end."

I finished breakfast and walked down the hill to Will and Tee's place.

"Hey pa, what's going on?"

"Figured I'd check with you and see when you planned to make the fall gather?"

"Figured the second week of next month. It seems to suit everyone. Tee is so excited, she and I were talking about the first gather we had after we got married. She told me that after that gather she really felt like she was a member of the family."

"Have you talked to Cookie son?"

"Talked to him last week, he and Martha are both looking forward to it, even though he doesn't have to do the cooking anymore."

"Son, I've got an idea."

"Lets hear it pa."

So our plan for the gather were worked out to the last detail.

When I got home I told Mary about my idea and she got excited.

"Oh James, that would be wonderful."

Mary made some suggestions that neither Will or I had thought about. This year's gather was going to be something special.

I drove into town and told Tom and the boys about my idea. It seemed everyone had an idea or two as to what should be done. Matt had an idea that everyone thought was great. So the next few weeks we were talking and planning, sneaking around and trying to get things done.

As sorting day got close things really began to get hectic.

Beth, Carrie and Joe came up from Tulsa to help Mary with the planning. Everyone was running around but yet things seemed to get done.

Finally the day of the gather came. I saddled my horse and met Will down at his barn. Inside sat Cookie's chuck wagon. I had never seen it look so good. New paint gleamed; a new canvas cover had been installed. The harness for the team had been oiled and all the brass polished.

"You've done a wonderful job Will, Cookie will be happy."

"I hope so pa, want to help me hook up the team? I need to get started, we sure don't want to be late."

I helped Will hook up the team and watched as our grandchildren rode up from the racing stables along with some of their friends.

I had to laugh; they were all dressed like we had been when we had brought the first herd to the tall grass. As they rode up to the barn I wiped a tear from my eye.

"Grandpa, do we look alright?"

"J.R. you all look great. Lets see with that mustache you look just like your great grandpa. Joe, I guess you're supposed to be playing me with the red shirt and paint horse. Lets see, Seth you have to be Harold, Becca, you are your grandma. Carrie you have to be Paco with your wide Mexican hat, but who is going to play Sam's part?"

"My grandson James."

Sam had come up to the back of the barn with his grandson whom I had never met.

"My daughter came in a couple of days ago so we had time to get Jimmy here outfitted. He already knew how to ride so everything is all set."

"Proud to meet you Jimmy, your grandfather has told me a lot about you."

"Thank you Uncle James, I've met all your grandkids and I'm looking forward to today."

"Well if that's the case you all fall in behind the chuck wagon and get going you've got a herd to drive."

Will looked at me and grinned.

"Pa it looks like its going to be one heck of a party."

"That it is son, I can hardly wait. Now get going we don't want you to be late."

I watched as the kids fell in behind Will on the chuck wagon laughing and talking as only youngsters can.

I walked back up the hill and saw Mary standing on the porch watching the chuck wagon and our grandchildren going down the road towards the holding pens.

"Looks like a sorry crew cowboy."

"Now Mary, I can't say that. They look like a pretty good bunch to me, especially the young feller on the paint horse. Did you notice his black hat has a hole in it?"

"I did notice that dear."

"How did you do it Mary?"

"We shot it James."

"You're kidding, right?"

"Not at all, it was Beth's idea."

That figures."

"She still remembers a couple of those hats James. Remember she was always wearing one of them around the house when she was small."

"I do now that you mention it. It was hard for me to not laugh when J.R. showed up wearing a mustache just like Pa used to wear."

"I know, Tee worked for two days trying to get it just right."

"She got it perfect Mary, but of course she usually does."

"James, go get your clothes changed we've got to get down to the pens. We sure enough don't want to be late."

"You've got that right, I'll only be a minute."

After I had changed clothes I found Mary waiting for me down by the corral. She was saddling her paint. My paint was tied and waiting. I quickly saddled up and we rode off towards the pens. A very happy couple indeed.

CHAPTER 28

▼

When Mary and I rode to the top of the rise overlooking the working pens we stopped our horses and starred.

Tents, automobiles, buggies and people it seemed were everywhere.

"James, remember the first sorting when only the tribal members were here?"

"Sure do Mary, it was a family affair more or less. Things have sure changed."

"That they have cowboy, I'm looking forward to the ceremony today."

"Me to Mary, lets ride down and see what's going on."

The Swinson's had built a small platform stage for today's activities, as we rode up we saw our daughter and daughter-in-laws talking to Martha over beside the stage. We tied our horses to the corral and walked over to where they stood.

"Morning ladies, is everything to your satisfaction?"

"Everything is fine James, but I have a question to ask."

"Ask away Martha."

"What is going on? Will came by a few minutes ago and asked Randall to go with him to look at something. I know that boy of yours well enough to know that something is up."

"Martha, you're right, something is up and if you'll wait a few minutes I think you'll be pleased with what you'll see. This is Cookie's day, our way of saying thanks to him and you for the things you've done for the people over the years."

Tom walked up the stairs and fired a shot from his pistol.

"Friends, gather round. We're here today to honor a man and his wife who has helped each and every one of you over the years. He helped bring the first herd of cattle up here and asked to stay and live among us. He and his wife helped when it was needed, fed folks who couldn't afford to pay but most of all has been a grand friend and neighbor to the Osage people."

"We've chosen today to honor both he and his wife."

"Martha, would you come up here please."

"James Howard!"

"Just go Martha, this is yours and Cookie's day. Enjoy it, and let us enjoy it too."

Martha walked up the stairs where Tom met her. A cheer went up from the hundreds of people gathered around the platform.

"Now folks, if you'll look to the East towards that little rise we've organized our own reenactment of that first day when our friends from Texas arrived with that first herd of cattle. See if you can remember how thankful you were on that day."

Tom fired his pistol in the air one more time as everyone watched the rise of ground to the east. A moment later Cookie's shinny wagon topped the rise with Cookie setting straight and tall on the wagon seat. Following along behind was a small bunch of cattle, which were being driven by our grandkids. I don't think I had ever been more proud than I was at that moment.

"Here James."

Mary was handing me a handkerchief. I needed it to wipe my eyes and was not ashamed to admit it. Mary and the girls were using theirs too.

Tom motioned for Cookie to drive his wagon up to the stage. Sam and other members of the tribe helped the kids pen the small bunch of cattle.

"Cookie, will you kindly join your lovely wife up here on the stage please."

Cookie was wiping his eyes as he climbed down from the wagon. He looked at Mary and I as he walked up the stairs to the stage.

Martha gave him a kiss, which brought another cheer from the crowd.

"Randall (Cookie) Smith the people of the Osage Nation have today made you an honorary member of our tribe. This is our way of saying thanks for everything you and Martha have done for us over the years. Our friend and yours, Mr. Conners has painted a picture of the two of you that will grace the hall of our new council house."

Mr. Conners with the help of two young men unveiled a portrait of Cookie and Martha standing at the back of his chuck wagon where everyone had seen them many times before. The picture was great; the crowd cheered as Cookie and Martha wiped tears from their eyes.

"Now lets get some of your friends or family as they prefer to be called up here with you. Mr. Howard, Carla, Paco, Rosa, Sam, Lesa, Harold, Flower and lets not forget James and Mary."

When everyone was on the stage and had hugged Cookie and Martha, Tom asked us to line up in a straight line. We lined up like Tom told us.

"Kids, get up here and stand in front of the character you portrayed in the cattle drive today."

The kids lined up in front of us.

"Now folks, what do you think?"

The crowd applauded and cheered. It was indeed a great day.

"Now folks lets have a good time. Later we all will have a fine meal and even some dancing."

The crowd cheered and began looking at all the goods the various vendors had in their booths.

"James, Mary is this whole thing your idea?"

"Nope, I guess the whole family would have to take credit for this Cookie. We sort of figured it was something long past due."

"Well by darn you shore enough caught us by surprise."

"James, we were caught completely by surprise. How did you manage all this and us not even hear a rumor?"

I guess you could say we've learned how to be sneaky from our brothers the Osage. Thumb tried for years to teach me, maybe I finally learned."

Martha gave Mary and I a hug and then everyone took off to have fun.

"Amigo, today you have again made me proud. Of course you have always made me proud."

"Thanks Paco, it was really quite a lot of fun."

"Your grandchildren did a wonderful job James, but I have to admit they were a lot cleaner than we were when we arrived."

"That's the truth but we did look better after Mary showed up."

"That is true, I think maybe you have been lucky."

"You bet I have, but don't forget you found Rosa and Pa found Carla."

"This is true, this country has been good to us."

"It sure has, now if we can help the tribe through this oil boom everything will be fine."

"James, all you can do is guide them. They too will have to find their way like you and I did. For some it will be hard, others will do well. Some will fall in between. Like I've heard you say, "The fit shall survive"."

"That's true Paco but I hate to see some of the folks fall."

"You cannot solve all their problems James. All you can do is help those who want help and listen to those who don't"

"Guess we'll have to just ride the bronc until we get him broke."

That evening Mary and I sat in the porch swing as the sun began to set. We could hear the music and laughter from the party down by the loading chutes. We had left early because we had had a long day.

Mary had boiled a pot of coffee and we were enjoying the cool evening.

"James, it was a wonderful day."

"It sure was, the trail drive the grandkids put on was great. The sight of Cookie setting up on that wagon seat was something I'll always remember."

"I know what you mean James, Martha was so pleased. She said it was something she would never forget. She said they felt so blessed by being thought of as family. She said she and Cookie only lived to see what would happen here next."

"I know Mary, he told me the same thing. He and I are both worried about the tribe."

"Well you can't do anything until you know what you have to fight."

"You're right Mary."

CHAPTER 29

▼

The day finally arrived for the first of the payments to the tribe. Mary and I stood outside the council house waiting for the checks to be handed out.

Our small town had boomed. New businesses had popped up everywhere.

"My Lord James this is a mess."

"I know Mary, I talked to Tom yesterday and he told me tomorrow he was going to sleep all day. He and the boys have been working night and day trying to get things ready. Payments to the tribe would be made every three months so maybe the boys would be able to get some rest."

"It's going to be a mess isn't it James?"

"I'm hoping not, but I'm afraid so Mary. Tom and the boys are looking for help. Tom said finding attorneys to help them handle the tribal affairs is going to be a nightmare. There are five new attorneys in town now, we can only hope they are honest men and not here to try and steal from the tribe."

"Thank goodness the major oil companies offices are in Tulsa."

"That could be both good and bad Mary. It means Tom and the boys may have to do a lot of traveling back and forth to get things settled."

"I guess the new field down South is going big time too."

"It sure is it's called the Glenpool field. They are having some of the same problems we are.

The next few weeks were a total mess. The people especially the older ones were like children in a candy store. They had never had much money and suddenly they had more than they knew what to do with.

Sales people were everywhere hawking their wares. One of the older members bought ten bathtubs. The gentlemen had them setting in his yard. He thought his wife could raise flower in them. The man didn't even have a bathroom in his house.

Other stories of people buying new automobiles who had no idea how to drive them. One man had driven out of town and had his automobile quit. He was walking back to town to buy another before a friend explained to him he was simply out of gas.

Stories that would have been humorous in a sense except the people were being taken advantage of.

New homes were started. Some contractors started homes, got a big payment and simply vanished, leaving the tribal members without their new home or any money for another three months.

Tom, Bill, Will and I were kept running for what seemed day and night. I helped settle disputes among tribal members where I could. I encouraged our older members to let their younger children read anything that someone wanted them to sign, or to take the papers to Tom's office.

The tribal police were kept busy trying to keep con men and whiskey peddlers out of our area.

Folks were robbed, murdered and threatened by all sorts of riffraff.

One of the most disturbing things was that outsiders were marrying into the tribe and older members were suddenly dying. At one time Tom was prosecuting or attempting to prosecute thirty something cases.

A salesman had tried to sell Bird half dozen corsets. She had laughed at him and told him to leave. People through out the area were trying to sell the people any and everything.

Tom came out to our place early one morning. He looked worn out.

"Need a cup of coffee Tom?"

"That would be nice James, thanks."

Mary poured Tom a cup and sat down.

"What's on your mind Tom?"

"What's not on my mind; land and mineral disputes, corrupt law officials, whiskey peddlers, scam artist, unsolved murders and about anything else you can think of James."

"Has it slowed down any at all?"

"Not much, scam artist are just working at getting better at their trade."

"I know we have run a half dozen or so off this last week. Problem is they just move off to another part of the peoples land. Change their name, a start another scheme."

"Tom, will it ever get better?"

"Yes Mary, but it's going to be a while. In the mean time we're going to be chasing our tails trying to keep the dishonest folks out of our town."

"James, the tribal police are doing a fine job. They have solved three murder cases this last week. We're beginning to get a handle on at least some of the cases."

"Folks over to the southwest are leasing their land for cattle grazing. At least some of our people are seeing the light and are making progress. The older people are beginning to listen to our younger people who we have educated and understand what some of these scam artist are trying to do to their folks."

"James, about the only thing going on that really makes me happy is that Sam, as we call her and Bill are seeing a lot of each other."

"Really, that's great Tom."

"It sure is they are like a couple of kids. She and Bill have both done so much for the tribe these last few months. I sure don't want to loose either one of them."

"Well, Tom at least something is going right. Boggs caught a couple of boys the other day who were butchering a steer over in our west pasture. They were planning on selling the meat. They tried to buy Boggs off and when they couldn't get that done they tried threatening him."

"To make a long story short, Boggs took his pistol out and turned them over to the tribal police."

"Were they local folks James?"

"No, they were from back east. The police here are checking to see if they are wanted back there before they let them go."

"This windfall of money definitely has had its down side."

"Sort of makes you want to go back in time doesn't it James?"

It sure does, things were a lot simpler then for sure."

Over the next couple of months we drove ourselves hour after hour, day after day trying to sort things out and keep the people out of trouble.

Little did I know that trouble was about to strike my family, up close and personal.

CHAPTER 30

▼

Ashooting occurred just to the south of town and the assailant had been caught.

It was pretty much of an open and shut case, due to the fact there were several witnesses. Matt had handled the case and the man was convicted. He had received the death sentence.

"Mr. Lawyer, you'll wish you'd never head of me before this is over. You'll remember the name of Mullins for as long as you live."

Will or no one else thought anything of the threat at the time. It was as Matt put it just another jailhouse threat.

That was until a week later when our granddaughter failed to come home from school. Seth had gone fishing with a friend after class and Mary Margaret had left school for the not to distant walk home.

Deb went to looking for her when she failed to get home on time. She and Deb were planning on baking a cake for her brother's birthday and had been planning it for a week.

When Deb didn't find her she went straight to Matt's office.

Matt of course was upset like Deb but hoped that she simply had forgot and went home with a friend.

A couple of hours later they knew that wasn't the case. When they returned home Tom was waiting for them.

It seemed a young man had delivered a note to Tom's office demanding they release the murderer if they ever wanted to see the girl again. Mary Margaret had been kidnapped.

I thought Mary was going to have a heart attack when we were told the news.

"James, you've got to get her back."

"I'll try my best Mary, while I'm gone why don't you go down and stay with Deb. This may take a while and lord only knows she'll need your help."

We drove down to Matt and Deb's house and after a few moments I headed into town.

By the time I got to town I'd gotten over the shock and was just plain mad. Not mad enough to not think.

I walked into the tribal police office. The men there all knew me and when I waved them to the room we had used for briefings, they followed me without question. When they were seated I told them what I wanted.

"Gentlemen my granddaughter has been stolen and I want her back. Alive if possible but to do this we'll need to get going in a hurry. Now here's what I want from you. Look at Mullins' file; I want to know where he was from, how many brothers and friends he had and where they live. Gentlemen forget formalities and standards my granddaughter's life may depend on how quickly we can find her. We let these boys get away with this, who knows whose child will be next. I'll be over at my brother-in-laws office. You find anything, anything at all, let me know."

"Mr. Howard, we'll do our best."

"Thank you gentlemen."

I walked into Tom's office and found Bill and Sammye pouring over papers.

"Anything I can do to help?"

"Grab a stack and get started, we're searching everything we have and can find on Mullins."

"Found anything yet?"

"Only that we sent his personal affects to a brother who lived down near Glenpool."

"Found anyone who may know who brought the note to Tom's office?"

"Tom said he had seen the young man around town but doesn't know him."

"Alright lets think, where would you find someone to deliver a note if you didn't want to do it yourself."

"Well I'd go to someplace where usually out of work men would hang out."

"Somewhere like the pool hall."

"You're right James, damn why didn't I think of that!"

"Bill, you've been working your tail off trying to find something that will help. Now tell me what Tom said."

"He said he was a tall skinny kid wearing a bright blue and white plaid shirt."

"Ok, I'll be back in a little while. Bill, Sammye, thanks for your help."

I left the office and headed across the street to where the billiard parlor was located. When I walked through the door I had to stop and let my eyes adjust to the dimly lit smoke filled room. I saw a man who worked the oil rigs that I had helped get his automobile working one morning. I wove my way through the crowd to where he stood talking to a couple of other oil field hands.

"Hank, can I have a moment of your time?"

"Mr. Howard, of course you can, pardon me boys."

"What can I do for you Mr. Howard?"

I explained what had happened and what I needed.

"Young fellow in a blue plaid shirt. Oh my!"

"What's wrong Hank?"

"I think I know who you're looking for sir. He couldn't find a job here so he was going to hitch a ride on a pipe truck over to Fairfax to see if he could find work over there."

"When did he leave Hank?"

"About thirty minutes ago."

"Would you know the truck if you saw it?"

"Sure I would Mr. Howard."

"Then grab your coat, we're going for a ride, now."

We ran through the front door, Hank right behind me. We reached my car and jumped in. Thank goodness the top was down.

I started the car and made a u-turn in the street as we headed west back toward my place I told Hank to hang on. A couple of miles from town I left the road and headed out across my pastures.

"Hang on Hank, I know every foot of this place and we'll cut about four miles off the drive. We may catch them at the creek crossing if we're lucky."

"Push it Mr. Howard, you're doing great."

We went across my pastures as fast as I dared. I just prayed we didn't have a flat. I needed to catch that truck. I saw men working on drilling rigs as we went by their well locations. We reached the creek and drove across the gravel bar and up the far bank then continued on towards the main road.

"Mr. Howard, we're going to beat the pipe truck to the road, it's just now coming up out of the creek bottom. He's really got a load of pipe on that ole truck."

Thank goodness we had caught up.

Hank jumped out of the car and waved the driver down. The driver slowed the truck down and stopped. I sighed a sigh of relief when I saw a young man sitting on the passenger side of the truck wearing a blue plaid shirt.

"What do you need Hank?"

"We need to talk to your passenger Jack. You know Mr. Howard?"

"Sure do, how are you sir?"

"I'm fine Jack."

The young man got out of the truck and walked around to my car.

"How can I help you Mr. Howard?"

"What's your name young man?"

"Steve Halett sir, why?"

"Well Steve did you by chance happen to take a letter to my brother-in-law's office today?"

"Yes sir I did."

"Good, can you tell me who gave you the letter?"

"Well yes sir, the man was tall with blond hair and had a small scar on his left cheek. He told me he owed the lawyer money and could only pay a small part of what he owed him. Said he was working down south and wanted to pay the lawyer off but the lawyer had cost him one job so he didn't want him to know where he was working. He offered me three dollars to deliver the letter. Mr. Howard, I needed that money to eat. I've been looking for a job for a week and I needed the money."

"I understand Steve, you didn't happen to see if they were driving an automobile did you?"

"Yes sir I did, after I delivered the letter I saw them pull out from between two buildings and take the road towards Tulsa."

"Steve, thank you. You've been a big help."

"Mr. Howard, the automobile they were driving was a dark green Ford roadster with yellow wheels."

"Thanks again Steve, here take this money. You'll be able to eat until you find a job."

"Mr. Howard!"

"Take the money Steve, the men who gave you the letter took my granddaughter this afternoon. The information you gave me may let us bring her home."

"Hank, lets get, I need to get back to town."

Hank waved to the boys and jumped back into the car.

I turned the car around and headed back to town. It looked as if it just me be a long night.

CHAPTER 31

▼

When we reached town I thanked Hank for his help and offered to pay him.

"No sir Mr. Howard. Anyone who steals a child doesn't deserve to live."

"He won't if I catch him Hank. If he's hurt that girl I'm not sure what I'll do."

"Mr. Howard I've got a couple of days off before we start our next job. Now sir I know the area south of Tulsa. I'd like to help if you'll let me."

"Come one over to the office Hank, we'll see what the boys have found out while we were gone."

We walked into the tribal police office and were greeted by the senior officer.

"Mr. Howard we've got some information for you. The Mullins fellow has a brother and a cousin. They have all been in trouble south of Tulsa. They have been looked at on several occasions but no one could prove anything on them."

"Is the brother blond headed?"

The officer looked at the papers in his hand.

"Yes sir he is, why?"

"I think he is the one who stole my granddaughter. Hank here helped me find the young man who delivered the letter to Tom. He gave us a description of the man and the automobile they were driving."

"Their home is in Glenpool Mr. Howard, you think they may have headed there?"

"They would need someplace they felt safe. I figure to head down that way and check it out."

"You're going to try and drive down tonight?"

"Sure am, but I'd like to borrow a gun and belt if you have a spare."

"Mr. Howard, I have one you can use."

The young man took an older colt with a holster from his desk. The holster looked almost like mine.

I felt the leather and found it well oiled and cared for. The Colt Forty-Four had a nice smooth action and was well balanced.

"Feels fine, got plenty of shells?"

"Here's a box Mr. Howard, I tried to make my holster like the one you have."

"Well young man it's close, real close."

"Anyone got a shotgun, I'm not much of a pistol shot but I'm darn good with a shotgun."

One of the officers brought a double barrel shotgun with a box of shells to Hank.

"Thanks, I'll take good care of it."

"Don't worry about it, just shoot straight."

"Can anyone join this party?"

Sam and Will stood in the doorway both wore a pistol and had a rifle across his arm.

"James, I thought you might need this."

Sam reached behind him and handed me my Sharps with its shell bag.

"Thanks Sam, now I feel dressed."

"Dressed for war pa, I've seen you upset before but never like this."

"Will, I have seen him like this several times. Usually somebody is in bad trouble."

"Uncle Sam, I've heard mother talk about things a few times but I'd never seen it."

"Son, you've not seen anything yet. Wait until we find and corner the skunks who stole my granddaughter."

"James, you lead out."

"That's how it's going to be Sam."

"Yes James, that's how it's going to be."

"James, James!"

I saw Bill running across the street holding some papers in his hand.

"James, Sammye wired the telegraph operator in Tulsa she knew and made some inquires. We just got this back, it seems the Mullins boys have been busy lately. We also managed to get directions to their parent's home. I thought you might need them."

"Bill, thank you. Be sure to give Sammye a kiss for me."

"Be glad to James, she's sort of special you know. Like your Mary."

"I know Bill, but be sure to thank her for me."

"Boys, let's get rolling I'm sure Mary Margaret is wanting to come home.

CHAPTER 32

▼

The drive to Tulsa took some time. The road was not that smooth and the vehicle lights weren't that great. We pulled into Tulsa about four in the morning. Sam knew where the Sheriff's office was located so Hank and I followed him.

"Holy cow, doesn't this town ever sleep?"

"There's an oil boom going on Hank, everyone's trying to reach the brass ring."

"I know Mr. Howard but a man has to sleep sometime."

We parked our automobile and walked into the Sheriff's office. People were running around like a bunch of ants.

Lawyers were trying to get folks out of jail; Drillers were trying to get their drunken crews out of jail and go to work.

I spotted a Marshal I knew and got his attention.

"Mr. Howard, what are you doing down here this time of the morning?"

I explained what had happened then he took us to the Sheriff's office.

"I think the Sheriff is in his office, we've had more than we can handle this last couple of months. I swear I think every crook and con man in the country has shown up here since the oil was found."

We found the Sheriff working on some paper work at his desk. The young Marshal introduced us to him.

"How may I help you gentlemen?"

"I thought we'd better stop by and let you know we were in your area."

I explained about Mary Margaret and our desire to find the Mullin's place.

"Those boys have been nothing but trouble over the last few years. I thought maybe the other one would settle down after you folks took his brother out of circulation. I guess that was just wishful thinking. Now tell me what you need."

"First we need to find their home and see if they are there. We have a description of their car. If they are there we'll have to make a plan as to how we get my granddaughter back."

The young Marshal spoke up.

"Mr. Howard I know one of the brothers, Phil is what he's called, he has a scar on his cheek."

"That is the one we're looking for."

"Then we got trouble. His folks live just south and west of Glenpool. I went out there just after I got my badge. They must have had fifteen hounds tied up in the front yard. Those hounds made one heck of a racket when we drove up."

"That's going to make it tough to sneak up on them."

"Yes sir, it sure will."

"Excuse me Marshal but are these hounds hunting dogs?"

"I think so sir, the father is from Arkansas and is a tough ole man to get along with. He doesn't have a lot of respect for the law, if you know what I mean."

"Sam, were you at the trial?"

"No I wasn't James, never had any reason to be, why?"

"I think we may just be in the market for a coon dog."

Sam began to smile, he was beginning to see where I was headed.

"James, I sure hope he has a blue tick, I do love a blue tick hound."

"Mr. Howard, maybe you'd better explain to us what you have in mind, your friend here seems to already know."

I explained my idea to the Sheriff who smiled.

"It just might work, at least it will get you close enough to see if the boy's at home."

"Sheriff, Sam and I will need a hat before we go out there just in case someone down there might figure out who we really are."

The Sheriff offered to send a couple of his deputies with us.

"Thanks Sheriff but the boy down there may recognize one of your folks and we don't want to get him on his guard. I think the four of us will be enough."

"You could be right sir, I sure hope it works for you."

"Me too, right now we've got to get down there and see if the boy is at home."

"Let me know if you need anything Mr. Howard, always willing to help another law officer."

I asked the young officer if he knew where we could get a couple of what Sam called street hats.

"Come on back to my office. I think I may be able to fix you up. There were several hats hanging on a rack there. I've not had time to throw them out."

We went to his office and found hats that we thought would work. A small narrow brimmed hat for me and a soft English style cap for Sam.

"Sam, you just became a driver."

"Yes suh Mr. James, I can suh enough do that. Yes sir!"

The young Marshal led us south across the Arkansas River. Traffic on the road was heavy even at this early hour. It was near daylight and it seemed everyone was on his way to work. It was almost eight when we arrived in the bustling community of Glenpool. Tents; people, trucks and teams of horses with equipment-laden wagons were everywhere.

The young Marshal pulled his automobile over into a clear area and waited for us.

"Quite a mess isn't it Mr. Howard?"

"It sure is, I thought our place was bad but my lord this is something else."

"Mr. Howard I have an idea."

"Speak up Marshal."

"You follow me until I wave you over, then let your son and his friend follow me. I'll point out the house to them and let them drive by for a look. If they see the car then we'll see about putting your plan into motion."

"Lead on Marshal, this is your territory."

Sam followed along behind the other two automobiles. The Marshal turned west on a road that said KIEFER 4 mi. we went about three quarters of a mile when the Marshal waved for Sam and I to pull over.

Sam pulled over to the side of the road being sure he wouldn't obstruct traffic flow. Traffic of all kinds was going both ways on the road.

"Set still James, I'm going to raise the hood and look at the engine just in case someone gets curious why we're setting here."

Sam walked around the car and raised the engine cover on my side of the car.

"I'm really trying to get it to run Mr. James."

"Sam, you're pushing me."

Sam was laughing when we saw the boys coming back toward us. They waited for the traffic to clear then pulled across the road and parked behind us.

"Pa, they are there, or at least the car is there. They must think they are safe."

"Didn't figure on anyone seeing them leave town. Sam, put the hood down."

"Think we need to look at some hounds?"

"I sure enough do."

"There's plenty of them around that place Pa, looked to be a dozen or so."

"They either hunt a lot or use them to let them know when someone's around."

"Pa there's a creek and some timber just behind the house. I thought Hank and I could follow the creek and hide in the woods just in back of the house, that way if they came out the back way we'll be ready."

"How much time do you need to get ready?"

"Give us fifteen minutes. Pa, can I take the Sharps?"

"It's under the blanket in the back seat, take a handful of shells."

"Thanks Pa."

The two boys left out in a hurry. Sam continued tinkering with the car. I unbuckled the belt and holster and put the pistol into my belt at my back. The light jacket I wore would hide it from anyone's view.

"James, reckon it's time."

"I think so Sam."

Sam put the hood down on the right side, came around the car and got in.

"Well brother lets get this show on the road."

We turned south on the next road and drove about a half mile then I saw the house off the east side of the road with the creek close behind like Will had said. The house had been here for a while and had little care. The yard fence was a patchwork of about every kind of wire I had ever seen. Inside the yard were at least a dozen hounds. There were red bones, back and tans and sure enough one big blue-tick. Just what I wanted.

Sam pulled our automobile into the narrow two-track road and I got out of the car. All of the hounds began to bark.

An older gray haired man walked through a battered screen door and out onto the porch.

"Well what do you want?"

He spoke with the accent of the Arkansas hill people.

"Yes sir, I'm Sam James. A man down at the store told me you had some of the finest hounds in the country. I'm needing some good hounds, my employer Acme Oil is bringing some folks down here from back east and they want to take them on a hunt."

"You ever run a hound?"

"Well no sir, but my employee here has. He'll be handling the hounds for me."

"You know hounds boy?"

"Yes suh, I shore do. My pappy used to breed and raise the finest hounds in Georgia."

"Sir will you sell me some hounds?"

"Well I might let a few of these boys go, but they won't be cheap. No sir!"

"Deacon, will you look the hounds over?"

"Yes suh."

Sam walked slowly among the hounds looking carefully at each one, finally stopping at the last one. The blue-tick.

"Suh, this one here is a fine dog, the one near you won't last all night. She's too narrow in the chest. The two red bones and that black and tan over there will make a nice pack."

"Damn boy, you've picked the best dogs I own. Your boss here better have plenty of money."

"Just tell me how much sir."

He quoted a price and I began bargaining, not to hard but hard enough to keep his attention. We finally settled on a price. One hundred and fifty dollars, just what I wanted.

I opened my billfold and handed the man two one hundred dollar bills. I could see his eyes light up.

"You don't got nothing smaller?"

"No sir I don't."

"Damn, I ain't got that much change. Wait a minute my boy may have some cash: Buddy, get yourself out here."

I eased closer to the porch and slowly moved my hand until I had the pistol in my hand.

A tall blonde headed man with a scar on his right cheek stepped out on to the porch.

"What do you need Pa?"

"Excuse me, but you're Buddy Mullins?"

"Yeah why?"

I spoke softly so no one in the house could hear.

I brought the pistol out from behind my back, cocking it and covering Buddy in one smooth movement.

He never hesitated he turned and dove for the door, shouting while doing it.

"Run Trey run!"

I shot him through his hip. The heavy slug slammed him into the doorframe where he lay groaning. Suddenly I heard two small caliber pistol shots then came the familiar sound of the Sharps.

"You, you've shot my boy!"

"He's not dead, but he will be if I don't find my granddaughter safe!"

"She's safe mister."

I looked up to see a gray haired woman standing in the doorway over her son.

"If you'll follow me I'll show you where she is."

"Sam, keep an eye on things."

"Done James, go get Mary Margaret."

I followed the woman into the house where she opened a door to a bedroom where Mary Margaret lay bound and gagged.

"May I go look after my boy now?"

"Just don't try and take him a gun, my friend is an excellent shot."

I removed the gag from Mary Margaret's mouth.

"Grandpa, I knew you'd come. I just knew it."

"Well I'm here baby, just lay still and I'll get you untied."

I freed her hands and then her feet and helped her to her feet.

"Follow me Mary and stay close, we've got some folks to talk too."

We walked to the front door where Buddy's mother was trying to stop the flow of blood from her son's wound.

"Mister, I'll get even with you for shooting my son."

"Mr. Mullins, you'd better get something straight in your head and do it right now. If my grandchild had been hurt, I'd have shot you as well as your son and never lost a wink of sleep. You may have bullied folks back where you come from but down here, you're not near tough enough or mean enough to get away with such stuff."

"How you expect us to live with both my boys gone?"

"Get a job, work like everyone else. Either get a job or get out."

Pa!"

"Yes Will"

"We got the other feller out back. He's going to need a doctor quick."

"The Marshal should be here any minute. Will, that's his car coming down the road."

The Marshal along with a local town Marshal pulled into the driveway and came quickly over.

"You've got your granddaughter Mr. Howard?"

"Sure do Marshal, but we're going to need a doctor. Buddy here took a bullet through the hip and there is one down out back of the house."

"Where is he shot?"

"Through the shoulder Marshal, he came out shooting at us."

"The city Marshal said he'd go get a doctor and would be back shortly.

"Mr. Howard."

"Yes Ma'am."

"I'd like to go home. My father begged me not to marry Raff here and as a young girl I didn't listen. Now I'm through with him. I still own that little farm back in Arkansas and I'd like to go home and forget this ugly life."

"Woman, get in the house!"

"No Raff, I'll not do that. You poisoned my boys with your evil talk. You've led them down this road and look where it's got them. They'll grow old in prison."

"Mister Howard, if you'd be so kind I've got a little money tucked back that Raff doesn't know about and I'd like to buy a train ticket home."

"Women, you're crazy. I'll whip you."

"No you won't Raff, you're going to jail too. The man out back told me it was your idea to steal Mr. Howard's granddaughter."

Well if that is the case you won't be needing this."

I took the two one hundred dollar bills from his shirt pocket and gave them to Mrs. Mullins.

"This should give you a little extra to settle in when you get home. Sam don't forget your Blue-tick when we leave."

"Don't worry James, he's one fine dog."

"His name is Tuck and he really is a fine dog sir. My husband wasn't much but he did raise some fine hounds."

"Mr. Howard I'll pack some things and be ready to leave when you are."

"Fine Mrs. Mullins, just take your time."

"Grandpa, she was nice to me, I'm glad you're helping her."

"Mary Margaret, sometimes folks get caught up in situations they can't control. Maybe now she can get a fresh start with the rest of her life."

"I hope so grandpa, she kept me in her room away from the others."

CHAPTER 33

▼

The local city marshal came back with the doctor who shook his head in disgust and went to work on Buddy. When he finished we walked around back of the house and found Hank watching the other wounded man who was leaning up against the house. He wasn't moving."

"Is he dead doctor?"

"No, but if we don't get him to my office he will be. His shoulder is smashed; I'll have to take his arm off. What in the world was he shot with?"

"My son shot him with my Sharps doc."

"That explains it, those things would drop a buffalo dead in his tracks."

"He wasn't shooting buffalo doc just a child stealer."

"I know this man, never been much good, he's been in and out of trouble most all his life."

"Maybe this will slow him down doc."

"I'm sure it will, that is if he survives the surgery."

"Send me the bill doc, I want this man to live. I want him to spend a longtime in jail."

"I'll do my best Mr. Howard."

We loaded the two wounded men into the city marshal's automobile and then helped Mrs. Mullins load her things in the boys automobile and headed back to Tulsa.

We followed the young Marshal who led us to the train station where I bought Mrs. Mullins a train ticket and saw her on her way. While we were there I sent a telegram to Tom to let him know everything was all right and that we would be home before sundown.

Mary Margaret was asleep not long after we left Tulsa her head resting against my side. Sam with ole Blue sitting in the floor of the automobile had his head in Sam's lap. Sam was rubbing his ears and the dog was groaning softly.

"Sam, by the time we get home that dog will be in love with you."

"Sure hope so James, I wasn't kidding about knowing hounds. The man I lived with as a boy did raise and train hounds. I had a Blue-tick pup when I was a boy, was really some kind of dog."

"What happened to him Sam?"

"The gentleman who owned the farm where I lived gave him to a brother who lived up north somewhere."

"You mean he just took him?"

"Sure did James, remember at the time I was a slave. The man owned me and the dog."

"Sam, I know that was the way things were done but it's still hard to believe. One thing for sure though Sam."

"What's that James?"

"Ole Blue there belongs to you."

"I know James, thank you."

"No thanks needed Sam, I paid for him and I sure enough didn't need a dog."

"You've never had a dog have you James."

Nope, couldn't have fed one when I was down Texas way and we just never seemed to need one."

"Man needs a dog, I've missed that blue pup my whole life."

As I drove the winding road towards home I thanked the Lord for letting me have my granddaughter back. Actually I was just beginning to feel the fear. I simply could not imagine loosing one of my grand kids.

As we neared town I saw Matt's car come flying down the road towards us. I pulled over to the side of the road and stopped. I could see Matt, Deb and my Mary all in the car.

Matt pulled the car over and everyone came running.

Mary Margaret was barley awake when everyone got to the car. The next few moments I would never forget for the rest of my life. Everyone was hugging Mary Margaret and crying at the same time. Mary came to me after a moment and just stood there, then gave me a kiss. A kiss that was something else. She drew away and looked at Sam.

"He's done it again Sam."

"Sure looks that way Mary, have you seen my Blue-tick?

"James, I don't know how but you got it done. I've never seen so many happy people before. When Tom got the telegram the whole town seemed to cheer. Oh James, I'm so happy."

"Grandmother, grandpa was like a knight in shining armor, just like in the books. He was wonderful. I told the men he would come get me."

"I know darling that's why I married him. He'll always be my knight."

"Hey folks lets get to town, it's been a long day and I'm hungry."

"Will, do you think we should feed him?"

"Mom, I think we'd better. Otherwise we'll have to listen to him all evening."

It was good to hear my family laugh again, even if it was at my expense.

Mary Margaret rode with Matt and Deb. Mary rode with Sam, Ole Blue and I.

Mary commented on what a beautiful dog Blue was.

Sam seemed to glow with her praise. He told Mary about his puppy and I saw the tears in Mary's eyes.

She wanted to know how we had found Mary Margaret. She asked Sam, not me.

"Mary!"

"Hush James, I want all the story.

As usual there were a few things happened that I didn't remember, but when Sam had finished Mary seemed happy.

When we rolled into town it seemed everyone in the country was there. People lined the main street on both sides. Everyone seemed to gathering in front of Tom's office. Matt stopped his car because the people blocked the street.

Tom, Bill and Sammye came out of their office and waved for silence. The crowd quieted down.

"Friends, as you can see my niece is back home where she belongs."

The crowd cheered.

"James, say a few words."

I hated talking to crowds but I was stuck.

"Thank you all for coming and for your prayers for my grand baby's return. She's home, safe and tired so if you folks don't mind we'll thank all our friends, Bill, Sammye and our local police force. Without their help we might never have gotten my granddaughter back. Remember they are here to help you so support them."

The crowd cheered and began to break up. We walked over to Tom's office where I shook hands with Tom, Bill and got a hug from Sammye. The Chief of the tribal police was there and I thanked him again for his help.

"Glad I could help Mr. Howard, we're all thrilled you managed to get her back unharmed."

"Pa, I've not got to hug your neck yet."

Deb came over and standing on her tiptoes gave me a kiss on the cheek and a hug.

"Thank you Pa, thank you so much."

"No thanks needed Deb, remember I love her too."

"I know Pa and so does she."

"That's all that matters Deb."

"You ready to head home Cowboy?"

"I sure am Mary, a hot bath and a good bed is the one thing I'm looking forward too."

As we walked through the door I spotted Hank.

"Hank, thanks for you help. Do you need a ride anywhere?"

"No thanks Mr. Howard I have a room over at the hotel."

"Hank, do me a favor."

"Yes sir."

"Call me James."

"Alright James, I'd be proud too."

"Mary, where is Sam?"

"Lesa drove their car into town when we got word you had rescued Mary Margaret."

A few moments later as we were leaving town we saw Sam and Lesa waiting by the side of the road. I pulled up beside them.

"Thanks again Sam."

"Thank you James, for Blue I mean."

"James Howard, I think he may sleep with this dog tonight."

"I'm glad he's got his dog Lesa, I think it is one of the few things I ever gave him that he had tears in his eyes. But after all he's done for me I'm thrilled I could give the dog to him."

"Sam, I'll talk to you tomorrow. Right now I want a hot bath and some sleep."

"That's two of us James, see you tomorrow."

CHAPTER 34

───────────── ▼ ─────────────

I awoke the next morning to find Mary was already up. I found she had laid out clean clothes for me at the foot of the bed. I got dressed and walked into the kitchen.

"Good morning dear, sleep well?"

"Like a log, what time is it?"

"Eight forty five."

"My Lord I was tired."

"Yes dear, you were up all night and should have been tired."

"I guess I was, been a long time since I slept this late."

"Well dear, you needed the rest. You've already had a guest this morning."

"I have, who was here?"

"Mary Margaret, she brought you some flowers, see!"

A vase on the table held a pretty bunch of flowers.

"That's nice, real nice."

"Yes it was, you've always been special to her and now you're her hero. She told me she prayed you'd come and get her and you did."

"Mary, I had a lot of help. Hank, the boys at the tribal office and the officers down at Tulsa."

"I know James, but you put it all together. That's all she knows and cares about."

"As long as she is home and safe is all I care about Mary. Do you have the coffee ready, it may take half a pot to get my eyes open."

"Made just the way you like it. Go out on the porch and set down, I'll bring both of us a cup."

I went out and sat down in our porch swing. It was a beautiful morning, just enough of a breeze to be comfortable. Mary brought our coffee out and sat down.

"Beautiful day isn't it?"

"I was thinking the same thing Mary. You know when the oil rigs came in I hated it. I didn't like the automobile. The sounds of the drilling rigs or the mess they made of our countryside. Worse yet I hated what the money did to the people. I know they have to learn but it hurts me to see them treated like children. I know there is nothing I can do but advise them but I wish there was."

"James, you've done everything for the tribe you can do. You've helped to build schools and sent their children off to college. You've told them to listen to the young educated ones. James you can't do anymore."

"I know Mary, but it still hurts to see them taken advantage of, I remember my promise to Thumb."

"James, Thumb never had any idea how big this thing would be, but remember he always said the fit would survive. You remember what he said about the tribe to the west; how they envied our way of life and the food we had because we worked."

"Yes I remember Mary, why?"

"It's what we have going on now. Those who have learned will survive in this new world and those who have refused to learn will perish."

"But Mary."

"But nothing James, it's how life will be, it's always been that way and darling there is no way you can change it. No matter how hard you may try."

"I guess you're right Mary, but it's going to be hard to watch."

"You'll do fine James, just fine."

We sat drinking our coffee until we saw our son Matt's car leave his place and head our way. When he stopped in front of our house he waved to us.

"Mother, you and dad seem to be real comfortable there in the swing."

"We are son, how's Mary Margaret?"

"She's fine, to hear her tell it she's got the greatest grandfather in the world."

"It will wear off son. She'll grow up and forget all about me."

"Dad, I don't think so. She and Deb baked you a cake this morning."

"They didn't need to do that son."

"I know dad, but I'm not about to argue with my wife. I listened to her talk about all the things you've done for us and for others. I swear she talked until almost daylight. Dad she thinks of you and mom as her second set of parents."

"Well Matt, she is our daughter you know. And we love her. She's made you happy and given you two lovely children. Matt, we could never ask for more in a daughter-in-law."

"I know mom but she feels she's so lucky to have you all."

"Matt, tell her we feel the same way about her and to relax. We plan on being around for a while."

Finally a week or so later things began to settle down. It was still about a month before we would have the annual party so I asked Mary if she wanted to take a trip.

"James, I'd love to but we'll have to wait. Will, Tee and your folks are going out to Jackson Hole to see Mel and go elk hunting. I've told Tee we'd watch the children and get them off to school."

"Well I guess we'll just take a trip in the spring. When are they planning on leaving?"

"Day after tomorrow. Mel had telegraphed them asking for them to come out. He and Will seemed to get a long real well when he was here, by the way he wants to come here for Christmas."

"Great, I'd love to see him. He is such a good friend."

CHAPTER 35

▼

Two days later we took Pa, Carla, Will and Tee to the train station. Will and Tee were so excited, it would be their first vacation as I had told them and was long overdue.

Mary had helped Tee pack, she was careful to see that Tee had plenty of warm clothes.

I had helped Will; he was so excited about going on the trip.

"Pa, I've never seen a live elk before."

"Don't worry son, Mel will help you. You'll see plenty before you get to take a shot."

"I know I can shoot but I just don't want to make a fool of myself in front of grandpa and Mel."

"You'll be fine son, by the time you've seen everything you're going to see the elk will be a snap."

Mary and I were going to stay down at our old place so the kids wouldn't have any adjustments to make.

The kids left to go down to pick up the folks. Our grand kids had already left for school so Mary and I had the day to pack a few things for our two-week stay. As Mary explained we would have every day to ourselves and would probably spend most of our time at our house anyway.

With Will gone I saddled my horse and made a swing to check the cattle. It was fun to once more be riding a good horse and looking the herds over. I checked the steers we would be shipping this fall and was very pleased with their condition. Will and the boys were doing a wonderful job of managing the herds. I was proud of my son.

When the kids got home from school it was like two small tornadoes had just blown into the house.

Mary had a snack ready and made sure the kids got their homework done before they were allowed to go outside and play.

Becca fed the chickens while J.R. and I took care of the horses, and a couple of sick calves.

J.R. had a yearling colt that he had bought from a ranch in Texas. His Uncle Matt and Aunt Deb had helped him make the deal.

The colt was a dandy, His Sire was a champion cutting horse and His Dam was a mare that I had even heard about. She had been a champion cutting horse herself and had been the dam of two more champions.

"What do you plan on doing with him?"

"I figured by the time he is old enough I'd have enough money saved to have Uncle Bill or one of his boys to train him for me."

"Sounds like a plan. J.R. he should make a dandy."

"I want him to be as good as your horse Slick grandpa. He's so pretty to watch when he's working cows."

"I'm proud of him J.R. but this colt could be way better."

"I sure hope so grandpa, I really do."

After supper when the kids went to bed, Mary and I sat in the living room in front of the fireplace having a cup of hot chocolate.

"I remember sitting here a lot of evenings when the children were small."

"So do I Mary, I remember moving in and how many times I moved the furniture that first week."

The next two weeks passed quickly. It was fun having time to spend with the grand kids and just really getting to know them.

Mary and I drove into town to meet the kids and my folks. I visited with Art who was getting ready to retire.

"It won't be the same without you here Art. I remember the telegrams you'd have delivered when the filly was running."

"Those were some sure enough good times weren't they James?"

"They sure were Art."

"My wife and I were talking about that the other day. We moved in here when there wasn't much to see, now look at what happened."

"Things have changed that's for sure."

We visited until Mary came back from her shopping. We heard the train whistle and watched for folks until the train pulled to a stop. Will and Tee were off first and helped Pa and Carla down from the train. Everyone was all smiles.

"Everyone have a good time?"

"It was wonderful son, your father and I had such a good time. Just watching the children enjoy themselves was worth the trip."

"Tee, you enjoy yourself?"

"Oh Pa, it was wonderful. You and mom had tried to tell us how beautiful it was but until you see it yourself there is no way it can be described."

"Son, did you get an elk?"

"Sure did dad, they'll unload the racks in a minute."

"Racks, did Pa get one too?"

"No he didn't hunt, but Tee did."

"Wait until you see the rack she got."

Tee was all smiles as the baggage folks unloaded the two sets of antlers from the baggage car.

Pa came over and shook my hand.

"Everything alright here son?"

"Fine Pa, have a good time?"

"Had a wonderful time. Just watching the kids was worth the trip, especially when Tee shot her bull."

"Mom, give me a hug."

Carla hugged me and gave me a kiss on the cheek.

"Folks, lets go down to the café and get a piece of pie, you all can fill us in on your trip."

We loaded their baggage into Will's automobile and tied the antlers onto the rear bumper. It was quite a sight in our small town. We
drove down to the café and ordered pie and coffee.

Pa said Mel would be in for Christmas.

"Son it looks like the government is going to make that country up
there into a National Park. Mel is sure happy."

"I can imagine he is. He's worked hard to get it done, it will be
nice to see him again."

"Now Tee, tell us about this elk you got."

"When we got to Mel's place and had seen deer, bear and elk on
the way I was just going along with Will and watch, but he suggested
I hunt with him. The day we began our hunt we had rode our horses
up the mountain we were camped on. We stopped at a beautiful
meadow. We had just tied our horses when Will spotted a bull elk,
but it was too far away for me to shoot so I told Will to shoot. He
took a rest on a log and shot. The bull fell where he stood. That was
when I saw my bull sneaking through the timber. He was close and
when I had an open shot I fired. He ran about fifty yards and went
down."

"Dad I didn't see her shoot, I was too busy watching my bull. I
sure didn't want him getting up and running off. When she fired I
first thought she'd fired by mistake, then I saw her bull lying at the
edge of the meadow. He was huge."

"Took you a while to get him dressed and back down to camp?"

"Oh no dad, Mel's boys showed up and did all the skinning and
packed the meat onto pack horses. The meat will arrive here sometime next week."

The kids and my folks had had a wonderful time. Mary and I visited with Tom for a few minutes then headed home.

"I've enjoyed my grand children James, but I'm glad to be home."

"I know what you mean, I'm going to saddle my horse and go
check the Angus."

"Fine James, I need to do some dusting and then I'm going to finish the book I started before we left."

"Sounds good to me dear, I'll be back in a while."

I rode down into the valley and rode among the Angus cows. I was pleased with them; over the years of culling and very careful breeding there was not a better herd anywhere. I was proud of them.

The pasture was in wonderful shape and would last well into the winter. We had hay crews come in and had the hay sheds full of good hay.

When I got back to the house I ate a sandwich and went into the bedroom for a nap. The grand kids had worn me out.

CHAPTER 36

▼

The time went quickly, it would soon be time for another oil check to be issued to the tribe. The checks were issued every three months. You could always tell when the checks were due. Merchants in town stocked their shelves and got ready. The tribal members would buy the things they thought they needed as soon as the money arrived.

Not only the local merchants, but merchants of every kind would begin to drift into town. The local police worked round the clock for two or three days. Folks had been robbed, shot and even murdered for the money they received for their oil.

Our money went straight into the bank. I hadn't even asked Mary how much it was. Strange, in years past I knew exactly to the penny how much money I had. I thought to myself, how times had changed.

The tribe wanted a new and larger school. With the new folks in town we had quickly out-gown our existing school. A council meeting was held where Tom explained the need for the new school.

One of the older council members surprised me when he said it was past time. He commented on how his grandson who had gone to our school had kept him from being cheated, only because he could read. As he put it, without the white mans education none of the people would survive.

The council voted and told Tom to take what ever funds were needed from the tribal fund and get started on the school as quickly as possible.

The council also approved the adding of four more police officers. The current men were in need of some relief. Petty thefts, whiskey peddlers and fights were everyday occurrences.

Whiskey was smuggled in at night and was sold to the people. I hated it worse than anything, but all that could be done was try and catch those responsible when the chance came to us.

One evening as the sun was setting Mary called to me from the front porch.

"James, some ones coming up the road."

I walked out onto the porch to see who was coming.

A truck pulled up and stopped. My driller friend Hank got out of the truck.

"Evening Hank."

"Evening James, Mrs. Howard."

"What brings you out this way Hank?"

"Thought I'd better come tell you of something I heard just a while ago."

"What was it you heard Hank?"

"Some fellers over west of here figger to move a bunch of your west herd tomorrow night. They know you've only got one man living over there; they figure he'll be easy pickings. Then they'll simply drive you cows west."

"But Hank, everyone knows my brand."

"Without the hide on, it's hard to read a brand James. They don't plan on taking them all, just thirty or forty head. They have half a dozen places ready and willing to take the beef."

"Hank, I appreciate your coming to tell me, we'll see what we can do to discourage these boys. How many of these boys are there?"

"Six that I know of, maybe a couple more."

"Thanks again Hank, I don't want anyone knowing you came over here."

"James, we've got to get a handle on things. I'm wanting to have my wife and family over here."

"I know what you mean Hank and if there were more folks like you things would get better in a hurry."

When Hank left I sat down next to Mary.

"James, you're thinking of how you're going to stop them."

"Well yes, but to keep anyone from suspecting Hank, I think we'll do a little something different."

"Different, how James?"

"I think I'll let the tribal police take care of it. It will do them a lot of good to catch these boys."

"Well, I have faith in you, you'll figure it out by tomorrow."

"I hope so Mary, I sure enough do."

As Mary had said I did have an idea the next morning. I'd thought about it most of the evening and thought I had it figured out.

I walked down to Will's place and told him what was going to happen. I explained my plan as he paced up and down.

"You're probably right pa, in fact I know you are. But it will be hard not to help."

"I know what you mean Will but I really believe we should let the police handle it."

"I'll catch Matt before he goes to town. He and Uncle Tom can set things up with the police. Like you say we need to be out of it. Let folks start to respect our police force. I'll make my rounds as usual but I'll be sure to inform Boggs about what's going to happen."

"That's a good idea, you'd better get moving if you're going to catch Matt before he leaves."

I walked back up the hill and had breakfast with Mary. I explained to her what we were going to do.

"It's a fine idea James, I think it will work and you'll accomplish what you're wanting to do for the police force. I only have one question."

"Alright, what do you want to know?"

"Where are you and Will going to hide?"

"Mary!"

"James, you and I both know you're going to go out tonight."

"I was thinking about it but I just haven't decided exactly what I'm going to do."

Mary went into the house laughing. When I went in a short while later I saw my Sharps and shell bag lying on the table. My wife was indeed a smart woman.

Sam and Lesa showed up late in the afternoon. I informed Sam about what was going to happen and he was ready to go.

"I'd love to have you go along Sam but what if they have someone watching the house?"

"James, I can answer that."

"How Mary?"

"We can set in our kitchen with the blinds half drawn with the light on and if we put on a big hat and stand near the shade. Now if anyone's watching they will think you're both home."

"Mary it will work. Come on Sam we've got work to do."

We caught two dark colored horses and rode them to a small stand of trees about a quarter of a mile from the house and were careful to not be seen coming back to the house in case someone was watching.

Later that evening Sam and I made ourselves visible to anyone who might be watching our place. As darkness approached we went into the house.

When darkness settled in Sam and I slipped out a bedroom window and headed out to the horses, rifles in our hands.

We rode our horses at a good speed until we were a mile or so from Boggs house then walked our horses until we reached a small knoll overlooking Boggs place.

"Reckon the boys from town are in place?"

"I don't know I hope so."

"James this is sure different."

"I know Sam but maybe this is what it will take to give the boys some confidence."

"Could be James, we'll see."

Boggs was still up because his light was still on. I know he was aware of the plan but I still didn't like him being the bait in this trap.

We lay on the grass and waited.

"James, there's someone down by Boggs house. I just spotted him when he went by the window light."

"Good, now get ready Sam, things should be getting ready the start."

A few minutes later Boggs light went out, only to come on and then go out again. It was a signal of some sort.

We could make out a group of riders come up from the creek area, an automobile coming along behind them.

"What in the world?"

"The boys have gone modern Sam."

"I'll bet whoever is in that automobile is the one running this operation."

"You could be right James."

"We'll keep an eye on things Sam, I don't want that fellow getting away."

We watched as the riders began gathering and sorting the cows. It didn't seem to me that any of the boys had worked many cattle before. They were trying to work the herd too fast. The cattle were getting stirred up and were beginning to give them trouble.

Suddenly all the men stopped and began raising their hands in the air. The tribal police were on the job. Suddenly the light in Boggs cabin came back on, it looked as if things were well in hand. That was when whoever was in the automobile started to try and make his getaway.

The tribal police began firing but the car never stopped. As he came by our location it was apparent he was going to succeed.

I brought the Sharps up and fired, the automobile began to slow. The heavy bullet from the Sharps had done its job. The automobile was coming to a stop. Two tribal policemen were at the car and had everything in hand.

"Lets go Sam, I don't want anyone to see us."

We walked back to our horses and headed home. We unsaddled the horses and turned them loose. Mary and Lesa would want to know what had happened.

About an hour later an automobile came up the hill. Sam and I walked out onto the porch. It was the head of the tribal police with one of his officers. They had two prisoners in the back seat. One was quite a surprise to me. It was the town Marshal from the small town to the south west of us.

"Mr. Howard, these gentlemen were with some others who attempted to steal some of your cattle tonight. The boys and I caught them. Just thought you'd like to know."

"Thank you sir, what about my employee over there?"

"Oh he's fine sir, he's mad but other than that he's fine."

"Thank you again sir, and tell your men how much I appreciate their help. Guess we've become a little soft these last few years."

"Don't worry Mr. Howard my men and I are on the job."

I thanked the men again and watched as they drove away.

"James, you've done it again."

"I don't know Sam, but if I have then I'm glad. I want those boys to gain confidence and find they can enforce the law."

The next morning Matt stopped by on his way to work.

"Morning Pa, guess you heard about the little incident last night?"

"Yes I did Matt, the head officer came by on his way to town."

Matt began to laugh.

"What's so funny Matt?"

"Pa, when they brought the car in last night and I saw the hole in the hood of the car, I knew you'd been there with your Sharps."

"Now son, you might think so but you know I turned this whole thing over to local police. I'm sure it was one of them."

"Alright dad, but it sure ruined the motor in that automobile.

"Is Boggs alright son?"

"Oh yes, he's fine. The police had a man hide out under his bed when the man came into his house and held a gun on Boggs. They let him make his signal then took control."

"As long as he's alright is all I care about. He's been with me for a while now."

"Pa, he's family and you know it."

When Will stopped and told him what was going to happen Will said he'd never seen Boggs so mad.

"Well Matt, you have to understand. Boggs has been taking care of that west herd now for a while, they are his responsibility and he takes that personal."

"He thinks that you and mother are the grandest folks in the world. He's told me numerous times how you gave him a new start, and how mother always made sure he had everything he needed to live comfortably."

"I know he's not just an employee, he's a friend."

"Have you been in his house lately dad?"

"Haven't had any occasion to son, I'd see him out checking the herd and we'd visit. Now that you mention it I've never been in his house."

"Its clean and neat dad. He has a small out building where he mounts the game animals we and others around here take to him.

"Like I've said Matt I wouldn't know, but if he's happy then so am I."

"He's happy dad, when your Sharps went off he giggled. He said someone had just had one hell of a shock, if he was still breathing."

"Wait a minute Matt, you were there?"

"Sure I was dad, you think I was going to trust one of the rookie lawmen with Boggs' life? He's my friend."

"I should have known son, I'm proud of you."

"Thanks dad, well I got to go to work. Oh by the way, you knew Bill is dating Sammye. They are like a couple of kids."

"Good lord, what next."

"Don't have a clue dad, I just set and watch things happen."

I watched our son drive down the hill; he stopped at the stables. He got a kiss from Deb, talked with Mac and Willie then got back into his automobile and drove off towards town. The boy was a mover; things just seemed to happen when he got involved.

"He's just like you dear."

"You really think so Mary?"

"No, I know so. He starts something, surrounds himself with good people, turns things over to them to run then moves on."

"I'd never noticed that Mary."

"I know, you've been busy. Speaking of busy, you'd better start thinking about the upcoming deer season. I seem to remember you promised your grandsons you'd take them hunting this year."

"You're right Mary, I think I'll talk to Sam about helping me."

"You'll need one other person, why not ask Bill. He might enjoy it."

"You know I would do that but I heard him tell Tom he wasn't a hunter, but what do you think about me asking Harold. His kids are gone and he might enjoy a couple of days visiting with Sam and I."

"That would be neat, maybe Flower can come down. I could get Lesa to come up and we can have a girl party."

"A girl party!"

"All right, a lady party then!"

"From that tone of voice I guess I'll have to go get my own coffee refill."

"My dear, you're getting smarter all the time.

I heard her giggle as I went through the door.

After I got my coffee refill I was looking out the front window and saw an automobile stop down at the race barn. I saw Deb talk to the driver and point our way.

"Looks like we've got company coming Mary."

"Do you know who it is James?"

"No I don't recognize the automobile."

"I guess I'd better make some fresh coffee."

The automobile came slowly up the hill as I walked out onto the porch. Two gentlemen got out of the vehicle when it stopped. It was easy to see they were cowmen. Their hats were sweat stained and their high-topped boots weren't shinned.

"Morning gentlemen, what brings you up our way?"

"If you're Mr. Howard we'd like a moment of your time if you don't mind. I'm Hank Thompson and this here is my son Gerald. We've got a lease over near the little settlement of Hominy."

"I've heard a lot of good things about you Mr. Thompson, I've heard you've got a real nice herd and have dealt fairly with the tribe."

"Thank you Mr. Howard we've sure enough tried. We heard all about you before we moved up here, saw some of your first crop of crossbred calves and bought a couple of Herford bulls for ourselves. I'd like to talk to you one of these days about a couple of your Angus bulls."

"We can do that, but what brings you boys over this way?"

"We've got a problem and we thought maybe you could help us with."

"Come up on the porch and set down, we might as well be comfortable."

I opened the gate for the Thompsons and they followed me up onto the porch. Everyone found a chair and sat down.

"Would you gentlemen care for a cup of coffee?"

"Yes Mamm, if you've got it made, we wouldn't want you to go to any trouble."

"It's made and it's no trouble at all."

As Mary stepped back into the house I noticed the younger Thompson was looking down at our ranch layout.

"Mr. Howard you've got a fine place here. Who was the lady down at the barn that gave us directions?"

"That was my daughter-in-law Deb. Our youngest son went down to Texas to buy a horse and found her at the same time. He didn't bother to tell his mother before hand either."

Mary handed us all a cup of coffee.

"Things like that happen Mrs. Howard. I found mine at a homesteader's place on a drive up to Dodge."

"I know sir, but all three of our kids got married and I only got to go to one of their weddings."

"All these deals have worked out fine?"

"Oh yes, we have a wonderful family and plenty of grandchildren."

"That's all that matters, we've got a bunch of grandkids ourselves."

"Well Mr. Thompson, tell me about your problem."

"We've got several sir, but would you call me Hank?"

"Glad too, call me James."

"Pleased too, James. We need help dealing with these oil folks. We're a good ways away from the agency office and don't have enough law enforcement folks to help me. We're trying to take care of the land and do right but there are some of the folks who just don't care."

"Hank, it looks to me as if we may already be working on your problem. The council and I have heard several other complaints and have four new tribal police who will be working over your way in the next couple of weeks. I'll have the men look you up when their training is finished. They should be ready in a week or so."

"That would really help. The salt water at some of the sights is a mess."

"I know what you mean, we had the same thing here until we got a handle on things. Have you all had any rustling problems?"

"We've had some, but we've managed to keep a hand on things."

"That's good to hear, we had some problems early on but things have settled down the last few years."

"James, we really appreciate your taking the time to talk with us."

"Not a problem Hank, I'm glad I could help."

"We've heard about your holiday you have each year. The wife and I just might wander over this way for the next one."

"You're more than welcome Hank but come early. The folks show up the day before and camp out. Everyone seems to have a good time."

"From what we've heard, half the country shows up."

"There's quite a bunch, it's become a tribal holiday."

"Mr. Howard, may I ask you a question?"

"Sure Gerald, ask away."

"Could I see your Sharps?"

I heard Mary laugh softly inside the house.

"Sure you can, would like to try shooting it?"

"Gerald, I'm ashamed of you!"

"Hank, don't get on his case. There are stories told about that rifle I don't even know about."

Mary came out onto the porch carrying the Sharps along with my shell bag.

"Lets go down back of the barn, there's a good place for you to try her there. Ever fired a Sharps Gerald?"

"Heck no sir, yours is the first I've ever seen."

"They have a pretty good kick so pull it up snug when you fire."

We walked around back of the barn where the boys and I had a couple of targets set up against a loose shale bank. I explained to Gerald about how the sight on the rifle worked and had him cock and dry fire it so he got the feel of the set trigger.

"Lordy! Mr. Howard, I barely touched the trigger and it went off."

"That's why I had you dry fire it Gerald."

I handed him a shell and told him to fire at an old can setting against the bank.

I winked at Hank as Gerald aimed the rifle and stepped behind him. The big rifle roared and I caught Gerald as he spun around and back.

I thought Hank was going to die laughing. Gerald was busy rubbing his shoulder and laughing along with his father.

"By dang son, you wanted to shoot that cannon."

"I sure did pa, but once was enough."

"Look what you did to the can Gerald."

When Gerald looked I saw the look of astonishment cross his face. The can was torn apart and was now a mess of torn metal.

Gerald walked over and picked up the can, all the time shaking his head.

"Mr. Howard, I've heard stories about you and this gun ever since we moved up here. Some as you say may not be true but, I figure most of them are."

"Gerald folks sometimes seem to add to the stories. Like I said don't believe everything you hear."

"I have one other question."

"Ask away."

"I'm bigger than you and that cannon almost broke my shoulder. How did you manage to shoot this thing and stay on your feet?"

"Once you learn how to hold and shoot her it's not so bad. Besides if your life depends on it you'll touch her off and reach for another shell."

"May I take this can home with me? I'd like to show it to the boys on the ranch."

"Take it home if you want, it's not much good as a target now anyway."

I shook hands with Hank and told him I'd been proud to meet him.

"James, it's been a pleasure to meet you. Tell the boys coming over our way to look me up. We'll make them feel at home and back them up if need be."

"Good enough. I'll have them look you up Hank."

I watched as Hank and Gerald drove down the hill.

"Did the Sharps live up to his expectations James?"

"Oh yes, I don't think he'll want to try it again."

We sat on our porch swing while I told her what they had wanted and about Gerald firing the Sharps."

"Dear, you and that Sharps are legends in the country. I know you didn't intend for it to happen but it has and who knows how many have heard the stories and decided not to come up here and try something."

"That could be Mary, I sure hope so because I'm beginning to like our life like it is right now. I guess I'd better go into town and see if the young officers are about ready to head over Hanks way."

"That would be a good idea. I might ride along with you and pick up a few things at the store."

"Holler when you're ready, we'll eat lunch at Cookies old cafe."

When we arrived in town Mary went to do her shopping while I went to the Tribal office to visit with the captain. I found out that the younger officers were almost ready but the captain had decided to send four of the more experienced officers over to Hank's area. He figured it would be easier to break the young men into what was expected of them in our area.

He was going to send the men over to Hank's area day after tomorrow. I told him to have them look up Hank when they got there. He told me one of the officers was from the area and had said he wanted to talk to Hank about some problems his relatives had been complaining to him about.

"Did he say what sort of problems?"

"No, Mr. Howard he didn't."

"Do you think he'd talk to me?"

"I'm sure he would, he has admired you for years. In fact he credits you with as he puts it, "Saving the Osage"."

"Now why would he think that?"

"Mr. Howard, years ago you gave a beef to a woman over west of here who had lost her husband in an accident. She had five kids and was about out of food."

"Captain, to be truthful I think I remember the woman but I gave several families a beef when times were hard."

"Well Mr. Howard the officer was one of those five kids and he'll never forget your kindness. Now if you want to talk to him I'll send him out to your place this afternoon."

"Captain, I'd appreciate it if he has the time to spare."

Not a problem Mr. Howard, besides I'm curious about this myself."

I found Mary talking to Cookie out on the sidewalk. I noticed for the first time that Cookie was getting old. I hated to see it but I wasn't getting any younger myself.

"Hey fellow, you flirting with my wife?"

"I would if my wife would let me."

We were all laughing when Matt, Tom, Bill and Sammye came out of their office.

"Did we miss something Dad?"

"Just caught this stranger here flirting with your mom."

"Want to barrow my Sharps dad?"

"A few years ago maybe. Now I'm not sure."

"Why you young pup!"

I ducked behind Mary to avoid his mock fighting stance.

"I knew it, I've known it all the time. You really were scared of her that first day."

"You bet I was, I've seen her mad."

"I have too dad, it's not a fun sight."

"Oh Matt, I tried to tell your father but he wouldn't listen."

"Brother, you're walking on thin ice."

"See what I mean!"

"Mary, I think we should quit cooking for a day or so and see just how tough these boys are."

"Good idea Sammye I don't think any of them will last a day."

"Wait a minute ladies, I never said a word."

"We know you didn't Bill but it's just because you've not been trapped yet."

"He will be day after tomorrow James. We're getting married Saturday morning. He'll either marry me or face a big law suit."

"All I said was will you. She said yes and said how about Saturday morning. What was I to do?"

After everyone quit laughing at Bill we enquired what time the wedding was to take place. It looked as though Saturday would be a big day.

Afterwards Mary and I laughed about Bill and Sammye's wedding. Mary had already bought a wedding gift a week or so before.

"You knew they were going to get married sometime soon."

"I had a good idea it would happen soon. I saw Sammye doing some shopping a couple of weeks ago and figured Bill's goose was about to be cooked."

"What we she buying Mary?"

"Things you need not know about dear."

"Oh!"

"Yes dear."

CHAPTER 37

▼

Later that afternoon I saw the tribal policeman drive his car up front. I walked out onto the porch and told him to come set.

"Thank you Mr. Howard, I'm officer Paul Walkingstick. I understand you wanted to talk to me."

"Yes I do Paul, please call me James."

"I'd be pleased to sir but I don't think my mother would approve."

"Officer what is your mother's name?"

"Her white man name is Bernice."

"No I mean what was her given name?"

"Little Dove, Mrs. Howard."

"Oh I remember her, she was a year or so behind me in school."

"She remembers you too. She had told me many times how you used to mount your paint pony and leave the school screaming at the top of your lungs. She said you were always trying to escape."

"She was right, I really didn't want to go to school."

"Now Paul, tell me what the folks over to the southwest are concerned about."

"Some folks over that way are hauling oil at night Mr. Howard, by that I mean they are hauling oil at night and the folks over that way aren't getting paid for it."

"What a deal, they drill the wells, pay for only part of what oil they get."

"Sounds to me like we might need to get some folks together and put a stop to this deal."

"Some of my friends tried to do that but were threatened. The men told them to keep their mouths shut or their homes just might blow up."

"Alright Paul, now that we know what's going on lets put a plan together and put a stop to this deal."

Sometime later after Paul was gone Mary and I sat talking.

"Well dear, looks like you've got yourself involved in another tribal problem."

"Family problem Mary, ever since Thumb had me appointed to the council the people became my family."

"You think your plan will work?"

"I sure hope so, it seems as though there's always someone out there figuring out a new way to cheat the tribe."

"That's true dear but you've done well in the past so I'll just keep my bet on you."

The next morning Paul and a friend of his stopped by on their way over to their new assigned area. We went over some details before they left.

Will, Matt and Sam rode up to the house a short time later looking the part of trail drovers.

"Morning boys, you all ready to do a little trail driving?"

"We sure are, but just what are we supposed to drive?"

"There are four young Angus bulls over at Bill and Willa's place. I want you boys to drive them down to the Thompson ranch over by Hominy."

"I reckon I'd better get the tent, bedrolls and the pack mare ready. I figure it will take two may three days to cover that distance."

"That's what I figured Sam, the tent, bedrolls and such are ready for you in the barn. The pack mare is in the lot."

"Dad, what is the deal, why isn't Mr. Thompson sending a couple of his hands to pick the bulls up?"

I explained to them what was going on over there and how I planned to cure the problem.

Sam reached into his saddlebags and brought out the pistol Pa had given him years before. He stepped off his horse and strapped it on.

"Figured something was up so I thought I'd just bring this thing along."

"Good thinking Sam, maybe you boys better get something for yourselves out of the cabinet in the house."

Matt turned his horse and I saw the Sharps in a scabbard under his leg.

Will grinned and showed me the lever action on his saddle. It seemed everyone was ready.

"We don't need to hurry, but if anyone wants to know what we're doing we have a good excuse. Once we're over there we'll see what we can do about the folks problems. I'm glad you're going along Matt, we may need a lawyer before this deal is over with."

"Bill is going to look after the office. Uncle Tom left this morning, he's going to check out a small tank farm and pump station down there. It's an independent outfit and is the most likely place to take the stolen oil. He took the Captain along with him. The last time I saw them they looked like two oilfield workers."

"Looks like everyone is involved."

"Sure they are dad, we've got a job to do. Will and I will go get the bulls, you and Uncle Sam get the pack mare ready while we're gone."

"Sounds like a plan, Sam and I will be ready when you get back."

"James."

"Yes Mary."

"I think Bill and Willa are driving the bulls up to the barn lot."

Sure enough, my Uncle Bill and his wife Willa were driving the four young bulls into the barn lot.

We walked down to the barn.

"Morning folks, Willa and I thought we'd just bring these youngsters over here to save you some time."

"Thanks Bill, Willa, we really appreciate your help."

"No thanks needed James, if I was a few years younger I'd be going along with you."

"I know Bill but I think I have enough help already. Besides we don't want to attract too much attention."

"I understand James, but you just remember, with this kind of money involved these boys will play for keeps. Remember James, there aren't any brands on the oil drums."

"I know Bill we'll be doing a bunch of sneaking as Thumb would say."

"I wish you boys luck."

"Thanks Bill."

We watched as Bill and Willa rode off towards their home.

"Boys, it looks like we'll get an early start."

"Suits us James, we're ready to get this party started."

"Mary, are you ready?"

"I'm ready for you to put my things into the car."

Car was a new word; it had suddenly replaced the word automobile. Surprisingly I liked it. I loaded Mary's bags into the car and laid a blanket over my Sharps and pistol. I was going prepared just like the boys.

"Boys we'll see you all in a couple of days at the Thompson's place. I'll need the time to get everything set."

"You all be careful Pa, we'll see you in a few days."

"As we started down the hill I looked into the top of Mary's purse. The short-barreled pistol I'd given her years before lay on top. My wife was prepared too.

CHAPTER 38

▼

Mary and I enjoyed the drive over to the Thompson's place. As Mary put it everything had changed so much. New homes had sprung up everywhere. The Osage people were prospering from the new-found oil money.

We met a lot of cars going the opposite direction. Everyone seemed to be in a good mood, we waved as we passed.

Mary could hardly believe how much the once small town of Hominy had grown. I stopped and filled the car with gas and got directions on how to get out to the Thompson's place.

There were three hotels on the main street that looked nice. We'd see the Thompsons and come back here for the night. I thanked the service station man and headed out of town. A few miles out of town we saw a sign saying Thompson Ranch pointing down a road. We turned down the road and a few minutes later came to a barbed wire string gate. A sign hanging on the gate got a chuckle out of both Mary and I. It read "Cattle Country, Close The Damn Gate". Needless to say we closed the gate.

A few miles later we drove into the Thompson's ranch yard. I saw Hank coming out of a large barn. I waved and stopped the car.

"Well I'll be, Mr. & Mrs. Howard. What brings you folks over this way?"

"Business of a sort Hank. My boys are bringing you four of my young Angus bulls for you to use. But if you've got time there's something I need to talk to you about."

"You get out and come up on the porch, my wife will be thrilled to meet you."

We followed the rock paved walk up to the front porch. I saw the way Mary was looking at the rock walkway; I knew I'd have a chore to do when I got home.

Hank's wife met us at the top of the porch and took Mary into the house. Hank and I found chairs and I asked him about the problem we wanted solved.

"James, I know something about the problem you're talking about. I'm sure some of my crew knows a lot more than I do. I'll talk to a couple of my hands who I know will keep their mouths shut."

"It seems there's always someone wanting to steal something from the Osage. We had a lot of murders over this way early on and it took a while to get things sorted out, but you know all about that."

"Most I suppose, but there's still a few undesirable boys around. I wouldn't be surprised if they aren't involved in this latest steal."

"More than likely, what can we do to help you James?"

"Talk to your men and lets see if we can't put a stop to this stealing."

"The boys will be in shortly, we'll talk to them then. You folks going to stay with us?"

"We thought we'd get a room in Hominy, we didn't want to put you out."

"Lord have mercy, have you seen my wife. She doesn't get much company out here and she'll probably talk your wife's leg off before sundown."

Shortly there after the women came out onto the porch with coffee, tea and some of the best peanut butter cookies I'd ever tasted. I told Mrs. Thompson so.

"Why thank you Mr. Howard, they are Hank's favorite too. I'll give Mary the recipe."

"I'd sure appreciate that ma'am."

"Call me Ann, James."

"I'll do that Ann, thank you."

We visited about the bulls the boys were bringing and when we could expect them to arrive.

"I'm really excited to see them James. We came to one of your production sales a couple of years back but the buyers from back east were paying way more than we could afford at the time."

"I figured we needed an excuse and you'd said something about the Angus so I figured it would make a perfect excuse for us to be here. Besides I've got more than I need but I want to see what two of these bulls look like in another hear or so.

"We'll sure enough take good care of them James, I'm going to sort some cows out for these bulls James, I'm going to take advantage of your generosity."

"I don't see why not, that's what they are for."

Later that afternoon the ranch hands began to drift into the ranch.

Hank waved to a couple of the men and we talked to them.

One of the men was reluctant to talk but finally told us what he knew.

"Mr. Thompson, you gave me a job when a lot of folks wouldn't so I guess I've got to tell you. One of our new boys is a part of the bunch you're after."

"You sure Red?"

"Yes sir, the new hand Gosset is working with the boys hauling the oil."

"Damn, I hate to hear that. I know his grandpa, a real fine feller. Anyone else you know of Red?"

"No sir, I've heard a few rumors but I don't know anything for sure. Maybe Mel here knows something."

"Well Mr. Thompson, I'm sort of like Red I've heard rumors but nothing for sure."

"Alright boys, lets talk about the rumors boys. You first Mel."

"I've heard they take the oil out to the independent pump station south of town. But I've heard the big boys in this deal are over in Bartlesville."

"I've heard the same thing Mel, I also heard they own a big percentage of the pump station."

"Now we're getting somewhere, did you hear a name?"

"Seems as though I heard the name Tucker."

"Tucker and Wise?"

"Say, I think that's it."

"It sure is, that's the same thing I heard."

"You know them James?"

"Sure do, they are a couple of crooked lawyers who we've finally run out of our area. They always seem to slip out of things."

"Maybe we can put a stop to them and their crooked games. Thanks boys for your help. I'd appreciate it if you'd just forget about this little talk. If any one asks about it just tell them we were talking about the new Angus bulls I've loaned Hank here."

"Angus bulls, how many?"

"Four, my men are driving them over this way right now. They should be here day after tomorrow."

"We going to sort cows Hank?"

"Just as soon as they get here."

"Hot dogs, it's just what we've been needing around here."

"This new man of yours, what sort of fellow is he Hank?"

"Nice mannered young fellow. Like I said I've know his grandpa for a long while. Came down here from Kansas City a year or so ago, been with me about three months."

"Think he'd listen to some straight talk?"

"He might, I can give it a try at least."

"We'll talk to him about it tomorrow, we need to figure out a way to nail the boys who are heading this thing up."

The evening went by quickly, Hank's wife was an excellent cook. As Ann explained the kids were all married and had their own homes so they had bedrooms to spare.

We got a good nights rest and after breakfast we saddled a couple of horses and Hank took me on a tour of his spread. We managed to check every set of storage tanks on his place. We were really looking at the remote locations. The problem was there were hundreds of such locations in the area. We needed to get someone in the gang to talk and we only knew of one. We'd have to work this out later.

After touring the ranch we visited with the different ranch hands we found out doing their job. Hank was going to send a man out at daylight to go meet the boys. There was a short cut the boys could take to the ranch.

We had just got back to the ranch house when an oilfield pickup pulled into the ranch yard. My brother-in-law was at the wheel.

I introduced Tom to Hank then inquired what he doing out here.

"Brother-in-law, it's a good thing you thought about the bulls. It's all over town that you're out here visiting the Thompsons. You're well known and when you stopped in town for gas it seemed as though half dozen folks recognized you and Mary."

"I was afraid of that but I guess it can't be helped."

"That's right it can't. But when the two biggest ranchers in the country get together people talk."

"Do they know about the bulls Tom?"

"Oh yes, the officer and I have dropped the word in a couple of spots and it's all over the country now."

"Good, now what are you doing in that oil field truck?"

"I'm the new tank gauger, I go around to all the company storage tanks and keep track of how much oil is stored in them. A friend of mine got me the job. James, no longer than I've been on the job I can tell you this is a big operation."

"What do you mean Tom?"

"I've ran into at least a dozen cases where oil has been taken out of tanks, they only take a couple of hundred gallons. At first I thought I'd miss read the tapes but not twenty times."

"Good lord, that's a bunch of oil. The gauger before you had to know Tom."

"I'm sure he did, he was probably getting a small kick back from the thieves."

"Tom, we need a plan, I've heard its Tucker and Wise who are behind this deal."

"Those two again, boy I'd love to see those two birds behind bars."

"I've got an idea Tom, how about we start taking oil before they get to it. I've discovered one of the men involved and if we can work a deal with him we can put these boys out of business. What we need to do is get those two boys over here."

"You start drying their money up and those two will be over here in a hurry, along with the two bodyguards they always have along."

"That doesn't worry me Tom, remember we've got help coming. I guess it's time Hank and I have a little talk with one of his hands. Have you found anything out since you got here?"

"There's an office in town where the operation is run. One of my friends told me the lawyer who works there was barely getting by a year or so ago but he has suddenly came into a lot of money. He has a new car and is having a nice house built out on the south end of town."

"Have you got a line on anyone else?"

"Not for sure but our police officer is working on getting inside the group. He's been hanging around a few of the local bars where we suspect some of the boys are hanging out evenings when they aren't working. He's pretending to be a son of one of the tribal members who has a large head-right. He's telling the story about how his father threw him out when he married a white women from down in Tulsa."

"I'll bet he's doing a real good job of it too."

"Oh yes, he's doing a real fine job."

"Good, Sam and the boys will be here tomorrow. Check in tomorrow night and we'll see what we've come up with."

"Fine, see you all later. I've got to get to work."

We watched as Tom drove off in the pickup truck, dust flying from underneath.

"That's your brother-in-law?"

"Sure is, he's the head lawyer for the tribe."

"He is, good lord I'd never have guessed he was anything like that."

"That means he's doing a good job."

"James, you've done this sort of thing before, haven't you?"

"A few times Hank, I helped set up the tribal police. I was a Federal Marshal for a number of years, so I've had some experience in law enforcement."

"Now I remember, you caught some boys who were blowing up homes a couple of years ago. I remember hearing about it when I got back up here. I was down in Texas selling our old place when it happened."

"I got lucky on that one, some of the tribal members came along and helped me out. In fact we just might use the same trick here if your young man doesn't want to help us."

"Just tell me what you want me to do, I'm sick of all the scum that's moved in here and tried to take over. We're on our fifth town marshal in just three years. The tribal folks just stay away from town. They do their shopping away from here. I don't blame them, the law around here is a joke."

"That's about to change Hank. We've got a couple of men over here now and I'll get in touch with the U.S. Marshal in Tulsa when I get back home. I have a feeling things are about to change around your little town."

"I sure hope so, we'd like to have things settle down around here. I want my grandkids to grow up in a normal surroundings."

"I know what you mean. There was a time when I wondered if things would ever settle down. Then when things began to settle down they discovered the oil, it seems there's always something."

The next day, just before noon the boys arrived with the bulls. Hank was somewhat excited.

The boys drove the bulls into a small lot for Hank to look over. I introduced Will, Matt and Sam to Hank. I introduced Will and Matt as my son's and Sam as my brother. I saw the look on Hank's face and then explained to him all the things we'd been through over the years.

"Sam, call me Hank, any brother of James here is a friend of mine."

"Besides, I've had several of your hams when we've been able to get one over here."

"Tell you what I'll do Hank, I'll send you all one over for your Christmas dinner. I can't sell them but I can give them away."

"By golly, I'll be looking forward to its arrival. James, these bulls are outstanding. They just don't have any legs."

"I know Hank but look at the weight they carry."

"Mr. Thompson, just don't take them for a trial drive, they sure don't walk very fast. Everyone got an eye full on our way over here. You'll probably be having some company this coming week."

"Let them come, I'm sure they've never seen anything like these bulls."

Later that day I filled the boys and Sam in on what we'd found out since being here.

"Sounds good Dad, looks like you all have been busy. What do you want us to do?"

"We've sort of got an idea but we'll wait until Tom shows up. He may know something we need to know."

Later that evening Tom drove into the yard. The smile on his face told me something was up."

"What's up Tom?"

"I'm a new employee, I just got hired to misread my tape."

"No joke, who hired you?"

"A trucker who hauls oil for the pump station down south. He stopped and visited with me this afternoon. Figured I could us an extra fifty a week. All I had to do was short my tanks fifty barrels a day. He and his friends will pick the oil up every other night."

"Now we got to find out exactly who he works for."

"Our officer may have some answers for us. I saw him today and he slipped me a note. Here James you read it."

The note was short but to the point.

"Got news <u>Big</u> news, see you at Mr. Thompsons."

"Well I guess we'll wait and see."

Shortly after dark officer Walkingstick drove into the yard, he was smiling as he got out of his car.

"Evening gentlemen."

"Officer Walkingstick, what do you have for us?"

"I've gotten to be pals with the fellow who works out at the pump station. It seems he feels as if he's not getting paid enough for all the work he's doing. He had a couple too many beers and got to talking."

"You just happened to have plenty of beer for him."

"Mr. Howard you know how Indians always have plenty with us."

Everyone laughed and waited for him to continue.

"There are eight of them on the trucks at night, two men to a truck. The gaugers are in on the deal also."

"We know that, they hired Tom today. Fifty dollars a week."

"Oh lord, if they only knew."

"Did he know who they were working for?"

"The lawyer hands out the money, but he's only the front man. He didn't have any idea who it was that runs the deal."

"My friends have four trucks we can use James, you still think we can pull this off?"

"It's certainly worth a try. We can get the guys here anytime. What we want are the boys who are really running this mess. Now what nights do they pick up the oil?"

"Tuesday, Thursday and Sunday. The boys don't like to work on Saturday."

"Well it looks like we'll make our pick ups on Monday, Wednesday and Saturday."

"What do you think they will do?"

"First off they are going to wonder what happened, then they'll figure it out and try and stop us. What they are not going to know is we're going to pick up the oil during the day. We'll let them stay up nights looking for us. Tom your friend can handle the oil for us right."

"He has two large storage tanks empty and waiting. James, this will drive this bunch crazy."

"That's what I'm hoping for Tom. Lets let them chase their tails for a while. Hank, we'll need to hide my car for a day or so just in case the boys send someone out to see if we're still around."

"What are we going to do about my hand who is in on the deal?"

"Lets have a talk with him. You seem to think his grandpa's a fine fellow."

"Non better James."

"Lets give him a chance to get out of the country and not break his grandfather's heart."

"If he doesn't want to do that?"

"We'll lock him up and tell everyone he left with some of your money until we're finished."

"Sounds good to me, lets get your boys here settled in the bunkhouse. We'll be able to get them some oil field clothes so they won't stand out from the crowd."

Later that evening the new hand Gosset rode in and after taking care of his horse went to the bunkhouse. Hank and I walked over in went inside.

All the hands including my bunch were visiting.

"Boys I'd like all of you to take a walk down towards the corral. My friend here needs to have a private talk with Mr. Gosset."

The men all left, leaving the young man setting on the side of his bed.

"Mr. Gosset we have a problem."

"What sort of problem?"

"Mr. Thompson here gave you a job because he's been a friend of your grandfather for along time."

"Yes sir, I know that. So what's the problem?"

"You're working with a group of thieves."

"Who said that?"

"Doesn't matter, we've checked and it's true. Now here's the deal. You can get your things and leave tonight. By leaving I mean get out of the country and don't talk to anyone. Get a fresh start and your grandfather will never know, or you will be locked up until we get this mess stopped and then go to jail and break your grandfather's heart."

"Doesn't look like I've got any choice. I'll leave now; I've got a sister down in Dallas who I haven't seen in a while. I reckon it's time I do."

"I've got your word on that son?"

"Yes sir, you do."

"I assume you'll not tell my grandfather."

"You have my word on it."

"Good enough for me, I'll be gone in five minutes and I won't be going through town."

We shook his hand and walked back to the house.

Hank waved to the boys down at the corral.

True to his word Gosset threw his things into his car and left a few minutes later. He waved as he drove out and started down the road.

"Well James, what do you think?"

"I think the boys in town are one man short. Maybe it's just the beginning of their troubles."

The next day was Saturday and we had oil to haul.

CHAPTER 39

▼

Everyone was up early. We were all dressed in oil field clothes so we would not attract attention. The trucks began to arrive a few minutes apart so they would not attract attention. I'd told Hank and his wife to go into town like the usually did on a Saturday. Today the boys, Sam and I would become oil field hands for the first time.

We all got into a different truck and pulled out. Our new adventure had started.

The driver of my truck's name was Melvin. He'd worked back east in the oil fields and had moved down here when he'd heard about the new field. He had a wife and four kids. Before the day was over I knew their names, their habits and dislikes.

Melvin taught me how to hook up the hoses and run the hand pump on the truck. I began to get a new respect for the men who worked in the oil fields. For the most part they were hard working, honest family men.

Before the day was over Melvin and I had hauled three truck loads to the tank farms. I saw the boys and Sam at various times that day. That evening I was going to need a rubdown. I wasn't as young as I once was."

When we all arrived back at the ranch we sat down and talked about our day.

"James, I'd a lot rather punch cows than work in the oil field."

"I know what you mean Sam, these boys work, and work hard."

My boys agreed with us.

We added up the tally sheets on how many barrels of oil we had hauled that day. I took the figure and multiplied it times the price of a barrel of oil and let out a sigh. This little deal was for sure a big deal.

When I told the boys how much we'd saved the tribe they were shocked.

"Anyone attract any attention today?"

"We didn't see that many people today dad. The folks who check the wells everyday were the only folks we saw."

"They ask any questions?"

"Nope, they recognized the trucks and Uncle Tom's friend had already talked to them. I think we're in good shape, all the folks I talked to want this mess to stop. One man said he had been threatened if he said anything. Seems they threatened his family."

"Sounds like the boys are operating just like they always have."

"Sure does pa, but another day like this and they'll begin to hurt."

"That's for sure Will, we'll get their attention in a hurry. Our lawyer in town is going to have a lot of explaining to do shortly."

"Thank goodness we get to rest tomorrow. I've not worked this hard in years."

"I know what you mean Sam. I can't decide which is the most tired, my body or my ears. I don't think Melvin quit talking all day."

Everyone was laughing when Tom walked into the room.

"Did I miss something?"

"Not really Tom we've just ran a tally sheet on the oil we hauled today. He looked at the figures and smiled."

"This will get the boys over east attention. I think from now on we'd better all carry a side arm. These boys aren't going to like their little deal going sour."

"Tom, I was thinking the same thing. Sam you and the boys are going to have to stay out of sight for the next day or so, just in case the boys in town send some out here to check on things."

"You think they'd do that James?"

"They just might Tom. Look at it this way, we show up in town and their oil starts disappearing. Wouldn't you want to check things out?"

"Good point, now what do you think we should do next?"

"The bunch is going to go out tomorrow night. They'll know something is wrong within an hour or so. I figure they are going to make a quick run either out to the pump station or into town to see the lawyer."

"Think we need someone watching both places tomorrow night?"

"Probably wouldn't hurt. We might want to have someone watching the telegraph office. It they send one, I'd like to know what it says."

"Let me talk to a friend of mine in town, he has a lot of friends who just might be able to help us."

"Sounds good Tom, Hank's pasture is just across the road from the pump station. One of our men could keep an eye on whoever shows up there."

"Good idea James, I'll bet Hank has a hand he can spare to help us out."

"I'm sure he does, he wants this mess over as bad as we do."

"Car coming in James."

The car was Officer Walkingstick.

"Officer, what brings you out here tonight?"

"News Mr. Howard, the boys are looking for the man Gosset. There's talk they may send someone out here to see where he is."

"Will, Matt, Sam grab your blankets and clothes. We'd better hustle down to the barn loft. If someone comes out we don't want them seeing us here."

Sam and the boys grabbed their things and headed down to the large barn. Officer Walkingstick left the ranch by a back road followed by Tom.

I walked back over to the house and filled Hank in on what was happening. He quickly rounded up his ranch hands and as he put it, had a war conference. One of the young single men volunteered to keep an eye on the pump station the next night. Hank told him it was his job until he was told different.

They made up a story that Gosset had gotten thrown by an older horse and had gotten mad when the boys had kidded him about it. He'd just up and left the next morning when he'd drawn what wages were coming to him.

With everything set Hank came back to the house and told me what had happened.

"Hank I sure appreciate all your help."

"Don't worry about it James, it's going to help us too."

Lord yes MR. Howard, it's not safe for a decent woman to be in town after dark. We're tired of it Mr. Howard, we want to have a nice normal town."

"We'll do our best Ann, so far our plan seems to be working."

"James, thank you for all your help, at least you're trying to solve our problem."

Later that evening a man drove in to the ranch and went straight to the bunkhouse. A few minutes later he came back out to his car and left. He didn't appear to be too happy.

Hank and I walked down to the bunkhouse and found the boys laughing.

"Mr. Thompson he bought our story hook, line and sinker."

"He sure did boss, when Red told him what had happened he cussed up a storm. He said Gosset owed him money and wanted to know where he went."

"We told him he'd said something about going to Texas but didn't say where."

"Good deal boys, thanks for helping us out."

"Not a problem Mr. Howard we want things to settle down around here too. Most of the oil field folks are nice God—fearing people. It's the bunch who only come to steal and swindle folks we need to get rid of."

"We're working on it boys, just go on doing your job and keep your eyes open. You may see something that will be valuable to us so keep your eyes open."

Late Sunday evening Sam and I slipped over to a storage tank location. We sat down in some brush to watch and wait. The boys had gone to another location.

Sam and I visited while we waited. Shortly before eleven we heard a truck coming up the hill towards the tanks.

We watched as the truck pulled up in front of the tanks and stopped. Two men got out and began to hook up their hoses so they could pump the oil from the tanks into their truck.

One man went up a ladder to check the oil level in the tanks. We could hear him curse all the way over to our location.

"Damn it all, there's no oil here either. Just like the other three locations."

"That can't be Jake."

"Well it's sure enough empty just like the others."

"What do you think has happened?"

"I don't know; these tanks should be better than half full. I guess we'd better tell Clint."

"He's sure enough not going to like it."

"There isn't anything we can do about it. We can't haul what's not here."

"I know but he'll really have a fit."

"Not our problem, let's get these hoses loaded and get."

Sam and I watched as the truck went out of sight then walked the road back to the house and told Hank what had happened. A short time later the boys came up laughing."

"Dad you should have heard the bunch over at our tank sight. They were furious. It seems they get paid for the amount of oil they haul and they weren't happy at all."

"Same thing at our site. Maybe we've gotten to this bunch finally."

An hour or so later Hank's ranch hand rode in on his horse.

"You all should have been over where I was. The ole boy over at the pump station is about to have a heart attack.

"Mr. Howard, I heard the name you folks mentioned the other night. Tucker and Wise."

"How did you hear that?"

"I slipped across the road and into the pump station yard. I was right beneath the office window. I heard it all."

"Well the information is great but I'd like you to be careful, we sure don't want you getting caught."

"I'll be careful sir, the man at the pump station left for town after the last empty truck showed up. He told the driver he had to send a telegram."

"Well if Tom's friend has any connections at the telegraph office we might find out something shortly."

"Tom showed up early the next morning on his way to work. He handed me a telegram sent by the pump station operator. It read: FOUR TRUCKS EMPTY (STOP) PRODUCT GONE (STOP) WAITING FOR INSTRUCTIONS."

The second telegram sent back to him was even more interesting. BE THERE TOMORROW (STOP) SEE LAWYER (STOP).

"Boys it looks like the rats are taking the cheese."

It certainly does James, but how do we tie them to this mess?"

"Tom, here's how I have it figured. Have your friend get his trucks running now. We drain every tank right now. When the rats get here I don't want a drop of oil in the tanks. We'll let you start a rumor that these truckers are selling the oil to your friend. We'll set up out there and see what happens."

We went to work. Several hours before daylight we unloaded the last oil truck and found a place to rest in the officer building. Now all we could do was wait.

Officer Walkingstick dropped by to let us know that he'd heard the truckers were selling the oil on their own.

It looked like our plan was working.

Later that morning we were informed that the lawyer in town was seen loading his car with his clothes. It looked as if he was leaving town.

I sent word out to the ranch for Hank to have someone watch the pump station and let us know if anyone strange showed up there.

Tom's friend already had someone keeping an eye on the lawyer's office. We would know when and if Mr. Tucker and Mr. Wise went there. I figured they would hear the rumor we had started and would show up out here at the office.

Shortly after two that afternoon the two men drove into town. They went to the lawyer's office and found it locked. The gentleman who was watching the office said he could hear them cussing clear across the street.

We formed a plan; Sam and the boys went outside to keep check on things. Everyone was armed and ready. Matt had smiled as he patted his Sharps and went out the door.

God help anyone who crossed him. I suddenly recognized what my wife had known for years. Matt was like me.

Tom and I were in separate rooms with the lights out but were watching his friend.

Shortly before ten that evening I heard Tom.

"James, there's a car coming into the tank farm gate."

"Thanks Tom, I'm ready."

Tom's friend Jerry shifted in his chair and laid a short-barreled pistol between his legs.

Everyone was ready.

The car stopped outside the office and four men got out.

"Tom, you take the right side."

"Fine James."

"Jerry relax, we've got you covered."

"I'm ready James, let them come."

Tucker and Wise walked into the office area and took a quick look around."

"Your name's Harrington?"

"Yes sir, what can I do for you?"

"You'll quit buying oil from independent truckers if you know what's good for you."

"Now why would I want to do that? The independent boys bring me most of my business. Don't see why I should stop, just who are you anyway?"

"My name's Tucker and his is Wise. We run Olympic Oil over in Bartlesville."

"Then sir, I'd suggest you go back to Bartlesville and run your own business."

Tucker turned red and turned to one of the men in the doorway.

"Set his tanks on fire Burt. We'll show him how we take care of folks who won't listen to reason."

As Burt turned to leave Jerry shifted in his chair.

"Mr. Tucker, you'd best not send him out to fire my tanks."

"I'll do what I want, Burt get gone."

Burt and his friend left the building.

"That Mr. Tucker was a mistake."

"Look Harrington, tonight I burn your tanks, if I come back I'll have you taken care of."

"Taken care of, you mean you'll have me killed?"

"I've done it before. If you were half smart you would have listened to me. No one is going to muscle in on my deal."

"You mean the truckers I have been buying from work for you?"

"That's right and I won't have some two bit nobody horning in on my business."

That's when I heard the Sharps.

"What was that?"

"The reason you shouldn't have sent Burt and his friend out there to fire my tanks Mr. Tucker. You've made a mistake; you've under estimated me. I'm not impressed with you or your partner Mr. Wise."

"Everyone around here knew you'd been stealing the oil but no one could prove it until now."

Mr. Tucker made a very stupid move he started to reach under his coat.

That's when Jerry brought his pistol out and covered him.

Tucker backed up, Mr. Wise just stood there frozen.

"Now look here Harrington maybe I have misjudged you. There's no reason we can't work together, there's plenty to go around."

"Partner with you?"

"Why not, together we could expand and really get rich."

"Heard enough James, Tom?"

"More than enough Jerry. Mr. Tucker, Mr. Wise, you're under arrest."

"You can't arrest me, you don't have any authority over here."

I showed him the U.S. Marshal's badge.

"Mr. Tucker I've arrested a lot of men in my lifetime but I'm really going to enjoy this. You've stolen, cheated and by your own admission killed. It's going to be a pleasure seeing you behind bars. Tom, you mind checking on the boys?"

"They are fine James, they have the two boys Mr. Tucker sent out to burn the tanks. One doesn't look well, it looks as if his shoulder might be broke."

"That would have been Matt and his Sharps."

"Thought I recognized that sound. Now let's get these boys in jail so we can get to sleep. Jerry, thanks friend."

"Tom, you're welcome. Mr. Howard it's been a pleasure to meet and work with you sir."

"Pleasure was all mine Jerry. You get over our way stop in, anytime."

CHAPTER 40

▼

We took the prisoners to the local sheriff's office and locked them up. A local doctor was called to come take care of the wounded man. He came into the sheriff's office after treating the man.

"Sheriff, the man needs to have surgery. He's probably going to loose the arm, his shoulder is a mess."

"Where do you want him doc? I'll have to send a deputy along with him."

"Get them over to my clinic as soon as possible otherwise he just might not make it."

I finished filling out my report and was just getting ready to leave when Officer Walkingstick came into the office wearing his uniform.

"Mr. Howard, where do you want me to put these boys?"

"What boys officer?"

"The truckers and the pump station operator."

"You've got them all?"

"Yes sir, Mr. Thompson and his boys came to help. As soon as our lookout out at the pump station heard they were coming over here he told Mr. Thompson and they just helped me gather the boys up."

"Bring them in officer, we'll see what they have to say. Even though they are small fish they may have some information we can use."

Hank and his boys brought the drivers into the office. They were indeed a sick looking bunch."

"Listen up! We've got your bosses locked up and they are going to jail. Now whether or not you boys go with them is going to depend upon what you have to tell us."

"You mean if we tell you what we know we may not go to jail?"

"That's right, but if you choose not to talk the Sheriff here has a bed ready for you."

One man stepped forward.

"Sir, I've got a wife and four kids. I took the job to help feed them, now what do you want to know."

Two hours later we had as Tom put it, everything we needed to know.

"Alright, here's how it's going to work. You drivers can go, but we're going to keep an eye on you all. If I have to come back over here again, you're going to go to jail, understood?"

"Yes sir!" The men said in unison.

"Now get out of here."

The pump station operator was going to be locked up and held until the trial. I'd let the judge decide what was going to happen to him.

I told the Sheriff I'd have the tribal officers come over and pick the prisoners up as soon as possible.

Hank and his boys led us all back out to his place where we finally got some rest after filling the women in on what had happened.

After a great breakfast the next morning we pulled out for home, a tired but happy bunch.

"James."

"Yes Mary."

"Uncle Thumb would have been proud of you."

"I hope so, right now though I just want to get home and get some rest."

CHAPTER 41

▼

Three days later I drove down to Sam's place. Ole Blue who was in the front yard announced my arrival.

"It's alright Blue, it's just family."

"Morning Sam looks like Blue's right at home here."

"Seems to like it fine James. I think Lesa's even taken up with him."

"That's great. Sam I need a favor."

"You want me to go along with you and your grandsons on a deer hunt."

"Well yes I do, I can handle one but three young ones with rifles are bit much."

"You're right there, I've already got my things ready but you know we do need a couple of things."

"What do we need Sam?"

"James we're going to need a couple of tents, in case it should rain."

"Sam you may be right, I guess that new store in town would have a tent."

"We can go see James. Let me tell Lesa, she may need something from town."

While Sam was gone I rubbed Blue's ears while I waited for Sam. He seemed to enjoy it.

Sam came out of his house ready to go. Lesa came to the door and waved as we drove off.

We drove into town and found that getting a tent would not be a problem. It seemed that since the oil boom had started they were in demand.

I bought two and decided I'd get six canvas cots to go with them. Tom and Bill came out of the bank and came over to where Sam and I were loading our purchases into my automobile.

"Planning on a camping trip James?"

"You bet, we're taking the grandsons deer hunting."

"All three of them?"

"Looks that way. Ever since Joe and I went last year it seems they all want to go this year."

"You'll have a great time."

"Oh yes, I'm going to ask Harold to go along and act as guide for one of them. It will make a good excuse for us to have a good visit."

"Sounds like a lot of fun. I guess we'll go the following week."

"How's everything going with the tribe?"

"We've still got some problems but it's mostly with the smaller companies. What's really troubling us is the way people are being murdered, or just plain disappear."

"The law officers are running night and day trying to solve some of the cases. They've caught a few but it seems there's always someone trying to steal something from the tribal members."

"I know, it seems as though we've collected the scum of the earth here. There's shootings and stabbings every night of the week. Add to that the alcohol that is being smuggled in and you've got a disaster on your hands."

"I know, one of the tribal members shot his wife the other night, then shot himself. They left five kids for their families to raise."

"James, I don't know what else we can do. We can't stop the female members or the male members from marrying outside the tribe."

"I know what you mean, and I for one can't say a thing."

Suddenly an automobile came sliding around the corner its horn blaring.

"Fire! We've got a well on fire and we need help!"

CHAPTER 42

▼

"**C**ome with me."

Sam and I jumped into Tom's automobile. It seemed as though everyone in town rushed out of town to help with the well fire. The only problem was that when Tom's car toped a low rise outside of town I asked him to stop.

"James, what's the matter?"

"Do you see any smoke?"

"No but."

"That's what I mean, I think someone wanted us out of town."

"The bank, Oh God!"

"Turn this thing around Tom!"

Tom turned the automobile around and headed back towards town driving across the tall grass because the road was filled with cars going the other direction. When the road cleared Tom steered the automobile back onto the road.

"James, I'm going to drive up behind the office. Bill, Sammye and Matt are there so maybe we'll be able to get inside without being seen."

Tom took us across several vacant lots and between homes until we finally stopped behind his office.

Sammye had seen us drive up and opened the door. Tom and I rushed into the office. Matt came out of his office.

"What's up dad?"

"Maybe nothing Matt but I think we may be fixing to have a bank robbery."

"If that's what you all think then let's get ready."

Matt walked back into his office and in a moment returned."

He handed me a box of shells and then handed me his brand new Sharps. Exactly like my own.

"Where in the world?"

I quickly loaded the rifle and put extra shells in my coat pocket.

Tom was looking across the street at the bank, everything looked normal.

"James, you think we may have made a mistake?"

"We could have Tom."

"Sammye, would you walk over to the bank and tell our banker friend what we are thinking."

"I'll go right now."

Sam as she liked to be called, picked up her purse and walked across the street. We watched as she entered the bank.

"Dad, Uncle Sam and I will go to out the back door and then cross the street. If you're right they may try to use the back door."

"Good thinking Matt."

"Matt, if you've got another rifle I'll go with you two. I don't care about hunting but I'm a damn good shot. Besides, I've got money in that bank myself.

Tom handed Bill a rifle with some shells and the three men went out the back door.

A few minutes later I saw Sammye came out of the bank just as a new shiny black automobile pulled up in front of the bank. Three men were in the automobile when it pulled to a stop. The man in the passenger side got out and started up the steps to the bank where he stopped. The man began visiting with Sammye, a moment later Sammye pointed to the law office and to two other locations. The man nodded his head and then spoke to the two men in the automobile. There seemed to be some heated talk but finally the man shook Sammye's hand and walked back to the automobile. We watched as the automobile drove slowly down the street and out of town.

Sammye came back across the street, a large smile on her face.

"Alright Sammye, what was that?"

"That gentlemen was a former client of a lawyer I worked for in Tulsa. His name is Arlis Flood."

"Arlis Flood, I thought he was in prison!"

"He just got out a week or so ago. He was told the bank here was loaded and ready to be picked. I convinced him it was a bad idea."

"How Sammye?

"I told him they were covered by riflemen at four different locations. What got his attention was when I told him you had him in your sights James. First thing he asked was what rifle you had. When I said your Sharps, he told the men in the car to relax. It just wasn't a good day to do any banking business."

"I told them to drive carefully and they did."

"Well dad, I guess I can have my Sharps back then."

"I reckon you can son, it seems I won't be needing it today."

Sammye later told us the story. The lawyer she worked for had defended Arlis in his last court case. At the time she had told him he needed to get into a new line of work, he had laughed and agreed with her.

People began to drift back into town and didn't think it had been a very funny joke someone had played on them. We agreed with them and never said anything about our near miss of a bank robbery.

Our banker friend however found no humor in the fouled attempt at all. He hired a bank guard for banking hours and another as a night watchman.

Matt wiped the Sharps down with a lightly oiled rag like he'd seen me do so many times when he was growing up.

"He handles that rifle just like you James."

"Dad, the school is coming along nicely."

"What does the council have in mind to do when it's finished?"

"Truthfully son I have no idea."

"A new courthouse would be nice."

"I hadn't thought about it son but it would be. The tribal police and the local town Marshal could all have an office there. I'll talk to some members of the council and get their input. It could go well with the new hotel that's going up on the triangle corner."

"It is going to be something isn't it?"

"Yes it is, can't say I ever saw one quite like it. Folks from down Tulsa way have come up to check it out. We're making headway with our little town."

"You got the tents for the big hunt?"

"Sure did, I even got six canvas cots so we won't have to sleep on the ground. It seems to have gotten a lot harder these last few yours."

"Well dad, if they would have had them years ago you couldn't have afforded them anyway."

"You know Matt, you're right. But by golly I can afford one now!"

We were laughing when Bill and Sammye walked into the office.

Sam, who had been setting quietly, began to laugh.

"What's so funny Sam?"

"James, if it's not Mary it's you."

"What do you mean?"

"We needed a top legal mind here to help the tribe so you found Bill here, problem was ole Bill here was a widower and just might not stay."

"Sam you've lost me."

"Why it's plumb simple James, you just ran down to Tulsa and rounded him up a new wife!"

"Sam I did no such thing!"

Everyone began to laugh.

CHAPTER 43

▼

$\mathbf{L}$ater, Sam and I headed for home. Driving down the dusty road Sam and I had a chance to visit and plan the up coming deer hunt.

"You know James, we go up to the same area every year."

"That's true Sam, but the reason we go there is it's some of the best deer area."

"I know that James but I was thinking maybe we should build a hunting cabin."

"Sam, I'd never thought about it before, you think we've got time to build one?"

"Don't see why not, we can use the oil field roads to go most of the way. We can have the lumber yard people deliver it to where the road quits and haul it on the wagon the rest of the way."

"Well at least we won't have to cut the trees, split the shingles and notch the logs."

"We could if we had to James."

"We could Sam but I'm afraid it would take us a little longer."

We were both laughing when Blue announced our arrival at Sam's place. Lesa came out to see what was so funny.

"We're entering our second childhood Lesa."

"I've known that for a while but what's going on, folks were driving all over the place this afternoon."

"Sam can tell you all about it Lesa, I got to get home."

As I drove up to the house Mary stood on the porch waiting on me.

"James, what's going on? People have been driving all over the place."

I sat down on the porch swing and told her what all had happened.

"You're telling me Sammye stood there in front of the bank and talked them out of robbing the bank."

"She sure did, she knew the man in charge and more or less told him this was one job he'd not walk away from. Mary she was cool as could be during the whole thing."

CHAPTER 44

▼

$\mathbf{I}$ told her about Sam and my idea to build a hunting cabin.

"I've wondered why you haven't done it before. Everyone goes hunting at Thanksgiving and personally dear I think it's a grand idea. When are you going to start?"

"Figure I'll order the lumber tomorrow. I need to get a hold of Harold and see if he will be able to help."

"Why don't we drive up to their place in the morning and see if he wants to help. I can invite Flower to come down and stay with me."

"Sounds good Mary we'll leave right after breakfast."

We had been in bed a couple of hours when we heard and felt a blast. I ran to the front door and could see the fire blazing high into the night sky.

"Oh my God James, what has happened?"

"I'm not sure Mary but I'll get my clothes on and go find out."

I quickly got dressed and drove as fast as I dared on the rough roads towards the well site. A couple of other automobiles were already parked a couple of hundred yards from the now flaming well.

I saw a group of men standing off to one side watching a couple of men try to help a man laying on the ground.

I asked one of the men what had happened.

"Mr. Howard, the man was a fool, he tried to shoot the well tonight instead of waiting until daylight. He was in a hurry and let one of the cans of nitro slip and fall."

"Good Lord, it's a wonder he wasn't blown to pieces."

"He's pretty well broken up. He's burned and I think one of his arms is broke."

"Boy, it looks like he blew the crown pulley off the rig."

"Oh yes, it's laying over there."

He pointed about fifty yard away. The heavy iron pulley, which would weight close to two hundred and fifty pounds, was a good hundred yards from the well.

"How are they going to put the fire out?"

"They've already sent for a crew from Tulsa who specialize in putting these kinds of fires out. They'll be here sometime tomorrow morning if they don't have another one going down south."

"Well in that case, I reckon I'll go back home."

"Not much anyone can do Mr. Howard except watch and make sure there's no grass fire. They boys on the crew have a pump and hose to spray water if a fire should get started."

"I'll see you boys later."

I drove back to the house amazed that anyone had survived the explosion. I told Mary what had happened when I got back to the house.

We ate breakfast the next morning and pulled out for Harold and Flower's house shortly after dawn. I had hated the automobiles when they had first come into our little town but had to admit they made traveling a lot easier. We drove into Harold and Flower's place a short time later.

"Hey you all, what are you all doing up this way?"

"Come to see if you had any coffee."

"Well light and set, I think we may have a cup or two left."

Flower and Mary hugged and disappeared into the house.

"James, what sort of fire did you all have down your way last night?"

I told him about the explosion down at the well.

"How many of these things have happened?"

"Three or four Harold, I don't even try and keep count."

"They are moving up this way. They were staking out well locations yesterday. You know they have eighteen wells on Thumbs old place."

"I knew there were a bunch, but I didn't know how many."

"Hey, what brought you up here today?"

"Well if you're not busy I thought you might want to help Sam and I build a hunting cabin down on my place."

"When you plan on starting?"

"Tomorrow, if I can get the lumber delivered."

"Sounds good to me, it means we'll have a good, dry and warm place to sleep. I'll be down around noon."

"Oh there's another thing Harold, I need your help with the my grandkids this deer season."

"Figured you would. Been sort of planning on it, Sam's going along isn't he?"

"He is if he can get away from Blue."

"Blue, who is Blue?"

"His new Blue-tick hound I bought him."

"You bought him a Blue-tick hound, now I want to hear the rest of the story."

"Where's that coffee, I'm getting mighty dry."

"James Howard, I've got your coffee so hush. Now tell us about the hound."

I told Harold and Flower about how Mary Margaret had been taken and how we'd got her back.

"I didn't know anything about it. We've been sorting steers and haven't even seen anyone. Guess we'd better start getting down your way more."

"James, I'll be down tomorrow morning. I'll bring my hammer and saw."

"Bring your bedroll, I'm sure we won't be done in a days time."

"Didn't figure we would, figured we would take the best part of a week."

"Partner, we don't have anything but time."

"By darn you're right"

"Nice isn't it, we'll have a week to visit."

"You men can visit all you want, Flower, Lesa and I are going to go down to Tulsa and do some shopping; sort of a girls day out."

"Mary you all do whatever you want; it's been a while since you all got together."

"You men better figure on taking Ole Blue along with you."

Later that evening we returned home. After a light supper we watched the kids lights go out from our porch swing.

Sam, Lesa, Pa and Carla's lights had gone off earlier.

"Nice isn't it James, to know everyone's warm, comfortable and nearby."

"Makes a man glad to be alive Mary, it's really all that matters."

"I know cowboy but if you're going to get things done tomorrow we'd better get to bed ourselves."

CHAPTER 45

▼

The next morning after an early breakfast I headed to town. I went to the local lumberyard and ordered lumber with the help of one of the men who worked there.

He assured me he'd have the lumber delivered as close to the cabin site as possible. He knew all the oil field roads out that way.

Before I left I stopped by the boy's law office; things were in a whirl, everyone was busy.

"James, come in and set. What brought you in town?"

"Plans Tom, I've been busy."

"What's going on?"

"We're getting ready to build a hunting cabin."

"Really, you going to build it west of Doves old place?"

"Figured we would, that way you boys can use it when the grandkids and I are through with it."

"That sounds great, the grounds getting a little bit hard."

"I know what you mean Tom, Mary suggested it so the grandkids wouldn't have to sleep out. I really think she was thinking of me."

"That might be James, but she'll never admit it."

"Say James, can I come along, I don't hunt but I'd enjoy watching the kids?"

"Bill you're welcome anytime, it's not going to be anything fancy. Just a place to stay warm and dry."

"That suits me to a tee James, besides I'm a pretty good cook."

"Now that really sounds good Bill, we'll look for you on opening day."

I stopped by Sam's place on the way home and told him we'd start the next day. He was more than ready. It seemed Mary have been down earlier and told Lesa about her and Flower's plans. Lesa was ready to go. Sam told me he'd be at the house shortly after daylight with Ole Blue.

The next morning Sam arrived just after daylight. We had coffee and then went out and hitched up the now seldom used team to the large wagon.

We loaded the food Mary had fixed for us and waved to her as we pulled out. The team was fresh and stepped right out. We arrived at the sight a short time later and went to work on the foundation. A nearby spring would supply all the water we needed.

"James, you think we'd better go check on the lumber?"

"Probably Sam, the fellow at the lumber yard promised me he'd be out early."

We drove the team and wagon down to where the lumber was to be delivered and arrived just as the lumber truck was pulling up.

With the help of the two men from the lumberyard we quickly loaded the wagon and headed back to the cabin site.

When the team topped the last rise in the ground we were surprised to see a bunch of folks waiting on us.

Harold, his youngest son and two of the younger Swinsons stood waiting on us. After handshakes all around we went to work.

Although they were teenagers, the two Swinson boys took over the construction job. They kept Harold, Sam and I busy carrying lumber and nails. They told me their grandfather had sent them to help.

By lunchtime the floor of the cabin was beginning to take shape and by the late afternoon we had the bare walls standing.

We were all tired but felt good. Sam had built a fire and had prepared a thick stew, which along the thick slices of bread was delicious.

We quickly hung tarps over the existing framework from our previous hunting trips and had shelter for the night.

The younger Swinsons asked a lot of questions about the time when we had first arrived. Sam told them about our first winter then Harold told them about the rustlers and thieves we'd had to deal with.

"Mr. Howard, is it true you could hit a target at a mile with your Sharps?"

"I don't know, I never tried a shot that far."

"Really, we heard you'd made several that far."

"Harold had to tell the story of how on the trail up I had scared some Comanches off simply by pointing my Sharps at them."

Sam verified Harold's story and told them how hard they had laughed afterwards.

We talked about the drive, and all the things we'd encountered on the way up to the tall grass. The young Swinsons had laughed and told us what they had heard, then it was out turn to laugh.

After Harold had told the tree cattle story we all turned in for the night. All in all it had been an enjoyable evening.

The next morning we ate a quick breakfast and began installing the rafters. Bill and Tom showed up in work clothes along with their hammers. With their help we were now making good progress. Bill was a pretty good carpenter and began installing the windows. By sundown we had almost all the roof on our new cabin.

Bill sat sipping on a cup of coffee with a smile on his face.

"Feeling good Bill?"

"You bet James, I'm tired but I feel great. Been a while since I built anything."

"You've built things before?"

"Sure have, my father and grandfather were both carpenters. I grew up building homes and such."

"Then how in the world did you become a lawyer?"

"I got tired of hitting my thumb."

We all laughed at his joke but found out later it was partially true. He'd become interested in the law practice while in high school and had went to work for a lawyer during the summer after his last year of high school.

Bill told us how he'd worked his way through college doing various jobs.

"How did you go to work for the oil company?"

"I went to work for a small firm. A short time later a client came in and wanted to sue them. I listened to his story and thought he had a good case. The firm I worked for didn't think we could win and said no. So I quit, took the case and ended up winning it a couple of months later. They hired me the following week."

"They didn't like getting beat."

"That's right, five years later I became a department head and a few years later became the company's lead attorney."

"Well we're sure glad you came here."

"That's for sure James, Will and I would still be tied up in knots without Bill's help."

"Say fellows, I've only done what I've wanted too. Besides thanks to you James, I've found my Sammye"

"Well there you go James, you've added another two people to the family list."

"Sam, two more isn't going to make any difference."

"Brother-in-law, that is a fact."

Everyone was laughing at my expense but it made no difference, friends were supposed to be enjoyed.

The next afternoon we finished the cabin.

"Wouldn't you have loved to have had this the first winter up here Harold?"

"I sure would, I like to have froze in my tent. Probably would have if Thumb hadn't shown me how to build a dugout."

"I forgot about that, you did make the first winter in a dugout."

"Sure did, was real cozy too. I wouldn't say it was anything to look at but it was easy to heat and that's all that mattered at the time."

I offered to pay the two young Swenson boys but they refused.

"No way Mr. Howard, dad sent us out here and said if we took a nickel from you he'd tan our hides."

Everyone was proud of our hunting cabin. The stove would allow us to heat and cook our meals. The canvas cots I had purchased would make getting a good nights rest easy after a hard day of hunting.

CHAPTER 46

▼

With the cabin done all I needed to do now was make a list for food. I sat down with my morning coffee and began to make the list.

Mary came out and set down next to me.

"Getting ready dear?"

"Trying to Mary, I just want the kids to have a good time."

"James, don't worry. They'll have a wonderful time. Truthfully I think Sam, Harold and you will have just as much fun."

"You're probably right, we really don't get together that much."

"Well at least you'll have something to look forward to each year now."

"That's true and we'll have a dry bed to sleep in too."

"James, there's a car coming this way. It looks like a tribal police car."

The car drove up to the house and the Captain of the tribal police got out.

"Good morning Captain. How about a cup?"

"I'd appreciate that Mrs. Howard."

"You men visit, I'll get your coffee."

"Captain what can I do for you?"

"Just thought you'd like to know what's happening with the oil thieves."

"Something new going on?"

"Oh yes, It seems Mr. Wise is trying to make a deal."

"A deal?"

"He doesn't want to go to jail for twenty years. He hopes to get a shorter sentence. He's told my deputy over there about an unsolved murder that happened over here several years ago."

"I'm sure Tucker was involved."

"Yes sir, Wise say's he will testify."

"That's great, it means we'll finally be rid of Mr. Tucker."

"Looks that way."

"Captain, officer Walkingstick did a good job."

"I know, he's now a Sergeant. I'm putting him in charge of the office over there. I'm sending four of the new recruits over there. We've got a handle on things now and we want to keep things that way. I came out here to thank you for all your help in the matter."

"Thank you Captain, but it's my responsibility too. As a member of the council I'm supposed to help."

"Yes sir I know but I just wanted to say thanks anyway."

"You're more than welcome Captain, feel free to call on me anytime."

Mary brought coffee out to us. We spent the next twenty minutes or so visiting. When the captain left I went back to work on my food list for the hunt.

Matt came up on his way to work.

"Sleep well dad?"

"You bet son. You doing alright?"

"I'm fine dad, I was just wondering if you'd heard anything about the man I shot?"

"He's going to live son, the doctor did have to remove his arm however."

"I didn't want to shoot him but when I saw what he and his friend were going to do I didn't have a choice."

"I know that Matt, but he left you no choice. You could have killed him."

"I know, at the last minute I shifted my aim to his shoulder."

"You did well son."

"Well I'd better get to work, I'm sure Tom and I will be swamped with work for a few days."

He gave Mary a kiss than went out to his car and drove slowly down the hill.

"There goes a man I'm proud to say is my son."

"I know James, I'm proud of him too. Deb and Tee came up while you all were away. We had a real hen session as you call them. I'm very proud of our sons, their wives and our grandchildren."

When I finished my list Mary and I drove into town where some how my list suddenly grew when Mary started doing my shopping. It was certain that everyone in camp was going to eat well.

When we returned home it seemed I carried groceries forever. I'd have to take the team and wagon to get the stuff up to the cabin.

Things worked out fine however; Sam, Lesa and Ole Blue all showed up an hour or so later.

While the women visited, Sam and I hooked up the team and wagon.

"You two might take along a shotgun, if you happen to see any prairie chickens. Three of four of those would make a nice dinner tonight."

"Sam, help yourself to a shotgun, I can already taste those chickens."

"You better take one too James, I'd like to take a couple home."

We each took a shotgun and drove the team towards the hunting cabin. Ole Blue lay in the back of the wagon. He seemed to enjoy the outing. We were visiting when Sam saw the chickens.

"Stop James, there's a flock of chickens scratching under those plum bushes."

I stopped the wagon; we quickly got our shotguns and loaded them. We walked towards the plum bushes intent on the birds. That's when Old Blue did his thing.

He raced past Sam just as a huge rattlesnake who had been sunning himself on a big rock struck at Sam's leg.

Ole Blue caught that rattler just behind its head and began shaking it. He snapped the snake's spine then gently laid it down at Sam's feet.

"Sam, that's the best dog I ever bought."

"James, he sure is something isn't he?"

We both patted Old Blue and went back to the wagon. The chickens had flushed when the rattler and Old Blue had got together. Some how it didn't seem to matter.

We unloaded the wagon then took another route back towards the house. We found several flocks of chickens and ended up with eight. Sam would have plenty to take home.

Lesa and Mary fixed us a fabulous meal that evening. We had told them about Ole Blue's rescue of Sam from the rattler. The women made sure Blue got some special table scraps that night. Mary even asked Sam for a pup if he ever raised any.

Thanksgiving and deer season were quickly approaching. It looked as though the whole family would be home for the holidays along with some old friends.

As usual we'd have the dinner at Will and Tee's place. The women had begun planning the meal a few days ago. It was always fun to watch the planning. The meal was always great but the women always had fun getting together.

Everything was ready for the grandkids to show up. Joe, J.R. and Seth had been in contact with each other for a couple of weeks. Joe living down in Tulsa was inconvenient for the boys but they had managed.

The weekend before Thanksgiving Joe and Carrie came up on the train. Carrie was going to stay with Becca and Joe was going to stay with Mary and I. He had brought his rifle and ammunition along. He asked if he could sight the rifle in so we did exactly that.

I was fun having him around, he had asked Mary if he could come up and spend a week or so this coming summer.

Joe was looking at the guns in the gun cabinet.

"Grandpa, is this your Sharps?

"Sure is Joe."

"May I take it out and look at it please?"

"Sure, go ahead Joe."

He took the rifle out and was careful to see if it was unloaded. He was shocked to find a shell in the chamber.

"Grandpa, it was loaded."

"Sure was Joe, if I need it I don't want to have to search for shells."

"But grandpa everyone says it's not safe to keep a gun loaded around a home."

"Why not Joe? Your grandpa and I know they are loaded, all of them."

"Grandma, you mean all of them are loaded?"

"Yes dear they are."

"Did you all keep them loaded when mother and my uncles were here?"

"Yes we did, we explained to them that they were loaded and that they would get hurt if they touched them."

"My mom would flip if she found my rifle loaded at home."

"I'm sure she would Joe but you live in a town and you have friends over who have never been around a gun before and they are curious. They might pick it up and pull the trigger. Up here everyone knows about guns and how to use them, therefore no one picks up a gun thinking it's unloaded."

"I can see how living up here is a lot different than living down in Tulsa."

"It's different yes, but we still treat guns with respect just like you did when you took the Sharps out of the cabinet and checked to see if it was loaded. By the way Joe, don't ask to shoot it. It kicks like a mule. Maybe in a couple of years you'll be big enough but be patient."

"Grandma, have you ever fired it?"

"Once Joe, but once was enough."

"Mother says it kicks something awful."

"She should know, she tried it once."

I had to chuckle, Matt had told me about Beth trying the Sharps and how it had kicked her right onto the seat of her pants.

"Grandpa, are you going to hunt?"

"I may Joe, your grandma and I like a venison steak every now and then."

"I'd like to get another buck this year grandpa but it's not that important. I'd like J.R. and Seth to get one. If you don't mind lets let them hunt the best places. We can hunt anywhere."

"That's awfully nice of you Joe, makes me proud to have you as my grandson."

"Me too, now would you two hunters care for a cup of hot chocolate?"

"You bet grandma, your going to add those good marshmallows?"

"Is there another way to fix hot chocolate?"

"No ma'am, No way!"

CHAPTER 47

▼

Finally the opening day of deer season came. Sam and Harold were ready to go. Our three grandsons had spent the night in the bunk-house room in the barn. I knew we'd have to wake them up but I didn't care, of course they wouldn't either.

We were all surprised when the three of them came into the kitchen smiling.

"We smelled grandma's pancakes."

"So much for having to wake them."

We were all laughing when we headed out the door.

We hitched up the team and after loading the wagon pulled out. Our adventure was starting. The kids were laughing and having a wonderful time. When we arrived at the cabin everyone helped unload the wagon and picked out a cot.

Sam got a fire started in the fireplace while Harold and the boys carried in wood for the night. I put the team in the small lot we had made for them. Water from the spring ran through the lot and the grass was knee deep. They went to grazing as soon as I turned them loose.

I could smell the ham Sam had brought along. Harold and J.R. were peeling potatoes while Seth and Joe peeled onions. A short time later the hunting cabin began to smell wonderful.

I filled the lamps and sat them around the room. After supper we formed a plan. Both Sam and Harold were familiar with the area. I told Harold who was guiding J.R. to pick the area he wanted to hunt. He said he and J.R. would hunt the west side. He'd seen a couple of nice bucks there last year.

Sam said he and Seth would go north.

"Well Joe, I guess we'll go east."

"Sounds good to me grandpa I'm ready to go but after the meal Uncle Sam fixed tonight I'm ready for bed."

"You boys stayed up a little late last night?"

"Yes we did, but grandpa we had such a good time."

"That's what it's all about Joe, having a good time with family and friends. Now if you boys are tired go turn it. I'll turn the light out when you're in bed."

The boys hit their cots and I turned out the two lamps on their side of the room.

Sam, Harold and I went out on the porch and sat down. It was quiet and peaceful the half-moon reflected off the tall grass was almost magical to see.

"James, we couldn't have even dreamed of a place or time like this when we left Texas."

"No joke, Lord only knows I never dreamed of anything like this."

"James, the place we left down in Texas was burnt up. This country has been good to us that's for sure. All of us."

"Harold, I remember when you first met Flower, and when Sam met Lesa. Now we all got nice homes, good families and a comfortable living. But it's things like this that make it all worth while."

"You bet, I wish I had my grandson down here to enjoy a weekend like this. But he's back east and will probably never know what he's missing."

"I know what you mean Sam it's hard for folks back there to realize what we've got, and to be truthful I don't care to share it with them."

"Boys I reckon we better get in bed, these big game hunters will be up early."

We went to bed and a short time later I heard Harold snoring lightly.

The next morning after a quick breakfast we all took off looking for the elusive white tail deer.

Joe and I followed a faint trail just below the hilltop. It was turning pink on the eastern horizon. We were heading towards a point where we could look down into a long shallow draw filled with pecan trees. A small stream ran through the draw. We arrived just as the sun began to come up over the horizon. We found a large log to sit on and began to watch the bottom.

Joe touched my leg a few moments later and with a slight move of his head indicated he saw deer. I watched for movement then saw four large doe coming along a faint trail on our side of the draw.

We watched as they passed below us and followed the trail east.

I touched Joe's leg; I'd spotted a nice buck following along behind the does. He traveled with his nose close to the ground unaware of our presence. He was a nice six point and would be good eating.

We both were startled by the shot; it came from the north. Seth had either got his deer or missed, but I doubted he had missed; Seth was a real fine shot.

Our deer on the other hand had jumped off the trail and was hidden from us by the thick brush. We were both searching for him with our eyes when we head the second shot off to the west. J.R. had tried his hand.

That's when we heard another deer coming over the hill and behind us. He was a beautiful eight point. When he stopped to look back over the hill Joe shot and dropped him in his tracks.

"Fine shot Joe, lets wait a couple of minutes and see if he stays down."

"Gosh grandpa, he was a beautiful thing wasn't he?"

"He sure was, he didn't have the points of the one you got last year but he's wide and has really long tines."

"You think Mr. Boggs will mount him for me?"

"I'm sure he will Joe, we'll go talk to him after we get home. Right now we've got a deer to clean Mr. deer hunter."

I was proud of Joe, he remembered how to dress the deer. While he was working I cut two green sticks and when he was finished we used the sticks to prop the deer open so it would cool out quickly.

When we finished we hung a white flag on a nearby bush and headed back to camp.

Sam was removing a buck from one of the work mares. It was a beautiful ten point, Seth stood nearby and was beaming.

"Dog gone Seth, that's one fine deer."

"Thanks grandpa. Joe did you get one?"

"Sure did, he's not a ten point but he's a nice buck."

"Sam, I take it that Harold has the other mare."

"She was gone when we got here James, so I guess he took her."

"That's great, that means J.R. has got his buck too. It's turning out to be a nice day."

"Sure is James, lets hang this deer and we'll go get Joe's"

We hung the deer from a large oak tree and led the mare over to where Joe's buck lay.

"Joe, he's got a wide rack. He's really something."

"Thanks Seth, I was actually going to shoot a smaller one when this one showed up."

We loaded the deer on the mare, talked and laughed all the way back to the cabin. We were all surprised Harold was still not back. We hung Joe's deer in the tree and had decided we'd go look for Howard and J.R. That's when we saw them come over the top of the hill.

"Good lord James, it looks like J.R. nailed the twin brother to the deer Joe got last year."

The buck was hanging on both sides of the mare had a rack that did look similar to the one Joe had gotten last year.

J.R. and Harold were beaming.

"Harold didn't you tell him deer that size are hard to load?"

"James, I did, but he's just like his grandpa. Go for the best."

Everyone laughed and admired the huge buck. After counting twice, to be sure we came up with sixteen points.

We got the buck hung up in the tree.

"Boys, what do you want to do now, no one expects us home until tomorrow evening?"

J.R. never to be outdone spoke up.

"Have one of Uncle Sam's ham sandwiches, a cup of chocolate and then get a nap."

Everyone laughed but Sam began slicing ham, while I sliced thick slices of bread. Harold had brought some of the last tomatoes he and Flower had managed to save from the first frost. He began slicing them and placed them on the bread. We soon had more than enough sandwiches. We heated milk from our underground cooler and soon had hot chocolate with marshmallows floating on top.

I had forgotten how much food a young boy could eat. Especially when he was out in the open air and having a great time.

All of the boys complimented their Uncle Sam on his ham. He thanked them and for a surprise got out a sack of home made dough-nuts. They disappeared as Harold put it, in nothing flat.

A short time later the boys were all stretched out on their cots and sound asleep.

Sam, Harold and I sat out on the porch drinking the last of the hot chocolate and telling how each of the boys had got their buck."

Harold told how he and J.R. had went west and set up on the side of a hill over looking a well worn game trail. They had heard Seth's shot and began looking that way in case any deer appeared.

Harold saw a nice buck and directed J.R's attention to it. He watched as J.R. shot. The buck turned and ran off.

"I swear I thought he missed, but he was hollering and saying he'd got him. What had happened was I saw one deer, he'd seen another. When I followed him I couldn't believe what he shot. It took us a while to get him dressed and loaded on the mare."

Well Seth and I went north and set up on that little creek bottom. We hadn't been there but a few minutes when along comes this nice buck. Seth put that little rifle on him and dropped him. He was one tickled boy."

"My story is sort of like Harold's we saw one deer which went into the brush when we heard Seth shoot. We were watching the brush when the bigger buck ran up behind us. Joe dropped him clean."

"By golly it's been a good hunt. How about we have a checker game tonight. I brought two sets, we can have a tournament of sorts."

"That will keep the boys interested James, what about in the morning?"

"Sam, we'll just let them entertain themselves. They'll figure things out."

"Sounds good to me, right now I'm going to get myself a nap."

We all took a nap.

Later we all went for a walk and tried to teach the boys what deer sign to look for, such as rubs and scrapes. Before the afternoon was over they had learned their lesson quite well.

The checker tournament was a success. J.R. came out the winner but I could see it wasn't nearly over. Before the Thanksgiving holidays were over the three would play again, it was a sure bet.

When we arrived home the whole family was ready for the Thanksgiving holiday. Our friend from Colorado Mel Foster was in. He was staying with my folks. This would make the third Thanksgiving he'd spent with us. Everyone considered him family and seemed to enjoy the situation.

He was at the house with the folks when we returned with the grandsons, and made a big deal out of every buck. The boys had beamed.

"James, I'd like to talk to you three when you have time."

"Guess we've got time now Mel. Harold, Sam, get over here."

"What's up James?"

"Mel here wants to talk to us."

We sat down next to the wagon and listened to Mel's idea. He wanted us to come up to his place for the upcoming elk season. They have opened the park and there's every sort of human up there during the summer months.

"That's what you wanted wasn't it Mel?"

"Sure was, out little town is doing well. Folks are seeing things they can't believe. They'll be a bigger bunch next year that's for sure. Some of the local folks are taking tours up into the park and looking to grow their business."

"I'd like your boys and Tom to come up and go elk hunting with me before I get to damn old. Conners is coming up so it will be like ole home week."

"He's been up your way a couple of times hasn't he?

"Sure has, have you seen the sketches he's done of the geysers?" Sure have, he's about to finish the one you all call "Old Faithful". It's really something to see."

I know I saw it yesterday. That man is a wonder. We talked about his home back east. He laughed and said he could hardly remember it. Said since he moved here he had never been so contented."

"He loves the folks here and told me to be a member of your family was the greatest thing that ever happened to him."

"I'm glad he feels that way Mel, we really enjoy having him here. Well boys what do you say, reckon we ought to go elk hunting with Mel next fall?"

"Sounds good to me James, what about you Sam?"

"By golly I'd like to go. I've got a new rifle I'd like to try out."

We'd talk to the ladies later.

We had missed Sammye and Bill's wedding but they were doing fine. They would be out for the dinner.

Will, Matt, Tom, Mike and Bill were going up to the deer cabin. They'd be back Thanksgiving morning. Sammye or Sam as Mary called her was going to stay with us. Bill said she made a killer cherry pie and I for one wanted to see if it was true.

The boys loaded the wagon and pulled out for camp. Bill was going to be camp cook and enjoy taking their money at night in the poker games. The boys were looking forward to seeing the cabin and getting away for a day or so. I'd get to check on the cattle while Will was gone. I'd need something to do to keep out of the women's way.

Next morning I saddled Slick and took off to check the herd kept near the main headquarters. I thought about riding over and checking in with Boggs. I figured I could get a cup of coffee and catch up on the news over that way at the same time.

The herd looked great, the new calves were running and playing while their mothers either ate the tall cured grass or lay down chewing their cuds.

I rode over to Boggs place just as he rode in from his rounds.

"Mr. Howard, good to see you. Tie up your fancy horse and lets have a cup."

"That's why I came by Boggs, I figured you'd have some ole fashioned cowboy coffee."

"Now Mr. Howard I know that woman of yours fixes you coffee the same way you like it."

"She does for a fact Boggs but the younger folks don't seem to care for it the way we like it."

"Times change sir, they surely do. I've been intending to come talk to you."

"What do you need Boggs?"

"Well, I've sort of found me a woman. She lost her husband a few years back and we've sort of been talking about getting hitched."

"That's great Boggs, anything you need me to do?"

"No sir not really, but I'd like to add a room to the cabin here."

"I'll send the Swenson boys out next week and get them started. Better add two rooms Boggs you'll need the extra room."

"Sure appreciate it Mr. Howard."

"My pleasure Boggs, I'm thrilled you finally found someone."

"You know Mr. Howard so am I. I never thought about getting married again after I lost my wife and daughter those long years ago."

"It's time Boggs, a man needs a woman."

"That's what I figured out."

"You going to bring her to dinner Thursday?"

"That's what I wanted to ask."

"You bring her Boggs, she'll be more than welcome."

"Thank you Mr. Howard, we'll be there."

We had our coffee and later I started back towards the house. Slick was fresh and more than ready to go. When I got Slick put away and walked into the house I began to suffer. The women were baking and the house smelled wonderful.

"I guess you're hungry?"

"Well I could eat something."

"How about a sandwich and a cherry pie?"

"You mean a whole cherry pie?"

"Not a full sized one James, Sammye made a small one just for you."

"Bring it on, I'm more than ready."

Bill was right Sammye did make a killer pie.

I complemented Sammye on the pie then went in and sat down in my easy chair. I was thinking a nap would be nice. It was a nice thought.

CHAPTER 48

▼

The next day I again checked the cattle and as I finished my circle I rode past the race barn just as Deb was working a two year old. I knew the colt was a late foal that had been to small to sell at the yearling sale they went to every year.

The colt looked really good to me. He seemed to float across the ground with an effortless stride. I could see that Deb had a good hold on the colt and was not about to let him get away and run full out.

After two full rounds around the track she began to pull the colt up. I watched as she turned him around and brought him back over to the track opening where I sat.

"Looks awful good Deb."

Deb turned the colt over to one of their stable boys and then walked over to where I sat on Slick.

"Pa, he's as good as he looks."

"Really?"

"Pa, I worked the Princess and I'm convinced this colt is as good or maybe better."

"My Lord Deb, you know what you're saying?"

"Yes Pa I do, but we've not had another like her since we've started this operation."

"Does Will know?"

"We've talked about him, but you know Will. Until he sees the time on the watch he's not going to get too excited."

Willie came out of the barn smiling.

"He's fine Deb, legs as cool as can be. Just the way we want them."

"Morning Mr. Howard."

"Morning Willie."

"Deb, where's your dad?"

"He's home, one of the weanlings kicked him in the knee yesterday. It was swelled up something awful, doc told him to rest it for a couple of days."

"I'll have to drop over and see how he's doing."

"He'd appreciate that."

"Willie, what's your opinion of this youngster?"

"Mr. Howard, he's a fine colt, real fine. In fact he may be in the class of the Princess."

"Well now, that's twice I've heard that statement in less than five minutes. Now I'm interested. What are your plans for him?"

"Dad and Matt are talking about him, but so far they haven't decided what to do. If he hadn't been such a late colt he'd have brought a good price at the sale."

"Well, if he were mine, I'd run him. You all have built a good reputation for your horses, looks to me as if you'd only help yourselves if you show up with a real fine horse."

"That's what I think but Matt and Dad are thinking maybe we should sell."

"Why, you all are making a fine profit each year. Your strings of horses have always done well so I don't understand."

"Pa you'll have to talk to Matt."

"I'm going to do that, just as soon as I talk to your dad and my son gets back from hunting."

I gave Deb a hug and told Willie we expected him and the boys for dinner.

"Looking forward to it Mr. Howard."

I kicked Slick into a long lope and headed for Mack and Birds place just down the road.

Doe was shaking dust from a small rug when I rode up."

"Good morning Doe."

"Good morning, tie your horse up and come in. Maybe you can help me settle my man down he's just been a bear this morning."

"We'll see what we can do Doe."

"I'll get you some coffee."

Mack was setting in a chair with his leg propped up on a stool.

"Morning James, what brings you over here this way?"

"Heard you were laid up and figured I'd check on you. How's the knee?"

"Doc says it's just a deep bruise but it hurts like thunder. It was my own fault, the colt that kicked me was actually kicking at another colt in the herd."

"Well those things happen if you're going to work around young horses."

"I know, but I still don't like it."

"That's understandable Mack but I need to talk to you about the young colt."

"I figured you'd be around sooner or later. Matt said if you saw the colt work you'd be down off the hill in a flash."

"Well he was right, I'm here and I'd like to know why you and Matt are setting back on this horse?"

"It's a little complicated James, but I'll try to explain."

"Every year we have our sale. Every year it gets bigger and better. We've developed a real good group of buyers which gets bigger every year."

"I know Mach, but what does the colt have to do with that?"

"Matt's afraid if we run the colt, some of the folks will think we held him out of the sale on purpose."

"Mack, I sell my Angus every year."

"Yes sir, I know that."

"Mack, I've never sold my best bull. I keep the best to keep improving my herd, no one expects me to sell my best. I'm sure none of your buyers expect you all to do that."

"Well Matt is worried, he's worked hard trying to make the stable pay."

"But he's done that Mack. Now's not the time to back up."

"James, there's not back up in that boy of yours. He just doesn't want to disappoint you."

"You're kidding aren't you Mack?"

"Not hardly, he looks up to you and doesn't want to fail."

"Oh my, I think I'd better get to town and have a talk with my son. Mack, how long will it take to have the colt ready to run?"

"Well first off he won't be ready to run for another ninety days or so. Then he should be turned out, or let rest for another thirty."

"Why Mack?"

"James, they don't write, or run two year old races until late August or early September. Now with as much talent and promise as this colt is showing we sure don't want him to get hurt or crippled."

"Mack, what would the colt have brought at the sale?"

"Maybe six or seven thousand, he's a late colt and a buyer would have had to wait on him to grow and mature."

"Fine, I'm going to town and buy the colt. As far as anyone is concerned he's been my colt all along. Now when you're up and around you take good care of him. I want to see him run this next summer late."

"James, you've just solved our problem. With you as owner no one will know the colt wasn't yours all along."

"Go to town and close the deal with Matt, don't worry about the colt."

"I told Doe good bye and headed to the house, Mary and I had to go to town. We had a horse to buy.

I unsaddled Slick and turned him out into the pasture. I headed to the house when it dawned on me. Matt was up in the deer camp and I'd just turned my horse loose.

I walked in the back door totally disgusted with myself.

"James, what is the matter?"

I told her about the colt and how I planned to buy him.

"So what's the problem?"

"I forgot Matt was up at the deer camp. I must be getting old."

"Not really dear, you just want to get things straightened out. Relax, the boys will be home this afternoon, you can talk to Matt then."

"James, your father is coming up the hill."

Sure enough Pa and Mel were pulling up in front of our house.

"They probably came up here because all you women are going to go down to Tee's."

That's right Sammye went down just before you came home. I've got to get down there myself."

I opened the door for Pa and Mel.

"Come on in, I'll get you a cup if you want one."

"None for me son, Mel and I have been up for a while and done nothing but sit and drink coffee."

"Carla needed to come up to Tee's so we figured you might could stand some company."

"Glad to have you, the boys should be back in an hour or so."

"They up at the new hunting lodge?"

"Yes, they left day before yesterday and are due back this afternoon."

"I saw you ride over to Mack's place this morning."

"Yes you did."

I told them about Mack's accident and the colt.

"Wait a minute son, how about Mel and me?"

"What do you mean Pa?"

"How about letting me and Mel in on the deal. Mel had a lot of fun out of the filly he bought and ran. She's in foal now and we've been talking about maybe buying a colt together."

"James, I've never felt more alive the I did when the filly was running. What I'm saying is, I miss it a bunch. So why don't we form a partnership and run this colt."

The partnership was formed; everyone agreed that we wanted Mack to do the training so all we had to do now was get a price from Matt.

"What's the colt's name?"

"I don't have any idea, never even thought to ask."

"Son, is that the boys with the wagon?"

It was the boys coming around the hill. From the looks of things they had a good hunt. I could see several sets of antlers sticking up above the wagon bed. They all seemed to be laughing as they pulled up."

We went out and looked at their deer. The grandsons came out of "their place" in the barn to check out what their fathers had managed to bag.

Mike it seemed had gotten the biggest buck, a pretty ten point. I could tell Joe was proud of his father.

After we got the deer hung up in the barn I called Matt aside.

"Son it seems you've got a horse that is giving you problems. Mel, your Grandpa and I are going to cure your problem. What's the price of the late colt?"

"Dad, I can't sell you all that colt."

"Why not, we've got money and you've got a problem. Now, price the colt!"

"Dad, I'll give him to you."

"No you won't, now price the colt!"

"Five thousand and five percent of what ever he wins."

I looked at pa and Mel, they shook their heads yes.

"Done, you just sold a horse."

"Dad, how did you know about the colt?"

"I watched Deb work him this morning. Now, what do we have to do to close the deal?"

"I'll let Deb take care of the paper work. You'll need a name for the colt, we haven't named him yet."

"Mel came up with a name "Three Ole Coots"."

"We all broke out laughing."

"Mel, how about we call him Three Dreams?"

Mel looked at Pa and smiled, it was settled. The colt had a name.

CHAPTER 49

▼

Thanksgiving was a blast, the meal was fantastic, the family was all together, and everyone was happy.

Mary was happy and that to me was all that mattered. I walked around the room and came up behind her. I slipped my arms around her and said "thank you" in her ear. She leaned back and snuggled into my arms. A man couldn't be any happier.

For the next couple of weeks Mary it seemed was running here and there with our daughter-in-laws. With Christmas only a couple of weeks away it dawned on me Mary's present hadn't arrived. I'd have to go into town and check on it.

Boggs and his fiancé Alma came over that afternoon and brought the tree he and I picked out the week before. We managed to get it in the frame and had it set up for Mary when she got back home.

Alma and Boggs asked Mary and I to go into town and stand up with them. They were getting married.

Tee saw us going down the drive and came out to give Mary some news. She asked where we were going and then wished the couple well.

Sometime later we finally managed to find the local minister. We had to wait thirty minutes so we went over to Cookies old restaurant and had coffee.

I checked my pocket watch.

"I guess we'd better go Boggs, the preacher should be there by now."

We walked the short distance to the church and all got a surprise.

The whole family was waiting outside.

Boggs wiped tears from his eyes."

"See what I mean Alma, they are the greatest family a man could have."

"Herbert, they most certainly are, how did they ever get here in time."

"Well Alma, we're not dressed for a wedding but we're here."

"Thank you all so much."

The wedding took place and afterwards we followed the couple out of town and watched as they drove their pick up on toward their new home. The day had been a grand one indeed; we'd added another member to our family.

The next day I found out that Mary's Christmas present was in and would be delivered Christmas Eve evening.

Finally, things were lining out.

The turkeys were baking and the ham Sam had supplied was being heated. Doe had brought here famous rolls and tiny desert cakes the grandchildren loved.

Will had gone over and picked up his grandmother and grandfather. When they arrived I helped Mary's father into his chair while Will carried the famous pecan pies into the house. I pushed Mary's father up the ramp and into the house, Mary's mom put her hand on my shoulder.

"Has it arrived yet?"

"Not yet, they told me it would be delivered at one this afternoon."

"She's going to have a fit."

"I know, but she'll get over it."

"James, I think I've figured out why I love you."

"Why."

"You're almost as ornery as me."

I gave her a hug and agreed with her.

Everyone was having a wonderful time; someone knocked on the door. Seth answered the door then called me. Mary's present had arrived.

I thanked the young man and after a moment called Mary.

"Yes James."

"Merry Christmas."

I handed her the keys to her new car.

She looked out the door and could see the new red roadster.

"Oh my God! James you shouldn't have done it."

"Why not, besides we need two cars. I'm running back and forth to town and you need a car."

"Thank you James, thank you for everything."

Mel, Pa and Mr. Conner came over.

"Son, we've been talking."

"Not to be disrespectful Pa, but when you three get together it's what you usually do."

"Well, we've been thinking, maybe Conners here could buy in on the colt. That is if you don't mind."

"I don't mind at all, but we'll have to change the colt's name."

"No way son, that's bad luck to change a horses name. Besides, Conners here likes the name."

"I have no objection you all go round up Deb and tell her before she starts the paperwork."

"We'll do it son. By nab this is going to be fun."

Mack came over after dinner and told me he'd heard about Conners buying in on the colt.

"It looks like the colt's going to be a family affair.

"Looks that way Mack but if it keeps them happy then everything will be fine."

"I'm surprised that didn't get Mary's folks involved."

"They asked them but Mary's dad isn't doing real well so they declined."

"I sure hope he gets better, they are such fine folks."

"I know, I thank God everyday that they get to stay here."

Later that evening after everyone had left Mary and I sat talking in front of the fireplace.

"It was a grand day wasn't it?"

"It sure was Mary, I'm still stuffed. Is there any pecan pie left?"

"I saved you a piece, you don't want it now do you?"

"Lord no, but tomorrow for lunch it will be great."

"Cowboy, I'm ready for bed."

"Me too, I'll turn out the lights."

CHAPTER 50

▼

We'd had a rather mild winter, the cows were fat and the new calves were doing great. The kids hadn't missed but a couple of days training down at the track. Mack and Deb had begun to get serious with the colt that seemed to enjoy it all.

We were fixing some loose wire on Mary's chicken pen when Mary suddenly straightened.

"What's the matter Mary?"

"You have plenty of hay put out?"

"Sure do, why?"

"Take a look to the northwest."

I stood up and saw immediately what she meant. The sky was blue and black; a major storm was heading our way. I quickly finished nailing the wire and put my tools away.

I caught Slick and Mary's paint gelding and put them in the barn. I filled their hay mangers and water buckets. We might need them in the days to come. The east door on the barn was partly open and I left it that way. I closed the west door and headed for the house. The wind was now coming out of the northwest and was cold.

Twenty minutes later the thermometer on the porch read thirty-two degrees. A short time earlier it had read sixty-four.

Two hours later the snow set in. It didn't stop overnight or the next day. When it did end we had twelve to fourteen inches on the level, the drifts were three to four feet deep.

I saw Will go out to his barn, I figured he could use come help so I got dressed and went in the east end of my barn and saddled Slick. A few minutes later I rode down the hill to meet Will.

Will waved as I rode up.

"Going to be a cold ride Pa."

"Figured so son, figured two would take only half the time."

We rode down the hill and began looking the cows and calves over. Everything seemed fine. There were plenty of draws where the tall bluestem stood tall and would provide plenty of feed for the cows.

When I met back up with Will his opinion was the same as mine. We headed back to his place.

"I appreciate the help Pa."

"No thanks needed son, I'll ride with you tomorrow. We need to keep an eye on them until this stuff starts to melt. I'll see you in the morning son."

I rode Slick up the hill and down to the barn. I think he was as happy as I was to be in out of the wind and cold.

I unsaddled him and rubbed him down good with a burlap sack, then gave him an extra ration of grain. I was ready to go to the house, I was cold.

It was three days before the wind shifted around to the south. The snow began to melt on the roofs; water began to run. I could live with the water and mud; I just wanted the snow gone.

Nothing but horses was going to move for a few days. I took the wagon to town and got groceries for everyone. By the time I got back home the team was give out. They'd not worked this hard in several years.

"Get every ones order James?"

"Finally Mary, seemed as if the storm caught everyone flat footed."

"Well its' the worst storm I can ever remember. I've never seen this much snow here.

"Lets just hope you don't see any like it ever again. That ride to town in the wagon was no fun, the team really had to work."

"I assume everyone was alright."

"Far as I could tell. You should have seen the streets in town. I saw a wagon being pulled out of the street. Mary they had three teams of horses pulling it and almost didn't get it pulled out."

"They probably had trouble finding that many teams."

"You know your right, now that I think about it the teams were a little light. Probably someone's old buggy team."

CHAPTER 51

▼

Springtime was coming in a hurry. Trees down along the creek bottom were putting on new leaves. The wild plum bushed were in full bloom. We sat and watched as Deb and Willie worked the young horses. It was always fun to see the young horses progress. The kids would have their yearling sale in two weeks, the two year olds they were working were horses that Mack would take to the track late this summer. Most of the colts were colts the kids had sold at the yearling sale last year. Mary and I were waiting for them to bring out Three Dreams.

Finally Willie led Deb out onto the track. The colt was on his toes, so to speak. He shook his head; he wanted to go to work.

Another one of the stable hands was led out onto the track on one of the older horses Mack had shipped home to rest. He'd developed a cold at the track and they had barley been able to save his life. Mack had sent him home to rest.

Willie had put him back in training about four months ago. It looked as if they were going to work him with Dreams, as Deb called him.

Deb and the other young man began to work the two horses slowly side by side. They worked around the track head and head until they come past Willie then began to extend themselves.

The older horse worked smoothly like a veteran of the track should. Dreams however was fighting Deb for his head, he wanted to go. Suddenly she released her hold on him.

It was beautiful to watch, he seemed to suddenly fly away from the older veteran. I had never seen a colt move so smoothly or so fast. Not even Princess.

"James, he's wonderful."

"He looks that way Mary, I have to say I'm very impressed. Now all we have to do is keep him from hurting himself."

"James, I'm sure Deb and Willie are taking every precaution with him."

"Oh I don't doubt that at all, its just part of the racehorse game. You do everything right and still some of them breakdown."

"Dear, you'll just have to pray a lot."

"That may be the only thing I can do."

Later that morning when I was on my way back to the house from the barn when I saw the tribal police car coming up the hill. I met the officer at the front gate.

"Good morning officer."

"Good morning sir, my Captain asked me to come and see if you could come see him at headquarters. He broke his foot yesterday and can't drive."

"Not a problem officer, tell him I'll be in his office in an hour or so."

"Thank you Mr. Howard. I'll tell him."

I watched as the young officer drove away, and then walked into the house.

"What do they want James?"

"No idea Mary, the Captain wants to talk to me about something."

"So I assume you are going into town."

"I thought I would, anything you need?"

"Would you give Sammye this cookbook, it's one the ladies at the church put together a year or so ago."

"Sure will Mary, just lay it there on the counter. I'll pick it up on my way out."

I changed clothes, kissed Mary then picked up the book on my way out. I wasn't about to forget the book. I wanted to come back home.

I drove into town wondering what the captain could want. I'd not heard of any problems the last month or so. As I pulled into a space in front of his office, Sammye came out of the law office carrying a stack of papers. She was in a hurry and almost ran into me as I stepped up onto the boardwalk.

"Oh James, I'm sorry!"

"Not a problem Sammye looks like you're in a hurry."

"Oh yes, I've got to file these papers at the courthouse."

"Don't let me hold you up, I've got to see the captain."

"If you're around when I get back maybe we can con Bill into buying us lunch."

"Sounds good, oh by the way Mary sent this cookbook to you."

"Oh good, it's filled with some of the tribes favorite dishes. I wanted to try some of them."

"I'll put it on your desk."

"Thanks James, tell Mary I'll take good care of it."

"See you later Sammye."

I went into the boys' law office and put the cookbook on Sammye's desk. I said hello to Will and Bill. Tom's office door was closed so I left and went next door to the Tribal Police office.

The Captain was waiting for me on his crutches when I walked through the office door.

"Mr. Howard thanks for coming sir."

"What can I do for you Captain?"

"It seems the folks over west have gotten together and have finally gotten a hand on things over there. Sergeant Walkingstick has done a wonderful job in the short time he's been over there."

"They have elected a new sheriff and a new city council. Folks were tired of what had been going on. The only thing they lacked was someone to take charge and lead them. Mr. Howard, you did that but managed to give the credit to Sergeant Walkingstick."

"Captain, Sergeant Walkingstick should have gotten the credit. He did a wonderful job before we even arrived."

"That's true Mr. Howard but it seems the folks over there got together and wanted to give you something. So they sent this token of thanks."

He handed me a long narrow box wrapped in brown paper.

I sat down in a chair and unwrapped the box. It turned out to be a new Winchester rifle with gold and silver inlay. It was a thing of beauty.

"Captain they didn't need to do this."

"Now Mr. Howard, I don't know about that, but they seemed to think they did."

"Sergeant Walkingstick said everyone in town helped buy the rifle. They like their new town and intend to keep it the way it is now."

"Captain, I don't even know who to thank."

"The whole town Mr. Howard and this time it's them that's thanking you. Mr. Howard, take the rifle. It's what the people want."

"Captain, I'll take the rifle and be proud to have it but I just don't think I deserve it."

"Mr. Howard, the folks who sent it thought you did."

I shook hands with the captain and went back over to Tom and the boys' office. When I walked in carrying the new rifle everyone applauded.

"You all knew about this already?"

"Knew about it yesterday James."

"Thanks for letting me know Tom."

"James, it was supposed to be a surprise."

"Well it was Tom, it surely was."

"I guess I might as well get home and show Mary this fancy new rifle."

"Dad, if you carry that rifle on Slick we'll all have to wear sun glasses."

"Son, that is a fact. I probably will have to wait for a cloudy day to carry it on him."

"James Howard, you're not going to use that rifle."

"Only if I should need it Sammye. It will hang in a place of honor as long as I don't need it."

"I don't understand."

"What dad is saying Sammye, is he'll hang it up for everyone to see and enjoy, but if he needs it he'll not hesitate to use it."

"But everything is settling down we've not had any major problems in months now."

"That's because those who would like to cause trouble know we'll take down our fancy rifles and come hunting."

"I know what you mean Sammye, but not that long ago everyone up here wore a gun strapped on his hip. It's taken a lot of hard work for the good and honest folks to get to where we are now and we're not about to give it up with out a fight."

"When you put it that way I understand. Bill even has a pistol at the house."

"Sammye, mom carries one in her purse."

"You're kidding?"

"No he's not, she has carried it for years. She's used it a time or two."

"I never had any idea."

"You weren't supposed to, her little gun is not for show. It's what she calls her "In case" gun. If you don't have one I think you should. I hope there is never a case where you have to use it but one never knows."

"I've suggested she carry one James but I've struck out."

"Bill, she first has to be comfortable around a gun, some folks never will be but it's up to every person to make that decision."

I left the boys office and drove back out to the house. When I walked through the back door carrying the fancy rifle Mary was shocked.

"My lord James, where in the world did you get the rifle?"

"The folks over west seemed to think I needed it."

"It's beautiful, but what in the world will you do with it?"

"Hang it up and look at it I guess."

"Where do you want to hang it dear?"

"I don't have any idea Mary, but I guess it should be where people can see it. I sure don't want to hurt the folks over that ways feelings."

"That's true, lets hang in over the doorway over there. That way everyone will be able to see it when they come in."

I handed the rifle to Mary while I hung two brackets over the doorway.

"James, this is a beautiful thing, do you have any idea what it cost?"

"Mary, I'd be afraid to even think what it cost."

"Well the people wanted you to have it so hang it up."

"Not until I do one thing Mary."

"What thing James?"

I opened the gun cabinet and took out a handful of shells.

"You're going to shoot it?"

"I sure am, I want to see if it shoots as good as it looks."

I stepped out back and fired at a tin can in back of the barn. The rifle shot fine, I kept the can moving until I ran out of shells.

I cleaned the rifle then hung it up for everyone to see. Someday one of my grandkids would own it.

CHAPTER 52

▼

The kids' yearling sale went great. I still couldn't believe folks would pay what they got for their colts.

Hank and his family as well as one of his neighboring rancher friends showed up to watch the sale.

"James, where did all these folks come from?"

"All over the country Hank. I mostly just stay out of the way."

"I sure don't blame you for that. I'm afraid to scratch my nose. I'd have to sell half my herd to pay for one of your boy's colts."

"I know what you mean Hank, but one of these colts could make a man wealthy if he gets lucky."

"James, I like to play a little poker every now and then but good lord this is really gambling."

After the sale ended Hank and his friend followed me up to the house where we had coffee and visited.

"James, Pat here and I have been talking. Between the three of us we've got the biggest spreads in the area."

"I know that Hank, so what's on your mind?"

"We've been thinking about forming a cattlemen's associations."

"For what reason Hank?"

"Just for fun James. Once every three months we'd get together for a feed and visit. There's half a dozen more boys up here who have never met you. The women would love it."

"What would you call this association?"

"R.C.B.A."

"R.C.B.A. What's that stand for Hank?"

"Ruthless Cattle Barons Association."

I had to laugh Hank was something else.

So the R.C.B.A. was formed. Our first meeting would be held at our place in about three months.

When Mary heard about the new association tears ran down he checks as she laughed.

"Ruthless Cattle Barons, Oh my."

"The Ruthless Cattle Barons, who only give cattle to hungry people and shut down their operations to help save the tribe from crooks and thieves. James I think it's a wonderful idea. We'll finally get to meet some of our neighbors."

Mary had gone to town for some "things" as she called them. I was getting ready to saddle Slick when Bill drove up to the front of the barn.

"Hey Bill, what are you up too this morning?"

"Well James, I need to talk to you about some business."

"Lets go to the house and get some coffee. We can set out on the porch. We might as well be comfortable."

We got coffee and went out and set on the porch.

"Now Bill what business do you want to talk over."

"I have two things, first off I want to buy a piece of land. There's a widow just over the north edge of town that wants to sell her place. But first she has to have the approval of the council."

"So you want me to represent you to the council?"

"If you would."

"Bill, after all you've done for the tribe there will be no problem at all."

"I sure hope so, I'd like to build Sammye a new home."

"I understand that."

"Now my second problem. I want to buy a half dozen of your Angus cows and a young bull."

"Well I normally don't sell my Angus outright Bill but for you and Sammye I'll make an exception. I'll sell you the six cows but not the bull. I'll loan you a young bull I want to keep but don't need just yet. I'll have a new bull for you every other year."

"Sounds fair to me, now one last question."

"Ask away."

"How or what do I have to do to join the cattlemen's association."

"You mean the R.C.B.A.?"

"That's the one Mary was telling Sammye about it yesterday."

"Well, first of all, you've got to own cattle. Then I don't have a clue but I'll find out for you. As far as I know it's a rather casual organization."

"Just what I'm looking for. Thank you James."

"I'll talk to the council about the land day after tomorrow. I'm sure there won't be a problem. I assume you'll have to have the place fenced before you want the cattle."

"That's correct, I'll have to have a barn built too. I've already talked to the Swinsons and if we can get the land deal cleared this week, they will start the house next week."

"Bill, Ill do my best."

"I know you will James. It looks as if I'm here stay, not that I ever planned on leaving. Say have you heard about Conners?"

"No I guess not."

"He's courting the new English teacher."

"You're kidding."

"No I'm not, they have been seeing each other for a couple of weeks. They met at the school. Conners has been helping the students with their art class for a couple of years now."

"Well I'm tickled for him, he's a fine man and a good friend."

"He sure is, Sammye has invited them to supper tonight so I guess I'd better get my tail home."

"That's for sure, you never want to make the cook mad."

"That's for sure James. See you later."

CHAPTER 53

▼

The council approved Bill's purchase of the widow's place. The Swinsons went to work on the new house and a couple of young men went to work putting up Bill's fence.

Mary and I were just coming out of the local grocery store when our banker waved to us from across the street.

"James, Mary, May I have a moment of your time?"

We walked across the street and followed him into his office.

"James, you remember a man by the name of Steve Hallot?"

"Sure I do, he was the man who helped us find my granddaughter when she was kidnapped why?"

"It seems he's come up with a couple of leases down in the Glenpool field near the town of Kiefer. It seems as though you gave him some money to eat on."

"Sure I did, he'd helped me and was looking for a job. It seemed the least I could do for him at the time. What does he want?"

"He'd like you to come down and look at a couple of leases he now has in his possession."

"Leases, you mean like oil leases?"

"That's right."

"They are west of Glenpool according to him, near the town of Kiefer."

"He thought you might be interested in financing the wells he wants to drill. He's willing to go fifty-fifty with you on deal."

"But I don't know anything about the oil business."

"Get your driller friend Hank, he could advise you on this deal. I know he's in town."

I looked at Mary.

"What do you think Mary?"

"James, we might as well go take a look. We've got the time and the money so why not take a look. I'm sure Hank will be more than willing to go along."

"Us, you mean you want to go along?"

"Sure I do, I've not been down that way and I'd like to see the country."

"In that case, lets go see if we can find Hank."

We found Hank down at the local café and explained the deal to him.

"Mr. Howard, I'm between jobs right now and I'd be glad to go along. When do you plan on leaving?"

"I'm thinking this afternoon. We can stay at a hotel in Tulsa then drive down and look the leases over tomorrow."

"Sounds good to me. I'm staying at the hotel just up the street. I'll be ready when you all come back."

Mary and I drove home. She packed a small suitcase and we headed back to town. True to his word Hank stood waiting for us in front of the hotel, he had a small bag at his side.

He got into the car and we headed south towards Tulsa. We visited on the way down.

"Mr. Howard, I've known Steve for a while. He's not one to make mistakes."

"What little I know of him he seemed to be a nice fellow."

"He is, he came down here looking for a job but was late getting here. He finally got on with a couple of the little independents but just never got the chance to get on with one of the major companies."

"Well, we'll take a look and see what you think. It's a fifty-fifty deal right now but we might be able to make it a three way split if you're interested."

"Oh I'm interested lets wait and see how this deal shapes up."

We spent the night in Tulsa and left shortly after daylight. We arrived in the bustling town of Glenpool and turned west at the sign that said Kiefer, four miles.

A short distance west and we began seeing oil wells everywhere. Drilling rigs were at work. Tents, sometimes three deep were on both sides of the road.

The town of Kiefer sat at the base of a range of hills running north and south. There were new buildings on both sides of the street. Stables for the teams that worked in the nearby fields were plentiful.

Hotels and bars that from the looks of things never closed. It was a true boomtown. We found the boarding house where Steve told us he'd be waiting. It was across the street from a hotel and two bars.

Steve came out and after shaking hands, got into the car.

"My God!"

"Mary, what's the matter?"

Then I saw what had shocked her. A woman was coming down the steps of the hotel. She was wearing a cowboy hat, a pistol in a belt on her waist and cowboy boots. That was it.

She came down the steps, then turned and went into the bar next door.

"What kind of town is this?"

"Boomtown Mr. Howard, it's quiet right now, you should see it after dark."

"Not if I can help it. Isn't there any law here?"

"Not much, law officers don't last long around here."

I backed the car around and headed east out of town. We drove two miles then headed south.

"My first lease starts right here Mr. Howard, the other is on the east side of the road."

Hank was looking.

"Mr. Howard, there are wells on all four sides of the leases. There has to be oil on them too. All we have to do is line up with the other wells and go to drilling. Mr. Howard this looks like a sure thing."

"Steve, how did you get these two leases?"

"They belong to my girlfriends parents. They are Creek Indians and let me have them after I proposed to my girl."

"How much money do you need?"

"Hank, what do you think. Five, six thousand dollars."

Not anymore than that Steve, if we can find a drilling machine."

"There's one in town that just came up for sale."

"Lets go look."

Later after looking the machine over we went to one of the three banks and inquired how much was owed on the machine.

Hank nodded his head at the price.

"It's a good deal Mr. Howard."

I had the bank telegraph my bank and have funds transferred.

The banker was pleased with the sale and later pleased with the money we deposited for Hank and Steve to operate on.

"Hank, are you going back with us?"

"Don't see any need too. I'll pick up what few things I need here in town. We'll get that drilling unit moved in the morning and start drilling the next day."

"We'll wire you a report every week."

"In that case boys we are leaving. I want to see the grandkids in Tulsa."

As Mary and I got ready to leave she pointed out where they were building a new school right at the base of the hill. A sign showed us it was built in the shape of a bird. They were about half done and it was indeed an impressive building.

We drove back to Tulsa and drove into Beth and Mike's place early in the afternoon.

Beth came running out of the house.

"Mother, Father, what a surprise."

"We were in town and thought we'd stop by."

"Can you spend the night?"

"I guess we can, the kids in school?"

"Of course, they'll be home in an hour or so. Joe got his mounted buck head last week. Mr. Boggs did a wonderful job on it. We had two days of sight seeing after he hung it up. He's quite the celebrity at school. All the boys envy his having his own rifle and his going deer hunting each fall with you dad."

"Well all that matters is that he had a good time. He's become quite a good hunter. How's Carrie doing with her horse?"

"She has a horse show week after next, I hope you all can come down for it."

"We'll certainly try dear, your father and I will do our best."

A short time later the kids come rushing into the house. Carrie was becoming quite a lady. I noticed Joe had begun to grow also. I was proud of them both.

Mike came home from work and shortly there after we had a wonderful supper after which we visited until bedtime.

The next morning after breakfast we got hugs and handshakes and headed back home.

CHAPTER 54

▼

The next week we started talking about taking a trip. Mary had been reading books about various places and was thinking about seeing some more of northeastern New Mexico. She was talking about Taos and Santa Fe.

It made no difference to me; the country out that way was beautiful so I could care less. I would enjoy it all; I loved the high desert country.

We got our first report from the boys down south. The report said the sand showed promise; they would send another report soon.

"Well what do the boys have to say?"

"They say the sand looks good, whatever that means."

"It must mean something good James or else they wouldn't have said anything about it."

"I hope so, I'm in to something I know nothing about."

"Those boys think the world of you and would never have started drilling if they didn't think they would find oil. Now I have a question for you. If the boys find oil what are you going to do with your share?"

"I've thought about it Mary and if the boys find oil, I'll put the money into a trust fund for all the grandkids for a college fund."

"That's wonderful James, you think there will be enough?"

"I really do Mary, I think the boys down south are good people and I trust them."

"Then I guess that answers your question. You trust them James."

"I guess it does Mary."

A week later the first well came in. It was flowing sixty-five barrels a day. The boys were already moving to a new location.

Within the next four months we had three more wells pumping the black gold as it was called. I got my first check the following week. I went to the bank and set up the trust fund.

My banker thought it was a wise decision. He said the interest would add to the trust over the years.

We decided we'd go the Taos and Santa Fe. We'd take the train to Raton then make arrangements to get to Taos when we got there.

Mary and I would be going alone. Harold, Flower, Sam and Lesa couldn't go.

Harold had some cattle buyers coming and Sam had just bought a new blue-tick female for Ole Blue. Sam needed to stay around make sure she and Ole Blue got together.

Mary and I caught the train on a pretty morning and enjoyed the train ride to Kansas City. We caught the westbound train and had a sleeper compartment. Later that evening we ate a fine meal in the dining car, a glass of wine after our meal was great.

We visited for an hour or so then retired to our compartment. We each had a book and read for a short time, then went to bed.

The next morning we arrived in Raton. The town had not changed that much since we'd been there years before.

We caught a small narrow gage train that ran from Raton to the small town of Eaglesnest on its way over to Taos.

The cars were small but the seats were comfortable; but most important of all was the scenery. The mountains were beautiful.

"James, aren't they beautiful?"

"They sure are, I'd like to have a summer home up here somewhere. Wouldn't the grandkids love it? They could fish, ride and just enjoy the scenery.

"It's a thought James, I wonder how long it will be until we reach Taos?"

A gentleman behind us spoke up.

"We're about twenty minutes out of town. It's pretty much down hill from here."

"Thank you sir."

"First time over this way?"

"Yes it is, we don't have mountains like this at home."

"Where are you folks from?"

"We're from Oklahoma."

"What part sir?"

"The northeastern part, we live about seventy miles north of Tulsa."

"Oh my, then you must know the Howards."

"Sir, we are the Howard's, or some of them at least. I'm James and this is my wife Mary."

"Good Lord, you're the one they used to call the boy rancher."

"I've heard that before."

"My cousin works for you."

"Your cousin."

"Yes sir, Herb Boggs."

"Good Lord yes, he's been with me for years. I didn't know he had nay relatives out this way."

"I left Kansas years ago but he and I have kept in touch. I feel like I've known you folks for years. What are your plans?"

"Figured to find a hotel and see the town. We plan on going on down to Santa Fe for a day or so."

"Alright, first off my wife and I own a small hotel. It's not the fancy thing you're probably used too, but it's clean and my wife sets the best table in town. Besides, I can show you all the sites. Herb would whip me if I didn't treat you folks right."

"Sir, your name is?"

"Alex Boggs, Mr. Howard."

"Mr. Boggs, we'll stay at your place. Fancy is not much of our style."

"Fine we'll get you settled and tomorrow I'll show you all the sites."

As Alex had said, the hotel wasn't fancy but as Mary put it, it's sure enough clean.

After supper we had to agree with Alex. His wife was a fantastic cook. We had fresh caught trout, baked potatoes, green beans and a fresh garden salad. The desert for the night was your choice of chocolate or cherry pie.

The cherry pie was almost as good as Sammye's. Mary went back to the kitchen and got the receipt for the chocolate pie from Alex's wife.

After a good nights rest and breakfast we followed Alex outside and began our tour.

We saw the home where Kit Carson lived and saw his grave. The town kept the house up for folks to see.

We drove out to see the old mission church. Mary and I were both impressed. We bought fresh fried bread from the local Indians who lived in what were called pueblos. They were the most unique homes I had ever seen. We met some of the folks and ended up spending most of the morning.

We returned to the town and began touring the various shops. Mary was looking at what was called a blanket jacket when I spotted the gun shop next door.

"Go on James, I saw it when we came in. You might as well go look, I'm going to be here for a while."

Alex and I went next door and began to look at the man's stock.

"Morning Alex, haven't seen you in a while."

"Been up to Trinadad for a week or so Charley. Meet my friend James Howard from Oklahoma."

"James Howard, I head your name before somewhere."

"I've got a ranch over that way."

"Wait a minute, you have any Thoroughbreds?"

"Yes sir, my son has a stable."

"Princess Mary, did you won her?"

"My son did."

"Hell of a horse, I made some money on her."

"Glad you did."

"Anything I can show you gentlemen?"

"I'm really just looking. Have more guns now that I know what to do with."

"But you don't have one of these."

He took a case from beneath the counter and took out a beautifully engraved Sharps, just like mine at home."

"Yes sir, I have one, same caliber; is this one for sale?"

"Well yes, but most folks aren't interested in a gun this size."

I picked up the Sharps and felt the balance. The rifle felt like an old friend.

"You sure enough interested in the rifle?"

"I am if the price is right, and of course I'd want to shoot it."

"There's a range just out back. I've got a few shells."

Alex and I followed him out back to the shooting range, which backed up to one of the mountains.

The targets were only a hundred or so down range. I spotted a white rock about three hundred yards off and sighted on it. Then let the rifle down.

I took a shell from the gunsmith and loaded the rifle then re-sighted on the white rock. The rifle roared and the white rock exploded.

"Good Lord, I don't believe it. That rock was three hundred yards."

"The trigger needs to be honed, it's a little rough."

"Let me see."

He took the rifle, cocked and pulled the trigger.

"You're right sir it is a little rough. I'll hone it down."

"You haven't priced it yet."

"Would you give two hundred?"

"I'd give one fifty."

"Split the difference?"

"Sold. Hone the trigger down fine."

"Yes sir I'll get it done."

"Good, I'll pick it up tomorrow before noon."

"Not a problem Mr. Howard, I'll have it ready for you."

Alex and I left the gun shop and met Mary as she was coming out of the clothing shop; she had her arms filled with packages. Boxes that Alex and I took and carried them to the car.

"Thank you gentlemen. James did you find anything?"

"Yes I did Mary."

"Did you find another Sharps dear?"

"Sure did."

"I thought I heard one being fired. Did you buy it?"

"Yes, I did. I figured I'd give it to Will, Matt already has one."

"Mr. Howard, what in the world do you do with those things? There's no buffalo left."

"Look at them mostly, the one I have was a big part of my life. It saved my life more than once."

"I see, Herb has written me letters and told me about your rifle."

"Mr. Boggs, my husband's rifle is or is almost as famous as he. When people meet him the first thing they want to see is the rifle."

"Mary, we need to make arrangements to have this stuff shipped home, there's no way we can carry all this stuff with us."

"I can take care of that Mr. Howard. The freight office is right down the street. Besides, there's something I want to show you all just west of town."

"We stopped at the fright office and I explained to the man where I wanted the things shipped too. I told him I'd bought a rifle and would bring it down the next morning."

We left the office and got back into Alex's car.

"Hang on folks we've got a little drive ahead of us but I'll guarantee you'll think it is worth the trouble."

We drove west on a decent road. We could see another range of mountains ahead of us. The high desert was beautiful to see and small; the Sage and other wild plants so different from our plants at home.

"We're almost there folks, look ahead of you."

Neither Mary nor I could see anything that was different, and then suddenly as Alex slowed the car we saw the opening in the ground ahead of us.

"My Lord Alex, what is this?"

"It's a gorge Mr. Howard, formed by the Rio Grande River, just wait until we get up close."

Alex pulled the car over into an area where it was plain to see many cars had parked before. He shut the engine off and we walked a short distance to where we could see down into the gorge. The river, which looked to be three quarters of a mile below, was a then fast moving ribbon of light.

"How in the world do you get to the other side?"

"You go south Mr. Howard, we've heard they plan on putting a bridge in here but I be darned if I can figure out how they'll do it."

"My Lord it seems impossible."

"It's huge yet so beautiful."

"Sure glad we didn't have something like this in our way up from Texas."

"You bet, you'd still be there James,"

We walked up and down the edge of the gorge and took in all the sights.

When we started back towards Taos Mary and I had a million questions for Alex. The drive back to town seemed short.

CHAPTER 55

▼

The next morning I picked up the Sharps and a case. I took it down to the freight office. The man there put the rifle in a wooden crate with out other things and explained to me it would go out on the next train. The same train Mary and I were taking down to Santa Fe.

We got our bags and Alex drove us down to the train station.

"You folks take care. Be sure and tell Herb I said hello."

"I'll do that Alex, thanks a lot for showing us the sites."

"No problem Mr. Howard, the pleasure was all mine."

We caught the train for the short run down to Santa Fe. The train ride was nice; we were leaving the tall mountains behind us.

Alex had told us what hotel to stay in while we were there. When we arrived we hired a hack to take us to the hotel.

Santa Fe was wonderful to see. The adobe building, some painted some not were each unique. There was a huge Church at the end of the street where the hotel was located. Our hotel was just across the street from the Governor's Palace.

The local Indians sat on blankets along the front displaying all sorts of jewelry and such. After Mary and I got settled in our room we went out to look around.

We found we could walk through the Governor's Palace and really enjoyed the tour. The lady who showed us through gave us many interesting facts about the history of New Mexico.

When we finished our tour we went outside and began looking at all the wares the Navajo's had for sale.

While Mary was looking at the jewelry, pots, blankets and such I stood nearby looking at buildings that were the treasures of the city.

"Traveling sir?"

The young man who had spoken to me was most assuredly a Navajo. He wore a black flat brimmed hat, high crowned with no crease. I had noticed several like it around the plaza as it was called.

"Yes we are, thought we'd come out and see the sites. We're from Oklahoma."

"Bet you have Indians there sir."

"Of course we do. My wife is Osage."

"You married an Osage woman?"

"Yes I did, why?"

"You wanted her oil money."

"Young man, my husband married me long before oil was even thought of. What he didn't tell you was that my tribe has made him a member and he now sets on our tribal council."

"Excuse me ma'am, your reservation must be different from ours."

"We don't have a reservation like yours young man. Even before the oil was discovered we were quickly becoming self-reliant. Each family had their own small herd of cattle.

"We have cattle and sheep but when we want to sell we have to let the agent sell them for us."

"Why would you have to do that?"

"It is just the way it is."

"You don't have to have your agents approval for such things."

"We wouldn't tolerate it. We deal when and as we wish. We have our own government and if there is a problem they try and solve it for us."

"I would like to see how this works."

"First thing young man we didn't rely on the government for food and clothing. We went to work and made ourselves self-sufficient. Maybe you should come see how our tribe has accomplished these things."

"So many of my people only want to be left alone and let the government take care of them. To some, all they want is enough money to buy alcohol."

"That is a problem. We have some who have taken that path but for the most part our people have been successful."

"Is this the reason your people sell their jewelry here in the plaza?"

"Yes, we don't really know how to go out into the world, our whole existence is right here."

"Sounds like to me you're being held hostage. This silver work you folks have here would sell for twice as much back at our place, it's beautiful, and I've never seen so much turquoise."

"It is a sacred stone to my people."

I pulled the thong around my neck and pulled out the stone I'd worn for years. I saw his eyes widen."

"Where did you get such a stone?"

"Lets get something to drink and I'll tell you the story.

We found a small café on the plaza and ordered iced tea.

The young man's name was Joe Walksalong. His family lived about ten miles outside of town. His grandfather and grandmother had raised him after his mother and father were killed in a mine accident. His grandfather was teaching him how to do the silver work.

"Mr. Howard, the stone you have is very old. Or at least I think so, my grandfather could tell you for sure. I think it came from a mine that was lost many years ago."

"Is your grandfather here?"

"No, but he will be here this evening at about four to pick up my grandmother and me."

"Do you come in everyday?"

"Everyday except Sunday, it is the only way we have of making any money. We usually don't make much money on our sheep, it seems the market is always down when we sell."

"You mean when your agent sells them."

"That is true sir."

"I'd like to meet your grandfather Joe."

"I would like you to meet him sir."

"Joe, are you busy tomorrow, I mean after you help your grandmother get set up?"

"Not really ma'am."

"Could we hire you to be our guide? You know the town."

"I would be proud to be your guide ma'am."

"It's settled then, we'll go back to our room. We'll be back to meet your grandfather."

"I will look forward to it ma'am."

We waved at Joe and headed back to our hotel. When we reached our room I could tell Mary was upset.

"James, I know there's nothing we can do but these people are being used by a corrupt system."

"It looks that way Mary, but like you said there's nothing we can do about it."

"I'm so glad we went the way we did when we moved south."

"Me too Mary, lets get a nap, I want to be fresh when I meet Joe's grandfather this evening."

We had a nap then walked back across the plaza to where Joe's grandmother had here blankets spread. A stocky gray haired man stood near Joe. He wore jeans, boots and the same sort of hat Joe wore. Joe waved to us as we walked up to them.

"Mr. and Mr. Howard, this is grandfather Frank Lonehorse."

"Pleased to meet you Mr. Lonehorse."

"I am pleased to meet you sir. My grandson has told me about you. I would like to sit and talk to you and your wife tomorrow if you have time."

"I think we can do that, we've hired Joe to show us around tomorrow afternoon."

"That would be good. May I see the stone you wear?"

I pulled the stone out from under my shirt and handed it to him.

He took the stone in his hands and studied it carefully.

"It is a very old stone sir, when my grandson told me about it I was sure he had to be wrong. It seems I must learn to trust his eye. He was right. The stone was taken from one of our sacred mountains many years ago. It is said the mountain became angry and caved in on those who were taking the sacred stones away."

"The mine was lost to my people and has never been found again. Your stone is the largest one I have ever seen."

"Well I'll be, I took the stone from a Comanche warrior years ago. I wanted my mother to have it but she said it was too large for her to wear. She told me to wear it."

"It is good, there is much good medicine in the stone. It is good you wear it, it was meant for a warrior."

He laid the stone on a piece of paper and with a pencil traced a line around it. When he finished he handed it back to me.

We visited for a few minutes then waved to them as they left the plaza. We walked back to the hotel and had a wonderful meal in the dining room.

We sat in our room, which overlooked the plaza and watched the lights go out.

"It's been a good day Mary, we've met some nice folks."

"Yes we have, even though it upsets me to see how they are being treated."

"I know Mary but there are some things we can't do anything about."

"I know James, I know."

CHAPTER 56

▼

After a good breakfast the next morning we walked across the plaza and found Joe waiting for us.

"Good morning, are you ready to see the sites?"

"That we are Joe."

"We'll get started then."

We had a wonderful morning. Joe showed us the old church and told us the history. We were shown where the fur traders and mountain men met every spring. He told us some of the stories his grandparents had told him of the times. He told us of how his people had been treated over the years and how the Spanish had been both good and bad for his people.

It seemed there were similarities between how his people and the Osage had been treated over the years.

We had a wonderful day. We returned to the plaza later that afternoon. We saw Joe's grandfather who motioned us to come over.

"Friend Howard, I have prayed and sought guidance, will you let me see the stone once more?"

I removed the stone from around my nick and handed it to him.

He took the stone and smiled then walked a few steps over to where his wife had her blankets spread and sat down. From a worn leather bag he began to lay out some tools and a small anvil. He brought out a rag and slowly unwrapped it. He took out the most beautiful piece of silver work I had ever seen. The engraving was like nothing I had ever seen.

He took the stone and set it into the grooves of the silver mounting. A smile crossed his face. He placed the piece on the small anvil and with a small hammer began tapping. A moment later he handed the stone, now mounted in silver back to me.

"Now friend Howard, the stone is complete."

I had always liked the stone but now it was a thing of beauty.

"Mr. Lonehorse, how can I pay you?"

"You can not pay me, I have just helped complete the circle. Just wear the stone with pride."

"Oh I'll do that."

"Mr. Lonehorse, I'd like to buy a couple of blankets. Do they sell them here on the plaza?"

"Not now, the agent sells all the blankets."

"What do you mean he sells them?"

"When a blanket is finished he picks it up and sells it for the weaver."

"I don't understand, you folks shear the sheep, dye the wool and do the weaving yet you can't sell your own things? Sir, that makes no sense."

"Friend Howard, it is the way it is."

"Do you know anyone who might have some blankets for sale?"

"The man at the trading post, we often have to pawn things so that we may feed our family."

"Where is the trading post?"

"My grandson can show you tomorrow, they are closed now."

"Joe, will you be free tomorrow?"

"If you need me sir."

"Meet us at the same time tomorrow."

"I took money from my pocket and paid Joe for his days work."

"Mr. Howard, this is too much."

"No it's not, you've spent the whole day showing us around and explaining to us the history of your wonderful town. Besides I just paid you what I pay all my employees for a day's work."

I saw Joe quickly glance at his grandfather.

"Friend Howard, you've paid my grandson more than he could make in several weeks guiding people. Our agent normally books the guided tours."

"If that's the case, maybe Joe should go to work for himself."

"Friend Howard, there is much you do not understand."

"That may be true, but I know when someone is being used and not paid for their work."

"Joe, be here in the morning."

"Yes sir."

Mary and I went to our room; I was upset.

"James Howard, I'm not sure I like the look on your face."

"I'm sorry Mary, it's just I hate to see people used like this."

"Then don't get mad James, start thinking."

"I am thinking Mary, but I simply don't know enough about this situation. The way it looks, it could take years to get things straightened out here."

"Maybe we can't solve all the problems James, but maybe we can bend some of the rules and help these folks."

"Alright Mary, let me hear your ideas."

The next morning Joe met us on the plaza. I rented a car from the hotel manager and with directions from Joe we drove to the trading post. I had given Joe instructions on the way. I wanted him to point out to me a rug that was made by the lady we were going to see.

We arrived at the store and went inside. The man who ran the store was in a hurry to help. Joe pointed to a table covered with Navajo rugs. They were beautiful.

Mary and I began to go through the stack, slowly looking at each one. Finally Joe nodded his head when we came upon a beautiful light gray and black rug.

The man finally came over to where we stood looking at the rug.

"Beautiful isn't it folks? It's all handmade."

"What's the price?"

"Two hundred and fifty dollars. It's a bargain at that price too."

"We'll take it, can you wrap it up for us?"

"Only take a minute folks, just go ahead and look around. You might find something else you like."

We browsed around the store while the clerk wrapped the rug.

When he finished I nodded to Joe to carry it out to the car. I paid the man and we left the store.

"Now Joe, where does the woman who wove this rug live?"

Joe gave me directions as we pulled out of town. Thirty minutes later he pointed to a Hagan a quarter mile distant.

"You know her well Joe?"

"She's my Aunt Mr. Howard."

"Good, then she'll talk to us if you ask her."

"I'm sure she will."

We pulled into the bare yard and saw a woman working on a rug under a brush arbor. She laid her things down and began walking to the car.

Joe got out of the car and went to meet her. The lady greeted Joe with a hug than listened to what he had to say. They talked for another moment then came over to the car.

"My nephew says you are good people, he says you are on the Osage tribal council."

"This is true, my wife Mary is a member of the Osage tribe also."

"My Christian name is Naomi. Now what is it that you want?"

"Naomi, did you weave this blanket?"

I unwrapped the paper on a corner of the blanket.

"Yes, it is one of mine."

"How much were you paid?"

She looked at Joe who nodded his head.

"Forty-five dollars sir, why?"

"Naomi, I just paid two hundred and fifty dollars for the rug."

The look of shock barely crossed her face.

"Doesn't that upset you?"

"It is the way things are."

"Would you be interested in changing them Naomi?"

"I don't understand."

"What if I were to offer you a hundred dollars for your rugs?"

"But the agent at the store?"

"Forget the agent at the store, Mary and I have been talking and we want to start a new business. We're going to ask Joe here to run it for us."

Joe was not nearly as good at hiding the shock as his aunt had been.

"Mr. Howard, what are you talking about? I don't know anything about business."

"Maybe not Joe, but you know good rugs from the bad. We'll supply the money. You buy the rugs and ship them to us or sell them in the plaza. Go around to the weavers and deal with them like I have your aunt."

"But Mr. Howard, the weavers are scattered all over the reservation, I have no way of getting around to them."

"You will have Joe, I'm sure your aunt knows all of the good weavers. They are the ones we want to go talk to first."

"Mr. Howard, we will cause trouble."

"Lets see Joe, all we can do is try."

"Alright Mr. Howard I'll give it a try."

CHAPTER 57

▼

We bought Joe a good used pickup that evening and with the list his aunt had given him he planned on leaving the next morning. He would report to Mary and I the next evening.

Mary and I spent the day shopping. As evening approached we were visiting with Joe's grandparents when he came walking up. He had a troubled look on his face.

"Joe, you have problems?"

"Well, yes and no. I saw eight of the weavers and have bought eleven rugs."

"What's bad about that?"

"At the last weaver's I ran into the man from the trading post. He was very upset with me and more upset with you."

"I'll bet he was, now lets go look at what you've bought."

Joe had done well. Mary began by saying this one will look wonderful in front of our fireplace.

By evenings end we had six rugs that would be shipped home in the morning. I explained to Joe how we would go to a bank and open an account for him to work with.

"Mr. Howard, why are you doing this?"

"Joe, my husband hates to see anyone cheated or taken advantage of. He has always been this way. He had helped my people time and time again. We can afford to set you up in business and help your people at the same time. If you're careful, you'll be able to run the business on your profits and make a good salary for yourself."

"I certainly hope so. Yesterday I enjoyed showing you all around. Today I've become a businessman. It's almost beyond belief."

Someone was knocking on our door, hard.

"James, it seems as if we have company."

I walked to the door and opened it.

Three men stood in the hall. The one in charge stepped past me and walked into our room. The other two stood in the doorway.

"Alright Howard, or whatever your name is. I'm here to tell you you'll not buy any more rugs. I've got a good deal going and I don't figure to let some stranger come in here and ruin it for me."

"And you are?"

"Jerry Albert, of Albert Sales."

"Well Mr. Albert, first off I don't really care if you like what I'm doing or not. You've been cheating these folks for a while and I guess if you want to stay in business you'll have to up the ante or go broke."

"Oh you think so, you don't have any idea about how things are done here. Now understand me, I came here to tell you not to buy anymore rugs, but if you won't listen to reason I'll have my boys here visit with you."

"James, don't worry about the boys."

"Thanks Mary."

"Lady you don't understand."

Suddenly, the man did understand.

Mary had the short-barreled pistol aimed right at them.

"Gentlemen, I assure you I know how to shoot. I also usually hit what I'm aiming at, and for your information you'd not be the first I've shot or killed."

"Gentlemen, come in and close the door, then sit down with your backs to the door."

"Boys, I'd move slow because my wife is upset so I'd be real careful."

"Now Mr. Albert we're on an even playing field, let me explain how things are going to work. You or your boys here give Joe any trouble and I'll have a dozen of the meanest boys you've ever seen in here in a day's time. First off they'll take your place apart, that is if they don't decide to start on you first."

"You see Albert, I'm a millionaire and I'll spend whatever it takes to see you suffer a hundred times more than this young man who now works for me."

"Now Mr. Albert, personally I think I could take you apart myself but right now I'm going to be nice. However if I ever see you or anyone associated with you around Joe or myself we'll take it personally. In fact someone just might get shot. Now do we understand each other?"

"Yes sir, I guess we do."

"Good, now get out of here and don't you ever come back. You've tried my patience to the limit."

"Gentlemen, you're getting off easy, my husband would have shot you back home. Now one at a time, get up slow and get out of here."

The men did as they were told. One look at Mary and that short-barreled pistol had been enough.

"Now you Mr. Albert, get out of here. I'm sick of looking at you."

Mr. Albert left and was tickled to do so. Mary walked to the window overlooking the plaza and watched as the men left the hotel.

She was suddenly laughing.

"What's so funny dear?"

"The men with Mr. Albert are somewhat upset with him. They took his wallet, took the money in it and then threw the wallet on the street. Mr. Albert is just standing there."

"Have the men left?"

"Oh yes, but he's still just standing there. Now he's moving. Oh my, now I understand."

"Understand what Mary?"

"Why he didn't move. He soiled his pants. Those boys must have really scared him."

"Mrs. Howard, may I ask a question?"

"Sure Joe, what do you want?"

"Would you have shot them?"

"Just like you'd shoot a rabbit for your pot Joe."

"She's telling the truth Joe, I've seen her in action."

"I had no idea you had a gun Mrs. Howard."

"You're not supposed to Joe. James gave me this little pistol a long time ago and it's come in handy a time or two before. Now lets order something to eat and work on this new business."

Just like Mary, eat and take care of business.

CHAPTER 58

▼

We spent two more days in Santa Fe and met many of the Navajo weavers and Silver smiths. Joe had suddenly become a very important man. We rented a small shop just off the plaza and Joe and some of his friends were busy fixing it up so they had a place to show and sell the blankets and such.

We had gone to a small bank and opened an account for Joe. The bank had contacted my bank and things were soon set in motion.

Mary and I spent one more day then caught the train for home.

Joe and his grandparents came to see us off. Joe's grandmother gave Mary a beautiful turquoise and silver necklace. Mary had tears in her eyes when we boarded the train for home.

We went from Santa Fe to Albuquerque where we had short layover. We had a sleeper car from Albuquerque all the way to Oklahoma City where we would change trains again.

We enjoyed the train ride. We reached Tucumcai late in the afternoon. We saw many Indians selling jewelry and such at the train station. We had a fine dinner in the dining car then went to our own sleeping compartment.

The train stopped in Amarillo shortly after we were in bed but I quickly went back to sleep.

We arrived in Oklahoma City early the next morning where we changed trains. We arrived in Pawhuska in the late afternoon. Mary visited with Art while I got our car. I loaded the suitcases into the car and we headed home. Art had told Mary he'd sent a bunch of freight out to our place. It was stacked on the porch.

We stopped at Will and Tee's.

"Hey kids, everything alright?"

"Things are fine Pa, we've had problems staying out of the way of the freight trucks running up and down the hill."

"Your mother bought a few things Will so be careful."

"I want to see what you've bought mom."

"Tee, I want you to see what we've got. J.R. will you run tell Matt and Deb to come up to the house?"

"Sure grandma won't take me long."

"Tell Matt to bring his hammer."

"Yes sir."

"You bring yours too Will, those boys at the freight station didn't spare the nails."

"We'll be up in a little while Pa, Tee won't let it be too long. She's been staring at those boxes for the best part of a week."

We drove up the hill and parked in front of the gate.

"Get the door Mary, I'll get the bags."

I put the bags in our bedroom and went back for the last load. I'd enjoyed our trip but I was glad to be home.

The kids showed up a few minutes later. Mary had put on a pot of coffee and it smelled great. I'd not had a good cup since we left home.

"Were do we start mom?"

"Open this one Will, it has things for Deb and Tee."

Matt and Will went to work, when they pried the top off the first box Mary began sorting through things. I looked at Deb and Tee's faces. It was almost as good as Christmas.

"This is yours Tee, and Deb this is yours."

The girls tore the paper off their gifts.

Tee began to cry as she saw the three quarter length blanket coat Mary had bought for her.

Deb looked at her jacket then slipped it on.

She and Tee modeled the coats for everyone. The girls were thrilled and both gave Mary a kiss. Mary took two more packages from the box and handed them to Becca and Mary Margaret. I watched as the girls removed the jackets that were like their mothers. Both girls were all smiles. Again Mary got hugs and kisses.

Mary had jackets for J.R. and Seth. They were similar to the others but had more leather trim.

"James, you want to give Will his present?"

I removed the rifle, which was wrapped in paper and handed it to Will.

Will tore the paper off the case and then uncased the rifle.

"Thanks Pa, I've always wanted one of these cannons."

"It shoots great son, I had the trigger worked over so it's just like mine."

"Thanks Pa thanks a bunch."

"Matt, I got you something too."

Matt took his present and unwrapped it. It was a beautiful vest, one he could wear to the office.

"Thanks mom, it will be great this fall."

"I've got things for, Beth, Mike, Carrie and Joe. We'll put them away for later. Now you boys undo the other crate."

The boys went to work and soon had the top off the crate.

Mary looked inside the crate and gave directions.

"Will, Matt, take this one into the house please."

The boys each got a hold of the rug and carried it into the house where Mary rolled it out.

"Oh Mom, it's beautiful."

"Oh yes, it just makes the room."

Mary stood smiling; she was pleased.

"Now lets go unload the rest."

"Will, this is yours and Tee's."

Will removed the rug and with Tee's help rolled it out on the porch.

"Mom, it's beautiful, you all must have spent a fortune."

"Not really son, your father owns the company who sells them for the tribe."

"Here Matt, this is yours and Deb's."

The two kids rolled out the rug to the delight of their kids.

Everyone was happy with their presents. It was a wonderful day to say the least.

Mary dug deeper into the crate and come out with another bag that she began sorting through.

"Tee, this is yours."

"Deb, this is yours."

"Becca, you and Mary Margaret see if any of these rings will fit you."

Mary had bought the girls necklaces with earrings to match.

It was fun for me to watch Tee. She had never had much until she had married Will and things like this always brought tears to her eyes.

Deb was a grand person in her own right but had been brought up in a different atmosphere. My sons had done well in their choice of wives.

The granddaughters both found rings that fit and were showing them off.

We all had coffee while Mary and I told them about our new rug and jewelry business.

"Dad, you mean you only paid a hundred and fifty dollars for these rugs?"

"That's right Matt, the folks were getting forty to fifty dollars. They are thrilled to deal with us. Take a look at this."

I pulled the stone from around my neck and showed them the new silver mounting.

"Dad, that is beautiful, who did the work for you?"

I told them about Joe's grandfather and told them the story behind the stone.

"You mean they've never found the mine?"

"Not since it caved in on some people."

"It makes you wonder, doesn't it?"

"Sure does, Joe's grandfather was very impressed with this stone."

"I can see why. You've worn it for years, I can't remember your ever not having it on."

"Son I've lived with him for many years now and haven't seen him take it off but a few times myself. He'll probably take it off less now."

We helped the kids load their things and went into the house.

Mary fixed what she called a supper breakfast. We had some of Sam's ham and eggs. It was great; we later sat on our porch swing and relaxed. Sleeping in our bed was going to be wonderful.

CHAPTER 59

▼

Everything was going well. We got our first report from Joe. Sales were going well. People were contacting him and wanting to buy rugs to sell in their stores. Everything was looking good. Mr. Albert had put his store up for sale. I wired Joe and told him to go look at the rugs and such and see if he could make a deal with Albert.

Joe had done what I told him and had bought a fair amount of Albert's inventory at a very good price. They had already sold more than half of the merchandise.

Joe explained how the people of the tribe were helping him with the business. The people on the plaza were sending customers to the shop. The weavers were very happy. He said he was also selling some artwork. They were branching out.

Mary and I were very happy to hear the good news.

"James, I've got an idea."

"Oh my, now I'm in trouble."

Mary told me her idea and I told her I'd think about it.

We got a letter from Hank. The members of the R.C.B.A. were due to have our first meeting. He wanted a suggestion as to who would host the first meeting.

Mary and I talked it over and decided we'd hold the first meeting. We'd have a lawn party a week from Saturday.

The following week we began setting things up. Sam, Lesa, Pa, Carla, Rosa and Paco were asked to help and were all excited about the party.

Tables were located and hauled and set up. Cookie and Martha showed up along with a couple of the young men Cookie had taught how to cook the pit beef. They dug a pit and got everything set. I sorted out a young Angus steer and drove him up into a lot next to the barn for the boys to use.

As far as I could see, everything was set and ready.

All the kids were going to help and were looking forward to the party.

When Saturday came Cookie and the boys had the beef in the ground. Everything was set. The first meeting of the R.C.B.A. was ready to go.

Folks began showing up about four. Some I had met, some I hadn't. Mary and I were kept busy. Hank and his crew showed up and we put him and his wife to work.

The kids seemed to be everywhere. They helped park cars, showed people around and in general worked hard.

I saw Mary visiting with a group of ladies I didn't know; she seemed to be having a good time. Our back yard was filled with people. Some I knew some I didn't but was looking forward to meeting them all.

The beef Cookie's boys fixed was great as usual. The guests were pleased and thanked the boys for preparing such a fine beef.

Local boys showed up and set up on a low wagon and began tuning their instruments. They began to play and people got up from their tables and began to dance. A short time later one of the men called for a square dance.

The evening was warm and I noticed more than a few damp shirts on the men.

As the evening began to wind down Hank got up on the wagon and thanked Mary and I for having the party. Everyone cheered.

Folks filed by thanking Mary and I as they went to their cars.

Pa, Carla, Sam, Lesa, Harold, Flower and our kids all sat down and had cold tea at one of the now vacant tables.

"Pa, it was a great party."

"It sure was James, who is going to have the next party?"

"Hank and his family plan on hosting the next one at their place."

"Sam, there were some awfully nice folks here tonight. Most of them were from Texas."

"I know Pa, one of the families lived about fifty miles from our old home place. They had some interesting stories about what went on down there after we left."

"I'll bet they did. Harold's folks have told us about the carpetbaggers coming in after we left."

"Pa, you still keeping the taxes paid on our old home place?"

"Sure have son, why?"

"I think Mary and I are going to take a trip down that way. I'd like to show Mary where mom is buried."

"I think you should James. You've never been back have you?"

"No sir, but I seem to think it's time.

"Then go son."

The kids began putting out the lamps around the yard; the party was over.

CHAPTER 60

▼

Two days later Mary and I caught a train south. I had a rather strange feeling, something I couldn't explain.

"You're nervous aren't you James?"

"Mary, I'm not sure how I feel. I can't figure it out. I'm not sure how I'm going to feel when we get there."

"James you'll be fine."

"In one since Mary, I'm feeling guilty. You know guilty for not coming back sooner."

"James, you weren't ready."

"How do you get ready Mary?"

"James, I'm not sure. But I know you and you've done your best. Your mother would have been proud of you."

"I sure hope so Mary."

"Relax James, just enjoy the trip."

We changed trains in Dallas and caught the next train going to San Angelo.

We arrived in San Angelo about nine in the morning. We inquired as to where the Ford dealership was located. A gentleman who had gotten off the train with us offered to give us a ride to the dealership.

During the ride we visited and as it happened he owned a ranch a few miles north of our old home place. He actually knew who I was.

"I'm Jack Smith Mr. Howard, you're some what of a legend down here."

"A legend, how can that be? This is the first time I've been back here since we left."

"Oh I'm well aware to that sir. We've always wondered if you'd ever come back."

"I'm back to see my mother's grave and the old home place, whatever is left of it."

"It's pretty much like it was when you left sir. The McCartney boys have kept it up all these years."

"That would be some of pa's doing."

"I don't know anything about that Mr. Howard, all I know is they've kept it up in good shape."

He pulled the car into the Ford dealership.

"Want me to wait, I know the roads and you can follow me out to your place. Things have changed a bunch since you lived here."

"Thank you sir, I appreciate that."

We went into the auto dealership and were greeted by a nice young man.

"May I help you folks?"

"Probably, we need a car."

"We have several sir, see anything you like?"

I looked at Mary who was looking at a new pickup at the end of the row.

"The pickup ready to go?"

"Yes sir, all it needs is gas."

"How much?"

"Don't you want to drive it sir?"

"Don't need too, got one at home just like it."

The young man quoted me a price and I paid him.

"Now where's the nearest gas station?"

"Oh sir, I'll have it filled right here. We'll have it out front in five minutes."

I thanked the young man then followed Mary out front. Our new-found friend was waiting for us. A few moments later we saw our new pickup being driven around to where we stood.

I thanked the young man then got under the wheel. I waved to our friend when Mary shut her door. An hour or so from now we'd be home, my old home. It seemed strange but suddenly I was relaxed and ready.

Some of the country I recognized some I didn't; homes and small farms now dotted what had once been open prairie.

Later I saw what I knew was Harold's folks old home place. It looked as if they were doing ok. Maybe later Mary and I would stop by for a visit.

Our guide of sorts pulled to the side of the road and stopped.

"Folks, this is where I turn off. That place up there is mine. Mr. Howard you just follow this road, it will lead you right to your front gate."

"Thank you sir, we really appreciate your help."

Thirty minutes later we arrived at the front gate. My mouth dropped open. Cars were parked everywhere, folks were walking around the old house and barn. I turned into the yard and was met by one of Harold's brothers.

"James, Mary how are you? We figured you'd be here this afternoon."

"Bill, how did you know I'd be here?"

"Your Pa sent us a telegram."

"You all get out and meet the rest of the family. Mary, I must say you're just as pretty now as you were the day this cowpoke found you."

"Well thank you Bill."

"No thanks needed, come over here I want you to meet the wife and family."

As Bill put it we met the family and had a wonderful visit.

"James why don't you show Mary around. The women say dinner will be ready in an hour or so."

"Thanks Bill, I'll do that."

The McCartney's had done a fine job of keeping the place up. I took Mary's hand and walked up the steps and into the house. Everything was just as we left it. My bunk along one wall, I showed Mary the fireplace and the place in it where we had hidden our money.

We walked into the bedroom and I remembered the cedar chest at the foot of the bed. I opened it and found it still filled with quilts my mother had made years before. I also found the pistol and holster that ma had given me to use when we fought the Comanche. I carefully picked it up and felt the grip.

"Bring back memories dear?"

"Sure does, it's like holding on old friend. Mary, I'm taking the chest home with us."

"That's fine with me, the blankets are beautiful. Maybe we can give one to each of the children."

"That is what I plan to do Mary."

I closed the chest and we walked out the back door and headed to the barn. I pointed to the stalls where I kept Devil and Comanche. I even found the rawhide reita I used to tie the horses. My eyes became misty when I remembered the two of them.

I showed Mary where I had found Sam and after a moment reached behind the feed bin and found the old double-barreled shotgun still wrapped in the sack like I had left it. I couldn't help but smile.

"You should take that home and give it to Sam, James."

"You're right Mary, I will."

After a few more minutes I took Mary's hand and led her up the hill to mom's grave. The grave area was well kept; fresh flowers were in a vase at the base of the headstone.

"James, the stone you carved is beautiful."

"Thanks Mary, lord know I tried hard enough."

The small cedar tree was now quite large. I looked at the grave and remembered how mom had helped to teach me to read, how we'd worked together to survive when Pa had left. I remembered the good times. I felt at ease, I think Ma would have been proud of how things had turned out.

I hugged Mary, and then we walked slowly down the hill to the waiting party.

I thanked the McCartney's for looking after things.

"Hell James, you and your Pa saved us from starving and saved our ranch. We felt it was the least we could do. The money we made on the two cattle drives left us in good shape."

"We've heard how you've helped our brothers over the years. James, you and your father are like family to us."

"Thanks Bill, we really appreciate that."

"Well lets eat, the women been working for almost two days. I sure don't want to disappoint them."

After a fine meal Mary and I decided we'd spend the night and leave early the next morning.

Bill told me the lamps were all filled with oil and later told us goodnight.

Mary and I sat out on the porch and relaxed.

"This country is certainly different from ours James."

"See why I was in awe of all the grass up home?"

"I certainly do. At the time I really didn't understand but after seeing this place I understand.

Where was the Comanche chief when you shot him off Comanche?"

"It was the hill right over there."

"James, know wonder you impressed the Comanche. That must be six hundred yards."

"Close Mary, but remember I had a rest on the window sill."

"True but it's still a long shot; even when you add your luck into the situation. I really wish I could have known your mother. The house shows she was a good woman."

"She was Mary, she always worked hard to keep the dust off things."

"I can imagine it was a hopeless case with the drought and the wind it would have been hopeless."

"It was but she always tried to keep things neat."

"James, lets go to bed, I'm tired and tomorrow is going to come early."

The next morning I loaded the chest after I had broke the shotgun down and packed it inside. The short reita was rolled up and in my suitcase.

We drove into a small town an hour later and stopped at a local café for breakfast. The coffee was just right, strong and black. The place was crowed with folks who worked in the area.

After breakfast we continued our drive back to San Angelo. I drove back to the Ford agency. The same young man came out to greet us.

"You have problems sir?"

"No, not any that I know of. I just wanted to know what you'd give me for this truck?"

"You want to sell it back to me?"

"That's right, I don't need it anymore. My wife and I need to catch the next train north to Dallas."

"Let me check with the owner sir, I've never had a situation like this before."

"The young man came back a few minutes later with an honest offer. I agreed to the deal if he would take us to the train depot.

He agreed and jumped into the back of the truck.

He helped unload the chest and our suitcases then with a wave drove off. I got our tickets then Mary and I had lunch at a local café. By the time we were finished it was almost time for our train to arrive.

We watched the chest being loaded then found our seats. Half way to Dallas Mary laid her head on my shoulder and napped.

We arrived in Dallas and after a short wait caught the train that would take us to Tulsa. We had a private compartment and after the train started we went to bed.

We arrived in Tulsa the next morning and caught the train for home. It had been a fine trip but I was ready to get home. Our home in the tall grass.

CHAPTER 61

▼

The day after we got home we drove down to Pa and Carla's place. I thanked him for having the McCartney's keep the place up. I explained to him how I felt that a chapter had been closed in my life.

"Son I'm glad that you went back down there. I know you had a hard time while I was gone but I think it helped make you the man you are today."

"You may be right Pa, but at the time it sure wasn't any fun."

"The folks down there treat you all alright."

"Pa, they treated us fine. Everyone was so gracious. I talked to one of Harold's older sisters. She was telling me how some of the folks down there still resented the fact that their family had helped make the first drive and prospered from it. She told me the girl who had done Harold wrong while he was on the drive had left the country a few years ago. She said she was bitter about Harold's success. She had told everyone about Harold's savage wife. It seemed to have backfired on her when Harold and Flower had gone down there a few years ago. Pa they love Flower."

"That's great Mary, I think all my boys did well in their choice of wives."

"We didn't do too bad, did we Pa?"

"Son, Carla and I thank the Lord everyday for the good life you boys have created for yourselves."

"Pa, I brought back Ma's cedar chest. I want the kids to each have one of her quilts. Mom, I hope that doesn't upset you?"

"James, I don't mind at all. I think it's a wonderful idea."

"Thanks mom, it was something I thought they should have. Pa I got the ole double barrel shotgun from the barn. I thought I'd give it to Sam if you don't mind."

"My Lord son, I'd forgotten all about that gun. Give it to him if you want, it was what may have saved his life."

"That's for sure Pa, I even brought back the short reita I used to tie up Comanche and Devil. Other than going up to Ma's grave that was the hardest thing for me to remember. Just looking at the stalls where I kept the two of them was tough."

"James, those two horses carried you a long ways and saved your life a time or two. It's something to be thankful for; a man doesn't get those kinds of horses very often. You were fortunate to have them."

"I know Pa, I look at Slick and the other paints I've got and smile."

We visited for a while then headed back to Will and Tee's place. Mary had sorted through the blankets and picked one out for each of our three children.

We gave the blanket to Will. He had tears in his eyes as he looked at the blanket.

"Will, we'll have to make a blanket rack and display it."

"We sure will Tee."

Later that evening we took Matt his blanket. He and Deb handled the blanket with care when they got it. They like Will and Tee said they would get a blanket rack and display it for everyone to see.

Beth would get her blanket next time she and her family came up to visit.

The next couple of months seemed to fly by. Mary and I were having coffee one morning when we saw Sam and Lesa drive up out front. Mary and I walked out to the gate.

"What brings you two up here?"

"I have something for Mary brother."

"Something for me, Sam what would that be?"

"This Mary."

He held up a beautiful Blue-tick puppy.

"Her name is Princess, it just seemed to fit her. I know you all have never had a dog and that's just not natural. So I picked this one for you."

Mary took the puppy and held it to her cheek, the puppy licking her all the time. I could see we had ourselves a dog.

"Well Sam, since you gave us a dog, I have something for you."

"For me, what is it James?"

I went into our bedroom and took the old double-barreled shotgun from the cedar chest. I quickly put it together and took it to Sam.

"Lord James, that's the gun you used to save me."

"That's right, Pa and I figured you should have it."

After wiping tears I got a big Sam hug.

Princess would be out first but not the last of our dogs. Later that evening after Mary had fed Princess I couldn't help but laugh. Princess long ears would fall into the bowl, which held the food Mary had prepared for her. Mary had found a short piece of bright red ribbon and tied her ears up on top of her head. It was too cute to talk about.

Mary looked at the pup and began to laugh. The puppy with her big sad eyes and ribbon wrapped ears began to wag her tail. I couldn't help but break out laughing too.

I found a small wooden box that Mary used to make the puppy a bed. She put the pup into the box and we went to bed. A short time later we heard the puppy's feet coming into the bedroom. She followed Mary's scent around to Mary's side of the bed and began to howl. For a small puppy, she had a very big voice.

Mary picked the puppy up and laid her on the bed next to her. The puppy snuggled up next to her and went to sleep.

After a month Mary finally got Princess to sleep on a bed Mary had made for her on the floor next to our bed. Princess was growing and would soon be way to big to sleep with us. The pup had become Mary's shadow; she followed her everywhere.

Princess proved her worth when she ran in front of Mary who was going to step into the chicken coop. Princess now half grown began to bark and stayed between Mary and the gate. After a moment Mary walked around the pen and saw a three-foot rattlesnake coiled just inside the gate. She called to me and asked me to bring a gun.

Mary got a hold of Princess and held her while I shot the snake, then disposed of it. Princess got a very special supper that night.

From that day forward Princess was officially a member of the Howard family.

CHAPTER 62

▼

Late one evening a week or so later Mary and I were both reading when a car came up the hill in a rush.

I walked to the door and saw the Captain of the Tribal Police came running towards our front gate.

"Captain, what's happened?"

"Attempted bank robbery Mr. Howard, we may need your help."

"Doing what?"

"The bank robbers managed to get out of town and made it as far as Mary's aunt's old place. One of my officers managed to shoot a tire out. They ran into the house. I thought you might want to be there."

"Let me get my guns."

Mary who had overheard the conversation already had my pistol belt and the Sharps ready for me. I grabbed my hat, a light jacket and I was ready.

We loaded into the car and started down the hill where we found Will standing by the road. The Captain stopped the car.

"What's wrong Pa?"

"Some boys tried to rob the bank, the tribal police broke up the deal but they managed to hold up in Dove's old place."

"Let me get my rifle, we don't want those boys getting away."

A moment later Will came back with his new Sharps and pistol belt. We turned onto the main road and raced off towards Dove's old place.

We arrived to find several tribal police cars. A young officer met us when we drove up.

"Captain, the men are still in the house. We have all four sides covered."

"Have you talked to them?"

"No sir we haven't."

"Captain, see if you can talk to them, if not Will and I will give them something to think about. Our rifles will shoot right through the walls of the house."

"I'll give it a try Mr. Howard."

The Captain moved forward and tried to talk to the men in the house. Their answer to him was short and to the point.

"Come get us!"

"Will, that feller is at the front window. Will, you shoot about a foot to the left, I'll shoot to the right, we just might get their attention. Captain, you count to three."

Will and I loaded our rifles then sighted them. The Captain began his count.

"One, two, three!"

Both rifles seemed to fire as one. We heard a man scream and others began to curse.

"Load up son, I think one more round will do it."

We reloaded and again the captain began his count. On three we again fired.

Suddenly the men in the house began to shout!

"Don't shoot anymore we're coming out."

The Captain and his men held their positions and waited.

"Come out with your hands in the air, one false move and we'll open up."

The men came through the door one at a time, their hands in the air.

"Where's the other man?"

"You'll have to go carry him out. His arm looks like it's half shot off. What kind of cannons were you all firing?"

"Sharps rifles."

"Never saw or heard one before, those slugs went through the walls of the house."

"We figured they would."

The men were handcuffed while a couple of the officers went into the house and carried out the wounded man. He had passed out and was loaded into a car that quickly pulled out for town.

"Mr. Howard, I'd like to thank you and your son for your help."

"You're more than welcome Captain, our money is in that bank too you know."

"I know sir, but with you alls help the situation was resolved easy."

The Captain drove Will and I home. Mary sat on the porch waiting for me.

"Captain, would you care for a cup of coffee? You're going to have a long night."

"Mrs. Howard, if it's made I'll sure have a cup. Like you say, it's going to be a long night."

We sat on the porch and talked. The Captain told Mary how Will and I had used our Sharps.

"No wonder they gave up, the walls of that little house wouldn't begin to stop the Sharps."

"It worked Mary, Will and I only had to fire twice."

The Captain finished his coffee, thanked Mary and I and left.

"James, how did Will feel about shooting someone?"

"He really doesn't know who shot the man, I really don't either. We never saw the man. But it didn't seem to bother him any."

Princess who lay next to Mary on the porch swing reached out a paw and touched my hand. She wanted her ears rubbed. Mary and I both laughed; Princess was just a little bit spoiled.

CHAPTER 63

▼

Tom and Bill came out one morning the following week with their fishing poles in the backseat of Tom's car.

"What are you two outlaws up to this morning?"

"We decided to go fishing. We've been hooked up for a while and decided we'd play hooky today."

"Sounds good to me, I think you boys deserve the time off."

"We thought you might just want to ride along, Sammye packed us a great lunch."

"Go on James there's nothing here that won't wait until tomorrow."

"Mary, I think I will, you boys give me a minute to find my fishing pole. I just hope the grandkids put it back where it belonged."

"They put them back James I saw them last week when I was cleaning."

I got my fishing pole and loaded it into the car with the others.

"Where you all plan on going?"

"How about the creek up in back of the hunting cabin?"

"Sounds good to me, there's some nice channel catfish in that creek."

"Good, now get in the car. I'm ready to get some fishing done."

I waved to Mary as Tom drove off.

Tom drove up near the stream a short distance from the hunting cabin. We unloaded our gear and walked quickly to the stream.

The boys opened the bait containers and we baited our hooks.

The fishing Gods as Bill called them we smiling on us. We each caught several nice catfish within the first thirty minutes or so. I had just hooked another nice cat when I heard the far distant shot, a moment or so later it was followed by another.

I looked at Tom who was now looking in the same direction.

"Lets go Tom, that's a Sharps for sure. Mary or Will is in trouble, bad trouble."

We dropped our poles and ran to the car. Tom quickly started the car and headed back the way we'd come. To this day I don't know how in the world we managed to travel as fast as we did. Tom slid the car onto the main road and we raced towards the house.

We heard another shot a short time later. I saw the smoke from up on the ridge in back of our house. Who ever was up there was in a small outcropping of rocks.

As we neared Will's house I hollered for Tom to stop the car.

I left the car running and raced to the back door of Will's house. Tee was standing just inside the door.

"Tee! Where is Will's Sharps?"

She quickly ran to the gun cabinet and grabbed the case that held the rifle and his shell belt.

I quickly uncased the rifle and loaded it as I was moving to the back door.

I rested the rifle on the doorframe while watching the rock outcropping where I'd last seen the smoke.

Suddenly I saw movement, sighted the rifle and fired.

The man jumped up from behind the rocks and swung the rifle around towards my position.

I quickly pushed Tee away from the doorway just as another shot sounded. The man on the hill suddenly was thrown back, his rifle flying into the air. Mary had fired from our home and it looked as if she'd done a fine job of it.

I quickly grabbed the shell belt and raced out the door.

"Stay away from the door Tee until I holler. The feller may be playing possum."

I ran to the car and jumped in as Tom gunned up the hill towards the house up the hill.

Tom slid the car to a stop as I raced up onto the porch.

"Mary, Mary! Are you alright?"

"No I'm not alright James, this cannon of yours almost broke my shoulder."

Her voice had never sounded better to me. She was standing by the back door with the Sharps still resting on the doorframe, just waiting to see if the man on the hill would get up.

I took the rifle from her and leaned it against the wall then took her in my arms and held her as she began to cry.

"James, just look at our house, there's holes everywhere. Just look at what he did to our table!"

The table had a leg shot off and now lay at an angle on the floor.

"Don't worry Mary we can get another one."

"I know James but I loved that table."

"You sit down and rest Mary, I've got to go check on the feller up on the hill."

Tom who was now standing in the doorway asked me to let him have Will's rifle, he was going with me.

Bill said he'd stay with Mary as Tom and I went out the door and headed up the hill.

We separated and each took a different route up towards the rocks above. As I neared the rocks I could hear a man groaning. I could also see the man's rifle laying a few feet from him. I had no need to worry about it, the stock was blown half off the rifle. Mary's shot must have hit the stock when the man had the gun to his shoulder.

I waited until Tom approached from his side then moved slowly forward. The man lying on the ground was covered in blood. Mary's shot had exploded the stock of his rifle before the heavy slug hit him. Half his face looked like raw meat.

Tom kept him covered as I rolled him over.

The man groaned and looked at me with his one clear eye.

"Damn it Marshal I guess you got me again."

"Again, what do you mean?"

"I was with some boys who held up a bank in Tulsa years ago. You and your wife shamed me. I just had to get even."

"You must have just gotten out of prison."

"About six weeks ago. I'd have been here sooner but I had a tough time finding myself a Sharps. Figured I might get away after I shot your place up."

"I'm sorry to tell you friend but my wife is the one who shot you."

"Well I guess she got me again, only this time I won't go to prison."

That was when I noticed the blood on the front of his shirt, Mary's bullet must have ricocheted down and gone down into his chest. The man coughed once and went limp.

"Is he dead James?"

I felt for a pulse and found none.

"He's gone Tom."

"James, the man must have been in prison for twenty years."

"Almost Tom, a long time for a man to hold a grudge."

"What a waste of a life."

"You're right Tom but some folks never seem to change."

"Look down at your place James, it looks as if your whole family is down there."

He was right, all the kids and grandkids were out standing in the yard. I waved my hat as Tom and I started back down the hill.

"Did Ma get him Pa?"

"She sure did Will."

"James, who was it up there?"

"The head of the bank robbers you and Mom helped us capture years ago Mary."

"You mean he came back after all this time?"

"Just got out of prison Mary, he just couldn't let it go."

"It's such a waste."

"I know dear but we're lucky that you weren't hurt. The house and furniture can either be fixed or replaced so lets just be thankful."

Mary, Tee and Deb made coffee and while we sat drinking it Mary told us what had happened. She had just sat down on the couch in our living room with a book when the kitchen window was blown out. A moment later the living room window on the east end of the house was blown out also.

She had crawled across the floor to the gun cabinet and got the Sharps. She had recognized the sound of the man's Sharps and figured he was firing from some distance away.

She said it seemed to last forever, every time she'd think about trying to get to a window to see where the man was hidden another shot would hit the house.

Finally when we had driven up to Will's place she had a chance to look up the hill through the now open back door. When I had fired the man had stood up and she had shot. She'd not seen what had happened because of the recoil of the big rifle. All she had known was that the shooting had stopped.

Will said he would drive into town and inform the tribal police, Matt and the Swinsons. We'd need the Swinsons to make the repairs to the house.

Bill said he'd ride along with Will and let Matt come home. I thanked him as he and Will left.

I wandered around the house and began to figure out what all would have to be replaced.

Five windows, the back door, my favorite chair, the couch and Lord only knows how many dishes. It was a strange feeling looking at all the damage but still being thankful that Mary hadn't been hurt.

Sam, Lesa, Ma and Pa showed up and to say the least all were upset.

Mary was calm and explained to everyone she was fine. Princess sat by her side and was getting her ears rubbed and loving it.

The Swinsons truck drove up right behind the tribal police. Tom took care of telling the police what had happened while I showed the Swinsons the damage to the house.

After a walk around the Swinsons said they would go into town and get what they needed then be back. They would replace the windows first then the door. They explained that plugging the holes in the house would take a while longer.

"Boys, just replace the boards. The place needs painting anyway."

Later that evening we sat in our porch swing and tried to relax after a trying day.

"James, you know we've been lucky."

"How do you figure that Mary?"

"You've put a lot of men in jail over the years and this is the first time any of them have come back."

"Well I guess you're right. I'd really never even thought about it. How's your shoulder?"

"Sore as all get out but I'll live."

"I'm glad."

"So am I dear, that rifle went off before I was ready. I didn't have it pulled up tight enough."

"You'll remember next time."

"You bet I will I hope there won't be a next time."

"That makes two of us Mary."

CHAPTER 64

▼

The Swinsons repaired the house then painted it.

Mary bought everything that needed to be replaced. She had the older Mr. Swinson make a new leg for the table. She loved that table.

Princess didn't mind all the goings on since everyone shared their lunch with her.

Things began to return to normal so one morning I told Mary I was going to saddle Slick and go get my fishing pole.

"Why don't you saddle my paint James, I'd just ride along with you."

"I'll have him saddled when you're ready. Be nice to have you along."

"Thank you dear, I'll be ready in a few minutes."

I caught and saddled our horses. I was leading them up to the house when Mary came out. I helped her mount and then stepped up on Slick.

"You know Mary, we ought to do this more often."

"You're right dear, it does feel good to be riding again. Besides, we'll not have to worry about having a flat."

We laughed and enjoyed the ride.

When we arrived at the cabin I tied our horses to the hitch rail. We walked to the spot on the creek where we had been fishing a couple of days before.

The fishing poles were still where we had dropped them. Bill's bait can still sat under the tree where he had left it. I stirred the dirt and found there were still plenty of live worms in the bucket.

"James, lets try our luck."

"I don't see why not, we're here."

An hour later we had a nice string of fish. We picked up the rods and headed back to the cabin.

I helped Mary get the woodstove going and a few minutes later we sat at the table and ate our fill of fish.

I dried the dishes after Mary washed them. We replaced everything in the cupboards and then headed back home. All in all it had been a great day.

We were relaxing the next day when we saw a strange car down at the racing stable.

"Wonder who is visiting the stables?"

"I don't have a clue Mary, there seems to be a never ending stream of folks going and coming down there."

We watched as Deb walked the gentleman to his car and waved as he left. A short time later we saw her coming up our way on one of the young horses. We walked to the gate to meet her.

"Hey folks, how are things going?"

"Things are fine dear, we saw you had company."

"Gentleman from Kansas City, he wanted to book a couple of mares to one of our studs."

"How many mares have you booked for the coming season Deb?"

"Thirty something Dad, it looks like we're going to have a great year. Bill is sending his horse here for us to stand you know."

"I didn't know, I figured he'd send him to stand at one of the big Kentucky farms."

"He had plenty of offers but said we'd raised him and besides he'd know he was being taken care of properly."

"How much did he make Deb?"

"Close to a half million dollars."

"That sure doesn't hurt the price of your colts."

"No we've done extremely well. I think it sometimes shocks your son."

"Well just remember how it all got started with one crippled mare."

"I know, when people ask us how we got our start they assume you bought a bunch of Kentucky breds for us. They are shocked when they hear the true story."

"Deb, James and my life together has been a story."

"I know mom, Matt and I were telling the children about some of the things that happened here the first few years you all were here. They were fascinated by them. It's hard for them to visualize this country with just a few homes."

"I can understand that, when I first heard about it I couldn't believe it myself. Then when we drove the first bunch of cattle through here it was like a dream come true."

"I know what you mean. Will had told me about this place while we were at the track up in Chicago but I couldn't really believe it was as great as he described. Then we got married and he brought me here. Like you said Dad it was like a dream come true. "We sit out on our porch in the summer time and watch the tall bluestem bend in the wind. It looks almost like an ocean when it moves."

"We do the same thing Deb, folks who come to visit say the same thing you did."

"Have you all heard anything from your friends out west?"

"We got a letter early this week. Things are going better but I think it will be a while before they get things lined out. There are too many government people involved."

"I'm glad you were here to help the Osage get things set up dad. Matt was describing how they had everything overseen by government people."

"It's not a good deal as far as I'm concerned, but I don't have any control over things out there."

"Well at least some of them are beginning to get control of their lives."

"That's true, but there are some who will never leave the reservation. It's going to be a tough go for some."

"I hope things turn out alright for them. I guess I'd better get this young horse moving he needs some pasture miles. He's having problems getting everything together so I figured we'd go riding in the pastures."

"He will either learn to handle his feet or fall down."

"That's what I figured. Anyway it's worth a try. I'll see you folks later."

We waved to Deb as she trotted the young horse up the trail in back of our house.

"That colt will learn to handle his feet. He's just outgrown himself."

"You think he'll be alright James."

"I sure do, I watched that colt play as a youngster and he was a real athlete. He's just grown so fast he's having trouble getting everything to work right. He'll be fine if they just give him time."

Later that morning we saw Deb coming around the hill from the west. The colt seemed to be doing fine. Maybe he was learning.

CHAPTER 65

▼

The tribe was prospering beyond our wildest dreams. Things were beginning to settle down. The youngsters of the tribe were talking about going off to college.

I was happy, Mary the children and our grandchildren were all healthy and prospering.

Sam and Lesa showed up one afternoon. Sam and I went fishing and got to have a visit.

"James, Lesa and I were talking last night about how things have improved since you and I first rode up here."

"I know what you mean Sam, Mary and I have done the same thing. I remember the trip Mary and I took back home. When I walked into the barn my mind was flooded with memories of Comanche, Devil and the time I found you trussed up like a turkey."

"I was all ready to go to Mexico and be put into slavery. You were indeed a welcomed sight. I've learned a lot from you brother, things I can't even explain but you know what I mean."

"I sure do Sam but it wasn't a one way street. I learned from you too, I learned about slavery and how folks managed to survive."

"That's what we talked about, we're so lucky to be here. My nephew is seeing a girl over west of here."

"I didn't know he was seeing anyone. I only see him about every other week or so. He made a fine hand so there isn't any need to check on him."

"He knows that and is proud of his job here. He's gained a lot of self respect since he first came here."

"He's earned it Sam. He's taken fine care of the east herd. He very seldom ever asks for help and is always ready to lend a hand when it's needed. Will thinks the world of him."

"Want to do it all over again James?"

"No thanks Sam, once was enough!"

We caught a nice stringer of fish and took them back to the house. While the women fixed a meal Sam and I sat on the porch and had coffee.

"Lesa and I are thinking of taking a trip back down south. I'd like to visit my mother's grave. I never got to see where she was buried."

"I understand how you feel Sam, sounds like a good idea to me. Is there anything I can do for you?"

"Not a thing James, we're even going to see if we can find any of Lesa's folks while we're down there."

"I wish you luck Sam."

"Thanks James."

After a fine meal Sam and Lesa left for home. Mary and I sat in our porch swing watching the sun set.

"Did Sam tell you they were planning a trip?"

"Yes he did, I never knew he'd not got to see his mother's grave."

"I hope the trip goes well, some of the folks down that way may cause trouble for them."

"They may find they got more than the bargained for if they mess with Sam."

"Lesa may be a handful too, she borrowed my short barreled pistol."

"Oh Lord, those two are going prepared for war."

"James, I hope they don't have any problems."

"I do too Mary."

A week and a half later we got Lesa's telegram.
JAMES (STOP) NEED HELP BAD (STOP) LESA.
Our hopes had been for nothing.

CHAPTER 66

▼

$\mathbf{M}$ary and I sent the young man back to town with a note for Matt to come out to the ranch at once.

"James, you'd better let your father know what's going on."

"I'll go right now."

I quickly drove down to Pa's place and told him what was going on.

"Son, we'd better get moving. Some of those folks down that way are still fighting the war."

"Mary is packing right now. We plan on taking the next train south."

"Stop by and pick me up, I'll be going with you."

I left Pa's and drove quickly back to the house. Will and Bill were talking to Mary on the porch.

"Pa, Bill, Sammye and I are going along with you all. I'll let Bill take my car back to town if you'll loan me yours. It won't take me long to pack."

"The keys are in the car son, get going."

"Bill I don't know how to thank you."

"James, Sam and Lesa are friends of mine. We can't see him getting railroaded for some trumped up charge. I'll talk to the new agent at the train depot. I'll be waiting when you all get there."

Mary quickly packed our bags. I was mad, madder than I'd been in years. I didn't know what sort of trouble Sam was in but I was going to do my best to help him get out of it.

Pa was waiting for us when we drove up to his place. He kissed Carla goodbye and got into our car. Carla waved as we pulled out.

Matt, Bill and Sammye stood at the railroad station when we drove up.

"You boys ready?"

"Sure are dad, Grandpa I didn't know you were coming along."

"Grandson, Sam is just like your father here. He's my son and if he has problems then I reckon the family needs to help him."

"When is the train due in Will?"

"Not for a couple of hours dad, but Mike is sending a short train as he calls it. He'll hold the eastbound train until we get there.

"Sure doesn't hurt to have a big shot railroad man as a son-in-law Mary."

"You've got that right James, besides being our son-in-law he's one fine man. Our daughter did well."

The short train as Mike called it arrived from Tulsa a few moments later. As we started to load our bags on the train Mary's mom drove up in a cloud of dust.

"James, may I have a moment please."

I walked over to her car.

"Son, you take care of things down there. You let my grandson do most of the talking, but if that doesn't work you might need this."

She handed me the small but deadly forty-four derringer I had given her years before.

"Son, you take care of things, I've gotten used to having you around. Now give me a kiss and get on with your business."

I kissed her check and tucked the small gun into my inside coat pocket.

I ran to the train as it began to slowly roll back down the tracks.

"Hey cowboy, I saw you kiss that woman."

"Really, I guess I still need to work on my sneaking.

Mary gave me a hug as we both laughed about my sneaking.

Mike and Beth met us at the Tulsa station.

"Dad; Mike has gotten clearance from the company to run a special train all the way down. You all will have to hurry to get in front of the next freight headed east."

"Mike thanks for the help!"

"Sir, Sam and Lesa are friends of mine too. The railroad made good money shipping his hams and such. It's the least they can do."

The train consisted of a dining and sleeping car. Mike was in charge of getting us a free run all the way to Macon.

We settled into seats in the dining car as our short train pulled out of the train station.

Matt and Bill began going through the stack of telegrams they had picked up at the telegraph station. Sammye was busy taking notes and organizing the telegrams for later reference.

"Dad, this is ridiculous. From what information we've got it seems Uncle Sam is charged with disturbing the peace and assaulting a police officer."

"That doesn't sound like Sam, I wonder what happened?"

"I'm not sure, I've contacted a friend of mine who has a practice in Macon. He is going to send us a telegram to the station in Memphis, we'll know more about what we're up against when we get his report."

Later that evening we arrived in Memphis where Matt ran to the telegraph office while our train was being switched to another track.

When Matt returned I could tell our son was mad.

"What's up son?"

"Dad, the whole thing is a mess. It seems Sam and Lesa arrived in the small town of Graden just outside of Macon in a new car. The police there wanted proof that the car wasn't stolen. That's when the trouble started. Sam opened his billfold to show the officer the receipt for the car. The officer saw what they claim was a large amount of money. He arrested Sam until he could explain where the money came from."

"My Lord, is it against the law for a man to have money?"

"Dad, Uncle Sam is a Negro and down here things are different than back home."

"Did you find out why Sam assaulted the police officer?"

"It seems when they arrested Sam, Lesa got upset. One of the officers said something to her that upset Uncle Sam."

"Well, what do you boys think?"

"Until we get there all we can do is try and figure out what can be done to get him released. We really can't do a whole lot until we get there and can read the charges. The folks down there don't want to release the information to my friend."

"In that case I guess all we can do is wait."

Later that evening after a nice dinner we went to the sleeper car and went to bed.

The next morning shortly before noon we arrived in Atlanta where we headed south to Macon. The boys picked up more telegrams but still didn't have a lot of information. Will's friend would have cars waiting for us when we arrived at the train station in Macon.

We settled back in our chairs and looked at the thick pines that grew on both sides of the railroad tracks.

We began to see more homes as we neared the city of Macon.

"James, I'm not sure I like this country. The pines are pretty but I feel like I'm living in a box."

"I know what you mean Mary, you're used to the wide open spaces at home. I'd get lost here in a hurry."

Our train pulled onto a special siding at the Macon station. As we got down from the train a young man walked quickly up to where we stood waiting. Will walked over to meet him.

"Folks this is Jim Stanley. We were in law school together."

We shook hands.

"I have the cars right over there. We'll get your bags and get you folks settled then get things rolling."

"I take it there's no place to stay over at Graden?"

"No sir, non that you'd be happy with. It's only a thirty minute drive so we've got plenty of time."

"Good, lets get this show on the road."

We were taken to a nice hotel where Jim had folks waiting on us. We quickly put our bags in our rooms and went back downstairs.

"You folks ready?"

"More than ready Jim, lets get started. My brother has suffered long enough."

We got into the two cars and pulled out for the small town of Graden. We made decent time and had little traffic because of the time of day.

We pulled into the small town and it was apparent we were expected. A small but loud crowd stood a short distance away from the local police office.

We heard a few racial slurs as we got out of the cars and went inside.

"James, I'd like to shoot a couple of these folks."

"Go easy Mary, these folks are different from the folks at home."

"I know James but the war's been over for a long time."

"I agree but some folks are going to take a little longer to realize that."

Matt, Bill and Sammye were in the local police office when we walked in. Matt was reading something the officer had handed him. When Matt handed the paper to Bill and turned to the officer.

"Officer, who is your boss?"

"Captain Ragsdale sir, why?"

"You better go get him!"

"He's gone fishing sir, and the Captain doesn't like to be bothered when he's fishing."

"That maybe officer, but if he's not here within the hour I'll have Federal Marshals go get him."

The officer shifted his feet.

"I'll see if I can find him."

"Officer, if you're not back within the hour tell your Captain to start running."

My son shocked me; I'd never seen him like this. The boy was spoiling for a fight he wanted one bad.

The officer left the room in a hurry.

"Dad, this is a trumped up charge. These folks just can't stand to see a Negro make something of himself."

"Son, it's your fight so get after it. Right now I want to see Sam."

"He should be here in the jail, lets see if we can find him."

"James, where is Lesa?"

"Mary I don't have a clue."

Suddenly outside the office the crowd grew loud. We listened a moment then I went over and looked out the front window of the office. It seemed our Captain had returned at the same time Lesa had come to see us. The crowd was giving her a hard time, much to the amusement of the Chief of Police.

I walked outside and walked through to the crowd. One big man in bib overalls was giving Lesa a hard time. Fact was he was being down right abusive. His language was something no woman should have to hear.

"Excuse me Chief, you going to let this go on?"

"Stranger we don't coddle these folks down here. They need to learn their place."

"You're telling me you're going to let this continue?"

"Not my problem."

"It is now, you can consider yourself under arrest, I'm a U.S. Marshal so stay here and stay out of my way."

I took his belt gun from his holster and walked up behind the big man who was still giving Lesa a hard time. I put the pistol up to the back of his head and cocked it. The man suddenly shut up.

"Now fellow, you turn around slow and head into the jail. I'm a U.S. Marshal and you're under arrest. So don't try anything stupid, right now I'd like nothing better than to shoot you!"

"Hank, you going to let him do this?"

"Shut up Frank, I'm under arrest myself."

I followed the two men into the police station.

"Where are the cells Captain?"

"In back."

"Lead on, I'll be right behind you."

Matt, along with the rest of our group stood as if paralyzed as I walked the police captain and the bibbed gentleman back to the jail cells.

I took a key ring from a hook on the wall and opened the door to a cell.

"Inside you two."

"You can't get away with this."

"I already have Captain."

I looked into another cell and found Sam standing at the bars waiting for me.

"I knew you'd be here brother."

"You were right, I couldn't let my brother sit in jail on some trumped up charge."

"James, I didn't do anything. We only stopped here to see if we could find an Aunt of Lesa's. First thing I knew the police here began giving us a hard time. Then one of the local boys said something to Lesa I couldn't let him get away with. I must have shook the police officer off when I got out of the car and tried to get to the man. Next thing I knew I was in jail with a terrible headache."

"We'll get things straightened out Sam. Matt, Bill and Sammye came along with us. That boy is mad Sam, madder than I've ever seen him."

"James, that boy is just like you. I feel better all over."

"Good, because you'll have to stay here until we get a judge."

"Fine with me James, have you seen Lesa?"

"She's in the office with Mary, I'll go get her."

I went into the office and found Bill and Matt talking to a tall gray haired gentleman.

"Dad, I'd like you to meet Judge Henry Farley."

"Glad to meet you sir."

"Mr. Howard I understand you are a Federal Marshal.

"Yes sir, I am."

"I also understand you've arrested our police chief and one of our citizens."

"That is correct Judge."

"What are the charges?"

"Dereliction of duty for the police officer and disturbing the peace for the other."

"Mr. Howard, I think we can settle this situation to everyone's satisfaction. What would you say if I were to drop all charges against your friend? Would you be willing to forget your charges against the two men you arrested?"

"I could do that your honor."

"Good, lets consider it done. Go get your friend while your attorneys and I take care of the paper work."

"Thank you sir, I'll do that right now."

I walked back to Sam's cell and unlocked the door.

"Come on out brother, we're going home if you're ready."

"More than ready brother, I've seen my mother's grave and that's all I came down here for."

Sam walked out of his cell and headed to the office. I heard Lesa call his name.

I stopped at the cell holding the Police Chief and his friend.

"I'm going to turn you boys loose but don't get any wild ideas. The judge and I have reached an agreement. You boys do something stupid and all bets are off, understand?"

"Why in the name of God do you care about that nig!"

"Hold on Chief, we don't use that word up our way. We judge a man by what he does not the color of his skin. It will be hard for you to understand but Sam, who is a very wealthy man, claims me as a brother. Chief, I'm honored that he does so. I've shot men who tried to treat him any different than they would treat me."

"Well you're not back home now."

354   North to the Tallgrass

"Friend, you're still fighting a war that ended years ago and is best forgotten. You keep thinking the way you are and your part of the country will be left behind. But I guess that's up to you."

"A nig!"

I reached into my coat pocket and pulled out the small but deadly forty-four derringer. Cocking it on the way out of my pocket.

"Finish that sentence."

"You'll shoot me?

"I sure will, no doubt about it."

"Marshal, you can't shoot him. I'd be a witness."

"Chief, there's two shots in this gun. There will only be one story told, it will be mine. I went to let you boys go and you jumped me. Case closed."

"You place rough."

"There's a bunch of boys pushing up daisies who would agree with you Chief. I'm not known for taking many prisoners. That's why I've lasted this long in the business of law enforcement. I'm going to unlock your cell door now but I think it would be best if you all stayed here until we have left. Sam will be armed by now and boys he's hell on wheels with a short gun."

I unlocked the cell door after I put the derringer back into my coat pocket.

"You boys behave now, we'll be gone shortly."

As I walked into the office Sam was signing some papers.

"You ready to go home Sam?"

"I am now brother, all I need is my money the Chief took from me."

"How much was there Sam?"

"Near six hundred James."

"Wait just a minute I'll find out where the money is located."

s I walked back into the cellblock the two men there were argu-

ief, my friend needs his money where is it?"

The Chief removed his billfold and took out some bills and handed them to me.

I quickly counted the money.

"Seems to be about two hundred short. Where's the rest?"

"I had to feed him."

"Not two hundred dollars worth, cough it up Chief or I'll arrest you again."

The Chief reopened his billfold and removed two folded up one hundred dollar bills.

"Thanks Chief, I'll not tell the judge about this."

Again I went out into the office area and handed Sam his money.

"Thanks James lets go home."

We drove back to Macon where we spent the night. After a good breakfast the next morning we boarded our train and headed home.

"Dad, what happened yesterday when you went outside?"

I told him what had happened.

"James Howard, you've not changed a bit over the years. You never tell it all."

"Now Lesa."

"Don't now Lesa me, I'll tell Matt and the rest all of the story."

And tell them she did. When she finished Sam standing next to her had a wide smile on his face.

"Uncle Sam, I don't know why Bill and I showed up to help. Dad just seems to take care of things."

"He always has Matt, he's not changed. For one I'm glad he hasn't."

"Me too Sam, his hair may be getting gray but he's still the same cowboy I married nearly fifty years ago."

The trip home took more time then the trip down; we had to wait for stretches of the track to clear. No one seemed to mind so everyone had a good time.

We all got a surprise when we got back home. It seemed that all the town was at the train depot when we arrived. Tears streamed down both Sam and Lesa's faces as we got off the train.

"Brother, I'm home. These folks are our family."

"That's true Sam, they have been for a long time."

"I know that now James, I just assumed they were nice to me because I was your friend. You know James it makes a man feel good."

"I know Sam, I'm just glad to have you home safe and sound."

"Me too brother, me too!"

C H A P T E R   67

▼

Pa and Carla left the station with Bill and Sammye. As we started to leave the station the new telegraph operator brought me a telegram.

CONGRATULATIONS ON SAVING BROTHER (STOP) WILL SEE YOU ALL SOON (STOP) YOUR WYOMING FRIEND MEL (STOP).

"Mary, Mel is coming down to see us."

"That's wonderful James, I always enjoy his visits. I know your folks will be thrilled."

"James, did I hear you say Mel was on his way down here?"

"That's what the telegram says Sam."

"By golly that's great. I sure enough like that man."

"I do too, but darned if I can figure out why he's coming down. He was just here a couple of months ago."

"Maybe he's coming down to check on his colt, who knows."

We loaded up and headed home. We left Sam and Lesa at their home and drove on up the hill to our home. It was great to be home.

The next few days Mary and I relaxed. Mary baked one of her chocolate cakes and I have to admit I ate too much.

"You're miserable aren't you James?"

"I sure am Mary, but I'd rather be miserably full than miserably hungry."

Mary laughed as she picked up our plates and carried them out to the kitchen. I leaned back in my chair and took a nap.

CHAPTER 68

▼

"James, do you know what day after tomorrow happens to be?"

"Yes Mary I do, we will have been married fifty years. I guess it is our golden anniversary."

"Does it seem like fifty years to you James?"

"Heck no Mary, I've been to busy to think about it. It seems like it's only a short time, then I look at our grandkids and realize how much time has passed."

"I know what you mean. I was down at Will and Tee's the other day and was shocked to see that Tee's hair was laced with gray."

"I know what you mean. I noticed Will had some gray in his side-burns. It was a shock to me too."

"It doesn't make any difference Mary, I still love you. Actually more than ever."

"James, you know I feel the same."

"I know and it's fun isn't it?"

"It sure is cowboy it's just grand."

Our friend Mel came in on the train the next morning. He and Pa came by to visit after they took a look at the studs down at the barn.

Mary and I worked in the yard all day and went to bed early.

The next morning we were awakened by the sound of a car coming up our hill.

"Now who in the world is up this early?"

"James, we've overslept!"

I drew on a pair of pants and headed to the door. I was surprised to see Will, Beth and Matt unloading out of Will's car.

"What are you kids doing up this time of morning?"

"Came to celebrate the fifty years you and Mom have made together Pa."

Well thank you kids I appreciate the thought."

"Not a problem dad, is mom up?"

"I am now."

"Good morning mother."

"Good morning you all, but don't push it. I've not had my coffee yet."

"Get your coffee mother we want you in a good mood."

"James, do you smell a rat?"

"I'm beginning to Mary."

"Mother, Father, why would you say something like that? You all could hurt our feelings."

"Mary, the rat is really beginning to smell."

"I know dear, when our oldest "Wild Child" calls us mother and father. I get nervous. Mom and Dad are one thing but you're right dear, the rat is really getting ripe."

"Will, I think our folks are suspicious about our coming up here to see them. I just can't understand them sometimes."

"It's age Matt, they become suspicious in their later years."

All three of the kids were grinning as they picked on us.

"James, get your Sharps. We may have to fight our way out of this!"

"Whoa mom! Get your coffee and settle down. We need to talk."

"At last we're going to find out what this bunch of outlaws are up too."

Our kids followed us into the house where Mary fixed coffee. When the cups were filled our youngest asked for our attention.

"Folks, you all have been married fifty years today. We wanted to do something special for you but we got out voted."

"What do you mean out voted, whose business is it but ours?"

"The family mom, the family out voted us. So if you all will get your coffee drank, we're going to have "Excuse me mother." "One hell of a party!"

"Matt, what are you talking about son?"

"Mother, Dad, Matt is telling it exactly the way things are. We were going to have a party for you but now that's all changed. It seems the family all had different ideas."

"What sis is saying mom is the family wants to do something special for you all. Mom, for once just go along and humor us."

"Mother, what Will is trying to say is please finish your coffee and then put on your buckskin riding shirt and fancy blouse."

"I'll braid your hair with the fancy ribbons."

"Dad, wear your fancy buckle and your new silver belly hat."

"Wait a minute kids, what's going on here?"

"Mother, father the family is throwing a party for you and we want you all to look nice."

"Will and I will saddle your two paint horses and have them ready."

"James, I think we're in trouble!"

"Mary, I think you're right but I guess we'd better go along with this bunch."

"You are probably right but I'm not sure I'm happy about things."

Mary and I went to our room and began dressing.

"James, what are these kids up too?"

"Your guess is as good as mine dear. They are up to something but what I'm not sure."

I finished dressing and went to the kitchen and got another cup of coffee. I took the pot into our bedroom where I found Beth braiding Mary's hair with pretty bright colored ribbons. I filled Mary's cup and left the room. I saw the boys down by the corral. They were saddling our two loud colored paint horses.

A short time later Mary and Beth came out of the bedroom. Mary had never looked better.

"Lord have mercy, you look great. I still can't believe I've had you for fifty years."

"Thank you kind sir, you look pretty neat yourself."

"Now lets find out what these kids of ours are up too."

We walked out of the house and met the boys who were holding our horses for us. Both were smiling big.

After we were mounted I asked the question.

"All right kids, where are we going?"

"Head down to the pens folks."

"The pens, why the pens son?"

"Because dad we didn't have room anywhere else."

I looked at Mary who was as confused as I was at the moment.

"Folks, we'll see you down at the pens. Enjoy your ride."

The kids walked quickly to the car and drove down the hill.

"I guess we'd better get started wife."

"Looks that way cowboy, it seems that folks are waiting!"

A short time later we topped the rise of ground that kept the pens from our view at the house. What we saw caused us to stop our horses and just stare.

"My Lord James, look!"

I was looking the area around the pens was covered with people. There were more people than when we had the gather each year.

"Where in the world did all these folks come from Mary?"

"I have no idea dear but I guess we'd better go on down. They seem to be waiting for us."

We rode down to the pens where people were clapping their hands and shouting well wishes to us as we rode by. I saw all the folks from the R.C.B.A. The Marshal now retired whom I had worked with from Tulsa waved to us as we rode by.

A lane was left for us up to the platform where Mary and my folks sat waiting. For once, Mary had nothing to say.

As we rode through the crowd I saw Tom walk up the steps to the top of the stage. Our kids stood at the foot of the stairway all smiling.

"Folks, our honored guests are here so we will begin the party."

The people cheered.

"Mary, James would you please come up here with your family?"

Two young men took our horses. Mary and I walked up onto the stage.

"Folks we're gathered here today to honor these two friends. For many years now they have worked with and for the betterment of our people. Today we are here to honor them, they have been married fifty years today."

Again the crowd cheered.

"Mr. Conner, will you come up please?"

Mr. Conner came up to the stage with two young men carrying a wrapped package.

"James, Mary your friends asked me to do a painting that will hang in our new council house. I was honored to be asked to do so. Boys would you unwrap the painting."

The two young men unwrapped the painting and then turned it around for the people to see.

The crowd began to cheer. The picture brought tears to both Mary and my eyes.

The picture showed Mary and I setting side by side on our paint horses. In the background you could see all our friends homes as well as the race stable. It was beautiful.

I took Mary into my arms and kissed her.

The crowd once more cheered.

When things quieted down I raised my hand for silence.

"Friends, we want to thank you for coming here today. My wife and I are honored that you have come here today. We are wondering if we deserve all this."

"Mr. Howard" a man shouted from the crowd.

"Sir you've helped so many folks in this community over the years that any one not here today better be in bed sick. Otherwise they will have to move. Sir we love you and your wife. Please sir enjoy the day with us."

What could I say, nothing, nothing at all!

The day was wonderful; we shook hands and had well wishes beyond our wildest dreams. The Lt. Governor of the state stood in line to talk to us.

After a wonderful meal the women from town had prepared, there was dancing and games for the kids. Mary and I had a wonderful day.

Our kids and grandkids were kept running all day. It was fun to watch.

Mary's mom and dad had to leave. Mary's father was tired and needed to rest. Tom had driven them home but not before I gave Mary's mom a kiss and returned the small derringer she had loaned me a few weeks before. She had smiled and gave me a hug and a kiss on the check.

When things began to slow down we finally got a chance to thank our kids for giving us this wonderful day.

"Mom, Dad we were going to have a small party at Will's place for you two but things sort of got out of hand."

"Folks began coming into the law office and wanting to know why they hadn't been invited, it became a mess. Finally Sammye came up with the solution, we'd invite everyone!"

"Leave it to Sammye to figure the problem out."

Finally just before sundown the party ended. Our grandsons brought us our horses. We mounted and after saying thanks we headed home.

I took the horses down to the barn and after unsaddling them I gave them their grain. I walked back to the house with a big smile on my face.

"Your cups out here waiting, James."

Mary was sitting in the porch swing my cup of coffee sat on the small table beside the swing. I sat down then took a sip and sighed.

"Some kind of day wasn't it cowboy?"

"It sure was Mary, I've never seen a crowd up here that big. My hand is sore from shaking hands."

"I know dear, everyone was so nice. James there were folks here today I've not seen in years."

"I know what you mean, the Marshal from Tulsa came up to wish us well. I'd not seen him for ten or fifteen years. It was nice to see him again.

"James, there was so many folks I felt like a ball bouncing; here and there."

"Well I doubt we'll make another fifty Mary but the first fifty have been a ball. Thank you."

"James, we'll work on making it day by day."

"Sounds good to me Mary, what's the plan?"

"Cowboy, you just follow me."

"Oh Wow!"

"Yeah, Wow cowboy!"

THE END

978-0-595-41685-1
0-595-41685-3

Printed in the United States
65629LVS00002B/32